UNEARTHED

AMIE KAUFMAN AND MEAGAN SPOONER

HYPERION

Los Angeles   New York

ALSO BY AMIE KAUFMAN AND MEAGAN SPOONER

The Starbound Trilogy
These Broken Stars
This Shattered World
Their Fractured Light

ALSO BY AMIE KAUFMAN

The Illuminae Files (with Jay Kristoff)
Illuminae
Gemina
Obsidio

The Elementals Trilogy
Ice Wolves

ALSO BY MEAGAN SPOONER

Hunted

The Skylark Trilogy
Skylark
Shadowlark
Lark Ascending

First Edition, January 2018
10 9 8 7 6 5 4 3 2 1
FAC-020093-17328
Printed in the United States of America

This book is set in Jenson Recut/Fontspring; Adobe Jenson Pro, Andale Mono,
Futura LT Pro/Monotype
Designed by Phil Caminiti

Library of Congress Cataloging-in-Publication Data
Names: Kaufman, Amie, author. • Spooner, Meagan, author.
Title: Unearthed / by Amie Kaufman and Meagan Spooner.
Description: First edition. • Los Angeles ; New York : Hyperion, 2018. •
Summary: Scholar Jules Addison and scavenger Amelia Radcliffe join forces to unravel
secrets of a long-extinct civilization, only to discover something that could spell
the end of the human race. • Description based on print version record and
CIP data provided by publisher; resource not viewed.
Identifiers: LCCN 2016059593 (print) • LCCN 2017029815 (ebook) •
ISBN 9781368012294 (ebook) • ISBN 9781484758052 (hardcover)
Subjects: • CYAC: Science fiction. • Extraterrestrial beings—Fiction. •
Ciphers—Fiction. • Puzzles—Fiction.
Classification: LCC PZ7.K1642 (ebook) • LCC PZ7.K1642 Une 2018 (print) •
DDC [FIc]—dc23
LC record available at https://lccn.loc.gov/2016059593

Reinforced binding

Visit www.hyperionteens.com

For Josh and Tracey, Abby and Jessie.
Family.

We are the last of our kind.

We will not fade into the dark. We will tell our story to the stars and in this
way we will never die—we will be Undying. Perhaps only the stars will hear
us until we are nothing more than a memory. But someday a race will find
the power we left behind—and they will be tested, for some things are
better left unknown. Some stories left untold. Some words left unsaid.

Some powers left alone.

Ours is a story of greed and destruction, of a people not ready for the treasure they
guarded. Our end came not from the stars but from within, from war and chaos.
We were not, and never had been, worthy of what had been given to us.

Within the mathematical cipher of this message lies a key to build a door into the
aether. Beyond the door, beyond the aether, you will face your trial. The worthy,
the chosen, will find the power we died to protect, and rise into the stars.

Know that the journey is unending. Know that the dangers ahead will be many. Know
that unlocking the door may lead to salvation or doom. So choose. Choose the stars
or the void; choose hope or despair; choose light or the undying dark of space.

Choose—and travel onward, if you dare.

—Excerpt from The Undying Broadcast (orig. "Unidentified Signal Alpha 312")
decoded and transliterated by Dr. Elliott Addison, University of Oxford

1

AMELIA

THIS IS REALLY, REALLY NOT GOING THE WAY I'D PLANNED.

The two scavengers below are talking to each other in Spanish, laughing and joking about something I can't understand. Lying facedown against the rock, I wriggle forward just enough to see the tops of their heads over the edge of the overhang. One of them is taller, bulky in the shoulders. He's around thirty or thirty-five, and easily twice my size. The other one's smaller, a woman, I'm guessing, by the way she stands—but even she'd have the edge on me if they knew I was here.

You were right, Mink, I should've taken that gun. At the time, it felt good to surprise the Contractor—to make her eyebrows shoot up underneath her bangs and stay there. "I don't need a gun," I'd scoffed, not bothering to add that I wouldn't know what to do with one anyway. "No one will ever even see me down there." Because if I were home, if I were scavenging a city on Earth, that would be true.

But studying the topographic surveys and satellite images of Gaia's surface didn't prepare me for just how barren this landscape is. This isn't like the ruins of Chicago, full of sewer tunnels and half-collapsed skyscrapers, with infinite places to hide and move around unseen. There aren't even any plants on this barren world—nothing but some microscopic bacteria in the oceans, and that's on the other side of the planet. Not surprising, given that something about Gaia's two suns gives off a flare every generation like clockwork and nukes the whole world. There's just open desert on either side of the canyon, and I'm screwed.

I'm screwed.

The raiders are filling up their canteens at the little spring under the overhang, the same spring marked on our pirated maps, which drew me to this spot. Though I can't understand their language, I don't need to know the words to tell that they're grumbling about the dusty, sandy quality of the water in the pool. Like they don't get how lucky they are that there's water *on* this planet in the first place. That there's air we can breathe—sort of—and the right temperature and gravity, though the solar flares dashed all hope of a permanent colony here.

It's still the closest thing we've ever found to a habitable planet, besides Earth and Centaurus. And one of those is rapidly dying, the other far beyond the reach of our technology.

We only found Gaia because we followed the instructions left by ancient creatures long dead. There's no telling when we'll find another world like it, unless we find more coordinates in the ruins left by the Undying. Ironic that the aliens called themselves that in the very broadcast describing the way they wiped themselves out.

I hold my breath, hoping that the scavengers don't look around while crouching to replenish their water. My pack isn't exactly well hidden, since I wasn't expecting company, but they haven't noticed it yet. *Idiots.* But I'm an even bigger idiot, because I broke my cardinal rule—I let go of my stuff. I put it down because I wanted to see what was over this ridge. The desert is marked by groupings of immense rock formations stretching up toward the sky, swept into shape by the wind, and by water that's long gone now. I'm going to end up marooned a billion light-years from home with no supplies because I wanted to admire the damned scenery. Just a few chunks of red-gray rock stand between the raiding duo and my only hope at survival in this terrain.

Not only does the pack contain my food rations, my climbing gear, my water, my sleeping mat, and everything else I need to live out here—it contains my breather. The atmosphere here's got just a little more nitrogen than Earth's. Eight hours a day or so, you need to strap on a breather and suck in oxygen-enriched air, or you stop being able to think straight, and then your body shuts down. And my breather—my lifeline—is in the bag a meter or two from a pair of raiders.

The man lifts his head and I jerk back, rolling over and gazing up at the empty blue sky. The light of the binary suns is harsh on my face even through the protection of the kerchief, but I don't move. If I don't get my stuff back, I'm dead. I won't even be alive when they come to get me in three weeks, much less carrying enough loot from the temples to pay my exit fee.

My mind scrambles for a solution. I could call Mink—except my sat-phone is in my pack, and the comms satellite won't be over this part of the planet for another six hours anyway. And even if I did find a way to signal her, she made it clear when she dropped me on this rock that I was only getting a ride back off the ground again if I had something to make it worth her while. It costs big to smuggle scavengers back and forth on official supply shuttles through the portal to Gaia, a shimmering gateway in space patrolled and guarded by International Alliance ships. She's not going to bother getting me back through to Earth unless I can pay.

I *have* to get that pack.

"Tengo que hacer pis," says the man, making his partner groan and walk off a few steps.

I hear the sound of a zipper and then a grunt, and then—after half a second—the sound of something trickling into the spring water.

Oh, for the love of— *Very nice, asshole. Like you're the only ones on this planet who might've wanted to use that spring.*

"Ugh," protests the woman, echoing my sentiments exactly. "En serio, Hugo?"

I tip my head just enough to get a glimpse of the guy standing, feet apart, over the spring, with his hands cupped around his groin—then I slam my eyes shut again before I can see any more. *I so* didn't *need that visual.*

I ought to try to get the jump on them while he's busy peeing, but my hands are shaking, and not from lack of O_2. I put up a good front with Mink, and even with the other scavengers I beat out for this job when Mink quietly put out word she was looking. A few knew me from the fences in Chicago, others had come from farther away and only met me while we all scrabbled to get hired. The kid, the little girl, the one who's going down all by herself to raid the temples. *What a badass,* they said, laughing. *What a punk.* But in Chicago, no one ever saw me.

The reason I was so good, the reason I convinced Mink to let me work for her, was because no one *ever* saw me. I never had to fight over turf. I never had to run anyone off. I never had to hold off two experienced and probably armed raiders while I retrieved my gear.

I try to breathe, sucking in air through the kerchief and making it clamp against my chapped lips. I feel for a moment like I'm suffocating, like someone's put a plastic bag over my head—I have to remind myself that it's only cloth, that I can breathe fine, that I don't need that extra oxygen dose for hours and I'm just scared. *Just wait,* I tell myself. *They haven't seen your pack yet. You're fine.*

But like that thought was a jinx, the very next sound I hear is the woman's voice, sharp with surprise, summoning her partner. The guy's fly zips back up and booted footsteps crunch across the loose stones and sand—heading toward the boulder half concealing my pack.

"¿Ésto pertenece al grupo?" A boot connects with fabric and something hard beneath it. They're kicking at my pack.

But that's not what makes my heart sink. Because while I don't understand what they're saying, I do know one of those words. Some of the gangs in Chicago spoke Spanish. *Grupo* means "group." These two aren't here alone. Mink warned me there were other contractors using this supply-and-survey mission to smuggle raiders down to Gaia's surface, but I assumed they'd be in ones and twos, like me.

Which means I either get my stuff back now, or they take it back to the rest of their gang, and I have to try to take it back from half a dozen looters instead of two.

I move before I can talk myself out of it and roll over to drop off the edge of the overhang, only a few meters from the scavengers.

The woman jerks backward, half stumbling in her surprise. "Qué chingados!" she blurts, hand going to her waist, where something in a holster glints in the light.

The guy's less jumpy, though, and merely tenses, watching me suspiciously—and standing between me and my gear.

"I just want my stuff," I say, deepening my voice until it makes my throat ache. I can't make myself look any bigger, but with all my gear on it's not blatantly obvious I'm a girl. Maybe if they think I'm just a short man, they'll think I'm less of a target. I point at the pack. "My stuff," I repeat, more loudly, glancing between them.

I'm wishing I'd paid more attention in Languages before I dropped out—maybe I'd speak more than a few words of Spanish. The only A I ever got was in math, and though it might be the universal language—the Undying broadcast proved that—it doesn't do me much good right now.

"Who the hell are you?" asks the man. Though he speaks with an accent, he tosses the English at me easily. *Well, at least that's something.*

"Amelio," I shoot back. Not exactly true, but close enough. "And I'm here same reason you are. Just give me my stuff and I'll be on my way."

The woman is recovering from her shock, and straightening as she comes to stand beside her cohort. She's in her mid-forties, I'd guess, with a sun-weathered face. The layer of dust coating her features lightens her skin by a few shades—the dust splits as she grins. "Just a kid."

The guy grunts agreement, and in an easy motion pushes his coat back so he can hook his thumb into his pants pocket—and, coincidentally, I'm sure, reveal the pistol resting in the holster at his side. "Maybe we take your stuff, enjoy the extra O_2, and you run back to Mamá, kid."

I suck in a lungful of air, waiting until I'm sure that frustration won't make my voice rise. "My 'mamá' isn't back for weeks, just like yours. Give me my stuff. Trespassing's bad enough, you really want to add murder? You're not gonna shoot me. I'm one of Mink's raiders. Cross her and you'll wake up dead once you get back to the station." It's a bluff—true, Mink's my backer, but I'm pretty sure she wouldn't give a damn if not all her crew came back from Gaia's surface.

The man, who's easily a head and a half taller than I am, rubs at his chin. There's a few days' worth of stubble there, and the movement rasps audibly through the dry air. "Nobody gonna find you here," he replies. "No body, no crime, eh?"

"Hugo," the woman breaks in, squinting at me. "No es niño, es niña."

Shit. I know enough Spanish to understand that. So much for trying to look less like an easy mark.

"Take off your helmet," the man orders.

My heart, slamming in my rib cage, overrides my brain. "No."

The guy steps forward, hand still lingering at his waist by his gun. "Take off your helmet or take off your shirt, your pick."

Instinct tries to make me reach for my knife, but I know it'd be a death sentence. I'm outmanned and outgunned. Trying to figure out if I'm a young man or a girl isn't going to keep him occupied for much longer, and the truth is these guys won't care I'm only sixteen. They won't care that they'd be killing a minor. They've already broken the IA's planetary embargo just by landing on Gaia, and that's a life sentence all by itself.

The International Alliance doesn't mess around when it comes to off-world law, not after it lost the project that brought Earth's nations together in the first place. Three hundred people boarded that ship headed for Alpha Centauri, the star system closest to ours in the vast emptiness of the cosmos, trying to reach the *only* potentially Earth-like planet we've ever found. Maybe the reason they failed, the reason they were left to drift and die in space, is because people like this managed to con their way on board and mutiny. The only way these two got here is the same way I did—by breaking the law—and breaking one more law isn't going to bother them.

I swallow hard, gritting my teeth. Millions of light-years from home, standing on the surface of an alien planet, it never truly hit me until now that the biggest thing I'd have to fear here would be another human being.

Tension sings through my body, the effort of staying put threatening to knock me down—half of me wants to run, the other half to fight, and caught between the impulses I just stand there, frozen. Waiting.

And then a new voice breaks into the conversation. "Oh, thank goodness, I thought everyone might have left!" The words cut through the tension like scissors through a rubber band, and all our heads go snapping toward the source.

A boy not much older than me appears over the lip of the overhang and then comes sliding down the slope of loose scree, laden with a pack so large I could fit inside it with room to spare. He drops it to the ground with a thud, straightening with a groan and rubbing at the small of his back. He's got brown skin and black hair in tight curls cut close to his head, and a broad smile that looks like it could charm the rocks right out of the ground.

His clothes scream money, with matching khaki cargo pants and vest, a spotless button-down shirt, and boots so new they're still shiny on the toes through their fine coating of dust. He's tall and lanky, with that slight stoop to the shoulders that comes from hours spent poring over tablet screens and keyboards.

Academic, my mind sneers. His type would show up occasionally in Chicago, studying the weather and the climate and whatever else contributed to the mass exodus, and they'd almost always get chased off by a scavenger gang. *What the hell are you doing here? The IA doesn't even have the surface open for research crews yet. Hence us bad guys taking advantage of the empty space while we've got it.*

He glances between the three of us, brow furrowing. "Where are the others?" he asks, the vowels elongated and the *R*s softened—English or something, like someone on TV. When he gets no reply, he tries again. "Da jia zai na li? Waar is almal? Wo sind alle? No?" He jumps from one language to another without skipping a beat.

Silence sweeps in to follow him, his smile dimming a few degrees in confusion. It hangs in the air, thickening and thickening until finally the woman snaps. "Who the *hell* are you?"

The boy's smile flashes back into brilliance at this, and as though he'd gotten the politest of greetings, he steps forward to hold out his hand. "Jules Thomas," he says, inclining his torso a little. He's bowing. *He's actually bowing, what the hell?* "It's a pleasure to meet you all. If you'd be so good as to direct me to the expedition leader, I can present my credentials and—"

He's cut off by the click of the safety coming off a pistol, as the woman pulls it out of her holster and levels it at the boy.

Jules stops short, smile fading and hand lowering. His eyes flick from the gun to the face of the woman holding it, then to the other raider, and then, finally, to me. And whatever he sees written on my face—fear, exhaustion, general *what-the-actual-hell-is-going-on* panic—makes his smile vanish.

"Oh," he says.

2

JULES

WELL, THIS COULD CERTAINLY BE GOING BETTER. "I'M THE LINGUISTICS and archaeology expert," I say, slowly and clearly, lifting both my hands to show them I mean no harm. "I was hired by Charlotte Stapleton—you're with the expedition from Global Energy Solutions, aren't you?"

"Global Energy," the woman echoes, gripping the gun like she'd really appreciate the opportunity to use it, if I'd just be so kind as to step a little bit closer.

Mehercule. It's all I can do not to utter the epithet out loud. I knew when I signed on with Global Energy Solutions' plan to bypass the law that the crew I'd be joining was rough around the edges, but I expected to live through my first five minutes of the expedition.

At least they've got decent security, I suppose. That'll be an advantage, once we've sorted this out.

"I'm Jules Thomas," I say again, in case it helps. It's not my real surname, of course. I didn't need Charlotte's repeated warnings not to reveal my true identity. I know better than to let anyone in this crew aside from its leader know who my father is.

"¿Quién carajo es esto?" asks the woman still sighting down her pistol at me.

"I told you," I say, starting to feel like a glitching audio file. "I'm Jules Thomas. These were the coordinates I was given—I'm supposed to meet the expedition leader here. Tengo instrucciones para reunirse con su jefe aquí."

"You can keep saying that as much as you want." The last guy— just a kid, to judge from the higher pitch of his voice—finally speaks up, gruff behind his kerchief. "But I really don't think these are your people, dude." The gun swings around to train on him for a moment when he speaks. But that would imply he's not part of their group—which means these are raiders, from more than one group. And that not all of them are as noble-minded as Global Energy Solutions.

"I'm beginning to think the same," I mutter.

"No talking," snaps the woman.

I risk one more question. "How likely is it they're about to shoot us?"

"Very," says the boy, easing his weight back as the gun swings around to me again. I can't make out his face behind the kerchief and goggles and helmet, but there's a tension in his voice that ratchets mine up another notch.

I wonder if they name a major landmark after you if you're one of the first people to die on a new planet.

"You can take my pack," I try, pointing at it, playing for time as a plan starts to slide together in my head. "I'll show you how my equipment works. You'll like it. I've got food, too. Chocolate."

Both the armed thugs fix their attention squarely on me for that last one—even if it's not to their taste, it's worth a fortune on the black market. And here, luxuries will be in short supply. Whoever they are, someone in their group will want it. I brought it to make friends with the other members of my expedition, a preemptive strike before any of them could decide that the smart kid would be a good target for mockery—but I'll just have to charm them without it.

The boy's edging around behind them while they're distracted, and as he reaches for his pack, I suddenly realize his intent. He's going to grab it and leave me here. *Can I blame him?* Maybe he'd go bring back help, but I don't think this can wait. This duo looks awfully trigger-happy. If he makes a break for it, I'll pay the price.

"You stay put," the woman orders me, then jerks her head at her companion. The big guy walks forward to pull open my pack, then tip it over, and I wince as something inside clanks against a rock. The boy jumps, eyes flicking from me to the pack they're searching and back.

"Please don't," I say quietly, risking a look straight at the boy for a moment.

The man rummaging through my pack only laughs, but I'm not talking about him banging my stuff against rocks. I'm speaking to the boy behind him, who's standing by his gear now, looking back at me. If he bolts, I'm not going to last long enough to catch up with my expedition.

"What is this?" The big man's holding up my set of picks and brushes, eyeing them with wary suspicion.

"It's for, ah, cleaning the rocks."

They both stare at me like I'm an idiot, and given they're the ones stealing my possessions at gunpoint while I look on helplessly, it's hard to argue with their assessment. "The tent," I say. "You'll like the tent, it's fully automated." My eyes flick up toward the boy, though it's hard to tell for sure if he's looking at me from behind his goggles. "Really surprising."

The boy shifts his weight, silent, light on his feet. A step closer to the woman with the gun. He's quick—he's at least picked up some inkling of my half-baked plan.

The man fishes out the bright blue package holding my tent, turning it over in his hands. He looks up at me, brow creasing. *Doesn't look surprising*, he's clearly thinking.

"Pull on the orange tab there," I say, standing a little straighter, sucking down a long lungful of air. Forcing my body to calm, be ready, like I do in the pool before a polo match. "Anaranjado."

He nods, turning it over in his hands once more, finding the tab. Without further hesitation, he tugs on it, leaning down to see what will be revealed.

The tent unfurls in 2.6 seconds, just like the manufacturer promised, struts shooting out and snapping into place, the bright blue canopy exploding into being. A tent pole strikes the big guy across the nose and I dive for him, slamming his body into the ground with mine, winding both of us. I'm gasping for breath as I push myself up far enough to punch him, pain shooting up my knuckles to my shoulder as his head snaps back. *Mehercule, I should've let Neal show me how to throw a punch without breaking my hand.* But before I can turn, a deafening sound cracks somewhere above my head, echoing off the rock all around us to come rolling back again and again.

I scramble to my feet, just in time to see my opponent start to lunge after me—then stop dead only a few centimeters away. I gasp for breath and stumble back, expecting to see his partner leveling her weapon at me—instead I see her on the ground, unmoving, and the boy's standing over her with the gun pointed at my assailant's face.

Except it's not a boy at all. *Her* helmet's on the ground, a bit dented where she must've used it to bludgeon the woman beside it. "Nice one," she pants, not taking her eyes from her target. She's short, with pale, freckled skin and choppy black hair streaked with pink and blue. Now is *not* the time to stop and admire the view, though *deus*, she's something else.

"Get his gun," she's saying, holding her own stolen weapon steady.

"His what?" I'm still staring at her, trying to process what's going on.

"His gun, genius." She nods at the pistol lying perhaps a meter away from the guy, who's practically snarling with rage, but unwilling to risk getting shot. "Their buddies will have heard the shot. Now would be an excellent time to run like hell."

I inch forward so the guy can't grab me, then hook my foot around the gun and pull it toward me. As I'm stooping to retrieve it, the girl's voice goes harsher again as she orders the man, "Take your shoes off."

"Shoes?" he repeats, brows raising.

"Zapatos," I translate, though from the guy's face it wasn't the language barrier making him hesitate. Shoving the gun in my jacket pocket, I shoot my own curious glance her way. "May I ask why?"

"So they can't follow us," she replies. "Not quickly, anyway. Grab hers too, in case she wakes up."

Clever. I reach down to pull the boots off the unconscious woman, who gives a tiny groan, but doesn't wake. "Have you done this before?"

I earn myself a quirk of a smile from the girl. "I'm improvising. But I've been doing that my whole life. Shove the boots in your pack, let's go."

"If we can spare another half a minute, I've got an idea." I jerk my chin toward the guy with his hands up. "Señor, quitarse los pantalones."

Evidently the girl knows the Spanish word for *trousers*—she starts laughing as the man spits furious curses. "This is going to be ugly," my new partner predicts, gesturing with the gun that the man should do as I've asked.

"I would imagine so," I agree. "But it'll be embarrassing, as well. They'll have to lie to their friends, say we were big, strong, many in number. They won't want to say a couple of teenagers did this. It might put the gang off trying to track us down."

She hikes up one corner of her mouth, grudgingly impressed,

and I tell my hormones to shut down the celebration—making her smile at me should *not* be my priority right now. Although it's a lot more fun to think about than the guy who's glaring furious daggers at me while pulling off his trousers. He kicks them toward me and I stuff them in my pack. With her gun still trained on him, the girl and I slowly back away from the clearing.

And then, once we're far away enough, we *run.*

We scramble past a pile of boulders until we're out of sight, then slither down into the nearest canyon, taking a path along the rubble at the bottom, where we won't leave footsteps. We run until my lungs are burning, pain shooting along my ribs, throat contracting.

Eventually, we slow by unspoken consent when we reach a stream—I double over to rest my hands on my knees, gasping, and she drops to one knee to dip a hand into the water, scooping it up to splash it across her face. Then she cuts a look sideways at me, eyes dancing with unexpected amusement. Relief forces its way out of me in a quick huff of laughter, which sets her off. Snickering isn't helping us recover, and the lower oxygen levels make running extremely ill-advised. I suppose I should be grateful to Gaia's oceanic populations of hardy little cyanobacteria for what oxygen there is, because I definitely wouldn't enjoy making this trek in a spacesuit. But it takes forever to catch my breath.

I fold down to sit beside her and spare my aching legs, leaning across to offer my hand. "We haven't been formally introduced. I suppose you heard me say it before all the unpleasantries began, but I'm Jules." I don't add my fake last name this time. The lie of it would feel too slimy, when offered to a girl who just saved my life.

Something about my voice seems to amuse her, making her mouth twitch. "Jeez, Oxford." She stares at my hand for a couple of beats, then leans across to slowly shake it, her palm warm against mine. "Nice to meet you."

I'm trying not to show my surprise—I wouldn't think she'd be able to tell where I'm from just by my accent. "Do I get to learn your name?"

I get the impression I've asked a much more personal question than I intended—she gazes at me, measuring, taking a long moment before she replies. "Amelia," she says eventually. I hope that pause was her deciding not to lie. "Mia."

"Well, I'm in your debt, Amelia." I don't ask for her last name. After all, she's not getting mine.

She shrugs. "We can afford to rest a little. They're not coming after us without shoes. Or pants."

"Is it possible we just committed the first robbery in the history of Gaia? I mean, they tried first, but we succeeded."

She just shakes her head as she stares at me, lips parted, breath still coming in heaves, skin smeared with dirt. I'm pretty sure I look just as bad. The last few days have been awful—my father's face on the vid-call screen as he understood my coded hints about my plan, the swell of my own fear as I walked onto the shuttle that would bring me to Gaia, not to mention the attempted holdup we've just escaped—but I can't deny that just now, despite it all, I feel *alive*.

In a few moments we'll have to pull out our breathers and let our lungs have a break, not to mention make a plan to try and salvage this fiasco, but for now we're still running on adrenaline.

And I'm not so sure about this planet, but I know I like this girl. Not having my expedition waiting for me—that's a blow I almost can't stop to think about now. But managing to run into someone who could help me in my mission . . . that's lucky enough to give me hope.

The girl eyes me, scratching the underside of her chin with the butt of the scavenger's gun. "Oxford?"

"Yes, Amelia?"

"You better not have been lying about that chocolate."

Deus. I *really* like this girl.

3

AMELIA

DESPITE THE GUNS, DESPITE THE FURIOUS SHOUTS AND THREATS IN TWO different languages trailing after us as we ran for it, despite the alien suns beating down on us and the thin air, I'm really not sure this guy fully gets the kind of danger we're in.

I'm not sure *I* even get it.

But by the time we get far enough ahead of them to stop and take a break with our breathers, he's grinning, whistling to himself in between breaths as he sorts through that monster of a pack he's carrying, checking a few pieces of equipment for damage. We've had to stop sooner than I'd have liked, though we made it farther than I'd expected. He's in better shape than he looks, under those brand-new khakis.

I pull my goggles back on, thumbing the dial on the side to switch them to a higher magnification, then scanning the canyon ridges behind us. I don't see any sign of our friends back there, but that doesn't mean we're alone. True, we'd be easier to spot up in the desert with no cover. But we'd also be able to tell if we'd *been* spotted. Here, obscured by the twists and turns of the canyon, we'll never be sure we're not being watched.

I tug the goggles down to dangle around my neck and pull my breather mask away from my face. "I should get going."

Jules pauses, looking up at me from where he's inspecting a handful of pebbles, turning them this way and that, eyes so intent he might as well be reading from a tablet. His brows lift as he considers my words. "I?" he echoes. "Singular?"

He sounds like a Languages lecture from my old lesson screen, the one covered in scratches and graffitied doodles from the generations of students who had it before me. I glance up again at the ridge, then drop into a crouch so I'm not looming over him. "Yeah, why? You've got your people to catch up with, I've got my own thing. I appreciate the help," I add, "but I've got to keep moving."

Jules's brows draw in—his face is so expressive, everything written there so clearly—as he considers that. "Well, I'm not entirely sure *where* I'm headed now," he says. "That was the only rendezvous point I had, and my expedition clearly wasn't there. If you don't think your people would mind, perhaps I could accompany you to your expedition, and shelter there until the station's overhead and I can call up for new coordinates?"

I find myself staring at him, torn between laughing at the sheer strangeness of this polite, put-together guy who'd be more at home in a library than in an alien desert, and saying yes just to see him smile that ridiculous smile again. He *is* charming. In an *oh-god-he's-gonna-get-his-head-blown-off* kind of way. "Um. You want to come with me until you can call home?"

"Yes, would that be all right?"

I hesitate, scanning his features. There's no sign of deception there, and if he were savvy enough to fool me, I don't think he'd have ambled, unarmed, into the middle of a standoff. Not without a better plan than "hit the dude with a tent," anyway.

"I don't have an expedition," I say finally. "I'm here on my own."

"You're here *alone*?"

"I move faster on my own." I hear the edge in my own voice, frustration at this detour coloring my tone before I can stop it.

Jules's eyes flick back down to the pack. "I see. Can you think of any reason my expedition would have left without me?"

Yeah, about a dozen, Oxford.

I swallow that urge and try to keep my voice civil. I beat out dozens of scavvers to get this job with Mink, I spent eighteen hours crammed in a packing crate to hide from IA security on the shuttle, I'm tracking every scrap of food and water and time and air I've got and praying I make it—and *this* egghead ends up here with all the know-how of a rock. "Time is money," I say finally. "And time is oxygen, come to that. You were probably late, and they figured you got cold feet or got caught up on the station."

"I was a little late, but only by an hour or so. They would've waited for me." He sounds pretty sure about that. "Maybe if I circle back, they'll be there."

"If they moved on, they're not coming back. An hour or so here, racing against the other groups, is worth a lot more than one English guy in shiny boots, no matter what he's paying them."

He falls silent, digesting that, looking down at those boots of his. I've got no idea why someone like him is here; maybe he's some rich private-school kid sticking it to his parents by taking an idiotic—albeit gutsy—joyride to the other end of the galaxy. Maybe he just bought his way into one of the scavver groups, and they took his money in advance and then left him here for the IA sweeps to pick up later. Of course, someone like him probably doesn't have much to lose. Lawyers like he could afford would probably have him out of one of the International Alliance's prison cells in a snap.

Instead of the tantrum I might have expected, or a demand that I help him, he stays where he is, silent, eyes on the interior of his pack. Then he lifts his head to look over his shoulder, down the canyon, and I get just the tiniest glimpse of his expression—there's something sharp there, something intense and unexpected.

Something I recognize from the mirror: desperation.

I swallow. "Hey, you'll be fine. You've got money, clearly. When the station comes back overhead tomorrow, send up a signal offering to buy your way back off the planet."

"No, I—" He stops and looks up, face now devoid of that faint, easy smile. "I can't leave yet. I'll figure it out. If the expedition's gone, I'll go on my own." Though his voice is steady, determined, his movements as he starts dumping things back into his pack are quick and jerky.

"Look, Oxford, you really don't want to be—"

"I'll be the judge of what I want, thank you." The reply is quick, snapped, a sign of temper he didn't betray even at gunpoint.

My own temper flares to match, and I lurch to my feet. "Fine. Do what you want, I guess." I turn my back and stalk the few steps to retrieve my own gear, slinging it onto my shoulders. But my annoyance tends to burn quickly, and it's already dimming. When I glance back Jules is still squatting by his enormous pack, pulling up a holographic map of the terrain from a device worn on his wrist.

This guy's going to get himself killed.

And I wouldn't wish dying a billion light-years from home on my worst enemy, not even on the assholes who were going to steal my stuff and leave me for dead.

"Hey, Oxford." I take a deep breath. I've already stopped, already lost time—I might as well make this my lunch break. "You hungry?"

Jules blinks and looks up. "What?"

"I've got some canned beans left. You hungry or not?"

I'd probably walk away from an offer from a stranger without a second thought. There'd be strings attached, or a trap, or some game to figure out. But instead, he nods. "I am, actually."

I nod and drop my pack so I can dig through it for the cans at the bottom. They've got to get eaten first anyway—they weigh so much more than the dried stuff—but at least it puts off the day when everything I eat is going to resemble rehydrated dog food. I find two and toss one his way, realizing only an instant after I throw it that this guy probably doesn't have the best reflexes. I jerk my head up to warn him—only to see him neatly catch the can and turn it over, inspecting the label with interest.

I drop down onto a rock, resting my elbows on my knees as I pull my multi-tool from my pocket. I click it a few notches to the right and then thumb the release button, and a hooked blade springs out of it. I jab it into the can, catching at the lid and tearing it free.

"High in protein," Jules muses, actually looking at the nutrition info printed along the label. "Not a bad idea, if a little bland. Five grams of protein per hundred, and the recommended daily intake is a little under a gram per kilo of body weight, so that's . . ." He pauses, frowning in calculation.

"About ten percent of my needs," I say, without thinking. "Less efficient for you."

He blinks, no doubt surprised I can count, much less anything beyond that—the look on his face needles me. "Yes," he agrees after a pause. "Ten percent. And in terms of regulation of blood sugar, and the vitamin complexes you find in them, they . . ." He trails off, because I'm staring at him.

"Wow," I reply, sarcasm oozing through my tone as I wipe off my multi-tool, still smarting a little over his surprise I could perform basic calculations. I fold my can's lid into a little trough to use as a spoon. "Nutrition too? So smart, I may faint."

Jules glances up with a grin, completely missing the sting in my tone. "I try not to show the smart in public too often. It's embarrassing when the girls swarm all over me. And demoralizing for the other guys, you know?"

A little laugh escapes me before I can stop it, and I find myself grinning at him for half a breath before I turn my attention to the can of beans, scooping up a mouthful. *Damn, Oxford. Be disarming, then.*

"Uh—" Jules interjects. "Don't you want to doctor that up a little first?"

I blink, the can lid loaded with beans halfway to my mouth. "Doctor? I'm not gonna cut myself, if that's what you mean. Spoons are extra weight, not worth carrying."

"I mean," Jules says carefully, "don't you want to heat it up, add some flavor? Give me five minutes and I can make it taste a little more like . . . I mean, do you really like it like that?" He reaches into his bag and pulls out one of the little cloth sacks he'd set aside earlier.

"I don't *like* it," I reply. "It's just food. You get hungry, you eat." What, does this guy think we're in some four-star restaurant in fancy-pants London? But curiosity's getting the better of me, and I kind of want to know what's in that sack that he thinks will turn cold canned beans into haute cuisine. I lean forward, holding out the can. "Have at it, Doctor."

"Thank you," he says gravely, like I'd just given him a compliment. Then he gets to work pulling out a few sachets of spices, a spoon, a box that looks like . . . oh, holy hell, he's got a wave-stove. Those things cost upward of a thousand bucks, and he's setting it up like it's nothing. I have only vague memories of how they work—something about electromagnets and kinetic energy—but no one I know actually has one in the field. I'd take the grand in cash over hot food, and so would every scavver I know.

He works for a time in silence, adding a pinch of spices and salt here and there, stirring at the can and placing it inside the box to heat. After a few minutes he glances up, expression curious. He has that intense, furrowed-brow gaze, the kind you see on billboards where they're trying to make you think buying cologne will make you so sexy that your shirt will fly off. I'm so distracted that I nearly miss his question: "When you called me Oxford before— can you really pick that just from my accent, or was it a crack about education?"

"Huh?" I blink, momentarily confused until my brain catches

up with my ears. "Wait, you mean you're actually *from* Oxford?" I peer closer, while somewhere at the back of my mind I'm trying to reconfigure what I thought I knew about this guy. "Aren't you kind of young to be in college?"

"I won't be starting until next year," he replies, stirring the beans as they heat. He doesn't *look* eighteen—he's tall, yes, but a lanky kind of tall, the kind guys get when they've only just hit a growth spurt and don't quite know what to do with their arms and legs yet. "And I'm starting early. I grew up there, though. It's complicated."

I bite my lip—the curiosity surges, making me want to ask more, to figure out this strange boy while I can. It's obvious he's not a raider like everyone else who's lied, cheated, or sneaked their way onto Gaia. I don't know what scam he fell for, but he mentioned being some sort of language expert for an expedition—not a raiding party. He's got that look, that *I'm-gonna-save-the-world* look, like his nobility weighs more than his ridiculous pack.

The second it occurs to him that I'm a raider just like the guys we ran from . . . well, that'll certainly be the end of this spontaneous little partnership. His kind don't exactly approve of mine. Even in Chicago we'd get academics screaming bloody murder about us tainting evidence and contaminating environmental whatevers. On pristine Gaia, untouched since the Undying were here, moving a rock is probably on a level with murdering a whole family to people like him.

Much less raiding temples for tech to sell on the black market.

"Here," he says briskly, interrupting my thoughts as he finishes up and nudges the can my way. "Use your sleeve, the tin's hot."

I've never seen a wave-stove at work, and the can doesn't *look* any different. I glance aside at him, but he's already at work on his own can. I reach out to grasp tentatively at the edges—and then yelp, drawing my fingers back as pain darts through them. "Ow, shit!" The words echo back at me from the canyon walls, and I level a dark glance in Jules's direction.

He says nothing, keeping his eyes on his own dinner, but I'm pretty sure I can see the corners of his mouth drawing back as he fights a smile.

I yank my jacket sleeve down over my hand and retrieve my can of beans. "Don't suppose you're carrying multiple spoons in that traveling cantina of yours?"

He offers up the spoon he'd been using to stir, pulling out a butter knife—he packed a freaking *butter knife*—to finish his own cooking. "Laugh at me if you want," he says, shrugging, "but tell me that's not an improvement over cold tinned beans."

I'm dying to say something in retort, a few possibilities flickering through my mind, but my nose catches a whiff of the steam rising off my meal, and all my snappy comebacks vanish. I blow at a mouthful until I'm sure my tongue won't suffer the same fate as my fingertips, then try a bite—and it's all I can do not to groan. It's delicious. More than delicious, it actually tastes like something you'd *get* at a fancy four-star London restaurant. Or what I'd imagine you'd get there, anyway.

"Ffff," I manage, and then forget all about the boy across from me as I focus on devouring my lunch.

He's quiet as we finish our meals—I'm trying to lick the inside of the can and making a mess of it—giving me time to study him surreptitiously under cover of scanning our surroundings through my goggles. So he's not completely useless. He can run, and he kept up with me—mostly—despite that giant pack. But half the gear in his pack is piled up next to it, and most of what I can identify is pointless in a place like this. The guy's got a pillow, and a little solar-powered fan, and a whole set of dinnerware. He's so far out of his element that it's like he's . . . well, it's like he's an alien here.

The terrain on this continent isn't all that different from the deserts in the southwest of the U.S., the ones creeping in across the continent toward the east coast bit by bit ever since the start of the climate decline. You can't tell when you breathe that the air here's not quite right—you only start getting tired and shaky if you go too long without your breather. If you don't notice that the only features are windswept rock formations, if you ignore the complete absence of any life, and if you don't look at the two distinct suns beside each other in the sky, you could almost forget you weren't on Earth.

Almost.

Most of my energy is going toward pretending that's the case, because every time I let myself think about the enormity of what I'm doing my thoughts start to spiral into a panic. I'm one of only a few dozen people who've ever set foot on this world—who've ever stood on another planet without a spacesuit, without breathing tubes, with nothing but the suns on my face and a breeze stirring my sweaty hair. I can't pull out my phone and text my sister. I can't ask it for tomorrow's weather. I can't check my feeds to see if anyone's bid on my latest salvage finds. There's no spot left on Earth where anyone is ever isolated from anyone else, but I'm *alone* here. The first people to explore Gaia on foot were trained IA astronauts, prepped over a lifetime of scientific study and practical training. And they died in the temples. I'm just a high-school dropout from the Midwest with half a dozen minimum-wage jobs under my belt and a juvie rap sheet too dull for the cops to bother with me.

And *he's* even more out of place here than I am.

"Jules," I say quietly as he finishes his lunch. "Listen. Are you sure you won't just head back up to the station? No offense, but you stick out here like a . . ." My thoughts screech to a halt. There's no good sentence that starts out with "no offense." I sigh. "Well, you stick out. You'll be a target."

He's silent for a while, looking first at me and then away, putting his can on the ground and pulling out a fresh white cloth with which to clean off his fingers and lips. Then, softly, he answers:

"I'm aware of how much I stick out." His eyes flick back toward my face. "But I wouldn't be here unless I had to be. I won't just turn and go back."

I want so badly to ask *why*, but then he'll ask me in return why I'm here, and if I know one thing about Jules Thomas already, it's that he wouldn't like my answer to that question. I can only assume the truth hasn't occurred to him yet because we've been on the run for most of our short acquaintance. I draw a breath. "Then will you at least let me give you some advice?"

He nods, folding the napkin and tucking it back into his pack. "I'd welcome it, please."

"How far from your rendezvous point did you get dropped?"

"It was . . ." He pauses, doing a quick mental calculation. "A little under ten kilometers. About three hours of walking."

"See, that's—three hours to cover ten Ks, that's too slow. That's why you were late, why your people left without you. I could cover that ground in half that time if I had to. I'm not trying to brag, I'm just—" I wave a hand at his pack, and the pile of stuff beside it. "You're trying to move with an entire outfitter's store on your back. You've got to get rid of some of this *stuff*."

"Well, the expedition I was joining was going to have grav-lifters," he answers, sounding only a little wounded. "What am I meant to do, just leave it all behind? I'm going to need these tools when I reach the temple."

"*When* you reach it?" I shake my head, willing him to understand. "You aren't *going* to reach it if you keep moving this slowly. And when you do, every raiding party on the planet will have beaten you there. It's a big temple, Jules, but it's not *that* big. It'll be stripped by the time you get within spitting distance."

"In my defense, I was anticipating grav-lifters, and I was *not* anticipating such a brutal race between capitalism and academia." Jules's face tightens—yeah, he *really* doesn't like raiders. "At least I'll be harder to spot on my own. And you never know, I might cross paths with another academically focused expedition, and they'll allow me to join up with them. It'll be a breach of contract with my employer, but surely they'd understand, given the circumstances. . . ."

I stare at him, heartbeat quickening. "Another—Jules, there *are* no expeditions looking to make new friends or discover the joys of learning. Don't you get that yet? I don't know who scammed you, or what fantasy-land you're living in, but it's all raiders down here. Scavengers. You don't stuff yourself in a packing crate and get smuggled halfway across the universe to . . . People don't become criminals for academic whatever, they do it for cash."

"*I* became a criminal for 'academic whatever,'" Jules says softly, his expression utterly calm, like he's used to listening to abuse without letting it get to him. "And you're wrong. I have reason to believe there *are* other academics here. Hybrid expeditions, combining research with gathering a few select artifacts, to justify the expense. Even those artifacts should stay where they are, really, but if we're careful, it's workable. I heard a couple of the guys from Yale were—"

"Don't be so naïve." A huge part of me hates being so cold, but he's not *getting* it. And if he doesn't figure it out, he's going to wind up dead. Even if it means he turns that disgust for scavengers on me, he should know what he's up against. "Maybe there are some scholars down here, but they're just here to guide the raiding parties. Your expedition was probably just a front for a raider operation, too, and duped you into working with them by promising you . . . whatever they promised you."

"You don't *know* everybody's a raider," he insists. "Maybe some are like me, academics hoping to stop the philistines from contaminating all the . . ." He trails off, the chill leaving his expression to make way for dawning realization, his gaze meeting mine.

Bingo. I've been waiting for him to realize I'm one of them, those *philistines*, no better than the duo whose shoes we stole.

I want to speak, but the tiny spark of guilt deep in my mind flares up into an anger I don't want to let out. I'm not going to let some pampered schoolboy make me feel guilty for doing whatever I can to come out of this alive. For doing whatever I have to do to take care of me and mine.

"You're here to steal from the temples?" Jules's voice is quiet, with a note of betrayal in it like we'd been partners, not just two strangers meeting by chance on the other side of the universe. "Do you have any idea—do you know the *damage* that does?" The ferocity of his voice makes me want to step back, but I hold my ground. "We have one chance, *one* tiny window, in which to learn about the race that built these structures, before they're destroyed. Before all they were is *gone*."

"Yes." I clench my jaw for a moment. I don't have to explain myself to him. I don't think he'd understand if I did. "Yes, I'm here to steal from the temples. Specifically, the big one where they found that first solar cell, the one that got the scientists all hot and bothered, the one that's single-handedly powering what's left of the west coast. Think whatever you like about me, but you're a smart guy, and you've got to see that, right now, I'm doing better than you are. Will you let me help you or not?"

He's still staring at me like I've killed his pet dog, that smile gone, his mouth pressed into a thin line.

"Look," I say, rising to my feet. "I'm offering to help. You can refuse on principle and get killed or left to die when you miss your pick-up—trust me, your expedition isn't going to circle back around to pick you up before they split—or you can let me help you. Then we can go our separate ways, and maybe someday you testify against me in IA court and clear your conscience."

He's silent and still, clearly fighting some war against himself, a muscle standing out in his jaw as he gazes at the nearby cliff face. He could be made of the same stone, totally unmoving, wrestling with whatever's slowing down his reply.

"All right," he says finally, as if every word is costing him. "Maybe we can help each other. You get me where I want to go, and I'll tell you what artifacts are going to be worth most to the collectors."

I take a step back, caught off-guard. "Hey, I was just offering to tell you how to slim down on your supplies. I'm not *taking* you anywhere. I've got somewhere to be, and you're just going to slow me down. You're not the only one trying to beat the other raiding parties to the temple—for all I know they're already there."

"They're definitely already there." Jules lifts his head, sounding anything but concerned. In fact, some of his anger is retreating and leaving something a lot like smugness in its wake. "But fine, go ahead. Run around the place and grab what scraps you can. Maybe you'll get lucky, and stumble across a solar cell everyone else miraculously, inexplicably missed, and make your fortune in a billion-to-one fairy-tale ending. Now, if you'd tell me what to leave out of my pack, I'd appreciate it."

For all his words are polite, the know-it-all attitude—so charming just a few minutes ago—makes me want to scream. "Those *scraps* are going to—" Save me. Save my sister. Be the difference between life and wishing I were dead. But my voice tangles in my throat. "You know what, never mind. I've lost too much time as it is. Screw you." I grab my pack, shoving its straps into place and reaching for my helmet and goggles.

"There's nothing there, you know," says Jules, not bothering to get up. I ignore him, buckling the straps of my helmet to my pack and slinging the goggles around my neck. "The original astronauts and survey teams brought back everything they could. All you'll find there is an empty tomb full of angry scavengers."

I kick my empty can of beans aside and scan the canyon ahead, mapping out my route, trying to figure out if there's any way to make up this lost time and get an edge over the others. His words are ringing in my head, though, with the horrible sting of truth to them: *an empty tomb full of angry scavengers.* If that's true, it's the end for me. No ticket back to Earth, no payday, no hope for . . .

I swallow. Then Jules adds, as calmly as if he were bidding me a good morning, "Amelia, every single one of those groups is looking in the wrong place."

The words freeze me, in spite of myself—and after a split second of hesitation, and of kicking myself, I turn back toward him. "What did you say?"

"Which part?" The question is polite, so polite I could punch him in his smug little . . . But he doesn't wait for me to answer and goes on. "I said that they're all looking in the wrong place. At the risk of being a little forward with a girl I just met, bigger isn't always better."

A little while ago, his innuendo would have made me laugh. But I can't care about any of that right now. The big temple complex to the east is the one the astronauts started exploring, the one where the Los Angeles solar cell came from, the one Mink and every other scavenger operation is aiming for. But if there aren't any artifacts left in there, or if I'm robbed or captured by another operation, I'll have nothing.

I'll be too far in debt with Mink to pay my way off the planet and back through the portal to Earth, much less have enough left over to get to my sister and—I gulp for a breath. "How would you know?" My voice shakes. "The International Alliance has had it under guard for months, that's the whole reason we all had to get dropped off way out here, to avoid IA satellite detection."

Jules seems to hear the shake in my voice, and some of the arrogance leaches out of his face. "It's a red herring," he says quietly, and there's a bitter note there now without that smugness to hide it. "I know the Undying Broadcast by heart, the words and equations that brought us all here, in its original language. It said the race who found Gaia would be tested. You really think the test is 'go in this fancy building and pick up our leftovers'? Amelia, Oxford's xenoarchaeology department is world-renowned, and I grew up falling asleep under the table as the world's top experts debated these very subjects. The big temple to the east is, yes, very big, and shiny, and attractive. And there might still be a few scraps in there worth some cash. But while humans are hardwired to think 'bigger is better,' there's no reason whatsoever an alien race would think that way as well. And I'm betting my own life on the fact that it's a decoy, because I've studied the data in that broadcast and I know which one of the smaller outlying temples holds the real treasure trove. And I can take you there." Now he does get to his feet, his amusement gone, face grave.

My heart's thrashing so hard it hurts, blood rushing in my ears and threatening to deafen me. I have only one shot at this. His distaste is obvious—he's no happier about offering his help to a scavenger and a raider than I am about having to put all my faith in this stranger, whose goals definitely aren't mine. If I trust him and leave the big temple to the others, and it turns out he's lying, I'll have nothing. Even if I survive the next few weeks, I'll come to wish I hadn't when I can't pay my way off and Mink leaves me here marooned millions of light-years from Earth without enough air to last more than a few days. And if I ignore him, and get to the complex even a day or two after the other parties, I'll be sifting through the dust they leave behind, trying to cobble together a fortune from broken tablets and scraps of stone.

My mouth is dry when my voice returns, and I blurt, "You know I'm one of dozens, right? Plenty of teams figured out how to get here, after the Addison interview." I swallow hard, trying to clear the rasp from my throat. "Misleading me won't do anything to preserve your precious artifacts, because someone else will be there anyway to take them. All you'd be doing is destroying me." Fear floods my voice with that last sentence, my eyes burning. I wish I were wearing my goggles, my breather mask. Maybe then he wouldn't see me fighting not to cry.

Jules's expression changes, the tight mouth softening, the brows lifting a little. He takes half a step toward me, but then thinks better of it and stops. "I'm not trying to do that," he says quietly. "I'm saying you're right. My only hope is to reach what I'm looking

31

for as quickly as I can." He takes a breath. "You're going to get a lot farther out here than I will alone, I think we can both agree on that. But there's a bigger payout, Mia. The technology the Undying have left behind . . . it's not in a few solar cells. There's something bigger at play, and to get to it we have to go deeper, get to the heart of the temple."

My heart is pounding. Now I *know* this boy's crazy. "What, past the kinds of traps and pitfalls that took out half the *Explorer IV* mission before they gave up?"

Jules looks away, one hand coming up to tug through his curls. He's staring at the cliff again. "I'm offering you a partnership. You help me get there, and . . ." He breaks off, and I wait. I can see what the words cost him, the way they're nearly dragged from him. "I'll help us get inside the temple. From there—I'll make sure you get your money."

I can hear the disgust behind his voice by the time he finishes speaking.

For a wild second I want to blurt out the truth, that I couldn't care less about *money*, that money's a means to an end, and that my end is something I'd die for a dozen times over if I thought it'd help—but there's no profit in my death, so I'm risking my life here instead. I take a deep breath, focusing on the air filling my lungs instead of the tears filling my eyes.

I was only ever going to be sneaking through the entrances to these temples, picking up what I could, never venturing far enough to trigger the Undying defenses they set up to guard their precious legacy, whatever it is. The International Alliance has been trying to put together a proper team to penetrate the temples for years, but when their top expert on the Undying lost his shit on live TV, it kind of put their plans on hold. In a weird way, I have Addison's meltdown—Elliott Addison, the guy who first cracked the Undying broadcast code, the guy who turned a sudden 180 and started claiming that Gaia was dangerous—to thank for being here at all. If he hadn't had that public breakdown and let slip all those top-secret codes, none of the illegal scavengers would've known how to get here to Gaia. He must be writhing in his jail cell, knowing that his attempt to prevent exploration of Gaia is what flooded the surface with people like me.

Not that we can get very far. Without Addison and his expertise, neither IA-led expeditions or scavver operations can get past the temples' myriad defenses. I was only ever supposed to lift artifacts from the entrances. I was only ever supposed to slip in, slip out, and hope I made enough money to satisfy Mink.

And now I'm standing here breathing alien air with alien suns beating down on my head and there's a boy not much older than me claiming he can do what the whole global scientific community hasn't managed yet and solve a zillion-year-old alien mystery if I help keep him alive long enough to do it. And whether he's right or not, I've lost too much time now to get to the bigger temple before others strip it.

"Fine," I say, firming up my voice. "But I can't guarantee you a ride off the ground. I can get you to someone who can do it, but you'll have to pay your own way, make your own deal with her."

"Understood," he agrees, businesslike again, smoothing away his distaste at working with a scavenger. "When does she come for you?"

"Three weeks." Assuming I have the money, of course, to pay her. If I don't, she won't bother sending a shuttle down for me at all. But I don't share that with Jules.

He must know I'm not telling him everything, but for now, he doesn't press for more information. He studies my face until I feel it start to warm, making me long to pull my goggles and kerchief into place. Then he nods. "In that case, we should get moving."

JULES

I WATCH HELPLESSLY AS SHE DISCARDS MORE THAN HALF MY BELONGINGS. The organization that recruited me supplied my breather, and a few other necessities, but I spent more than I'd care to admit on the rest of it, this equipment she's tossing aside like it's worthless. I had to buy it all new, because I couldn't access most of my belongings at home.

She's obsessed with the idea that everything must serve more than one function—she brandishes her own tool, like one of those old Swiss Army knives people used to carry, as if it's worth more than my wave-stove. I want to tell her that you can order one exactly like it for twenty quid online, but when she mentions having made a number of alterations to it herself, and demonstrates its spring-loaded settings, I have to admit it's clever.

And this is why I need her. Without the relative luxury of a whole expedition to back me, I don't know how I'm going to make it to the temple intact when I know next to nothing about this underworld that she's a part of, this network of raiders and thieves.

Back home, these are the kinds of people who start looting stores and hospitals the second a city's people are forced to abandon it. It's worst in the U.S., according to the news—they're seeing the most drastic climate changes, with deserts sweeping across the continent and sandstorms violent enough to claim lives. Families get packed up and carted elsewhere once the city shuts down, and their sofas aren't even cold before these scavenger gangs move in and start divvying up what's left. The thought of working with one of them makes me sick to my stomach, but at least she's only one, and not a whole gang, and at least she's . . . not really what I expected, I suppose.

She seems to take particular relish in lecturing me on the ways my gear is redundant—any item of mine that can't justify its existence in half a dozen ways is stashed in a shallow cave, there to stay until the end of time, I suppose. Or until the next spacefaring civilization comes through, following the same trail we did.

Still, once we start walking, I'm grateful for the lighter load. We have several hours of daylight left, and we ought to dispose of quite some distance before we camp for the night. The two suns bear down overhead, and without trees for shade, it's hot. It's hard to wrap my head around the idea that I'm genuinely walking on *another planet*, and I occasionally push at the idea, worrying at it like a loose tooth, trying to provoke a response.

We thought we were done with our chance at this when the Alpha Centauri colony mission failed, calling out to Earth for help that they knew couldn't come, then vanishing forever into the blackness of space. But here I am, Jules Thomas Addison, literally going where no one has gone before.

And I'm lying to the one ally I have.

It's not bragging or exaggeration to say that right now, I'm the most important person on this planet. I *have* to reach that temple. Not just for me, not just for my father, but for all of us, every person on Earth. Including Amelia. That's justification enough for the lie. And odds are there will be something of value there she can take, so it probably isn't even a lie.

It's justification enough for teaming up with a scavver—and I've promised myself that I *will* find her a way to earn her money, however distasteful looting is. I was prepared to do it to a small degree for Global Energy to earn my ride here—helping her is no different.

But it's hard to reconcile this girl with what she's here to do. It's easier to hate vultures and carrion scavengers when they're not standing in front of you with freckles and dye-streaked hair and a razor-sharp wit. But then again, I'd like to think I'm a fundamentally honest person, and I'm in the middle of lying to her about what we'll find when we reach our destination.

She's made it clear she's here to make money, and I need to remember she'd walk away from me in a heartbeat if she thought there was a better profit in it. Which means that I need to be prepared to tell her whatever will keep her by my side.

If we're not moving at the speed I'd hoped for in a larger group, equipped with vehicles, it's better than nothing. We should be at the temple I'm after in under a week, traveling on foot. We're heading for a long, winding canyon, a landmark I memorized from the endless swaths of satellite images that used to litter my father's study back at Oxford. If we're lucky, it should provide us with a highway that will take us most of the way to our destination. It has a stream running the better part of its length, which will take care of our water needs as well.

The only problem is that for a while, at least, it's the same path all the other groups will be following. The canyon branches in a number of places, and eventually we'll be taking a different branch, but until we do, we've got to keep our profile as low and quiet as we can to avoid attracting attention from scavengers who'd be just as happy to raid our packs as the temples themselves, and perhaps remove a little competition at the same time.

My father would be horrified.

Dr. Elliott Addison used to be the last word on the Undying. There was no one more dedicated to unraveling their secrets, no one more passionate about learning from them. But the International Alliance, haunted by their decades-old promise to find a solution to Earth's decline, accused him of wasting time.

And the harder they pushed, the more my father began to resist. When the *Explorer IV* crew entered that main temple—without my father's guidance—he raged for a week. And that was when he began fighting, trying to make them understand, making passionate pleas to the IA authorities and the public alike that some of mankind's most important, practical discoveries came out of pure research. That the time spent to truly explore Gaia would be anything but wasted. That more power cells would certainly help now—but only until we outgrew those like we outgrew our oil reserves.

He desperately believed that the key to our salvation lay in understanding the Undying—in understanding why they destroyed themselves, after reaching such heights in their civilization. Their warnings, my father said, were to stop us doing exactly what the International Alliance would have us do: rush in, take as much profitable and useful technology as we could carry, and start shoving it anywhere it'd fit in Earth's infrastructure.

He wanted us to take our time, to focus on the science, to let ourselves be drawn on by exploration, curiosity, and discovery instead of driven by greed. He was ridiculed for his insistence that we needed to open our minds, to explore this place with the thoughtfulness and reverence—and caution—it deserved, not run so hungrily for the one benefit we could see that we missed others . . . or missed dangers.

They used to come to our flat in Oxford, the suits from the International Alliance, and I'd put my ear to the door of his office while they argued with my father for hours. My father wanted to learn about Gaia and the Undying as badly as they did—wanted to help those who needed it as badly as they did—and he tried longer than most scientists would have to find alternate explanations for the dangers and inconsistencies he was finding in the broadcast. First they came to debate him—then to argue with him—then to plead with him to change his position. Pleading turned to cajoling turned to peer exile turned to threats, but he never seemed to falter.

I didn't realize he'd stopped trying to convince the world until after he snapped on live television. I'm not sure he even knew he was going to commit treason that night until it was happening. But halfway through the program, the interviewer abandoned the usual, courteous dance and pushed and baited him, started accusing him of sacrificing the welfare of others—people like Mia, who desperately need the IA to solve Earth's energy problems—merely to satisfy his own academic curiosity.

And I saw the moment he broke. A few security clearance codes blurted in frustration and anger—he already knew at that point they were going to drag him away, I'm sure of it—and in seconds hundreds of log-ins around the world had downloaded every document the IA had kept classified about Gaia, the temples, and the Undying tech.

He meant to give the world transparency. Instead he handed them the keys to pillaging this planet.

I remember the moment he met my eyes, as they held me back and dragged him out of the studio after shutting down his interview. I haven't met his eyes since, except through a vidscreen once a week.

He's sacrificed everything, from his reputation to his happiness to his future, to *my* future, for his cause. And I have, too, because I believe he's right. I trust him.

My father is certain that we need to enter Gaia slowly, carefully, recognizing that the true wealth of these ruins lies in scientific study and understanding. And yet here we all are, charging on in like shoppers at a holiday sale looking for the shiniest baubles to bring home.

Nobody is supposed to be on the surface at present—the space station in orbit is tasked with enforcing that ban, and conducting satellite surveillance to continue building the maps and surveys the IA's expedition will use when trying to solve the riddle of the Undying temples. Of course, as I discovered through my contact at Global Energy, for the right price, the staff on the station won't just look the other way, they'll even get you down to the surface. Thanks to what my father said on a live broadcast, it's not just the International Alliance that knows how to reach Gaia now.

It must have been quite an investment for Amelia to get down here on her own. I'm about to ask her whether she raised the money herself, or has backers, when she stops at the crest of a hill, dropping to a crouch with a low curse. I thump down beside her, easing forward to prop up on my elbows and peer over the ridge to see what stopped her in her tracks.

The creek we were aiming for is a silvery line stretching along the red valley, looking strangely barren without plants taking advantage of the water. My eyes are used to Earth in ways I didn't even realize until I landed here. But it's not the lack of plant life that makes Mia groan at my side.

Camped all along one side of the river is a sizable expedition that's paused for their evening meal, crates and grav-lifters visible, and a row of skimmer bikes. For a brief moment I think maybe it's the expedition I was meant to join, and my heart lifts—but then I recognize the woman from our little encounter by the spring. *Raiders.* I count at least four people moving back and forth between their possessions. They'll have visibility for the length of the canyon. *Perfututi.* There goes our plan.

"So," I say, gazing down at them. "Head on down and introduce ourselves, yes?"

Amelia lets out a snort, then taps her goggles to activate their zoom setting. "Wait here, Oxford, okay? I got this." Apparently that's all the warning I'm getting before she starts to clamber down into the canyon without further consultation. I grab hold of her pack, and after a couple of tugs she realizes she's not going anywhere until I let go. "What?"

"Well, I suppose most pressingly, where are you going?" I venture, still holding on.

She eyeballs me, disapproving of this new streak of curiosity. "I'm going to steal one of those bikes," she says, in the same nonchalant tone with which she might say, *I'm going to go for a nice stroll.*

I tighten my grip as I turn that one over in my mind. How am I meant to work with this kind of impulsiveness? I was kidding when I said it, but was she really just going to saunter on down there and hope it all unfolded according to plan? Assuming she even has a plan.

When she tugs against my grip, I return to the question of the bike. On one hand, it would be enormously risky to try to steal one. On the other, a skimmer bike could cut our travel from a whole week to less than a day. *And,* a tiny voice says in my mind, *if they catch her, she's one of them anyway, isn't she? What's the worst that could happen to her?*

The fact that I just asked myself that makes me a little bit sick, but I *have* to remember that what I'm here to do is more important than me, than her, or than any individual. And I have to remember that she's a scavver, and I have no way of knowing if she's even interested in returning loyalty, let alone capable of it.

The skimmer would get us there in less than a day.

Also, if there's one thing I've worked out about Amelia already, it's that there's very little point arguing with her once she's made up her mind. "Then let me help," I say, instead. "Your safety is my safety, now."

She eyeballs me again, and I wait out her disapproval until she adjusts her goggles with a muttered opinion that she chooses to keep under her breath. "Stay close. If they spot us, make for the ridge to the east. It's too rocky for skimmer bikes, so at least it'll be a footrace."

"Yes ma'am," I say, just to provoke that little line between her eyes that shows up when she glares at me. I need to stop noticing that.

Though we've got to move slowly to avoid triggering any major rockslides down the canyon walls, the breeze running through the valley masks our smaller movements. So really, it's just a case of patience. Sweat runs into the small cuts on my hands and face, and my back aches steadily—but Amelia moves without complaint, and I'm not going to give her another reason to think twice about agreeing to partner up. This skimmer bike idea alone has proved that I was right to recruit her help—I'd have carefully avoided this group, and spent another week making my way to the temple.

Presumably because there are only a few dozen people on the planet, the camp doesn't have any guards posted. I see a lean man with dark hair sprawled on the grass, eating, talking to the woman Mia decked with her helmet by the spring where we met. That means our other friend must be somewhere nearby too, with or without his trousers.

It's not a huge coincidence that it's the same group, given how difficult it is just to get to Gaia's surface, but my stomach tightens.

Until we peel away from the main route along the canyon, heading to my smaller target, we're going to be up close and personal with these other groups—groups that clearly have no qualms about shooting the competition. I think about the scavenger's gun tucked into my bag, one of the few pieces of equipment Amelia put into the "keep" pile without discussion. Even if I'd thought to make it accessible before crawling into danger, though, I'm not sure I could really point it at someone with the intent to pull the trigger.

I'm rather regretting my impulsive order to that big guy to leave his trousers behind. Perhaps under other circumstances they might have held off on shooting, afraid of ruining their skimmer—but I have a feeling he won't hesitate to aim straight at us. A couple of the other raiders are filling their canteens at the spring, and one's standing some distance away, face lit by the screen of his phone or tablet as he hunches over it.

Most important for us, nobody's paying attention to the row of skimmers.

The lack of order also means there's no discernible pattern to their movements, though we watch for a little as Amelia taps her finger softly against a pebble. She's counting the seconds, I realize, looking for the best gap. She's not holding her stolen gun either, but I'm betting hers is in a pocket somewhere she can reach it if she has to. I ease my knife out of my own pocket—happily, it has several extra tools built into the handle, so I was permitted to keep it. All hell's going to break loose when we make off with one of their bikes, but I think I know how to slow down their pursuit.

I'm jolted from my planning when Amelia tilts her head at me and, crouching low, heads toward the bikes.

My height means I'm a liability, but I can at least keep up, even if I can't crouch as low. Amelia drops to one knee to work on the ignition of her chosen skimmer, and I drop down beside her, crawling along the row to the farthest bike. Time to see if all those hours of putting up with my cousin Neal's obsession with *his* bike were worth it—time to see if I can remember how to find the power cables. I check the casing with one finger to make sure it's not still hot, then reach up inside to grope around blindly, sending up a silent prayer of thanks as my fingers close over the nest of cords. Heart thumping, hands sweating, I yank the knife through them, severing the connections, then crawl down to the next one.

A shower of sand hits the back of my neck as I reach the third, and my heart surges up into my throat. I jerk around, to find Amelia silently shooting me a *what-the-hell* look. But there's no way to explain what I'm doing without speaking, so I immobilize the final bike and start crawling back to her side. Once I'm close enough, I drop my head to whisper into her ear, "Nobody's going to chase us now."

She's silent for an instant, then a huff of air hints at the laughter neither of us can risk. I feel myself wanting to laugh, too—some combination of adrenaline and terror and utterly mad abandon. My mind is shrieking that this isn't me, that I belong back at Oxford, that this girl and her insane ideas are going to get me killed, that I'm no daredevil and my best bet would be to stay put and call back up to the station when it's back overhead.

And yet I feel myself wanting to laugh. Because there's some part of this that's . . . *fun.*

It turns out she's using an ancient paperclip to short out the thumbprint scanner, and with a satisfying hiss, it gives up the ghost. She winks, then rises to her feet to swing one leg over the bike. She shifts her pack around to her front to make room for me to slide on behind her. I'm momentarily stuck on where to put my hands— wrapping them around her waist seems overly familiar—when a voice rings out behind us and steps approach.

"Rasa said to leave the skimmers there." The owner of the voice has clearly mistaken us for members of his gang, and every nerve in my body lights up as adrenaline goes crashing through me. *Oh, perfututi, we're screwed, where did he come from?* "She wants to make sure they're sheltered if the wind—" And then the voice rises abruptly to a shout. "Hey, who—"

I end my debate and throw my arms around Amelia, and she jams her thumb into the ignition. The bike hums to life, lifting up off the sand to about knee height, and as she turns her head to look back at the bike's old owner, her smile's pure mischief. "Thanks for the ride!"

Then we're accelerating away, gathering speed rapidly as she weaves her way through the boulders, making for level ground. I've only been on the back of Neal's bike a couple of times, but I know enough to lean when it turns, and as the wind rushes past us, I'm resisting the urge to tip my head back and shout our victory.

Then the rocks to our right explode into flying bits of gravel that strike my back like shrapnel. I twist my head to see the scavengers lining the edge of their camp, aiming their weapons after us. Explosive ammunition. Amelia's curse is whipped away by the wind, and she accelerates so fast that she risks a spectacular crash as bullets fly past us.

And abruptly, the world snaps into focus.

What the *hell* am I doing?

This isn't a game.

This is my *life*, and if one of those things so much as grazes us, I won't live long enough to feel it. I'll be dead on an alien planet, and nobody at home will ever know what happened to me. My heart surges up through my throat, and every movement, every sound, is turned up high. My whole body is pins and needles, twitching in anticipation of a bullet right between my shoulder blades.

This isn't a game, and I'm way, way out of my depth. *I shouldn't be here.*

The skimmer tips at a crazy angle with no warning, and I tighten my arms around Amelia while desperately trying to make sense of the world as it flies past. We're careening down the side of a canyon, and for three terrifying heartbeats it seems as though there's no way we can stop—we're going to cartwheel end over end, to lie broken at the bottom until they come for us.

Then the bike levels out, and Amelia's thumping on my forearm with one fist to get me to loosen my grip—when I remember how to make my arms work and do so, she takes a long, shuddering breath. We're racing along the bottom of the canyon, taking the twists and turns like we have nothing to lose, and though I crane my neck to look behind us, I have no way of knowing if they're following.

Then the canyon fork looms up as we take another curve, and somehow through my streaming eyes and lurching stomach I realize how much ground we've covered. "Take the left fork!" I scream to be heard over the roar of the wind and the engine.

"What?" Mia's voice is half torn away by the wind. "But the temples—"

"Trust me!" I give her a squeeze, the only way I have to emphasize my words.

She hesitates a moment longer, then says something in reply that I'm glad I can't decipher over the wind. She throws her weight to the left and the bike goes lurching down the narrower canyon path, away from the soon-to-be-well-traveled path to the central temple.

Some time later, she abruptly skids over to the side and cuts the engine, the sound echoing off the canyon walls, then dying away. The skimmer thuds down onto the ground, the jolt traveling all the way up my spine. We both hold perfectly still, her thumb hovering over the ignition, straining our ears for the sound of pursuit. There's nothing but silence. The walls of the canyon stretch up above us, lips tilting in to obscure most of the afternoon sky, and it seems we're hidden.

"Are we dead?" I whisper, breath still coming in short, sharp gasps, my body still a bundle of nerves.

"Don't think so," she whispers back. "They tried pretty hard, though. You're *sure* this is the way?"

"Positive," I reply, trying to make myself sound certain. Because I *am* certain *I'm* going the right way—just not so certain that it's the way she'd choose, if she had all the facts.

"Then let's get a little more distance." She starts up the skimmer again, taking the corners with only a little more caution as we race away down the canyon. My insides are churning, and I'm pretty sure my stomach's trying to climb up my throat to join my heart there, and the things I'm repeating to myself like a litany aren't making much difference at all.

They're not following us, I tell myself. *We made it. We'll get to the temple faster. This was a good idea.* I'm clenching and unclenching my fists, as if by sheer physical force I can make these things true despite the one thought that keeps ringing around and around in my head.

I'm not just out of my depth, I'm realizing I don't even know how to swim.

I can't imagine my father's face, if they even bothered to tell him about my death. They might think it would compromise their chance of getting him to start cooperating again. I can't imagine my cousin Neal's, or my mother's—though there's a lot I can't imagine about her, lately.

I shove all of it out of my mind. We're closer to the temple than we were before. Closer to its spiral shape and stone curves, and the answers I hope to find there.

Finally Amelia pulls over, parking the skimmer behind a boulder, and turning it off once more. It crunches down to the ground, and we both climb off. My hands are shaking. I clear my throat before I speak, hoping at least my voice will be level. "That was good driving."

"It's easy here," she replies, shrugging away the compliment. "I'm used to much tighter quarters. Skid on some loose gravel here, you're in trouble. Crash into a skyscraper on Earth, and you're done. Let's take a few minutes, stretch, use our breathers, then keep moving. Even if they repair their bikes, they've got no way of finding us now, and we'll hear them coming if they get close."

I try for normal conversation, stretching my back, willing my arms and legs to start working properly as my system tries to process the shock of what's happened. "Where did you learn to ride like that?"

"Chicago." She glances at me, sees that isn't answer enough, and shakes her head. "You wouldn't want to know."

And of course, immediately, I do. It's a distraction, and I need to do more than stretch my arms and legs to get myself back to rights. "Why not?" I unhook my breather from my belt and take a long drag of oxygen-rich air from its attached tank. The oxygen in the tank goes a long way, just a little added to the air I'm drawing in naturally, but that extra percent or two makes a real difference.

"Because it'll give you all the more reason to think I'm a terrible person," she replies, not sounding particularly guilty about it.

"I've committed just as much crime today as you have," I point out.

"True," she allows. "But look on the bright side. Grand theft skimmer bike isn't as bad as breaking International Alliance planetary embargoes. You're clearly on the path back toward the light."

"You're right, I'm de-escalating. I'll be reformed in no time. You're a good influence."

She laughs for that, shaking her head. "You're unexpected, Oxford."

"I'm reaching for the last vestiges of composure," I admit. "Please tell me that terrified you half as much as it terrified me."

"It did." She eases off her pack and leans back against the canyon wall, soaking up the heat from the sun-warmed rock, folding her arms around her mid-section to hug herself. "The reason I've lived so long is that I avoid people like that. I thought they were going to hit us."

"I'm glad we stole that guy's trousers this morning," I say. "I'm pretty sure I need a new pair."

That startles a proper laugh out of her, and the noise thaws something inside me a little. We could have been shot. *But we weren't.* "If you won't tell me how you learned to drive, tell me something else about yourself," I try, just to see if I can keep her talking. Let my nerves settle. And keep her from asking any questions about me, because I'm not sure my poker face is any good right now.

She considers the question for a minute or so before she replies. "When I was little," she says eventually, "I wanted to be an astronomer when I grew up." Which isn't quite the same thing as telling me something about herself *now*, but—actually, I take that back. She's clearly not an astronomer, so in a way, I do know something about her. How things turned out for her. I want to ask what happened to get in the way of that dream, but I bury the question for the present.

"When I was small, I wanted to be an airplane." The embarrassment is worth it, for her quick snort of laughter, even if it's probably half fueled by adrenaline from our heist and ensuing escape. "There was logic behind it," I protest. "I wanted to fly, but birds seemed very fragile. My father tried to explain it wasn't feasible, but I kept pointing out every new cybernetic upgrade that came along. I was completely confident they'd have the plane question sorted by the time I grew up, which would of course be far, far into the future. My father said I might see some drawbacks to being a plane by adulthood, though, and turns out he was right."

"I don't know." She's still grinning, and the sight of it warms my core a little more, almost banishing the pang I feel at the mention of my father. Almost banishing the fear that's still pulsing through me. "Being an airplane sounds pretty good to me. For a start, you'd have a way to get off the ground, instead of being stuck here. Better the pilot—or the shuttle, I guess—than the cargo."

The image of the portal between Earth and Gaia comes back to me for a moment. My backer's representative, Charlotte, somehow got me formal International Alliance identification—albeit in the name of Francois LaRoux—and I posed as a junior technician being posted to the orbital station around Gaia. I pretended to speak nothing but French, which helped avoid most conversation during transit. "The view on the way here was pretty spectacular," I admit. "The portal itself, the way it shimmered, you know? Even if the jump through it was disconcertingly like being . . . stretched."

"No," she replies, grimacing. "I don't know. I spent my trip stuffed in a packing crate." Her tone does not invite more conversation on the subject of our trip here, and I move along quickly.

"Well, I haven't entirely ruled the plane option out," I say. "If this life of crime continues, and I become some sort of evil mastermind, I'll certainly have the funds. I'll take you for a ride." And then, almost as much to convince myself as to comfort her: "I don't think you're a terrible person, Mia."

"You think what I do is terrible," she replies, looking away finally to locate her own breather mask. "Same thing, really, for you."

And that shuts me up. I don't know how to argue with what's essentially true. Amelia and the others here on Gaia are destroying the only chance we have at unlocking the secrets of the Undying.

It's unfathomable to me, this willingness to disregard everything we could learn—and to take such unthinkable risks with humanity's safety—just for the sake of quick cash. But I can't say any of that out loud, not and keep her here with me, so I fall silent.

We'd always thought we were alone in the universe—or that any other life was so unimaginably far away that we might as well be. The quickening decline of our planet, the worldwide realization that we were doomed, was what sparked the formation of the International Alliance. Created to realize the idea of building a ship capable of traveling to the next solar system and the planet astronomers had dubbed Centaurus so that humanity might endure, the IA represented the power of ideas, faith in the future, the infinite vision and reach of our species. It represented hope.

It was such a thing to have done—the whole of humanity pulling together, pooling resources, launching our colonists, an inspired act of cooperation unimaginable before the rapidly changing climate put all our other petty grievances on hold.

But then, eight years into their journey—just over fifty years ago now—something went catastrophically wrong. Their final transmission was a plea for help playing over and over, for the International Alliance to save them. But the IA couldn't—or perhaps wouldn't—commit the colossal resources required for a second mission, a rescue mission able to reach them beyond the edge of our solar system. That had always been the understanding—that the Centauri colonists would be on their own once they left the heliosphere for interstellar space.

We're sorry, was Earth's response. *Godspeed.*

There was a camp that thought we should've salvaged the Centauri mission at any cost. That we weren't just saving lives, we were saving our last hope, a journey we *had* to take. But others argued we simply didn't have the money, the resources—that we couldn't afford to attempt rescuing three hundred souls most likely lost already by the time their distress call reached Earth, at the cost of projects that could aid hundreds of thousands, even millions, of people suffering now on Earth.

Eventually their looped distress call simply faded away.

All those lives, those resources, the unprecedented global cooperation . . . for nothing. The mission's failure convinced mankind the stars didn't hold any solutions for us, not that our technology could reach. What we had was all we'd ever have—we couldn't simply flee the world we were destroying to find another. The International Alliance rebranded itself, turning away from the stars in order to find ways to extend the remaining resources on Earth.

Until, that is, the small handful of astronomers still searching for confirmation of the Centauri mission's demise picked up a new signal. Until my father, the famed mathematician and linguist Elliott Addison, decoded the Undying broadcast. Until that broadcast led us to Gaia, a planet with secrets and technologies so powerful an entire species destroyed itself fighting over them.

I'm not so naïve as to think that the companies hiring people like me are trying to solve the mystery of the Undying for the good of humanity. They want the alien tech for themselves, a monopoly. After seeing what the solar cell could do in Los Angeles, most of the world thinks this tech will solve all of Earth's energy problems. The company that manages to unlock Gaia's secrets will make a killing.

But their vision is locked so firmly on this one earthly goal that they forget to lift their gazes. They forget to see the stars, as humanity once did, as we all used to do when we were children. When we learned about other stories and cultures for the sake of doing so, for how those revelations changed us, what they made us. Gaia is the chance to learn on a scale we've never imagined before, and instead we've become traitors and thieves.

I accepted Global Energy's offer to lead their expedition because they could get me here. Their sleek executive, Charlotte, found me through my cousin—and best friend—Neal. He's an engineering major, and he's interning with them this year. He and Charlotte got to talking, and she came to understand what others didn't— that I'm my father's son in many ways, and knowledgeable enough about Gaia to help achieve both our ends.

So she made me an offer I couldn't refuse. They could put me on Gaia's surface, and as long as I shared my findings with them, I could choose my own course. Nobody's pretending they're not in this race for their own corporate interests, but Charlotte understands there are bigger questions to be answered here, and she cares about more than profit.

I still didn't tell her which temple I was heading for, of course— Mia may think I'm an idiot, but I'm not stupid enough to give away the existence and location of what my father believes will be the defining discovery on Gaia, the one that proves once and for all whether we're saving or dooming ourselves. I intended to hit a couple of smaller temples first as misdirection, to keep them from realizing I'm not here to uncover tech. The one upside to having missed my exploration party is that I don't have to hide my goal and its significance, and I can head straight for the spiral-shaped temple.

There, I can look for an explanation that will prove my father right, once and for all—or, though I can't imagine it, prove him wrong.

Somehow, the fact that there was a third option never really sank in. That I might not prove the danger of the tech or uncover it, because I could die without ever making it to the temple or penetrating its defenses. Mouth dry, palms damp, with a girl symbolizing everything my father stands against, everything I stand against—I'm suddenly wondering how much my life is worth.

When I look up, Mia's frowning, scanning the ridge with her goggles in place—from the way she adjusts a dial on the side, I'm assuming she's got some kind of magnification lens in there.

"What is it?"

"Maybe nothing," she replies, though there's a tension in her voice that makes me question her nonchalance. "Thought I saw a flash up there on the rim, but it's hard to tell with light coming from two different suns—it's weird here, eyes play tricks on you."

"Think someone's following us?" My thoughts summon up the trouser-less man's face as he glared daggers at me. I have no doubt he's both re-armed and re-trousered by now. But would they really deviate from the path they believe holds all the riches and glory just to take revenge on a couple of teenagers?

"I don't think they'd bother coming after us for just one bike," Mia replies, echoing my own thoughts. "But we'd better keep moving, just in case. The farther away from the other path we get, the less likely they are to keep following us. If they're following us at all."

We remount the skimmer in silence after that.

My stomach is in knots, and I know it's not just the twists and turns of the skimmer bike. I don't like misleading her. I've never really experienced . . . is this *camaraderie?* I'm not sure I'd know. I've just never been very good at knowing what to do with people my own age. Even when we were all very small, the other children knew I wasn't quite the same as them, and try as I might, I could never fit into their games. I asked too many questions, I think.

My cousin Neal was the nearest I came, with his quick grin and quicker wit. Popular with the ladies, even more popular with the gentlemen, Neal. He more or less harassed me into joining him on the university water polo team against my protestations, and to everyone's surprise, I loved it. To our collective astonishment, I was *good* at it.

He dragged me onto the back of his bike as well, giving me the practice I'd need here on Gaia, though neither of us ever could have imagined that. He dragged me out to see and do new things over and over, trying with all his might to breathe some youth into me. When the few friends I'd managed to accumulate left after my father's disgrace, Neal was the one who stayed. He was the one who kept me on the team. I heard him arguing with the captain when I arrived for practice the night after my father's arrest, wondering if I'd still be welcome.

"He's just a kid!" I can still hear the anger in my cousin's voice—a note I'd never heard before.

"He's not *just* anything," the captain replied.

I nearly turned around and walked out again, but some stubbornness made me continue on to the change rooms. Something in me decided that if I wasn't welcome there, then they'd have to tell me to my face.

And maybe I was just very good at polo, because nobody ever did. And so I stayed, though the early green shoots of friendship with my teammates died away.

Nothing survives for long in the desert of our disgrace.

• • •

Amelia's the one to restart the conversation a couple of hours later, when we take another break to stretch. She pulls down her kerchief so she can snag a few lungfuls from her breather, silent long enough that I'm surprised when she breaks the quiet to speak. "How do you *know* you're taking us to the right temple?"

"How much do you know about the Undying?" The basics of what we know about the ancient aliens are taught even in regular schools, I assume—except I'm not sure how much school Amelia actually attended, so I'm treading carefully.

She shifts, leaning back against a rock and eyeing me. "I know enough."

Not helpful. I hunt for my least lecture-y tone. "The broadcast that reached us fifty years ago, the one m—Dr. Addison decoded when he was at university, didn't just give the instructions on how to build the portal to Gaia."

"It also talked about how they destroyed themselves," she

interrupts. "That the precious technology they've hidden here on Gaia is their legacy, that only worthy people can inherit it, blah blah blah. I'm not a total idiot, Jules, I didn't come here knowing nothing."

"Ah, but see, what most people don't know is that there's a code within the code." My father was the one who discovered the second layer of encoding in the Undying's message. "It's classified. Originally they all thought it was just a distortion in the message, but actually, it was intentional." And this is where I lie to her. Not about the existence of the second layer of the code—that part is true. Just about what it says. "Beneath the instructions for the portal were a set of coordinates showing which of their structures held the key to finding their precious technology."

"There's a what now?" Amelia's frowning at me. "If there were more information, telling us where to look, we'd know it. The IA's good at keeping secrets, but not *that* good."

I wipe my brow, glad I thought to pull out a handkerchief from the discard pile when Amelia was throwing away half my gear. "They kept this one. And anyway, only a handful of academics know how to translate it."

The frown's graduated to a scowl, though it makes lying to her no easier—the scowl's almost as appealing as her smile. But some of Amelia's skepticism is fading away in favor of curiosity, and she leans forward. "You're still talking about Elliott Addison, aren't you? This is the warning he was trying to give on TV, before they cut the feed. This is what he went to jail for. You're saying you know what he knows?"

I'm treading on dangerous ground here. I know even more than that, but I don't want her to realize she's talking about my father. She's a scavver, and I won't ever be able to entirely trust her. She certainly wouldn't trust me, if she knew whose son I am. "I do. And before you ask, no, I'm not telling you how I know. That's not a part of this deal."

She closes her mouth, frowning again. But the expression shifts as she mulls my words over, and eventually she's eyeing me with cautious interest. "So you're telling me that you have, essentially, a secret map to all the good stuff that no one else has?"

"Not exactly how I'd put it, but . . . yes." I'm lying. *I'm lying.* But I have no choice.

She squints at me for a long moment, a dimple in her cheek suggesting that she's chewing at her lip. "I don't suppose you've also got a map outlining the locations of all the traps and pitfalls and puzzles inside, like the ones at the big temple that pulverized half the astronauts in *Explorer IV.*"

"Not as such, no."

"But you can read their writing? Understand their language?"

"As well as anyone can." I pause. "Except for Elliott Addison, of course."

She's watching me, eyes narrowed, and for a long, breathless moment I'm certain she's figured it out. I have lighter skin than my father due to my mother's genetic contribution, but we've got the same hair, the same eyes, the same jaw. I'm waiting for her to ask me how I could possibly know what I know. Someone as savvy as she is wouldn't just take the word of a near stranger on any of this—she's going to demand answers. Any second now.

I've only told her a fraction of the whole story.

It's true, about the layers of coding. There's the first layer, telling us of the riches of the Undying, waiting to be claimed by the worthy.

And then there's the second. The layer we thought was a distortion in the signal, a blip of no consequence, ignored for decades. It's different from the first, shoved in there like an afterthought. It's inelegant, messy . . . inconsistent, in ways that are hard to quantify. There's a *not-rightness* about it that's hard to pin down. And the message it conveys is much, much smaller than the first.

When you graph it, the mathematical equation in that second layer of code marks out a shape resembling a Fibonacci spiral, like a Nautilus shell or our own Milky Way, but subtly altered. And there's just one word, its isolation making it all the more difficult to translate. But we think we know what it means.

Catastrophe. Apocalypse. The end of all things.

It's this secret layer, with its scientific inconsistencies, that stopped my father in his tracks. He was already begging the IA to slow down, to try to understand what the words meant before looting Gaia like the world was clamoring for them to do. But that second layer of code changed everything, for him. Here was proof, he claimed, of what he'd been saying all along—the Undying themselves were sending us a message of danger, and if the IA couldn't justify slowing down for the sake of discovery, surely they'd *have* to slow down for practical reasons, for the safety of their expeditions and Earth itself.

But the leaders of the International Alliance weighed the good of the many—already, Los Angeles has a fresh water plant powered by just one small piece of Undying tech—against the "unfounded" warnings of an academic already out of favor, and of course they decided against him.

So he defied them. Tried to warn the world. And now he's locked away.

I only worked out what I had to do a couple of weeks ago. I was staring at the topographical maps of Gaia again, studying the now familiar lines for the thousandth time, when suddenly I blinked out of my daze, and pulled the map in closer, my breath catching in my throat.

Because there it was, at the end of a canyon, backed against a wall of cliffs: a small, otherwise unremarkable temple in the shape of a spiral. Shaped into the same Nautilus spiral as the second, secret layer of code. Only a handful of us even know about the Nautilus, and it's barely a speck on most of the maps, which is why none of the other scavengers are likely to bother with it.

That temple is where I'll learn what the message means. Where I'll learn why they paired this shape with the warning they did:

the end of all things. That's where I'll find the answers to my father's questions.

And if I have to lie to her, so be it. She's all I have to replace the expedition that was supposed to back me up, and my chances without her are slim at best. So I'll make sure she has reason to *want* to get to the temple. Even if it means lying to her about what we'll find there.

I expect her to read all of this on my face, to somehow know. To call me out, to walk away, chasing her loot and leaving me to survive alone.

But instead she just leans forward and shoves to her feet with a groan for sore muscles, and reaches for her pack. "Then we'd better keep moving."

• • •

The bike chews up the ground between us and the temple, and though the canyon's twists and turns make my stomach lurch, it provides us at least a little bit of cover in case our new friends manage to repair their bikes and pick up our trail. For the last part of our journey, though, we have to work together to heave the skimmer up the steep canyon wall. According to my maps, the temple should be just beyond the stone rim.

Once we reach the top, I see it. A huge stone structure juts out of the cliff face at the end of the valley, its walls curving ever so slightly around in the start of the Fibonacci spiral it forms from above. I've studied every satellite photo of this temple, imagined myself standing before the huge pillars supporting the entrance a thousand times in the last few weeks, but nothing prepared me for the reality of a structure built by an alien species.

This moment feels holy.

"Hey, Oxford!" It's only when Amelia shoves the bike into me that I realize I've dropped my end, leaving her to haul it over the lip of the cliff by herself. I grab the seat, pulling it onto level ground, then turn my attention back to the temple's façade.

"That it?" she pants, clearly needing a few minutes with her breather.

"That's it." I can't contain myself—I can see the entrance chamber in my mind's eye. If this temple is anything like the one *Explorer IV*'s astronauts photographed, there'll be carvings in the anteroom, frenzied and abstract. The patterns and waves of glyphs will be etched into the stone surfaces with the kind of violent exuberance that makes me want to get to know their creators—and makes me a little afraid of them. Dropping my pack, I'm walking toward it before I've even decided to move.

"Jules, stop!" Amelia grabs my arm, dragging me to a halt. "It's been there a zillion years, it'll probably still be there in the morning. Let's not get blown up or melted or sliced and diced tonight, okay? It'll be dark soon. We can hole up here tonight, the temple walls will hide the light from our camp from the canyon floor."

I grit my teeth, forcing down a noise of frustration. She's right. Deus, I know she's right, and this is exactly the sort of thing I need her around for. But it's *right there*. I've spent my whole life dreaming of this. My father spent most of *his* life dreaming of this. A pang shoots through my heart, making my eyes water. *He should be here.* With an entire expedition of experts at his back, and the world holding its breath to see what he would uncover.

I'll have to feel it for him. I breathe deep, gazing at the temple and letting the euphoria in. "There's nowhere left on Earth," I say, the excitement bubbling up again, overruling my frustration. "Not the highest mountain, not the remotest desert, or the deepest trenches of the ocean. Nowhere someone else hasn't been first. But this, Mia, this is ours. Everybody else who comes here, they'll be walking in *our* footsteps. We have the privilege of this first glimpse of another culture. Another species. Another *world*."

I can't help it, the excitement rising in me—she's still holding my arm to keep me from running forward, and I grab hers in return, reeling her in so I can throw my arms around her, lifting her clean off her feet to turn in a wild circle. "Us! First!"

She gives a startled squawk as we whirl, and she swats at one of my arms, and it's the feel of her—wiry and tense and strong—that reminds me who she is. What she is. *Scavenger.* I set her down, trying for nonchalance but getting only so far as awkward. She's got a smile on her face, small and a bit baffled though it is.

"Let's make sure our first steps inside the temple aren't our last," she says breathlessly, dismissively, but I can see an answering glimmer of excitement in her eyes. Some part of her gets it, that this isn't just about scavenging—that it can't be, no matter how badly you want money. For just an instant, she's not one of them. She's just a girl, standing at my side, while we linger before the doorway to an ancient alien world.

I have to clear my throat, then clear it again. "Right. You're right. I just—I want so badly to know why they led us here. What secret they're hiding, what really happened to them."

Her mouth quirks. "So long as you're not *dying* to know."

I can't hide my smile, despite her horrendous pun. And maybe a tiny bit because of it. "Just think, Mia. We could find anything in there. And tomorrow, we'll be the first humans in the universe to set foot inside that temple."

5

AMELIA

THE DESERT SURFACE OF GAIA GETS BITTER COLD ONCE THE SUNS GO DOWN.

My phone's thermometer cheerfully announced to me that it was only a few degrees above freezing by the time we found a good spot to camp in the lee of the temple walls. Fortunately for me, I have some experience with deserts in my scavving territory, so I wasn't exactly caught with my pants down.

To be fair, neither was Jules. Caught with his pants down, I mean. Though, watching him now as he pulls a sweater on over that not-so-spotless-anymore buttoned shirt, I can't say I would've minded much.

Mia. Get your head in the game.

I have to stay focused on why I'm here. Before I register the impulse, my hand's slipping into my pocket to pull out my phone again. It's set to automatically download incoming messages whenever the station or the relay satellite's overhead, but I'm not really expecting anything when I unlock its screen and check my inbox. A few notices pop up that there's been bidding activity on some of my Chicago salvage auctions, but it's hard to care much this far away. If I die here, the auction site'll just confiscate my earnings. So it's not until the alert I've set up with a little icon of a pair of heart-shaped sunglasses pops up that my heart does an instant flip-flop.

Evie.

I glance at Oxford, who's hunched over the wave-stove, and I stroll some distance away. I put in one of my earbuds, then play my sister's video message.

"Miiiiiiiiia!" Her voice, loud and bright in my right ear, instantly makes my eyes sting. I haven't seen her in five months. "Dunno if you'll get this, but if you do, you should already be on Gaia—on *Gaia!* I mean, WTF, you're listening to me talk to you in another galaxy." She recorded this after a shift waitressing at the club, I can tell. Though she's changed into sweatpants and a tank top and taken off her makeup, I can see traces of the lipstick they make her wear and her arms shimmer with the holographic glitter lotion that's supposed to make her look hotter.

Hotter. My fourteen-year-old baby sister.

This is why I have to get her out. Right now she just takes drink orders. But once she turns eighteen . . . her contract doesn't let her stay a waitress forever.

"I wish I could be there with you," she goes on. "Well, actually, not really. Actually, it sounds horrible. Impossible. But you like doing impossible things. I can't wait for you to get back. I'll meet you in Amsterdam."

We saw a movie once, which we siphoned off a neighbor's net connection, where these two lovers had a plan to meet in Amsterdam when they'd both taken care of the obstacles between them. Our stolen connection cut out before the end of the movie, but Amsterdam became our end goal, our code for a future with-out hiding and stealing, without our constant fights about her staying in school while I worked, without the constant fear of being found out as illegal sisters. Of course, neither of us is ever going to be able to afford to go to Europe—our Amsterdam has always been Los Angeles, where the Undying solar cell means there's clean water. It also means it's not cheap to live there, but expensive places are often safer, and with what I could make in a place like this . . .

After Evie managed to get herself tangled up with the club while trying to help pay our bills, I found that movie again and watched the ending. One of the lovers killed himself and the other took a fast-food job in New Jersey where he had to wear a clown suit and advertise on street corners. I never had the heart to tell Evie.

Evie's gone quiet in the video, her expression torn. She never wants to say anything that's hard. Everything's bright and hopeful, and to speak of fears and worries and hardships is to summon them closer, invite them to hover over us. I can see her struggling not to pour out her fear for me. Finally, she plasters a wide, brittle smile on her face and says, "I miss you. Stay safe." And then, softly, almost as though she hopes her mic won't pick it up: "I wish you weren't there alone."

She stares at me across the millions of light-years between us. Then she presses her fingers to her lips and blows me a kiss, and the screen goes black.

I wish you weren't there alone.

I glance over at Oxford, who's still puttering around the wave-stove, looking like a mad scientist from an old movie.

He's shivering as he "doctors" our dinners, but I can't tell if that's from cold, the thin air, or from the fact that his body, despite its lanky size, is clearly too small to contain the sheer volume of excitement coursing through it from being this close to an Undying temple. I thought I knew excited—I mean, that time I found a '24 Chevy Air-bike almost intact in the remains of a collapsed garage had to be one of the highlights of my whole life. But this . . . if I weren't here, Jules would be through that temple entrance already, stumbling around in the dark and probably on his way to being impaled by some spike trap by now.

I feel like I've got a dog on a leash smelling freedom. And

metaphorical or not, that leash is stretched to the snapping point. I can feel his tension, as real as the cold creeping in the collar of my polar fleece hoodie. There are about a million questions swirling around in my head, and I have a feeling the answers could be dangerous—but Jules is clearly set on keeping his secrets.

If I push him too hard, he might decide he doesn't need me after all, not now that I've gotten him to the temple. But some teenaged kid doesn't just wind up here conveniently possessing the knowledge the entire human race has been trying to pry out of Elliott Addison's head. I'm going to figure out how he knows what he knows, and what it means for me. But right now, when he sees his goal within reach, isn't the time to ask hard questions. Better to wait until he can't avoid them by leaving me behind. And I'm not naïve enough to believe he won't drop the scavver scum he's had to team up with as soon as he thinks it's safe to kick me to the curb. Arming myself with as much information as possible is the best way to make sure that if anyone's getting a jump on anyone, *I'm* going to get one on *him*.

"What's on the menu, Oxford?" I ask instead, as his eyes wander yet again to the sandy, dusty, and otherwise featureless wall of the temple next to us. Academic excitement or not, dinner smells good, and I'm not letting some doe-eyed professor type burn it because he thinks maybe one of those sand grains is gonna tell him how the Undying used to live.

"Hmm?" His eyes snap back after a moment's hesitation. He's got a flashlight that pulls apart into a lantern, and on its dimmest setting I can make out the glimmer of his eyes meeting mine. "Oh. Lime-glazed chicken and wild rice with porcini and kale."

I blink back at him. "I think I heard *chicken*."

His lips twitch, and as those eyes flash, I wonder if he's trying to size me up like I am him. "It'll be delicious, I promise. I have a few days of real food, vacuum sealed, before we've got to resort to more drastic measures for our nutrition."

"Canned beans isn't drastic measures," I point out, feeling defensive. "It's good."

"After some cayenne and brown sugar and about half a dozen other things to make it palatable." He removes the dish from the wave-stove box and carefully splits its contents evenly into a second bowl for me. Part of me wants to point out I'm like half his size, and that he's gonna need more food than I will. But the bigger part of me wants to eat the hell out of that chicken and lime rice thing, so I shut my mouth and take the bowl he holds out to me.

I do speak up, though, when he starts to pack the wave-stove up again.

"Hey, wait. Throw some rocks in there."

He pauses, his thick brows drawing inward in that way they do when he thinks I'm a whack-job. "Throw some what now?"

"That thing heats stuff other than food, right? That can from the beans earlier today about burned my fingerprints off."

"It heats inorganic matter too, yes."

"Well, heat up those rocks, wrap 'em up in your blanket with you when you sleep, and you'll be toasty warm. Not as nice as having another person to curl up with, but almost as good." I flash him a bright smile, just to see what happens. Even if the light was brighter I'm not sure I could tell with his dark skin whether he was blushing, but when he swallows hard and turns away to locate some suitable rocks among the rubble, I know what I'm seeing.

Score. He may think scavengers are scum, and that the tomb raiders here on Gaia are the scummiest of the scum, but he plays for my team and he thinks I'm cute. And I can work with that.

Sometimes cute gets you into trouble when you're traveling alone. I'm not an idiot. But one look at Jules and you know he's not *that* guy. I'm pretty sure he's one of those guys who would've apologized the first time he kissed a girl just in case he did it wrong.

If, somewhere deep down inside, he still thinks I'm cute even after learning that I'm basically his archnemesis, maybe we can work together anyway.

I snuggle down into my blanket, cradle my bowl close to my chest, and watch him through the curls of aromatic steam rising around my chin.

I'm trying to judge what's under the khakis, the button-down, the argyle sweater—not *that* way, though a girl's hormones will do what they do, not my fault—to figure out if he's got any athletic ability at all to go with his self-proclaimed genius. He's got strength, more than I'd have thought from an academic type—he about cut off my air supply with how hard he held on while we were on the bike—and he kept up with me when we were running. But I can't tell if he's got the conditioning we're going to need once we get inside. Hell, to be honest, I don't know *what* kind of conditioning we'll need once we get inside. I was only going to skim through the temple antechambers like the rest of the scavvers— none of us has the ability to navigate the Undying's network of traps and pitfalls that killed the *Explorer* astronauts. I don't know if I'll eventually have to ditch him so I can move faster, once he's gotten me past the Undying security checks.

I don't want to ditch him. And not just because his know-how will be handy in figuring out whatever traps the Undying have left to try to kill unworthy looters. I like this guy. He's cute, in a *don't-kick-the-puppy* way. Hell, he's cute in a *come-back-to-my-place-and-meet-my-puppy* way.

But I'm on Gaia. I'm on an alien planet. I've risked my life, everything I own, everything I could *ever* own or be or do, for this chance. A pair of big brown eyes and a sheepish smile that flashes white in the dark when he sees me watching him . . . that, I can find somewhere else once I get home. Maybe not the same smile. Maybe not the same eyes. But something.

I let my breath out in a sigh and take a bite of my dinner.

Oh, holy crap.

I must've made some kind of happy-place noise, because when

I manage to lift my head, I find Jules staring at me, mouth half open. He shuts it with a pop. Definitely blushing, but just now, I don't care.

"This is fricking *awesome*," I blurt, blankets falling away as I sit bolt upright and start devouring my dinner. All thoughts of allies and betrayals and the color of his eyes go flying straight out the airlock. *Chicken. And whatever a porcini is, I'm in.*

It isn't until we're finished and the bowls are wiped clean and the hot rocks from the wave-stove are tucked inside our sleeping mats—mine, a single thick-weave blanket I can roll up in; his, a true space-age marvel of engineering with zippers and quilted pockets of god knows what and a self-inflating pillow at one end—that we can actually talk again. I have vague memories of him trying to start up conversation over dinner, but at that point I was more interested in what my spoon had to say.

Now, though, as I look into the cool blue light of the dim lantern and the desert chill creeps in around my face, all that's left of the chicken is a warmth in my stomach and fingertips that smell like lime. And I feel reality setting in once more.

Cute or not . . . he basically thinks I'm a monster. He thinks of what I do back home as pillaging, stealing, criminal in every sense—though it's not like anyone's coming back for all the crap that got left behind when the sandstorms started sweeping through Lincoln Square. But if he thinks my regular work is a problem, he sees what I'm here to do as even worse, by a magnitude of infinity. To him I'm here to kill what he's clearly devoted his life to discovering and preserving. I'm a *monster.*

"Why Gaia?"

His words come out of the dark so abruptly that I startle, jerking my gaze from the lantern and searching for him on the other side of it. My eyes are so dazzled by the light that all I can see is the red-green afterimage, lantern shaped, dancing this way and that. "What?"

"Why come to Gaia to do this? The raider gangs, that I can . . .

well, I can't *understand* that, but I know why they're here. Money will make people do a lot of stupid things, but you—you can't be more than what, fifteen? You should be in school, you should be . . . you should be home."

He's been thinking about exactly the same thing I was. There's so much I want to say. *What home? And I haven't been in school since I was thirteen. I'm not like you, I don't get to think about what I "should" do, only what I've gotta do. You don't get to decide my choices are stupid when you don't know a thing about me.*

Instead what bursts out, in a voice so sullen I might as well still be thirteen, is: "I'm *sixteen*, Oxford."

"Regardless," he replies, unfazed, "even if you have some reason not to be with your parents right now, or in school, you could be looking for a job with a little less 'almost certain death' in the fine print. You're young, you could—"

"Oh, and you're what, thirty, Mister 'I'm starting college early next year'?"

With the afterimages from the lantern fading, I can see that he's frowning now. "Seventeen," he admits finally. "Look, Amelia, this is all coming out wrong. I'm not trying to—just—what could someone like you possibly need with the kind of money you get from a dangerous expedition like this that a normal job wouldn't get you?"

"Someone *like me*?" I know what he means when he says *someone like you*. He's seen the grimy blue-and-pink hair with two-inch brown roots showing, the worn boots, the gear cobbled together from ancient finds in old warehouses; he's heard the bad grammar, the advice from someone who's already seen years as a criminal. "You think I'm just some stupid punk slum scavver who thought, 'Oh, hey, I'll up my game and hop a spaceship to the other side of the galaxy,' but since I'm clearly poor as dirt and dumb to boot and couldn't tell you what the hell a porcini is, I couldn't possibly know what to do with a couple hundred grand in smuggled Undying artifacts, so I should just find the nearest fast-food joint and—"

"I think you're smart," Jules interrupts me, voice quiet. "And clever, which isn't the same thing. I think you're hurting about something and I don't think you like what you're here to do, but you're too proud to admit that, so you're putting words in my mouth. And I think you'll find I don't really care for that."

The silence that swarms in around us when he stops speaking makes my throat hurt. My head feels fuzzy, a combination of the exhaustion of the day and richer food than I'm used to eating and the lack of proper air. And something about what he's said makes me want to pull my blanket over my head and cry, just a little, where no one can hear me. But *he's* there, and he'd hear.

Jules clears his throat, warning me this time that he's about to speak. "What I meant to say was that you seem to me like a clever, beautiful girl who could more than support herself in any of a dozen ways on Earth, which either means I'm wrong about you, and I don't think I am, although come to think of it I didn't really mean to say *beautiful* because I'm not really sure how that plays into anything—" He stops, clears his throat a second time to regroup. "Either I'm wrong about you, or else you have some other reason for being here."

Who the hell calls someone beautiful *anymore?* My thoughts are reeling. *This isn't some after-school feel-good movie special.* But I resist the urge to pull my blanket over my head and ignore him. My face isn't feeling the cold anymore anyway.

Goodnight, Oxford.

The words form clearly in my mind. But then I see Evie's face, the stain of rouge on her lips as she blows me a kiss, the hope in her face when she breathes the word *Amsterdam*. And when my mouth opens, I say something else entirely.

"I'm trying to buy back my little sister."

6

JULES

THE MORNING DAWNS COLD AND THIN, AS GAIA'S DUAL SUNS CREEP OVER
the canyon rim. One half of the sky is still inky black, stars scattered carelessly across it, but the other is slowly shifting from a
metallic gray to a soft orange. By noon it'll be baking hot again,
but just now the air is crisp, and I could live inside my little silver
cocoon forever with no complaints.

Except, that is, for the temple beside us, beckoning me with a
pull so strong I'd almost think it was supernatural, if I hadn't felt
it ever since I first learned about the Undying from my father. My
earliest memory is of sitting on his lap while he tried to work, and
I alternated between trying to take off his glasses and trying to use
my best pencils to color in the glyphs he was working on, the paper
charts stretched out across his desk. This has been my journey as
long as I've been alive. I'm not sure how much I actually slept last
night, buzzing with the need to just leap out of my sleeping bag
and sprint toward the temple's entrance.

Beside me, Mia sits up, tearing her breather mask away and

71

squinting at the canyon rim as though it's to blame for all her woes. "Stupid goddamn alien suns," she mutters, transferring the blame neatly. "How the hell do I know what time it is when there's two of them?"

I wriggle around until I can free my hands, hitting the display and bringing my wrist unit to life. I pull my own mask away. "Six," I croak, my voice still rusty with sleep and the bone-dry air from the breather.

Mia fixes me with a look that adds me to the list of things she's blaming for her current predicament, but keeping her blanket wrapped around her like a cloak, she slowly clambers to her feet, shifting from one foot to the other to get the blood flowing. "I'll check the canyon, see if there's any sign of other camps."

"I'll make breakfast." I force myself to move, wincing as every muscle in my body lines up to file a complaint about yesterday's trials. *And I thought I was fit.* "If you see any hostiles incoming, let them know we need about an hour or so before we're ready to flee for our lives."

That earns me a sound that's certainly not a laugh, but might be a distant relative hovering uncertainly at the edge of the family photograph. I set to work with the wave-stove, pulling together the quickest breakfast I can manage. I only really won one argument the whole of yesterday, but as the scent of porridge and cinnamon slowly revives me, I'm bloody glad it was the one about keeping my spices.

While she's gone, I can't help thinking again about what she said last night. *Her sister.* She wouldn't say anything more after that, pretending to be asleep, though I know she was faking it by the way her breath kept varying. A sister should be illegal, especially in the U.S., where the population control laws are incredibly strict. I'm not quite as naïve as she thinks I am, though. I can guess what happened.

We received the first Undying transmission over fifty years ago, but decoding it, building the portal, testing it with probes, unmanned drones, and finally manned missions took decades. It was only about fifteen years ago, when Mia and I were toddlers, that the first clear images came back of Gaia. It was then that some people started breaking the "one child" laws, thinking we'd settle the planet in a year or two and there'd be space for everyone to raise more than one kid.

Mia and I were still children when geologists and astronomers worked out that one of Gaia's suns gives off a solar flare every few decades, like a cosmological Old Faithful, and dashed any hope that Gaia could be a permanent second home for us. Only the simple, single-celled bacteria in the oceans survive each flare. The discovery of tangible life on another planet knocked the scientific community flat when the first samples came back, but the rest of the world was more focused on the extinct race of sentient beings trying to communicate with us. For most of us, the bacteria are just a reminder that nothing more complex could ever live on Gaia.

Without those solar flares, though, we wouldn't have been able to date the Undying ruins. The cut stones of their structures have been absorbing radiation with every solar eruption since they were built—for less time than the surrounding ground and cliffs— which allowed my father and his colleagues to calculate the age of the temples to a staggering fifty thousand years.

But whether or not Gaia was ever going to be the answer to Earth's overpopulation problems, Mia's parents still broke the law.

Her sister's existence is illegal—which explains why Mia might have to think outside the box when it comes to helping her out of whatever circumstances she's in. It also complicates my role in all of this. Whatever aversion I feel to bringing a scavver inside the temple with me, I can't deny the urgency of her mission. I might not come from the same kind of underworld as Mia—I might never have set foot in it—but I know enough to understand it's not hyperbole when she says "buy back." It's not just about money for her, any more than it is for me. And I'm still lying to her.

We're both quiet as we down breakfast and pack up our things. Mia's more or less stopped scowling, tamed by the porridge, though her pink-and-blue hair's still sticking up every which way, her eyes sleepy. Clearly not a morning person. I reluctantly learned to be, after years of early rising for polo practice at the pool, but now doesn't seem the time to rub that in.

"I suppose we should get an early start on today's law-breaking," I venture, groping for a logical next step. Despite my eagerness to enter the temple, however, it's proving more difficult than I would've thought to turn my mind to the magnificent stone façade above us. It wants to stay focused on the sleep-rumpled girl beside me instead. After years of being told I'm growing up too fast, that I should relax and act more like the teenager I am, this is *not* the time for my hormones to kick in and decide to do exactly that.

Except, apparently, logic doesn't get a vote.

We both stare up at the temple we're about to brave. Columns line the steps, inviting, leading up to a shadowy maw of an entrance. At first glance, a passerby—if there were passersby on Gaia—might think it a relic from our own past, at home next to the stone city of Petra or ancient Egypt's grand Abu Simbel. But the Undying temple seems to grow out of the cliff as though it were organic, part of Gaia, in a way no human civilization could have attempted. The stones are so precisely cut it's impossible to see the seams between them, except in a few places where sand and wind have nibbled a corner away over the eons. And though the façade before us is of the same red-brown rock of the canyon below and the cliffs above, a glimmer in the dark doorway reminds me we could find anything once we step inside this temple.

Temple isn't really the right word—my father and his colleagues used to wince whenever they heard it, preferring *structure* or *complex,* anything that didn't hold a spiritual connotation—because there's no evidence of religion in the Undying's broadcast or glyphed messages on Gaia. There's no evidence any of the structures were built to honor a deity or house their dead. But standing here, my breath steaming in what's left of the desert night and dawn edging the cliffs with gold, the word *structure* leaves me hollow.

And I understand why the first astronauts on Gaia's surface, scientists themselves, whispered the word *temple*.

Banks and supermarkets are structures. Structures are built and used and torn down and rebuilt and recycled and end up just so much cardboard and plastic wrap. This place . . . this place is heavy with importance. It calls, the way a church's bells call a congregation to mass or the cry of the muezzin summons the faithful to prayer. It waits with gravity and consequence, with the ancient serenity of a massive oak. I don't have to scan the radiation levels in its stones to know how long it's been waiting for us, because it's how long I've been waiting too: *always*.

The moment takes me so abruptly that my knees want to buckle, leaving me floundering, floating, as unable to move as if I were in zero-G. I tear my eyes away to see Mia, her eyes wide and breath quickening as she gazes at the temple. I watch her face, see how the fear in her eyes gains not a scrap of ground against the absolute determination in the set of her mouth. And suddenly my feet are on the ground again.

"We have to be careful." My voice is dry and dusty, like the sand underfoot, as I order my feet to start moving. "Once we're inside we can't get separated, can't run ahead, can't so much as step through a doorway without thinking it through."

I'm rewarded with a roll of her eyes as we make our way toward the steps. "You mean I *shouldn't* sprint headlong into an alien tomb full of booby-traps and pitfalls? I saw what happened to the *Explorer IV* team. I'm not volunteering for the same fate."

I wince. *Everybody* saw what happened to the *Explorer IV* team, the very first astronauts to land here on Gaia. In their desperation for some positive PR, the International Alliance agreed to broadcast the exploration live via satellite relay, like the moon landings were, once upon a time. Which means everybody heard the screams when half the team was pulverized a few rooms in.

After that, it became clear that without somebody to serve as a guide, someone able to translate the temple's warnings and instructions, any exploration past the temples' antechambers would be next to impossible. And though other people can read the glyphs, there's *reading* them, and then there's *understanding* them. There's a nuance to translating the Undying language that few people have ever mastered.

Mia shifts her weight, the laces of her boots creaking in protest. "Look, Oxford," she says, voice softening. "This ain't my first rodeo. I can take care of myself."

"And I've trained for a moment like this for years," I say, though privately I'm suddenly thinking that summer spent sifting early hominid bone fragments in South Africa didn't exactly prepare me for this. "But neither of us has done anything like this before. You're going to have to trust me when it comes to interpreting their writings, passing on their warnings. We need to watch out for each other." *Trust me*, I keep saying, my own voice echoing around my mind like a mocking chorus. The words taste like sand.

She doesn't reply at first, reaching the bottom of the steps and pausing to glance across at me. Whatever she sees there makes her smile—though her lips don't curve, her eyes shift, warm, crinkle at the edges. "You go on," she says softly, watching my face. "I don't mind being second in history."

I know I'm smiling back at her like an idiot, but I can't bring myself to care. *She gets it.*

At the big complex, the *Explorer IV* team didn't trigger any traps until several rooms into the temple. Still, my body's taut with caution, every nerve on high alert as we climb the stone steps, the soft sound of our footfalls the only break in the dawn's silence. We have to clamber up them—they're just a little higher than is comfortable, even for someone as tall as me. Not quite built on our scale, but almost. The world has spent years speculating on what the Undying might have looked like, from the sensationalized frenzy of movies and books about the Undying to the scientific community's painstakingly crafted theories, but even the more plausible theories are still little more than guesses. We know they must have been only a little larger than us, judging by the scale of the structures they built, but beyond that . . . there were no images of themselves among the glyphs photographed by the *Explorer* team. Unless the images are hidden at the unexplored hearts of the temples, the Undying left behind no traces of what they looked like.

I reach up to switch on my head torch as we reach the threshold, even the tips of my fingers seeming to shiver in anticipation. The first humans ever to step into this place. "Just one step into the anteroom," I murmur, and beside me she nods. "Then we stop and look for instructions."

And then, with a step like any other—except that it's perhaps the most important step of my life—I ease in through the doorway, and onto the first flagstone.

I wait a moment, and when nothing happens, I shift to the side so Mia can join me, and together we lift our heads to scan the walls around us. We're in a soaring chamber, several meters across in each direction. A huge spiral made up of long strings of Undying glyphs is carved into the wall. My eyes jump to them immediately, and my heart just about thumps right out of my chest—this is the Nautilus spiral, the hidden shape in the code that brought me here. I'm in the right place to unravel the mystery.

There's an energy about the carvings, despite their static nature, and as motes of dust dance in the torch beam, the designs almost seem to move. It's hauntingly familiar and utterly foreign all at once. It raises the hairs on the back of my neck.

"Holy hell," Mia breathes beside me. She doesn't have a torch on her helmet like mine, but she switches on a light affixed to her wrist, a crude fiber-optic set-up that lets her illuminate whatever she's pointing at. "The images *Explorer IV* sent back didn't look like *this*."

"The site they explored isn't the important one," I murmur. "I've never seen a pattern like this either. The transmission Dr. Addison decoded doesn't allow for aesthetics, and the *Explorer IV* team was more interested in getting out alive than taking proper visual records. These glyphs are almost artistic, although that could simply be projection, since we're hardwired to see symmetry and pattern and—"

"Oxford." When I glance at her, she's got one eyebrow lifted, that bemused expression on her face, arms folded.

"Right." She has no reason to take an interest in the sweeping spiral shape, of course. And I need to see more than this—I need to see as much as possible, if I'm to understand what the warning pertains to. We need to keep moving. "I'll just take some pictures—there's text all over the place in here, not just these large ones over the entrance. Maybe when we take a break I can decode some of it." Though I want to sit down on the floor and pull out my journal right here, I force myself to sweep my wrist unit in an arc around us, recording the images. "Let's see . . . The language of the original broadcast was mathematical in nature, and this written language is too. Each glyph's lines are determined by numeric values that correspond to words and concepts from the broadcast, but once you learn the glyphs you can read it almost like any other language."

"Almost?" Amelia's voice is tense.

"Well, some of them are more like letters, like an alphabet, and others are complete words, even complete ideas. And their abstract concepts aren't always the easiest to understand. This group here, these convey a sense of . . ." I'm forced to pause and hunt for the right words. "There will be consequences, for treading here. Moving up toward the top of the arch, we have the symbol the Undying used for themselves, the one that looks like a meteor arcing through the sky. They're saying this is their place, their territory."

"Huh," she mutters. "You really *can* read it. Does it say where the tech will be?"

I choose to ignore her surprise, as well as her question— an uncomfortable reminder that she's *not* just here for the joy of discovery—and press on. "This next section down the other side of the arch is for learning or education, meaning we will need to apply knowledge to make our way through the temple. And this section here is denoting this temple's importance above the others in this area—told you our friends are looking in the wrong place—and that what we're looking for will be at the very center of the temple. Or possibly the bottom, they don't seem to think quite like we do when it comes to three-dimensional spatial relationships."

"At the very center," she echoes, though that deadpan response is lightened by her clear relief that I was right to lead her here instead of the bigger temple. "Of course. Past all the traps."

"Indeed."

"And you're absolutely certain there'll be tech here I can grab? I can't pay my debts with interesting facts and cultural insights, Oxford."

I can't bring myself to look at her as I reply. Suddenly *she's just a scavver* doesn't feel like a remotely good enough reason for sacrificing her interests in favor of mine. I promise myself again I'll find a way for her to earn some money out of this. "This is exactly what I was hoping for," I say.

She doesn't seem to notice it's not an answer to her question. "I don't suppose all these carvings tell us what sort of traps we can expect?"

"I'm afraid that's on a room-by-room basis," I say, carefully testing the next paving stone with my foot, and stepping forward. "We can take some educated guesses, based on what happened to *Explorer IV*. Some of it will be good, old-fashioned stuff designed to stand the test of time. Falling rocks, spikes that come out of nowhere, that sort of thing. Some of it will be a little more high-tech."

"I've watched all the *Explorer* videos available online," she says, taking her lead from me and carefully probing each paving stone with her foot before she steps forward. "And a few classified ones that Mink—that's my backer—could get hold of. But you're the expert. What next?"

"That," I murmur, staring up at the glyphs, "is the question. This sequence here tells us this room is clear, but that the next

79

room will contain our first test." I move forward gingerly anyway, aware that while I *think* I can read the glyphs on the walls, I could very easily miss something simply by not seeing the world the way their creators did.

I realize Mia's not following me and pause. Her expression is troubled, lip caught between her teeth. I'm starting to recognize that as her "thinking" face, but the way her lip dimples is distracting, and I have to stop myself staring. "Mia?"

"I don't know." She gives a little shiver, as if trying to shake off a chill. "I just expected this to feel more . . . alien."

"What do you mean?"

"I mean, this place is like the Pyramids, or that thing in like . . . Cambodia or wherever—"

"Angkor Wat," I interrupt, unable to control the impulse.

"Right," she continues absently, not missing a beat. "That. Or Stonehenge. I mean, isn't it weird that these temples are even here? Space is infinite, practically, with infinite possibilities and forms for life to take, and we're exploring a temple that has steps and doorways. It just feels . . . strange. This could've been built by our own ancestors."

She's a lot more perceptive than she seems, and I find myself wondering how much of that is my own prejudice, and how much is the fact that she doesn't let on just how clever she is. "True," I admit. "Except that the Undying were traveling the stars before our ancestors learned how to make fire—they wrote these messages and went extinct before the first human had figured out *how* to write."

"But that's an estimate," Mia protests. "They date it with the radiation, right? It could be wrong."

"Off by a few hundred years, sure. But the stones of this temple have been absorbing that solar radiation for the last fifty thousand years."

"And still . . ." she murmurs.

"It's not *so* strange. It happens on Earth all the time. Convergent evolution. Two totally unrelated creatures wind up with the same traits because they evolved in similar environments. Think of birds and bats and butterflies. They don't share any common ancestor with wings, but it turns out it's a useful development, and so they all ended up with them. Or dolphins and sharks. Completely unrelated, but ended up roughly the same shape, and with a lot of the same features, because they found a niche where those worked."

"So you're saying we fill the same niche as the Undying did?" she asks, looking down at herself, then across at me, like she's sizing us up.

"Could be," I say. "We can't know how similar to us they were physiologically, but perhaps there's something about the way we evolved that made us the most likely to be the dominant species on our planet, and that held true elsewhere. True, there's no cities or record to indicate they evolved here, but the fact that the Undying chose Gaia to build these structures suggests they could breathe this atmosphere, just like us. It would make sense for two intelligent species who need similar environments to survive to share some traits."

Mia's frown lessens a little and she shivers again. "Let's just get going."

The archway opens up into a vast cavern, with a yawning abyss a few meters from our feet. Only a narrow stone bridge crosses the chasm to the far side, where a stone door blocks the exit. The bridge itself is beautifully symmetrical, as mathematically precise as one of our own suspension bridges. And though it seems intact, it's not hard to figure out what fate awaits anyone who makes a wrong step.

"You think it's as simple as walking across?" Mia's beside me, the LED on her wrist shining futilely down into the impenetrable darkness below.

I'm scanning the walls, searching for the carvings that will tell me how to solve whatever challenge the Undying have set for us. I stare at the strings of glyphs, letting the translations slowly unravel in my mind. It's a narrative—a repeat of the story in the original transmission, I think. I take a careful shot of it with my wrist unit. I can translate it tonight, when we stop for time with our breathers.

What's not among those glyphs, though, is anything by way of instructions for tackling the bridge.

The only thing I can't account for is a gentle curve etched into the stone above the far door, nothing like the glyphs I've been studying, and nothing like the spiral I'm here to find out more about.

There must be an answer here somewhere, but if there is, it's not in the glyphs I've been trained to read. I spend a full hour examining every centimeter of the walls our lights can reach, searching for clues. Eventually, heart in my mouth, I simply step out onto the bridge.

It feels reassuringly solid, though I can feel my heart slamming against my rib cage. Now that I'm shining my light down directly onto the stone of the bridge, I can see it's not the same stone as the room all around us. It hasn't simply been carved or built from the rock of the cliffs.

The stone of the bridge is oddly crystalline, striations running through it with faint glimmers that dance away from my vision as soon as I try to focus on them. One moment there's a pattern to them, and the next moment, just as I think I'm about to grasp it, it's gone. It's not quite circuitry, but it's . . . something.

And this, the unknown glimmering at me from the stones of the bridge, is what scares me even more than the bridge itself.

Fortunately, the bridge isn't that long—and it's been so expertly constructed that despite a chip here and a missing chunk there, it doesn't even tremble once before I reach the other side, which butts up against the sealed stone doorway to the next chamber. I take my time, searching the surface of the door for any warnings, before placing my hand on it, gingerly. Then my shoulder—then the weight of my whole body. It doesn't budge. There's not even a shower of sand or debris for my efforts. And no sign of a handle or any mechanism that would open it.

"*Perfututi*," I mutter. After a time I'm forced to carefully make my way back, and that's when I see it. Scratched into a stone on the side of the bridge, a small shape. Like an afterthought, a quick, last-minute addition carved with nothing like the care of the proper glyphs.

It's the Nautilus, tucked in out of the way where nobody would see it, unless they were hunting all over the chamber for a clue about how to safely cross the bridge. The word that was with it in the original broadcast isn't there, but my memory helpfully supplies the grim translation: *Catastrophe. Apocalypse. The end of all things.*

I suppose at least I can be sure I'm in the right place to solve my mystery. I just wish my spine was crawling a little less while I tried to do it. I drop to my knees, pretending to inspect the bridge itself. Explaining the Nautilus to Amelia would mean exposing my lie.

"Do you hear that?" Mia's frowning, flashing her light about the room. "A rattling?"

"The room's probably channeling wind from the desert outside," I answer, my eyes still on the shape in front of me.

"Hmm . . ." Mia's wandering off to one side, following the sound of that rattling wind. She keeps on talking, but her voice is a buzz in the back of my consciousness, as I carefully photograph the Nautilus—and the line radiating from it, which I haven't seen before—with my wrist unit.

"Yes," I say, when there's a pause that seems to suggest she's waiting on me, only realizing a moment too late that I don't know what I've agreed to. I snap my head up, and my heart stops. She's climbed up on a platform to the side of the entrance, one hidden when you stand in the doorway as I was doing. "Check this out, it's like a latch or something."

"Wait—wait, don't—"

But she's already grasping it, and the ancient mechanism gives way under her fingers, allowing some kind of stone shutter to slide down, away into the rock, opening a channel that unleashes a small-scale gale that half knocks her back with surprise.

While the wind itself is shocking, neither of us are prepared for what it causes—a series of jangling, discordant notes flood the room, forcing us both to clap our hands over our ears. Mia shouts something, trying without success to pull the shutter back up out of its groove to block the wind again.

Forgetting the Nautilus, I run to join her, half furious, half thrilled. "You've got to be more careful!" I say over the jarring notes, which are hollow and resonant like a deep-voiced bassoon.

"You said yes!" she retorts.

Deus, I have to pay more attention to what I'm agreeing to.

She spares me the need to explain myself, jabbing a finger downward, where into the stone platform are sunk a series of five holes, arranged in the same curve depicted over the immovable door. "You tell me, Oxford. Think there might be some connection?"

If it were quiet, I'd be forced to admit she's right. As it is, the noise of the "music," such as it is, lets me answer her with a shake of my head, and we both lean forward to inspect the shutter, the wind plastering Mia's hair back away from her face. She drops to her knees, reaching out to cover one of the holes with her hand—and one of the notes cuts out.

"It's like blowing across a bottle," she says, moving so her body can cover more of the holes, muffling the cacophony a little.

"It's bloody awful, is what it is." I want so badly to admire the Undying in this moment, but the remaining two uncovered holes are just slightly out of tune with each other, making my teeth hurt.

She glances at me, jerks her head to the side. "Stand there in front of the wind, will you? Buy us some quiet."

I brace my shoulders obediently against the channel, feeling the wind trying to force me away, the holes drilled into the platform are mostly silent now, except for the occasional eddy that slips around me. Now that things are a little calmer, I can see the stone shutter that slid away was that same odd crystalline stone that made up the bridge.

"What do those mean?" she asks, pointing to the few glyphs carved into the wall.

"Nothing useful," I say. "They're telling us what we already know—that we have to pass tests—and I think they're starting to tell the story of the Undying."

"And that?" she asks, pointing to the curve over the far door, then tracing the holes in the ground.

"I don't know—it's not an Undying glyph."

"Well, it has to mean something, right? Otherwise, why put it there?" She leans forward to shine her light down into the holes, thoughtful. "Maybe it's not language. Maybe it's math."

"Math?" I eye her sidelong, fighting to keep my back pressed against the wind tunnel.

"Yeah. You said their letters are based on math, and the original broadcast was math, right?" She glances up at me. "So maybe this is, too. Like—you know, when you put points on a graph, they make shapes."

I pause, glancing back at the bridge. From here, you can't see the Nautilus shape scratched into its other side. What she's talking about is exactly how my father first found the spiral—equations hidden deep in the Undying code that, when graphed, formed the image that brought me here. I take a careful breath. "There aren't any numbers, though, no glyphs to—"

"No, not the glyphs—look." She jumps down long enough to pick up a loose stone, then climbs up again beside me.

Before I can stop her, she's using the rock to etch lines against the platform. I'm so shocked by her casual defacement of this ancient place that I can't summon the speech to stop her—I just stare.

She marks out a crossed pair of lines for the axes of a graph, then scratches a curve connecting the holes sunk into the rock. Then she frowns, lip caught between her teeth as she examines the result, tapping her rock against her chin and looking for all the world like one of my father's colleagues at a tablet with stylus in hand. Then she's making more marks, a horizontal line through the first hole, another through the second, and so on.

My foot slips, and I give up trying to block the wind. There's a flood of discordant sound for a few moments before I drop to my knees beside her and cover as many of the holes as my hands and one foot will reach. "I know it's been fifty thousand years or so, but one might've hoped they'd take better care tuning their instruments."

She blinks, and looks up at me. "Tuning?" But before I can answer, she's flashing me a huge smile. "Tuning—you're a genius, Jules. That's the puzzle. We have to *tune* this."

"How does one tune holes in the floor?" I ask dubiously.

"Well . . ." Mia hesitates, experimenting with placing a hand over the second hole and removing it again, and listening to the awful dissonance between it and the first hole. "If they were pipes you'd just shorten the pipe to . . ." She looks up abruptly. "Give me your water bottle."

"My water bottle?"

"Yeah, you've got one of those fancy air condenser things, right? It'll fill itself back up by sucking water out of the air. So we can use that, pour it in the holes here, shorten the pipes."

I'm reaching for the bottle, all too aware of the preciousness of what I'm handing over. But then, if we don't make it past the first door, we might as well have an entire swimming pool full of water for all the good it'll do us. "How do we know what to 'tune' the holes to?"

"The glyph. Or graph. Or whatever it is." She's gesturing to her etched lines with pride—it's all I can do not to burst out with all the reasons she shouldn't have done what she did, scratching graffiti into such a precious find. "The holes are points on this curve, numbers in the equation. If you think of the first hole as a pipe or a bottle full of air, we need to make the second hole half-full—because its point on the graph is halfway down from the top."

I'm staring at her. "Uh . . . what?"

She waves away my incredulity. "Just trust me. Math is like the one thing about school I actually miss. Numbers are my thing, they always make sense, they're always the same. These are fractions. One over one, one over two—half—one over three . . ." One by one, she's adding water to the holes. And one by one, the notes are rising in pitch. The second hole, half-full, matches the note the empty hole is playing, only an octave higher. The third note rises until it's suddenly harmonizing with the first two, making the air resonate.

Suddenly, the defacement of the stone below us isn't on the top of my list of concerns. The simple brilliance of the puzzle makes me ache to see my father. I'd give anything to hear the intake of breath that always marks a new realization for him, to see the way the lines come in around his eyes when he grins like a teenager. He'd lean in so close his nose nearly touched the stone, then remember his glasses and slide them down, drawing back a little.

"You're making harmonies with an ancient alien temple, Mia," I murmur, just to see her look up and flash me a delighted smile. It's not my father's smile, but it's hard to look away from. *She's* hard to look away from, lit up like that.

We finish her work together, filling each hole to the amount specified by the arc etched into the stone, and this time, when I move out of the way, the whole set plays at once.

And it's a chord. Beautiful, haunting, resonating with the room until the soles of my feet ache with it, until my head's ringing, the room swaying around me . . .

But the room *isn't* swaying. It's the bridge.

And with Mia's voice ringing in my ears, the reminder that maths is music and music maths—somehow, the Undying have *tuned* this bridge to the same frequency as that chord. It's twisting on itself, the very stone warping, glimmering in the beams of our flashlights. And just as my heart's sinking, as I'm thinking we've ended our journey before we ever really got started, and the bridge'll crumble into the chasm at any moment . . . The door shifts.

The bridge itself is rooted under the door, and with each fluctuation the bridge is nudging the solid stone just a fraction more to the side. A few more seconds and the doorway will be wide enough to slip through.

I don't have to speak to know Mia's thinking exactly what I am—that crossing the beautiful stone bridge was one thing when the room was still and quiet. Now, with each side buckling up and down like a wave . . .

"We just have to go," I manage, trying not to think of the drop below. "If we stay in the center, the waves won't knock us off. They'll just twist around us. I—I'll go first. You hang back, in case anything goes wrong, maybe you can make it back to the beginning."

Mia starts to protest, but she glances back at the temple entrance, and I know she's thinking of the sister she mentioned. She can't help her if she's dead. "Fine," she whispers. "The tech on the other side of that door had better be worth a freaking *fortune*. Let's go."

The buckling bridge under my feet makes me want to throw myself to the stone and hold on for dear life, but I force myself to focus on the destination, not the shifting, wavering path below me. My legs feel more and more rubbery with each step, but I'm telling myself over and over it's just fear, it's just exhaustion, it's just—

"Is it getting worse?" Mia's voice, several paces behind me, is high with panic.

I make the mistake of looking over my shoulder at her. And from where I stand I can see almost the whole bridge behind me, buckling so hard now that the sides are almost over Mia's head, and she's having to fight to stay upright.

It's clear the bridge was designed to move, to open the door. But this . . . Something's wrong. Time, or miscalculation, or some

error on our part—the buckling bridge is tearing itself apart, the harmonic waves building on one another. And Mia's only halfway across.

"Run!" I shout, and she doesn't hesitate to obey. But then there's a scream of rock that rises above the eerie song of the Undying stone flute, and a huge chunk of the bridge behind Mia collapses.

I lift my gaze to hers just in time for our eyes to lock.

And then the stone gives way beneath her feet.

She vanishes with a shriek as the bridge falls apart, the first two-thirds of it ripping free of the other side and sliding down, down toward the abyss. The screech of splintering stone and the roar of rock crashing drowns out the rest of her scream and the music, as the bridge tears the platform asunder, silencing the ancient flute forever. I can't move. I can't think.

It's only then that my ears make out a breathless string of curses, and my mind snaps back into gear. My eyes find something pale in the gloom and I realize it's a hand, clinging white-knuckled to an outcropping of rock. Mia must've thrown herself across empty space to reach it before the rest of the bridge fell.

I'm diving toward the edge before I can even process that she's alive, before my brain can point out that throwing myself after her might be a somewhat fatal plan. But when the stone beneath me quivers, making my whole body shrink and lurch, I have to force myself to edge toward her with agonizing care to avoid another collapse of the rock. My heart's pounding in time with the *no-no-no-no* drumming through my brain as I make myself test each stone before transferring my weight, checking to see whether any more of the bridge is going to break apart. "Hold on."

"You think?" she gasps, her other hand appearing over the lip of the stone as she grunts with effort.

I reach out to push on, moving too quickly in my impatience, and a chunk of stone gives way. As part of the remaining bridge crumbles into the chasm, my arm slides down the gap in its wake, my fingertips grasping at nothing. I swear for a moment I see circuitry, but I can't spare it a second glance. Adrenaline surging, breath coming in quick gasps, I scramble back, and force myself to climb over it, checking the rock on the other side.

It takes me a moment to realize I didn't hear the falling rubble hit anything below. It's a *long* way down.

One of Mia's hands disappears, then reappears a moment later holding that multi-tool of hers. She bangs it against the lip of the stone a few times, and it suddenly sprouts tines, digging into the rock to give her a better grip. She grunts again, and for an instant her face appears over the ledge just a meter away, her eyes so wide the whites are showing all around. Then the stone groans a warning, and she thinks better of hauling herself up, freezing in place.

Finally, *finally* I'm there, lowering myself onto my front, praying the pathway holds as I reach down to grip her bicep, letting her grip mine in return. "I won't let you fall," I murmur, bracing to hold her in place. "Deus, this is my fault, I told you to hang back."

"Can we divide up the blame later?" she asks through gritted teeth, clinging to my sleeve, her feet swinging free in the void.

Just a weight at the gym, I tell myself, closing my eyes for a moment, and checking my grip on her, slowing my breathing. *Stay calm, don't screw this up.* Then I exhale hard and push backward, onto my hands and knees, pulling her with me. She slams the tool down on the rock once more, using her grip to pull herself up and over the rim, and as soon as I get her a little farther back, she swings her leg out to the side, hooking her boot over the lip of the stone. She moves like one of the climbers at the gym, lithe and quick—of course, she'd have been practicing on skyscrapers. And probably didn't have anyone to catch her if she fell.

I keep hold of her and she keeps hold of me, and together we crawl back along the remaining fragment of the bridge, me backward and her forward, until we can collapse together in the now wide-open doorway between this chamber and the next.

"The Undying certainly knew how to roll out the welcome mat," I manage, meeting her gaze. She's as rattled as me, and I know that endless fall will be flashing behind her eyelids as she tries to sleep tonight—just as it will behind mine. *Assuming we survive until bedtime.*

"If this is the welcome mat, I'd hate to see their 'do not disturb,'" she manages, with a weak laugh.

I try to join her, and we realize about the same time that we're still holding each other, arms and legs tangled together. Our gazes are still locked, and I see her face flush even as she lets out her breath, visibly deciding for the moment not to care that I'm holding her. I don't think either of us gives a damn about pride just now. And I'm not ashamed to say that the solid warmth of her is keeping me from shaking.

"Thanks for coming back to get me," Mia whispers, sober now, as reality catches up.

"Of course," I murmur, unable to summon even the ghost of a glib comment, or a joke about how I didn't have anything better to do.

Because it was *of course.*

I realize now that I didn't even think before I threw myself after her. Maybe I didn't know this girl a couple of days ago, but I know her now.

I know she's fierce and smart, determined and wryly funny.

And I know I'm not just drawing out the time I'm lying here tangled up with her because I'm too exhausted to move. This is a terrible time to discover she makes my heart beat faster just as surely as danger does, but there it is.

And I know that I've lied to her, brought her here without any idea whether she'll find the tech she needs, with her sister's life on the line. And whether or not I'm trying to save the lives of everyone on my planet, I know that won't matter when Mia finds out what I've done. I can't even blame her—because as much as I'm doing this for the people my father wanted to protect, I'm doing this for him, too. I'm here for one person, just like she is.

I don't know how this ends between us, but I know it doesn't end well. And I wish it were different.

"Snack?" I ask, forcing myself into safer territory, making my mind focus on practicalities. I can't imagine moving enough to wrestle my pack out from behind me, and getting up seems beyond me. For now, at least, I can unhook my breather mask and take a few long lungfuls.

"Snack," she agrees, reaching down and slipping a couple of granola bars out of a pocket on her thigh. "If we make it through the next room, I'm expecting some kind of fancy celebration dinner."

Deus, the next *one.* As one, we turn our heads, shining our torches through the archway.

The next puzzle awaits.

7

AMELIA

I'M DOUBLE-CHECKING THE BANDS OF MY CLIMBING HARNESS AND listening with half an ear while Jules talks to himself. Every chance he gets he starts scribbling in his little journal, working through ideas aloud and staring at pictures of glyphs from his wrist unit. He's translating those damn things as though his life depends on it. *I guess maybe it does. Or could.* Still, I had to remind him to chew on his granola bar. Then I had to remind him to swallow.

When the next room proved to be little more than a massive pit, he ordered me to stand to the side on the ledge while he investigated, certain that this was some new kind of puzzle. But there are barely any glyphs to be seen. Just some in an archway, and then on the ledge by our feet, a spiral shape, with a line radiating from it. He said that one wasn't a glyph, but he did snap a surreptitious picture of it with his wrist unit. Maybe he's not as sure as he claims to be when it comes to the glyphs.

The ceiling soars so high above us that it's mostly lost in the dark, the beams of our lights only dimly illuminating cables and glimmering stone up there. Just inside the doorway we stand on our ledge, and the rest of the room is one giant hole in the ground. To me, it looks more like a puzzle that fell apart—a trap that time had sprung, maybe, given how long ago this place was built.

I don't mind the break, though. It gives me time to mull over the mystery that is Jules.

Oxford University was where Elliott Addison worked, before the IA threw him in prison for treason after his famous TV appearance. Oxford was where he first decoded the Undying broadcast, when he was only a little older than Jules and I are now. I'm wishing I could get a signal on my phone here, pull up pictures of Addison from back then. Gazing at Jules now, with that eager gleam in his eye as he tries to figure out what our next move should be, it's hard not to wonder. He said his last name was Thomas. But if I were related to a world-renowned lunatic and traitor, I'd lie about my name, too.

"Maybe some trick of the light," Jules is murmuring to himself, moving his head this way and that, so that the beam of light from his helmet flashes around the empty cavern, half blinding me. "A bridge, something that looks invisible unless you get just the right light—I don't see the exit, though, so unless that's camouflaged too . . ."

I give myself a shake, letting him talk as I dig in one of my cargo pockets until I come up with a handful of mini chem-lights. I snap half a dozen and give them a good shake until my handful starts to glow an increasingly bright green. Then, with all my strength, I hurl them down and across the chasm.

"Wait—what are you *doing?*" Jules half-reaches for me, almost like he thinks I'm about to hurl myself in after them.

"You think two-dimensionally," I retort, watching as the sticks fall—one bounces off the far wall, ricocheting back toward the center of the chasm. Eventually they hit the bottom, revealing a surface strewn with broken rock, some pieces big as boulders. The rock seems to glint at me in the light. "You said when we came in that the Undying don't necessarily think of space and distances and stuff like we do. Whatever maze or test was in here, it's long gone now. But the next chamber might not be across some invisible bridge, it might be . . . oh, for the love of—turn that flashlight off, will you?"

I'm blinded by his light, but I can hear his intake of breath and can imagine the annoyance on his features. He complies, though, and after a few seconds, I can see the dim glow at the bottom of the pit again. It's maybe five or six stories down—farther than I'd originally thought.

"There—see?" I lean closer to Jules so I can point, letting him sight along my outstretched hand. There's a section of the ragged circular wall down at the base of the pit that's darker than the rest. An opening. Jules ducks down to see what I see, his cheek a hair's breadth from mine, and I can feel the warmth of his skin.

"Mehercule, this path led downward," Jules breathes. He may be predisposed to think two-dimensionally, but he certainly catches on quick. "But how—" I switch on the tiny LED flashlight on my wrist, and he breaks off, looking at me. His eyes rake across the climbing harness I'd been fiddling with while he talks. "You know, you could have just said something when you got there first."

"And ruin your fun?" I flash him a grin. "Think all the traps or whatever are broken here, too?"

"Well, I don't see any of their writing," Jules replies, easing his pack off and dumping it on the ledge so he can rummage through it for his own climbing gear. "If there were instructions, or warnings, they're down there with the rest of the path." He inclines his head down toward the bottom of the drop-off, where huge chunks of debris rest in shattered pieces. As if to underline the risk, there's the sound of a couple of pieces of rubble falling from the collapsed bridge we left behind, the rattle of rock breaking away from rock.

I pull out my multi-tool, ignoring the flash of remembered panic from when I last used it—getting purchase on the rock, dangling over an abyss, trying to hang on until Jules could get to me. I twist it until I hit the drill-bit setting, then thumb the button. Drilling a climbing anchor is hard work at the best of times, and my hands are already exhausted from my mad scramble earlier. But I pull my hammer from my belt and start anyway, tapping the rock floor to make sure it's sound. The structure and the tech of the Undying are built from a kind of metallic stone, but this temple is built into the cliff, and the place I'm drilling is just good old-fashioned rock. Gritting my teeth, I grip and twist downward with the multi-tool while tapping at it with the hammer.

Jules is watching intently as he pulls on his climbing harness, brows drawn in, and I want to make some biting remark at him— *Gee, don't offer to help or anything*—but I remember the way he flung himself down on the crumbling bridge to grab for my arm. And I keep my mouth shut.

It's not until he's got himself strapped in that he ambles over. He switches on his helmet light so he can watch what I'm doing. "Can I have a go?" He crouches, like it's some fascinating new skill, and not something making my whole body ache and sweat drip— oh-so-sexily, I'm sure—down my face.

"It has to be done right to be safe," I reply breathlessly, though I stop as I speak, and the second my grip relaxes, cramps go shooting up the hand holding the drill. *Yeah, maybe take him up on that when you're done criticizing him for not helping.*

"I'm a quick study," Jules promises.

I look up and eye his equipment. It takes half a second to tell it's brand-new—the creases from the manufacturer's packaging are still visible against his thighs, and the straps are a shiny new red. "This isn't something you pick up cramming late at night in the library, Oxford."

But I'm exhausted. And he just raises one of those expressive brows at me, and I shift over so he can take my place. His fingers brush mine as he grasps the tool, and I flex my hand.

"You've got to keep a steady downward, twisting pressure on the drill bit while you hit it with the hammer." I drop to my knees beside him so I can keep a close eye on proceedings. "And don't hit it hard, just tapping. Too hard and you'll crumble the stone."

Jules starts tapping at the base of the multi-tool, strokes almost exactly imitating mine. I watch his hands as he works to make sure he's doing it right. While I can't tell exactly how much pressure he's putting on the drill bit, I'm not hearing any of the telltale cracks that would suggest he's breaking the edges of the hole we're making.

"Like this?" he asks.

The question catches me off-guard—I'm still staring at his hands, which bear no calluses like mine, but nonetheless grip the tool with strength. "What? Oh. Yeah, you're doing fine." I pause, trying to think of a way to ask this without sounding like some boy-crazy idiot—because it's not about the way the tendons stand out on his forearms when he's got his sleeves rolled up.

It's curiosity, that's all.

Mostly curiosity, anyway.

I let my gaze slide away, studying the rock wall below us, lit dimly by the far-off glow sticks. "So . . . get a good workout carrying all those books around, huh?"

Jules pauses, and I can feel his eyes on me for a moment. "Can I say yes? You'll hate me if I tell you the truth."

"C'mon," I retort. "You're a college boy camping with a full set of cutlery and a freaking wave-stove worth more than everything I own put together. Can't get much worse than that."

"Hey, good table manners are the last bastion of—" He cuts himself off with a grunt, renewing his efforts with the drill. "I play water polo." He says it like it ought to have meaning, weight, like the words are somehow going to ignite some furious response.

"What the hell is water polo?"

He stops, looking up at me with lifted brows. "Oh. Um. Well, it's a sport. You play in a swimming pool, and there's two teams swimming about and generally mauling each other and trying to get the ball into the goals at either end."

I swallow, just the thought of that much water instantly turning my throat dry. Now I know why he expected me to flip out. I've seen swimming pools before—dozens of 'em. But none with anything in them besides garbage and old deflated pool toys. Swimming pools are a luxury of the past, when fresh water was everywhere. A luxury of the past—or of the unbelievably rich. Even in LA, with the fresh water they get from the solar cell there, they don't waste a drop—certainly not for swimming pools.

"Holy shit, Oxford. And like . . . you practice in this pool? Whenever you want, you get to just splash around and—god, I don't even know how to *swim*. That's drinking water that dozens of people, maybe hundreds, could . . ."

Silence falls, even the tapping of the hammer ceases. It feels like midnight, in this underground gloom broken only by the lights we brought with us, and the stillness between us is as intimate as if we really were huddled together in the middle of the night.

"We're not even from the same world, are we?" I whisper.

He seems to get that I'm not really expecting him to answer, and he resumes drilling after a few more moments of that strange, tense quiet.

"Tell me about your world, then," he says finally.

"My world?"

"About your life, how you came to be here."

"There's not much to tell." I'm flipping through the string of events that led me here, trying to think of any that don't make me look like . . . well, like what I am, in front of a guy like this. Guess the best way is to just tell it quick, like ripping off a Band-Aid. "Dropped out of school a few years back so I could work odd jobs to try to pay down Evie's debt. Got nowhere with it. Started scavenging sort of by accident—I got fired from this diner because I wouldn't . . ." I pause, remembering the diner owner's greasy apron and the smell of onion rings with a swell of nausea. "Anyway, got fired, had no place to stay, and hitched out to Chicago because I'd heard of some tent cities out there, and it was still close enough that I could get back home when I needed. Once I saw the kind of cash the scavver gangs took in, reclaiming and recycling all the junk people left behind, well . . . I realized I could do that too. Some of the scavvers are good sorts—taught me a bit about it, you know. What's worth taking, what's worth stripping for parts, what's not worth a second glance. Others not so much with the helpful, had to sneak after them, learn their techniques on the fly."

He's listening—though the hammer's continuing its steady *tap-tap-tap*, I can see the troubled furrow of his brow that tells me he's thinking.

"Anyway, I worked solo until about six months ago, when this honcho Mink needed new operatives and one of my fences dropped her my name. I impressed her, and she offered me this, in the end. Gaia. I had to decide right there whether to go or not, and I have a feeling if I'd said no, Mink would've been making damn well sure I couldn't tell anyone else about her plan. But the money's too good. I had to try." I sigh, stretching my hand and massaging the palm, which is still protesting the drill work. "So here I am. Not exactly one of your epic literature whatnots."

"On the contrary." Jules's words are punctuated by his breathing—he's getting winded, and I can tell by the slight quiver in his arm that the drill work is getting to him, too. "The epics are filled with litanies of tests and trials for their heroes. And the best stories are always about heroes who work their way up from nothing."

"Hah." It's all I can think of to say. This dumbass guy comparing me to heroes from his great stories—there's a ghost city full of "heroes" just like me back in Chicago, waist-deep in dumpsters and old department stores. I just happened to be the one Mink sent here. "Let me take back over, it's almost deep enough."

Jules relinquishes the drill, and I test the rock a few times before giving the multi-tool a little wiggle to dislodge it and pull it free. I dig in my cargo pockets until I find the tubing I'm looking for, only a hand-length long, and feed it into the hole so I can put my lips to the other end and blow the rock dust out of the hole, then use the tube to measure how deep it is.

I'm searching in my pack for my climbing bolts when he breaks the silence again.

"Tell me about Evie."

My fingers close around a bolt as I look up.

"That's your sister's name, I'm guessing. The reason it was important to you that Chicago was close enough you could still get back home to visit?"

I let my breath out, fitting the end of the bolt to the hole. I'm trying not to let Evie's face, the last time I saw her, blind me to my task. *Just keep working*, I tell myself. I start hammering in the bolt, fully intending to ignore Jules until he gives up. But instead I find myself speaking, almost before the words form in my mind. "She's a terror. She never thinks, she just *does*, you know?"

"I don't know anyone like that," he replies, wry, teasing.

"Shut up," I reply automatically, still hammering.

"It's not an insult," Jules replies, and something in his voice makes me glance up. He seems almost as surprised by his words as I am. "Maybe for her it is, I don't know, but you . . . you don't waste time. You figure out what you need to do and you do it."

I swallow, blinking and forcing my gaze back to the bolt. "That's why I'm alive." I shrug. "Stop to weigh your options too long in the field, and someone either beats you to your next score or scams you out of your last one."

"So maybe Evie's just trying to be more like you."

"Maybe." My hands stop, but my heart's too tight for me to think of a way to disguise how much that hurts me. "I think a lot about why she did what she did—applied for a job at the club, I mean, the company that owns her contract. She didn't know what she was doing, she was just a kid. Thought she was helping me." I breathe out, the bolt before my eyes blurring. "Trying to be like me."

Jules is quiet, and it gives me time to collect myself. I drive the bolt home and shove the hammer back into its slot in my belt, wiping at my brow. I'm probably covered in dirt by now, rock dust and sand and god knows what, mixing with my sweat. At least it's dark.

I switch the multi-tool over to its wrench setting, and twist until it's the right width for the anchor bolt. I yank it tight against the rock, throwing my weight behind it until it doesn't budge anymore. I reset the multi-tool, slip it back into its pocket in my sleeve, and take a breath. Nothing left now but to make the descent.

Softly, into the darkness, I find myself whispering, "I miss her."

Jules doesn't answer, but the quiet that envelops us is soft, and for a strange moment it's almost like I can feel his sympathy in the air between us. I take a deep breath of it, then pull the coil of rope from my pack and start tying in.

I've done it so many times that tying these knots is easier than signing my own name, but when it comes time to do Jules's rope— shiny and new, of course, just like his harness—my fingers fumble. I tell myself it's because I never had to do it on someone else, that in mirrored reverse the movements are harder. I tell myself that because the alternative is that I'm fumbling because, to tie him in, I am by necessity right by his crotch, and climbing harnesses fit guys in such a way that leaves little to the imagination.

Focus, idiot. I grit my teeth and finally get the S-curve of the knot right, and tied through both loops of his harness. I run my fingers along the thigh loops, fingers scraping against the khaki of his pants and warming along his leg. I give one of them a quick tighten. When I glance up, he's staring hard at the ceiling, the beam of his helmet light fixed on a featureless chunk of rock.

I exhale noisily and stand up, giving him a chance to start and take a step back. I can't tell, even when I point my wrist LED at his face, whether he's blushing. But the too-casual way in which he tries to shove his hands into his pockets, then finds them blocked by the harness, then crosses his arms . . . that's better than a blush. I resist the urge to laugh, mostly because even flustered, he's hot. Especially in climbing gear.

"Okay, I'm gonna go first." I lift up my ropes, looped through the brake. "Once I get down I'll be able to—"

"Wait, what?" Jules's arms fall to his sides and the beam of his helmet swings over to blind me as it fixes on my face. "We should stick together. You shouldn't head off alone."

"So chivalrous." I roll my eyes, knowing he can see it in that helmet beam of his. "I *have* to go first—I've only got the one belay device for a brake, and besides, it takes practice to rappel without a belayer."

Jules looks down, where I'm gripping the gear at my waist, unblinding me enough so I can see his face and the blankness of his features. For once, I'm the one using the big words he doesn't understand.

"Look," I say slowly, relishing in the fact that I get to lecture *him* for a change. *See how he likes it.* "I rappel down, using this brake. Then once I'm on the bottom, I can belay you—I can hold your rope while you come down the cliff. I can tie in on the ground so that even though I'm lighter than you, I can still use my brake to slow your descent."

The light swings over to the abyss and quivers once. Abruptly, I realize something—maybe it's not misplaced chivalry at all. His gear's brand-new, his rope stiff and unused. He's not a climber. A cliff like this has got to look like death on a tea sandwich to someone like him.

"It'll be easy," I promise him, softening my voice. "And I promise I won't let you fall. I've done this more times than I can count." Then, while his focus is on the drop and the ropes and his fear, I decide to take my opportunity to see if I can even the scales a little. I just told him about Evie, and I want to know more about him. So I add a few more words: "Trust me, Jules Addison."

It takes him a few seconds before what I've said sinks in. His eyes stay on the drop, and he's letting his breath out and nodding absently—and then he freezes. And in that moment, I know I'm right about who he is. Because when he looks back at me, there's guilt and fear in his face, not confusion. I can see him panicking; I can see him trying to figure out if there's any point in denying that he's the son of Elliott Addison.

Then he closes his eyes. "How long have you known?"

"About two seconds," I reply, my own heart rate climbing as I try not to dwell on the implications. "But I've been wondering ever since you showed up. Mostly after you claimed to know what he knows, what the IA would kill to know."

"You figured it out just from that?"

"Well, you look like him too. And you've mentioned your father a bunch of times, but never a mother. It was all over the net when Dr. Addison's wife left him after he started up with the 'Undying tech is dangerous' bullsh—" Too late I realize that might not be the most tactful approach. "Sorry. Um."

"Mehercule." He turns, pacing a few steps away from me. "Sorry for the lie," he says finally, stiffly. "I was told I should keep my identity secret."

This is my moment, the one I've been waiting for. He needs me, my climbing expertise, to keep moving forward. This is where I get to ask every question I've wanted to ask him—hell, every question and accusation I've ever wanted to level at his father. But when I open my mouth, the only thing that comes out is, "We really *aren't* from the same planet."

Jules's head snaps up. "What do you mean?"

"Did you ever have any intention at all of helping me, helping Evie? Your dad refused to even come here—I'm supposed to believe you're going to let me profit off the Undying tech that your father sacrificed his career, his freedom, to keep mankind away from?"

Jules is tense, that much I can see even in the gloom. "I gave you my word," he says, voice stiff. But despite that insistence, my gut tells me there's something he isn't saying.

Now that I know, I can see Elliott Addison in his face. His skin's lighter—that's his mom's genes, I guess—and he doesn't have a beard, but the nose is the same, the brow, even the slight stoop to his shoulders. I've been traveling with the son of *Elliott Addison.*

When the first broadcast arrived fifty years ago, before we discovered Gaia, Addison pioneered the field of xenoarchaeology. As a young man, he became the first to decode their transmission. He's a freak, basically—mathematics, linguistics, archaeology, all coming together in perfect combination, so this guy was the first one to understand what the aliens were saying. He figured it out at *eighteen*.

And then a couple of years ago he went totally bonkers in a live newscast that then went viral online.

Overnight his tune had changed—suddenly he was babbling about how dangerous it was to use the Undying technology, just as they started using the solar cell *Explorer IV* brought back to power LA and its water purifying plant. Just as scientists started to realize that this near-magical power source could be just the miracle our energy-starved planet needed to survive, if only we could find more, or discover how to produce these cells ourselves—he started preaching to anyone who would listen that the cell ought to be destroyed, and further exploration of Gaia's temples put on hold until we were sure we knew what we were doing.

Put on hold, while people like me—people like Evie—suffered.

Though I had my suspicions before, everything is different now that I *know*. Now he knows. I want to tell him I don't believe him, that if he shares his dad's eyes and academic zeal then he probably shares his ideals too, that maybe we're better off separating and going our own ways. Except that I can't read these stupid glyphs, and I won't get much farther than the *Explorer IV* team did at the other temple without him. This revelation just proves he does know what he's talking about, that as much as I might hate his pampered life and his roadblock of a father, he really is the one person who could get me into the heart of an Undying temple, past the outskirts I'd planned to ransack.

And he won't get very far without me.

The truth is that I have absolutely no idea what to say.

Fortunately, I have another way out. I angle the rope in my brake up enough for me to slip over the edge of the pit and start making my descent into the dark.

8

JULES

MIA'S A THIRD OF THE WAY DOWN ALREADY, GRIPPING THE ROPE BY HER HIP, her feet planted against the rock, pushing off to bounce slowly down like she's jumping in low gravity. I'm leaning over the edge of the cliff to watch her, my head torch illuminating her path, motes of dust and debris dancing in the beam of light.

She's silent all the way down to the ground, letting me stew in my fear—and the fact that *she knows who I am*—the whole time. This is terrifying on all possible counts.

I took a basic course on climbing before I left, because I didn't count on having Mia here to help, but the clean, predictable wall of the gym was nothing like the ancient, crumbling rock face below me. I didn't like the idea of climbing then, and I *hate* it now.

Once she hits the floor of the cavern, she's quick to unlace the rope in movements I can't make out, then uses both hands to roll a boulder into place beside her. When she shouts up, her voice is steady, and I'm trying to pretend to myself that my breath isn't sticking in my throat and my hands aren't fumbling as I thread my rope through the anchor point and drop it down to her. The prospect of the climb is crowding out what I should really be focusing on, which is that my cover is blown. But how can I think about that when I'm about to rely on an anchor we just drilled into the rock ourselves?

The rope slithers as it unwinds, whispering like the wind, taking forever to reach the bottom. Though I suppose those few seconds won't seem very long if I'm the one falling. She secures one end of the rope under the boulder—she's too light to be my counterweight all on her own—and calls up that I should launch myself off into space. Just like that, no big deal.

You've done this in the gym, I remind myself, carefully turning and backing up to the edge of the cliff. If I'm to make my way down like her, feet planted against the rock face, body bent like an L-shape, I'm going to have to lower myself backward over the cliff, against every instinct I have, my gut and my brain screaming at me in chorus to stay safely perched up here, where gravity can't hurt me.

Deus, I'm going to die.

Prickles run up and down my spine, the back of my neck tingling, trying to warn me danger's nearby. I have to wait until I'm almost not thinking about it, until the image of my father's face—and of Mia's face, when she worked out who I am—is floating in the forefront of my mind, and then I let myself ease back, catching my warring instincts unawares.

It's not so bad, once I'm underway. I don't make long leaps like her, but instead simply walk down, carefully placing each foot before I move the next, craning my head back occasionally to eyeball the rope. It seems like the anchor point is holding. After a few moments I even dare to look sideways, along the ragged edge of the cliff. Far into the distance, I think I can see cables sticking out of the rock, thick as my arm, trailing down into the darkness below. Some part of the mechanism behind this broken trap, I suppose, but I can't make out more than that.

A pebble slides away beneath my foot, and I yank my attention back to the rock face in front of me. But I'm not just moving slowly because I'm inexpert—it's because I need to know what I'm going to say by the time I reach the bottom.

She's heard the stories about my father, and she believes them, that much I could see in her face. And I understand. The thing is, he tried every possible channel before he went public.

He was the one who decoded the language of the Undying. He studied every text, every second of the footage from first our probes, and then the *Explorer IV* crew. He's devoted his life to this ancient civilization since before I was born.

When we discovered we could use Undying tech as an almost endless energy source, he understood what that meant for Earth. People said he didn't—they called him a cloistered academic, an elitist, accused him of being so distant from the real world that he couldn't imagine what the energy to filter water, to light up cities, to protect crops could mean to . . . well, to people like Amelia.

But those people weren't there with him as he struggled with his decades-old translations, obsessed over them, let them consume him. They didn't watch him endlessly coding and decoding the broadcast, and the fragments of text from the *Explorer* mission, praying out loud by lamplight that he was wrong. They weren't raised by a man desperate to disprove his own life's work so that he wouldn't have to tell the world we hadn't discovered a way to save ourselves after all.

Nothing stopped him, not even my mother leaving. At the time I hated him for it, for ignoring us in favor of a bunch of stupid maths problems on the walls of his study. My parents were—are—so different from one another. A chemist and a linguist. You'd think his mathematics specialty would help him stay in her world, her scientific sphere of yes and no, right and wrong, thesis and proof.

But mathematics and linguistics always came together for him as a merging of art and science, a world full of shades of gray, where hers was black and white. The two of them were like oil and water, never quite mixing, and when it all became too much for her, the answer was clear. It was like a chemical response.

When unyielding husband is added to desperate social pressure and worldwide publicity, normality evaporates and stressors multiply. Solution? Remove husband.

So she cut her losses and asked me to come with her. But somebody had to stay, to try to keep him from drowning completely. And I had already started to learn the language he was reading— not just the Undying glyphs, but the language of mystery and secrets.

My father's office walls were covered with translations from the original broadcast, along with sticky notes and satellite images and pictures from early exploratory missions. I can still picture a particular passage that had spawned dozens of notes: *Know unlocking the door may lead to salvation or doom.*

Whose salvation? he had written underneath in black marker on the faded chevron wallpaper. *Whose doom?*

It's easy for the International Alliance to say they'll be careful on Gaia. It's easy for them to dismiss the warnings from the Undying, the stories of their own civilization's downfall. But the human race has been dismissing the decline of our planet and the destruction of its resources for centuries now. We've gotten pretty good at it.

I don't know what I want to find here. I'll follow the Nautilus, try to understand why that strange, inelegant warning was crammed into the broadcast. A part of me wants my father to be right. I don't want him to have thrown our lives away for nothing.

Another part of me, of course, wants him to be wrong. Because if he's not, that's the end. Not this generation, probably not the next, but it'll happen pretty soon. Our world will fall apart. And Mia is one of the billions who need this tech, whose lives will be changed if we can find enough of it, or better yet, find a way to replicate it. If I told her he wants to withhold it for her own good, she'd punch me, and I wouldn't blame her.

I've left it far too late to tell her what I'm really chasing here—to tell her about the mystery of the Nautilus spiral, and the one glyph of warning. But if I'd told her any earlier, she wouldn't have come, she wouldn't have helped me.

So? says a tiny voice in my head. *That would have been her choice. You made it for her.*

Another voice pushes back. *And if I did? It was for the good of everyone on Earth, everyone she cares about. She was here to steal—she is here to steal. To desecrate this place before we can learn from it.*

I'm still searching for the right words when I realize I'm only a half a meter from the ground, and I can lower my feet until my boots hit the gravelly surface and shift my weight so I'm standing once more. We're standing amid the ruins, and near the entrance to another chamber.

My hands are still trembling from the descent as I start to unbuckle my harness. And though I still haven't found the right words, Amelia's the one to break the silence.

"It explains a lot, actually. If he's your father."

Familiar frustration surges up in me, though it's a little hard to tell it apart from the adrenaline. "Deus, you think he brainwashed me? That's the usual assumption. My age means that nobody credits me with the ability to form my own opinions. This, despite the fact that I finished my schooling at thirteen, have been auditing university courses ever since, and if you'll forgive the lack of modesty, can go toe-to-toe with any academic in the field, at any level. I formed my own opinions, including deciding how to weight his expertise, and I believe him."

"Actually," she says, and stepping forward to help me with removing the last of the harness—an intimacy I try unsuccessfully to ignore—"I just meant that what you're doing makes more sense now. Risking your life for a bunch of rocks, that I don't get. It's different when you're doing it for someone you love."

"Oh," I say, in one of my more eloquent moments.

"You're going to keep up your end of our bargain?" she asks quietly.

"Yes." I mean it. *Somehow, I will.*

She nods, some of the tension going out of her frame. "For what it's worth," she adds, "I'm more or less the same age as you, and I think we can make our own decisions just fine."

"We may be the only ones who think that braving a series of crumbling deathtraps is proof of good decision-making," I joke weakly, the strength starting to come back to my limbs, though when she flashes me a grin, I find my knees aren't quite as recovered as I thought.

I *like* this girl.

And I've lied to her.

"Also," Mia says, interrupting my scattered thoughts, "it explains why you're such a freak. I mean, your dad was a freak, he decoded the broadcast when he was . . . well, our age. Makes sense you're some crazy genius too."

That's always been a sticking point, for me. The people around me who treat me like a genius—which, perversely, generally involves assuming I can't tie my own shoelaces, so lost am I in brilliant thoughts. And the ones who don't think I can be, not at my age.

For my part, I've always known that I have in me what my father has in him. It's not arrogance. It's just truth. I didn't earn it—I was born with it, gifted it.

The part that's on me is the challenge—the pressure—to make something of it.

My father's always told me that my integrity matters more than any other part of me, and he's shown his over and over, in the face of unbearable pressure, to protect even those who don't want his protection.

"Well," I say. "You think *I'm* a genius—you've never met him. Now I'm the only one my father has left in his corner, freak or not. And that's why I'm here."

"That, and you get all hot and bothered about walking where no human foot has trod before," she teases.

You *get me hot and bothered, Mia.*

"Um," I say, shoving that thought aside. "Well, true. Have you heard of Walt Whitman? He was one of your American poets. He said, 'I am large, I contain multitudes.'" I shrug. "I can be here for more than one reason. I *am* here for more than one reason."

"Can I ask you a question?" she says quietly.

"I've heard the worst of it from every possible angle," I say, though my mind is already bracing itself against whatever blow is coming. "Ask, I won't mind."

"Helping your father, finding something to prove the tech is dangerous, finding something that will get him out of jail, that I get. But learning about the Undying . . . why does it matter?" She pauses, to see if I'm offended, and I nod that she should go on. "I understand archaeology. I understand looking at our past to figure ourselves out, that makes sense to me. But these . . . beings . . . were completely different from us, not connected at all. They've left tech we can use, sure, and it's worth learning about that and how to use it. But why does it matter who they were and why they died? Aren't there better things we could spend our effort on?"

I consider the question, as a trickle of rock falls gently down the cliff face above me. "Well, who says learning those things *isn't* the same as ensuring our own survival and well-being?" I say eventually. "For a start, we don't know how different they really were. You said yourself, this place reminds you of Angkor Wat, of the Pyramids. They set us puzzles with musical harmonies that sound good to our ears, they built doorways the right size for us to go through."

"Say you're right," she counters. "My question still stands. I understand wanting to learn about the tech, prove your father right or wrong. But their stories? What good does that do?"

"The Undying went extinct," I say. "And while the broadcast didn't get specific, it does say that they did it to themselves. How many times have we, as a species, tried to annihilate one another? How long will the IA's authority hold, as things get worse and worse on Earth? The Undying had the tech we think we need so badly, and they still destroyed themselves. I think we ought to know why and how."

She's quiet for a time. "You think the puzzles, the set-up of this place means they might think like us," she says eventually. "So we might fall into the same mistakes they made. We know humans are capable of violence, deception. You think the Undying were the same?"

I wish I could answer that honestly. I know there was a warning hidden deep in their broadcast, and someone, or something, had to put it there. "I . . . I don't know," I say. "They mentioned war, in the broadcast. But they're the only other intelligent species we've ever discovered. Given the distances between Earth and even the next closest star to our sun, they're probably the only intelligent species we'll ever encounter, even long extinct. We should know who they were. They're gone now, but somebody should know their story."

"Is it worth dying for?" she asks.

"Maybe." The word is out before I've had the chance to consider my answer—though really, I decided that long ago, as I took the first steps on my path to Gaia. "Though I'm not volunteering to be another *Explorer IV* team, if I can help it." Everybody remembers the fates of the astronauts who died discovering that the temples on Gaia were full of traps and pitfalls. It was messy. And publicly broadcast, thanks to a live relay feeding through the portal to Earth.

We both stand in silence when I've finished my impromptu lecture, and she's gazing at me in a way I can't make sense of, though I want to. Like she's adding together all the things she knows about me, and perhaps the answer she's getting doesn't completely displease her. Eventually, she nods. "I hope you find what you're looking for, Jules."

The sincerity in her voice shakes me, and all I can do is nod in return.

The next moment she's clearing her throat and turning businesslike. "Let's make camp here. It's been a . . . a busy day." Her voice is wry, and I don't blame her. Tuning ancient temples, falling off bridges, drilling holes, and rappelling down cliffs . . . Busy is an understatement. "We'll just do something stupid, if we try for the next puzzle tonight." She pauses, then quirks a smile. "Well, stupider than coming here in the first place."

I can't disagree, and together we get to work setting up camp, in what feels like companionable silence. Even with this trap triggered already, we don't trust it not to yield up some final, nasty surprise. So she clears a space in the rocks at the base of the cliff just large enough for the two of us to lie down to sleep, and I sit at one end of it preparing dinner. We're amid the debris from whatever trap was here, and once again I'm reminded this couldn't just be any cave back on Earth. Metallic lines streak the nearest boulder, no thicker than the hairs on my head. They intersect and weave together in endlessly intricate patterns—this rock is unlike anything we have at home.

But staring at the ruins of a broken trap won't help me now, and I return my attention to our meal. Once I've eaten, I can keep translating the glyphs we've seen in the first few chambers.

I've had my water bottle strapped to the outside of my pack all day, and the idea behind the outrageously expensive fitting on it is that it should condense water from the air, and continually refill itself by way of a slow drip. When I lift it to inspect it by the light of my head torch, it's only half-full—the air in here is too dry for it to be totally effective.

I show it to Amelia, and she looks up from where she's gathering a small layer of rocks to stop us rolling into danger in our sleep, and grimaces. We had to use that water or we wouldn't have gotten this far, but I'd always figured our breathers would be our limiting resource—not water.

I abandon my plan to soak dried noodles and make us something hot to eat, and instead unpack flatbread, covering it with slices of thick yellow cheese, the crumbs of it sharp as I lick them off my fingers. I cut fat slices of salami to layer on top of it, the rich, salty smell setting my mouth watering.

Amelia sets aside our breathers for when we need them at bedtime, and edges along to sit cross-legged beside me, her fingers touching mine as she accepts her slices of flatbread. "Salt and fat and protein," she says, around a huge mouthful. "Talk about the holy trinity."

For a time, there's nothing but the sound of blissful chewing, as we sit together with our backs against the cliff, lit by the light of just one torch to conserve power. We end up licking the grease of the salami off our fingers and picking crumbs of cheese off our clothes, sharing the use of my handkerchief to clean ourselves up.

Her shoulder's a hair's breadth from mine, and I'm hyper-aware of her presence. There's something about being in a place like this—not just another planet, but deep inside a temple, where nobody else could reach us, together in the dark. Something that inspires a closeness, a confidence . . . an intimacy. A place like this encourages truths, and confessions.

My own confession's on the tip of my tongue, but as I draw in breath to speak, she breaks the silence instead.

"I learned about your father at school," she says. "Before I dropped out."

"You mentioned that." My curiosity's killing me, though I don't want to offend her. But it should be impossible to do what she did. "How did you drop out of school? They didn't send truancy officers to find you?"

She snorts. "You've never heard of attendance drones, I assume. Kids'll rent out their time, answer questions for you every now and then, along with the twelve other accounts they're running. You don't get good grades, not without paying extra, but you pass."

"I've never heard of attendance drones," I admit, which I'm pretty sure doesn't surprise her even one iota. "How does one work around the retinal scan? I did most of my classes in person, Oxford tradition and all that, but I took two remotely, and a constant retinal presence was required."

"The retinal scanners just need an eye," she replies. "Not specifically my eye, and turns out, not even a *human* eye." I'm trying very hard not to think about what that means, when she continues. "What do you mean, your classes were in person?"

This is going to be the water polo pool all over again, and I'm an idiot for bringing it up. "I mean the teacher and the students are all physically in the same room," I say. "Not virtual."

She nearly drops her last piece of flatbread, scrambling to catch it, her hand brushing against my leg. "What, like the guy on the screen is a real person for you? You can talk to him?"

"And he can talk to you," I reply. "Or shout at you for daydreaming. Then tell your father all about it at tea." Which, now I think about it, doesn't really stack up against her own list of misfortunes. I try to change direction before I can shove my foot any further into my mouth. "You said maths was the school subject you missed the most," I venture. And of course, now it just sounds like I'm trying to work out how little education she has, which isn't what I mean at all—her ingenuity fascinates me. I admire it.

"It makes sense to me," she replies. "It's beautiful. When you really get math right, it's perfectly streamlined. Everything has a job, everything has a purpose, and all the elements work together in harmony. You know exactly where you are, with math, and what's required to make it right. It's not much use in my current line of work, though." Her voice has dropped low, and as we sit shoulder to shoulder, she's turned her head, and I've turned mine, so we're whispering to each other in the near dark.

The small light illuminates one half of her face—the freckles, the tug of her lips to a wistful smile, the graceful swoop of her lashes. The other half is cast entirely in darkness, unknowable.

"I hate it sometimes," she continues. "Picking through the remains of people's lives, like vultures, taking anything that can be sold or stripped down for parts or recycled. But early on I started a collection, you know? Things that didn't have any value, wouldn't help Evie, but still held *something*. Like little snapshots. Stories about the people who used to be there. Most of the personal stuff is gone, but you can put a lot of it together from the pieces you do find. I love that part."

My own lips curve to match her smile, though mine's more warm than wistful. "That's archaeology, you know," I say, just as quietly. "Putting together stories from what's left behind. That's what I do."

And it turns out she does understand it after all, and as our eyes meet, we both share that knowledge for a few seconds: that in each other we can see the same love of uncovering a hidden story. I wish we shared more than that—I wish I truly knew her mind. We're from two different worlds in every possible sense. I ought to hate her just for being here. I ought to resent everything she's done, and everything she'll do, if we escape this place. But just like the left-behind histories we uncover—hers in ruined buildings, mine in vanished civilizations—our own story is more complicated than one simple truth.

Here's a very simple truth, though: I could tip forward just a fraction, and if she did too, our lips would meet. Her gaze flickers down to my mouth and lights a spark inside me—a moment's hope that she's thinking the same thing as me.

She clears her throat and turns away, head dipping so she can open her pack and rummage through it, like she's taking inventory. "It must be killing you not being able to take your time and study everything we're finding here."

You're killing me.

But I let my breath out in a rush and tip my head back against the wall. "Pretty much," I agree. "But we're here for something more important." Above us yawns the black emptiness of the pit walls we scaled earlier, the darkness heavy with all the knowledge, all the stories, haste has forced me to leave behind. I'm struck with a sudden sense of vertigo, as if our little pool of lantern light is clinging to the rock and I'd fall up into the dark if it weren't for Mia tethering me to the ground.

"What about those pictures?"

Her voice makes me jump. "What pictures?"

She frowns at me, then jerks her chin toward my arm. "The ones you took when we came in, of the walls and stuff. The ones you were going over when we stopped after the bridge."

"Mehercule, I for—" I stop, blinking. I *do*. I have brand-new pictures, new glyphs to study. Forgotten because of this baffling, pink-and-blue-haired criminal at my side. I jerk my eyes downward and bring my wrist display to life with a shaking twist of my hand. Some of the pictures are blurry from my rush to record the glyphs in that first room, but others are clearer, and as the Mia-fog recedes from my brain, they start to click into focus. I grope around with my other hand until I find my journal in my pack and pull it onto my lap, eyes still on the pictures.

Mia snorts beside me. "Aaaaand he's gone."

I could tell her she's as fascinating a puzzle as the coded messages the Undying left behind. That if she wanted it, she could have my full attention. But she broke that moment earlier, she looked away first—and I know when not to push my luck. It wouldn't be honest, anyway. I've lied to her, and she believes I'm something I'm not. So I try to put her—and the sound of her humming, the flicker of shadows as she fiddles with one of the carabiners, the scent of her in the still air—out of my mind and focus on my translation.

I have no idea how much time has passed when I finally look up again. With every new image I feel like I'm sinking deeper into the language of the Undying, understanding the nuances better. But none of it says anything about the Nautilus—and judging by the way it was carved so sneakily in the two places I found it so far, I'm not sure any of the formal carvings *will* help with it. So far, all I've seen is a retelling of the story from the original broadcast.

Mia's moved a bit away from me, and she's looking down at her handheld phone. The display's on its dimmest setting, but I can see the flicker of it against her face—she's watching a video. The sound's muted, but she's gazing at it intently. We're way too far underground now for there to be a signal, even if the station were directly overhead. I'm guessing it's the video message I saw her get last night.

Her face in the glow of the screen is tired and miserable and dirty, and her shoulders droop forward. I start to speak and stop myself—but I must make some sound, because her eyes snap up and she's immediately scowling at me and thumbing the button to turn her phone display off.

"What?" Her voice is a challenge, daring me to comment.

"Nothing." I let my wrist unit go dark and stick my pen inside my journal to hold the page. "Just thinking about my dad. Doing this kind of work reminds me how much I miss him, I guess."

Mia's shoulders lose a bit of their tension, and after a few seconds she crawls closer again so she can reach her pack to slip her phone back into its protected pocket, then resume her spot at my side. "Any luck with the translations?"

"Some." It's nearly impossible to keep from reaching for my journal again—but my utter exhaustion helps. I may have pulled a lot of all-nighters in my life, but never after a day spent fighting for my life in an alien temple. "These glyphs are a lot less formal than the ones in the main temple that the *Explorer* crew photographed. Almost conversational."

"Well, you can save the rest as a treat for tomorrow."

I grin, and together we bunk down on the chilly stone floor, clearing spots of debris for our bedrolls. We pull on our breathers, settling them over our noses and mouths to supplement our air with oxygen as we sleep. My body's ready for the boost, that much I can tell as soon as I inhale.

We're necessarily close to each other—the larger debris forms a maze-like path that leaves us little room to spread out. But I notice that there's only a thin line of rocks and pebbles between my sleeping bag and her blanket nest, and I'm racking my brain trying to remember who put their bed down first and who was second. Was it me? Or was she the one to choose this closeness?

My conscience beats at me again, even as I ask that question. *You're lying to her. You're lying to her.*

She flicks off the lamp without much warning, before I can read her face, or what's visible of it behind the breather. Before she can read mine and see my guilt.

I hear the rustle of fabric as she nestles down, and I follow suit, thoughts spinning. There's a few breaths of silence, and then her voice comes low and soft, a little muffled by the breather.

"So, the translations—what do they say?"

"It'll take a while for me to figure it all out." Again, the urge to turn on my torch and study my notes by its dim light flares, and I have to suppress it. Easier, with Mia just a hand's width away from me. "And we don't have the whole of the story yet, but it's elaborating on what they said in their original broadcast. I think it's the history of their civilization. How they rose, how they fell. Why they left these places behind for a new race to find."

"It must be so much bigger than ours," she murmurs, and for a moment I have to force my mind back, to remember what I just said. "Ours is all the story of one planet. Of one brief attempt to leave it, the Alpha Centauri mission, and otherwise, not even a blip until now."

"And the history they're telling in this temple says they've seen the whole galaxy. Can you imagine the stories they could tell?"

"Stories," Mia echoes, voice weighty with meaning. "Uncovering things left behind."

It's hard to know exactly what she's referring to—the Undying, perhaps, or our conversation about scavenging versus archaeology. Or she's talking about Evie and my father, the family we've left behind. My ruined academic career and her dangerous work in

Chicago. The sun and the sky and her skyscrapers and my pool—our lives, maybe. Neither of us are writing the stories we thought we would.

But her next words tell me exactly what part of home is on her mind: "Jules," she says, quiet. "We're a few rooms in now, and there's been nothing I could take back with me to sell. You're sure there'll be something?"

My silence lasts a beat too long. I know that even as it's happening, as I'm groping for words that won't be a lie. "I promised I'd help you," I say eventually, a lifetime too late.

The lamp flicks back on, and she's propping up on her elbow, expression wary as she looks at me. "Jules?" It's a warning. A question.

"This is absolutely the most important place on Gaia we could possibly be." The words come tumbling out of my mouth, defensive.

"Because of the second layer of code," she says, her voice flat, and for a moment my heart jumps. Then I remember the lie I told her—that the second layer mapped out the locations of the best tech.

"Yes," I say slowly, heavily. Because I can't lie, not again. Not to Mia, and not when she's asking me directly. I should—this is *that* important—but I can't. "Because of the second layer. But the second layer doesn't lead us to hidden tech. At least, I don't think it does."

I look over, finally, my eyes finding her face. And suddenly, like water pouring from a broken dam, I'm telling her what I do know—I explain the equation in that second layer of coding that forms the start of a perfect Fibonacci spiral when you graph it. Forms a shape found over and over in nature, including in the nautilus shell I've named the spiral after. I tell her about the glyph, with its fluid meaning, difficult to translate.

Catastrophe. Apocalypse. The end of all things.

"And from the air, this temple looks identical to the perfect spiral, just like the graph," I say. "I don't know if someone was warning us that this temple is full of danger, or that this temple will tell us how to identify the danger, but I'm the only one who knows, and nobody's listening to me now that my father's . . ." I fall silent, searching for a word. *Incarcerated? In detention?*

When I worked out what I was seeing on the satellite images, my brain suddenly sparking as I matched the spiral shape to the roof of this temple, I knew what I had to do. I tried to tell my father, in our last vid-call. *Remember my very first dig?* I'd said, holding up the arrowhead my five-year-old fingers had pried out of the dirt. His face softened, and then I held up a nautilus shell, the rusty red-and-cream stripes lining its curves. He went very still, then—he knew the shell didn't come from any dig I'd ever been on. He knew what that shape meant. *I think I'm going to go back,* I told him, willing him to hold his poker face. *See what else I can find. I love you, Dad.*

And before he could protest, I shut down the call. He knew where I was going. He knew why. And the IA operatives monitoring our weekly call thought I was off to entertain myself on some university excursion.

I drag myself back to the present. "I had to come here, Mia. This shape, this spiral, it means something. And this is the place that will tell me what."

She stares at me in the dim light, still propped on her elbow, and she blinks once, swallows slowly. When she speaks, her voice is careful and composed in a way I've never heard it before. "The spiral means danger," she says. "But you don't know if this place is *full* of danger, or just teaches us *about* danger."

"No," I admit. "But we're in the right place, I know that. Right before we walked out onto the bridge, I saw the Nautilus scratched into the rock, like a sign. I saw it at the top of the cliff, as well. This is where we're meant to be, to find out more about it."

"You don't know if this place is deadly." Though her pose is one of relaxation, even in the dark I can tell her body is tense. "And you brought me in here, without even—you just *brought me here*, without ever asking if I was willing to take that risk. And then you saw a symbol that probably means freaking *apocalypse*, and you just strolled on by without sharing that information?"

I gaze at her in silence. There's no defense I can offer. She's right.

"Do you have any idea if there's anything valuable in here at all for me? For Evie?" she asks, controlled once more.

My heart wants to shrink away. "I don't know," I whisper. *There could be*, my mind says. *I hope there is. I want there to be.* But none of those words make it past the lump in my throat.

She pushes up to sit in a sharp, sudden movement, lifting her hands to weave them through her hair, her knuckles white with the strength of her grip. "You don't know," she repeats, cold as ice. And then in a blink, the ice is gone, seared away with the heat of her fury. "*You don't know?* My sister's *life* depends on me, my only family, my little sister—everything I care about in the world, and you just decided to merrily lead me in here to play some stupid detective game, because you're Jules Addison, and you know better than everyone else. You knew I had one goal here, just one thing I came to do. I needed tech and you . . . you *lied* to me. This isn't a game, this isn't—even if you don't care at all about helping my sister, without something valuable, I won't be able to buy my way off the planet. I'll *die* here, Jules."

"I'll help you," I try, when she pauses for a breath that sounds more like a sob. "I gave you my word. I meant it."

"With what money?" Her voice breaks, and the crack of it makes me want to melt back into the rocks and debris. "Where's this magical money coming from? Are you that rich, Jules?"

And I'm not, of course. I might live in the plush surrounds of Oxford, but my father's on a professor's salary. I don't have the kind of money Mia will need to buy her sister's freedom. "We'll find something," I mumble, unconvincing even to my own ears. "There's no way of knowing what we'll find at the end of this trail."

Mia's eyes burn in the torchlight. "Is that what you've been telling yourself this whole time? Making yourself feel better?"

I don't answer—I can't. Because she's right, and we both know it, and even though I know I'm doing the right thing, even though I know I have to get to the center of this temple to discover what's so dangerous about the Undying tech . . . looking at her face, all the things I know don't seem so certain anymore.

She's right. And my silence acknowledges it.

She stares at me a beat longer, then two, her angry gaze measuring me, and finding me wanting in every possible way. Then she's looking over toward her gear, her climbing harness, before glancing up—my heart shrinks—at the cliff. I can see in the furious set of her jaw that she wants nothing more than to get away, leave me and try to salvage her original plan. But if she's even half as exhausted as I am, she'll never make it. So instead, she reaches for the lamp and plunges us both into the dark once more.

I want to convince her that I *will* find a way to help her.

I want to try and explain one more time that we could be in the middle of making the most important discovery on Gaia—that we could be saving our whole world.

I want to . . .

"Mia—"

"Don't."

The word is a bullet, and it silences me.

9

AMELIA

WHEN I WAKE UP, I KNOW TIME HAS PASSED, BUT NOT ENOUGH—MY EYELIDS
are still heavy, my gut churning with the nausea that comes from
waking too soon when you're already sleep-deprived. Something's
touching my face, and it's a moment before I realize it's my breather,
and it's meant to be there.

A light flashes past my vision, and a rock clicks against another
up by my head. Is Jules clearing a path to go take a leak or something? Wait, no—he's still curled up behind me. We've moved
closer together in our sleep—*because it's cold*, I tell myself, *and it's
warmer to stay close*—and the curve of my back is fitted in against his
front. When I take a deep, shaky breath, I discover that he's got an
arm wrapped around me. It's like he knew what I was thinking last
night about leaving—like even his subconscious wants to keep me
here with him.

Time to go, Mia, I tell myself, letting last night's anger wash over
me. I knew he was naïve, idealistic, single-minded—but somehow,

somewhere in the brief time since we met, I started trusting him. *Stupid*, rages that voice in my head.

The light flashes across my eyes again, and suddenly I'm awake, adrenaline surging through me as I sit up. Jules groans a protest, but the same instinct must take him, because a moment later he's sitting up behind me.

"Did we wake you, lovebirds?" It's a woman's voice, American, hard-edged.

"Who are you?" I snap, my heart slamming in my chest, forcing myself to move slowly as I slide my hand under the covers for my multi-tool. I need to hide it somewhere I can get to it—there's no circumstance in which these people are friendly, and I can't let myself get taken captive. Jules can't know what I'm doing, but he keeps his arm around me, providing cover for the movement.

"My name's Liz, sweetheart," the woman replies, dropping the flashlight a little, so I can make out the silhouettes of four more people ranged around us. They must have come down the cliffs while we slept. I can hear the sneer in Liz's voice. "You didn't think Mink put all her eggs in one basket, did you?"

Shit. Shit shit shit.

"Mink?" I blink blindly in the light on my face, unable to see much past its glare. I need to buy time. Somewhere in my pack is one of the guns we took off the raiders back at the spring, but there's no chance I'd reach that without them noticing—and they'll be looking for weapons if we're searched. But the multi-tool in my hand—if I could hide it somewhere . . . "I don't know who you're—"

"Don't play dumb," she interrupts. "We're way beyond that, kiddos."

I briefly consider slipping the multi-tool into my boot, but that's the first place anyone with half a brain checks when they're frisking you.

So instead I shove the tool down the front of my pants, inside my underwear, sideways so hopefully it'll feel like part of the waistband. Scavvers aren't above using a frisk to cop a feel, but they usually go for the boobs or the ass.

"What's going on?" Jules is going out of his way to sound bewildered, following my lead. When he pulls down his breather to speak, I can feel his breath on my neck. He keeps it down, as though this will somehow help him get a better look at them, understand them. It's like a befuddled academic peering through his spectacles, the way he does it.

Liz just laughs, a chilly sort of chuckle. Behind her, a shadow moves and I hear the sound of a flare being struck. An orange light blossoms in the dark, then drops to the ground.

My heart sinks. There's five of them, and while Jules is taller than a few of them, Liz's men are bulky with muscle where he's lean—and they're all bigger than me. I don't recognize any of them from the group whose guns and skimmer bike we stole, but that brings me little comfort. It means I don't know what these guys are after, which gives me zero leverage.

My first instinct, that they're IA crews sent to stop raiders, is clearly wrong—Liz mentioned Mink, and Mink's gone to a *lot* of time and effort to make sure her little side operation is off the IA's radar. She'd have had to bribe a bunch of lower-level IA employees to get herself and her crews on board the orbital station, and the employees couldn't rat her out without exposing themselves too. If this Liz knows who Mink is, she isn't IA.

Liz's team starts tearing through our packs, locating the guns with grunts of acknowledgment and confiscating them. Most of our other gear is left in the bags, though they take careful inventory and snag a few choice items from Jules's pack, including the valuable wave-stove. My stuff, I guess, is all too battered and cheap to be of interest.

Then she turns to us, snapping her fingers and holding out her hand. We both stare at her blankly, waiting for the instruction to become clear.

"Your breathers, lovebirds," she says, impatient.

My heart sinks even further down into the pit of my stomach. Our lifelines. Without them, we'll be dead in a few days. One of her gang comes up beside her with a gun hefted meaningfully in one hand, and we both unstrap them, handing them over. It's the smartest move she could make. We can't run now, even if we could escape five armed raiders barehanded.

"Get up," Liz orders, moving the flashlight from my face to gesture with it and rise from her crouch. She's in her mid-forties, with a hard-lined face that would've been quite pretty if it weren't for the chilly, narrowed eyes and the thin set to her mouth.

"We're getting." I give Jules's arm a squeeze under our shared blankets, then get slowly to my feet. He does the same, a half beat behind me. I was ready to leave when I woke, to climb out of this spiral deathtrap of his and try to salvage my original plan. But just because I can't bring myself to look at his face—and god, I wish I could—doesn't mean I want to see his brains splattered all over the cliff behind us. I want to get out of this alive, and I want to get him out alive too, if I can manage it. So I thank whatever deities or spirit ancestors or spaghetti monsters that might be listening that he's keeping his mouth shut, recognizing that of the two of us, I've got the better chance of talking our way out of this. "Let me get this straight—Mink sent you?"

"That's right, sugar." Liz rakes her eyes up and down first me, then Jules. Her sharp eyes linger on him, no doubt taking in the same qualities I noticed about him. Although his brand-new clothes aren't quite so spotless now, his expensive boots no longer so shiny.

"Well, at least we're on the same side." It's worth a try. I do my best to look relaxed, though it's hard with the adrenaline surging through my body.

"We work for the same employer." Liz is watching me, hawk-eyed. "Doesn't put us on the same side."

I have to act fast. I only have one big play here, one piece of information I can use to convince them I'm worth my weight, and the second they find it out on their own, it's useless to me. This is what scavver life has trained me for—weighing up risks and opportunities in the blink of an eye, and acting on them without hesitation.

"Hey," I say, raising my voice, putting just a hint of irritation in it, like they're wasting my time. "Do you know who this guy is? How valuable he is? This is Jules Addison, Elliott Addison's only kid." I hear Jules's sharp, shocked intake of breath behind me, and force myself to ignore him, my voice hard. "He knows more about Gaia than everyone else on this planet put together, and I've been keeping him alive so far. So let's all stop posturing, and just figure out our way forward, yeah?"

Liz fixes me with a long look, and the corner of her mouth lifts like she wants to laugh at a joke only she gets. "Honey, we know who he is."

That robs me of breath to respond, leaving me scrambling. His identity was the only currency I had, my only bargaining chip.

Liz grins, the twist of her lips making me want to lunge at her. "Mink knows all about him. Why stumble around blindly when you can follow the trained rat right to the center of the maze?" She's enjoying herself, that much is obvious—one of those people who gets a twisted pleasure out of holding all the cards. But information's not worth nothing. If I keep her talking, maybe she'll let something slip I can use.

"But—" I stammer, and though I'm playing it up, I don't have to look far to find a quaver for my voice. "But I'm one of Mink's, she would've told me . . ."

"You were supposed to go to the main temple with the other dumbass scavvers." Liz shifts her weight, impatience starting to overtake her enjoyment. "Insurance. Bottom-feeding carrion crawlers—nothing to lose by putting more feet on the ground, and if one or two of you make it back with something valuable, bonus payday."

My mind's reeling. But Liz's eyes shift toward Jules, and when I glance at him out of the corner of my eye, his expression is stone.

He heard me betray his identity—it doesn't matter that Liz already knew who he was, or that I was trying to save both our lives by making it more profitable to keep us breathing. From his point of view, we fought last night, and I've turned against him.

Whatever fragile chance we had of acting like a team is in pieces now. Maybe it was doomed from the beginning. Maybe that moment lying together after that bridge collapsed was the lie.

After all, I'm a scavenger. I'm a raider. I'm a thief, and a vandal, and a criminal. And he's a privileged, idealistic scholar who'd call the cops on me if he could, in another life, on another world.

We were always going to fracture. I take a breath and harden myself against the regret and loss in my heart. This is what I do. I shut out the hurt and keep going, no matter what happens. *Stay alive. Save Evie. Do what you came here to do.*

Liz cuts her inspection of Jules short with a snapped order, and two of her men step forward to empty our pockets and pat us down for weapons while the others load up our packs again. I'm hyper-aware of the multi-tool against my lower belly, warming slowly to skin temperature. The guy frisking me is a scruffy-faced twenty-something in dire need of a shower—but then, aren't we all?—and a change of clothes. He keeps it professional until he gets to my waist. But as he starts to cup his hand around my ass, I flinch away and snap, "Hey, you wanna lose that hand?"

He starts to bristle, but the guy frisking a blank-faced Jules, a middle-aged Latino guy, snaps, "Cut it out, Hansen. She's just a kid."

"Whatever." Hansen's reply is sullen, and he finishes his search of my pockets as quickly as possible. He gives my boots a cursory check and then stalks off, leaving me shaking and trying not to show my relief that he didn't take my multi-tool. There's a blade in there. I'm not defenseless. He leaves the other man to keep an eye on me and Jules while Liz holds an indistinct conversation with the others in her group, some distance away. One's a short guy with fair hair, the other's wearing a newsboy cap that shades his face, and has stupid-looking facial hair crawling down his cheeks.

"Sorry about him," says the Latino guy, who's about Liz's age, maybe late thirties or forties. He's following my gaze as I watch Hansen retreat. "My name's Javier. Just do what she says and you guys'll be fine."

"Thanks." I offer him a nod even though I feel like throwing his "apology" in his teeth. He's still helping her waylay us. But it never hurts to try the friendly approach. Maybe it'll buy me a second or two of hesitation if Liz orders him to shoot me in the head.

Jules says nothing, gazing at some fixed point in the distance, as if he's withdrawn entirely to his own world. Part of me wishes I could explain that his name was currency, that I was trying to buy a measure of trust so I could get us both out of here—and part of me recoils, still furious, insisting that I don't owe him a scrap of loyalty.

They finish searching us and then put our packs back on our shoulders. They bind our hands with my climbing rope, tying us together and leaving a length of it hanging out like a leash. *Great. We're pack mules.* Hansen's the one who does the knots, and he yanks mine extra tight with a grunt of satisfaction. Javier might have some sympathy for us, but Hansen's certainly not a fan of mine anymore.

Liz finishes her confab with her team and strolls back toward us to pick up the "leash" end of the rope. "You'll go first," she informs Jules, plunking his helmet down on his head and switching on his head lamp. "Seeing as you've been so good at decoding these little traps and pitfalls so far. It'll be a lot easier following you now, without needing grappling hooks and harnesses. You made a mess of that first room up there."

"Our breathers?" I ask. I didn't see where they went—no doubt they meant us not to. I know it's a futile effort, that they took them on purpose to make sure we couldn't run, even if we got out of our ropes. "We didn't get a full night with them."

Liz wraps the leash end around her hand. "You'll get them when we make camp. If you do as I've said, and lead us through safely. Bury us under half a ton of rock, and your breathers go with us."

I asked Jules if the Undying were capable of violence and deception, like humans are. I should have stuck to worrying about my own species.

Jules swallows, eyes swinging from Liz to me before turning toward the yawning darkness at the edge of the field of rubble. There's fear there, in his gaze—but not nearly enough. I didn't exactly tell Jules everything about my past, about the kinds of people you encounter as a scavenger. I told him there were some decent folks, and there were.

But I didn't tell him about people like Liz. People who'll shoot you as soon as talk to you, who'll leave you trussed up for the desert to suck dry just to make off with a handful of your gear.

To people like her, everything, every*one*, has a value. It's no different from the way I sorted through Jules's gear at the start of our little partnership—anything that's not worth carrying goes.

The fact that they haven't decided to kill me right now doesn't mean it won't happen—it just means they haven't made up their minds, or they want to use me like a canary in an old mine to spring any traps Jules might miss. If it serves her purposes later, I have no doubt Liz is capable of killing me without a second thought.

Jules has a use to them, but right now I'm on borrowed time.

I've got to make sure we're both worth carrying.

• • •

The next chamber seems relatively intact, though given how much easier it was to climb down the broken puzzle before we made camp than it was to solve the tuning puzzle and then make it across that deathtrap of a bridge, that's not necessarily a good thing. But after only a cursory examination of the glyphs scattered about the walls,

Jules begins leading the expedition on a circuitous path through the room.

It's some time before I recognize it—it's not all that different from one of the early puzzle rooms in the *Explorer IV* temple. I watched the videos of those astronauts dozens of times, studying up in the weeks after Mink recruited me. This one isn't exactly the same, but it's a relatively simple grid puzzle—and while I can't read the glyphs, Jules can.

Each time he steps onto the correct paving stone, a glimmer of light seems to run through it, the silvery filaments coming to life for an instant. It's unnerving, this stone-that's-not-stone. It's just as unnerving to think that fifty thousand years ago, when we'd just begun to replace spears with bows and arrows, before we'd developed anything we'd call a language, the Undying were building this place, broadcasting their final message into space for their successors, creating tech we still can't comprehend.

We continue on, waiting as Jules figures out where we can safely step, minutes stretching into hours. I can tell by the way he lifts his bound wrists that he's still taking pictures of the glyphs, as if translating the sagas of the Undying matters at all now. He's got no clue how bad this is, how screwed we are. How unlikely it is that he'll ever have the chance to go home and share these pictures. There's nothing to do but stay close, though, and make sure the ropes binding us together don't tug either of us off our course, onto unsafe ground.

Following closely on his heels gives me time to think. They know who Jules is, somehow—Mink knew he was coming to Gaia, knew he'd be their ticket through this deathtrap of a temple. And that he'd be worth following. That brings the tiniest flicker of hope. Mink's not the type to care about academic research unless there's a payout. Maybe, just maybe, there's still a chance I'll be able to earn enough to help Evie.

With Liz holding the rope attaching me to Jules, there's no

chance for him and me to have a private conversation, which is probably just as well. Any given moment I don't know whether I want to save him or punt him down one of these bottomless chasms for lying to me the way he did.

I tear my thoughts away from Jules with an effort, and concentrate on walking. But then, as I listen to the occasional rock shifting behind us or pebble skittering across the floor, I realize something.

I heard them. I *saw* them. What I thought was just the broken maze shifting after we passed, what I dismissed as glare from an alien sun on the canyon rim—those were the telltale signs we were being followed.

I could scream my frustration. *I'm better than this.* I should've been on the alert for . . . but we were so sure there was no reason for anyone to come this way in our wake. Jules thought he was following some second, secret spiral code in the original transmission— something nobody else would know about—and I thought he was leading me to a payout nobody else had discovered. We couldn't have guessed Mink would have a team on his heels. We couldn't have guessed she even knew he was here.

My eyes burn—*exhaustion,* I tell myself—and I squeeze them shut. No telling what kind of water rations they'll give to their prisoners. Can't afford to lose any in the form of tears.

Down here, with no windows to the surface, it's impossible to tell the passage of time without a clock, and I can't get at my phone with my hands bound. But some time later—it feels like hours—after the grid chamber and corridor open into a debris-filled antechamber, Liz calls a halt.

She gives a jerk on the rope holding us without a warning, wrenching my shoulders, and a quick cry of pain escapes me before I can clamp my lips together. Jules, attached to me, stops too, stumbling to his knees and almost dragging me with him.

"You," she orders, jerking her chin at Jules. "This another broken puzzle?"

Jules turns his head enough to look at her out of the corner of his eye. "Looks like it." I can see the muscles clenching in his jaw.

"Safe to make camp here?"

"I'd imagine so."

Liz's eyes narrow. "Look, cutie, anything happens to my team because you 'miss' something, on purpose or not, and I'm gonna make sure it happens to you, too. Now, once more, with feeling: is this a safe place to make camp?"

Jules grits his teeth, then scans the room for a few long, tense seconds. "To the best of my estimation, yes."

"Fine." She strides forward and ushers us off to the side, forcing Jules to scramble from his knees. She orders us to sit, then anchors her end of the rope around a massive boulder. Then she and her men—there's Javier and Hansen, and I haven't caught the names of the other two yet—spread out, gingerly inspecting the room and testing the floor, not wholly trusting Jules's assurances. I can't blame them—I wouldn't trust him, in their shoes.

Our bindings offer no other way to rest, so I slump back against Jules, letting exhaustion claim me for a few breaths. Even if we could get free, where would we run? Straight into more traps, and with them on our heels, we wouldn't have time to reason out the solutions. And we'd only last a day or two without our breathers.

"Are you okay?" Jules's voice is quiet, and the question sounds like it pains him to ask.

The freaked, exhausted, one-step-away-from-hysterics part of my mind wants to laugh. Such a gentleman, even when tied to a dirty, sweaty, traitorous girl in the bottom of a deadly temple, surrounded by mercs ready to shoot us in the face. "Fine. You?"

"Fine." He pauses a beat. "Really bloody annoyed."

This time I do grin, fueled by a flicker of relief, or hope, that he understands why I betrayed his identity. "Glad to hear it." I lean my head back, greatly daring, to rest it against his shoulder in some silent display of solidarity—and he jerks it away. The flicker of warmth in my chest vanishes.

135

Around us, the members of Liz's team are making a rudimentary camp, setting their bags down and clearing spaces for their sleeping bags. I watch them a moment, until I'm sure nobody can overhear my murmur. "Jules, the only reason I gave them your name—"

"Don't." He grinds the word out between his teeth, eyes closed. "I don't want to hear your excuse."

I find myself gritting my own teeth. "You don't get to be pissed at me." My voice is chilly. "I wouldn't be here if you hadn't lied to me."

"Maybe I wouldn't have brought you along if I'd known you'd spill my identity at the first sign of trouble."

"Let's just survive this." I keep my voice cold. "Then we can go our separate ways."

I can feel him, tense, against my back. The forced intimacy of being tied together makes his every shift and reaction feel almost like my own. I reach for resolve, trying to harden my thoughts. I don't owe Jules anything. I cling to that thought and keep my body as stiff as I can where we're touching.

"Fine," he says eventually.

"I'm pretty sure they've been following us since the canyon." I take a breath, watching to make sure none of Liz's gang drift close enough to hear. "Someone'll be guarding us soon, we don't have much time. Any idea who these people are?"

"None. Never seen them, don't know the name Liz."

"The group you were supposed to meet when you landed? When you thought you were meeting a research expedition?"

I feel Jules shake his head, his ear brushing my hair. "Not what was described to me, anyway."

"Mink's a notorious puppet master." I'm thinking aloud, head spinning with hunger and exhaustion. "Maybe somehow she found out you were on board the ship and . . . and put together a team to follow you, knowing wherever you went, it would be somewhere worthwhile."

"Maybe." Jules's voice is soft, but weary rather than gentle.

"The company that hired me, the woman who approached me, Charlotte, took a lot of precautions. I vetted them for weeks, traced everyone involved back for years online, but if Mink's that well-connected . . . maybe she had someone on the inside at Global Energy, someone who tipped her off."

I close my eyes, wishing I could shut out the sounds of Liz's gang settling in. I'd thought the silence of only the two of us, alone in an ancient alien temple, was unsettling—now I long for it.

If Mink got a tip-off from a spy—or however she found out—then she could've known from the start that the main temple might not be the prime target for looting. Jules never would've helped a gang of raiders, mercs as ruthless and efficient as Liz's gang, if they'd taken him prisoner from the start.

Mink's smart enough to have done her research, and she'd know he'd be too principled for that. They'd let him go on Global Energy's dime, wipe out the party that was meant to meet and support him, let him lead them to the right spot, and wait until there was no turning back before springing their trap.

It's a brilliant plan, and my gut twists at the tiny flicker of admiration I feel for that. But it's the cruelty of it that really makes my stomach churn. Liz would've had orders not to interfere, not to show a sign of her presence, until he was far enough inside the temple that he couldn't run. Then truss him up, use him like a bloodhound, make him watch while they stripped this place of every scrap of evidence that could help his father. And the whole plan is unfolding smooth as butter.

Except for one thing: me.

I was supposed to head for the main temple. A backup policy, I guess, in case her hunch was wrong or Jules had given up or died. I was never supposed to meet him, and was certainly never supposed to join him. Jules was supposed to be alone.

Which means I'm dead weight to Liz.

Fear, hot and tangible, runs up my spine so viscerally I'm half certain Jules can feel it where we're pressed together.

I'm not worth carrying.

"Jules," I breathe, careful not to whisper—in caves like this, a breathy whisper carries a lot farther than a soft voice. "We've got to get free."

"No, really?" His sarcasm would normally make me grin, but I'm too scared.

"No, I mean *I* have to—"

But one of the men is coming toward us, and I break off. It's Javier, the one who stopped Hansen from groping me, the one who showed the tiniest flicker of sympathy for our lot.

"We're stopping here for the night," he announces. Though there's no telling what time it actually is, it doesn't really matter down here in the perpetual darkness. "Gotta get you two settled."

By *settled* he means *secured.*

He crouches beside us and grimaces when he sees the knots Hansen tied earlier. I can't feel my fingers anymore, and it's some time before I register the pressure of Javier's hands as he starts loosening the ropes. "I can give you guys a minute or two to get your circulation going again."

"I need my journal from my pack," Jules says, so icily polite that it's a wonder Javier doesn't freeze solid on the spot. "I need to keep working on my translations, if you want to make any progress tomorrow."

Javier considers the question, but apparently he's willing to risk a weapon as fearsome as a pencil in Jules's hands, because he hands it over, then turns his attention to my bindings.

The blood comes shooting back into my fingertips, burning and tingling enough to make me bite my lip. But I force myself to massage my hands despite the pain, as Jules does the same. We're both able to turn a little, and now I can see his face. What I see there makes my heart constrict.

He's *angry.* I've never seen him like this, and though I've only known him a few days, I know him enough to see that this kind of fury is alien to him, too. He's seen, maybe for the first time, just how mercenary and calculating people can be. For someone like Jules—smart, dedicated, passionate—to realize that nothing he can say will make these people understand him, make them look at the bigger picture he cares about so much, has to be beyond devastating.

I, at least, grew up in a world of smaller, more self-interested views. For him, this kind of betrayal is new.

I'm getting us the hell out of this mess. Me *and* Jules.

"I've gotta pee," I blurt, plan forming as I go. "Before you tie us up again."

The rest of the camp overhears, and one of the other men, whose name I don't know yet—the short, fair-haired guy—sniggers. He tosses an empty plastic bottle our way so that it skitters to a halt against my thigh.

I look down at it, then up again with exaggerated horror. "Are you *serious?* Girls can't pee in bottles, you dumbass. Look—your boss can take me. I can go in the hallway we just came from. That's safe, right?"

That's for Jules, and he looks at me for a long moment before nodding. I wish I could explain the plan to him, tell him to trust me, but all I can do is gaze at him for half a breath before Liz gets to her feet with a shrug.

"Girl's got a point, Alex. I can always shoot her if she tries anything."

I try not to let that hit me, but it does, and my extremities tingle with the desire to run and hide, as I'd do if I were confronted with heavily armed scavver gangs back in Chicago. There, I'd have half a dozen bolt-holes within running distance of wherever I was operating. Here, there's just fatal traps ahead of me and a sheer cliff behind me.

Liz takes me back the way we came, into the corridor, until we're out of sight of the rest of the group. My spine tingles, knowing she's on my heels—though I didn't see a gun on her, I know she'll have one. And it'd be just as easy for her to use this opportunity to get rid of the dead weight as to let me do my business.

So I talk fast.

"Look," I blurt, coming to a halt. I turn, lifting my hands to show my sudden movement isn't an attempt to overpower her. Still, by the time I can see her, she's got a weapon trained on my face. I swallow. "I didn't really need the bathroom, I just wanted a chance to talk to you away from him." I tilt my head back toward the group, where I can dimly hear Jules asking the rest of the gang about something to eat.

Liz raises an eyebrow, but the gun doesn't waver. "Then talk. You've got ten seconds to get interesting."

"You know who he is? So do I. He was dumb enough to tell me straight out when we ran into each other." The lies come easily, quickly. This is what I'm good at. "I'm pretty sure I know why you're here—and it's why I'm here too. You're right that I was supposed to head for the main temple, but when I met Jules, I realized he was heading somewhere else, and he'd *know* where the good stuff is. So I went with him."

"I'm getting bored." Liz is little more than a silhouette in the dark, but I can hear impatience in her voice.

"I'm a scavver, just like you." I talk faster. "You think I give a crap about this guy's academic whatever? But thing is, he's not going to help you. You've seen him—sheltered, pampered Oxford life. His head's full of loyalty and heroism and honor and all that bullshit, and he's dumb enough to die rather than help scavvers get to the artifacts he's trying to save."

"People like to say things like that, but they tend to change their minds when they're looking down the barrel of a gun."

"Not this guy. I've gotten to know him. He's the real deal. He's as crazy as his dad, and Elliott Addison let them dismantle his life's work and stick him in jail rather than help the IA get here."

I take a deep breath, head spinning with the gamble I'm about to take. "You think I'm worthless to you. Just one of Mink's backup plans. That dumbass in there is the real prize, and you're right. But I'm the key to unlocking it."

Liz shifts her weight from one leg to the other. "The hell you talking about?"

"He's not gonna help you—but I already got him to help me. Fed him a sob story about a fake illegal sister, a debt that needs paying." My heart tightens, part of me wanting to burst into tears just saying these words. Evie's not some sob story. She's all I have. But I harden my voice. "And you said it yourself when you found us. Lovebirds. He's smitten, never met a girl like me before. He's already thinking of a way to escape, I guarantee it. He might be naïve, but you're trying to hold on to a genius, and it's not gonna work. He'll get loose. But if I'm with you—if I join your team— he'll stay. I can convince him it's in his best interests to work with you and take you to the loot."

"And what's in it for you?"

"Well, not getting shot in the face, for one."

Liz's mouth twists to something like a smile, and she lowers her gun. "And?"

"Our breathers." I hear Liz draw breath to argue and I talk over her, quickly. "You've still got him tied up, and it's not like I can go anywhere—I don't know how to solve these stupid puzzles any more than you do. But having our breathers would go a long way toward convincing him to go along with you."

Liz arches an eyebrow and cocks the gun, its click echoing around the stone walls like an explosion. "Killing his little friend would go a long way toward convincing him we're serious."

It takes every ounce of strength I have not to shatter, to let fear take over and turn me into a blubbering mass of terror. But my mouth knows what to say, even if my brain is begging me to curl into a fetal position and cry. "Kill me and you destroy the only leverage you've got over him. First thing he said, when we stopped? That he'll go headlong into the next bottomless pit before he leads you to the loot."

Liz's eyes narrow. "I find that hard to believe."

I shrug, hoping it looks nonchalant. "Believe what you want. But if he's the reason Mink sent you here, *I* find it hard to believe that she'd pay to get you back off Gaia if she knew you'd let him take a swan-dive off a cliff."

Liz chews on the inside of her cheek for a few seconds, then tucks her gun away. She's got a holster somewhere under her jacket, but in the gloom I can't see exactly where. "Fine," she says, and a tension snaps around my lungs like a rubber band. "But you'll stay a prisoner for appearances—better than him thinking you double-crossed him."

Damn, I was hoping she wouldn't think of that. I need to be free, even trusted, if I'm going to get us through this. This is what Jules brought me here for, even if he didn't know it at the time—this is my world, half a universe away from home. "If I'm a prisoner, he'll be thinking of ways for us to escape. And eventually he'll come up with something good enough that I can't say no without it being obvious I don't *want* him to escape. No, I've got to make him think *helping* the group is what'll see him though this, and to do that I've got to be one of you. He'll be pissed, sure. But I know when I've got a guy on the hook." I summon a grin from lord knows where. "He likes me more than he'll be pissed at me, and I can convince him that I'm just pretending to side with you. Make him think I'm really still on his side."

Liz is quiet a long time, considering. "All right. But the guys are all going to have their eye on you, and they're all trained to shoot first so that there *aren't* any questions later. Understand?"

I feel like dropping to the ground—the tightrope I'm laying down for myself is exhausting just to contemplate. "Got it."

"And *I'll* be watching you, too."

Somehow, that's worse than the rest of her group combined.

We head back down the corridor toward the gang's camp, my stomach roiling. I can't help but think how much easier it'd be if I wasn't lying—if I did switch sides. I'd stand a better chance of keeping Jules alive, not to mention myself. And if I'm a member of their little crew, and Mink really did send them . . . maybe I'd share in their payday. Jules would probably get his answers, too, even if he'd be a prisoner while getting them.

He lied to me. The words repeat in my mind, resounding with every echoing step as we walk. *I don't owe him anything, especially not loyalty.*

When we reach the camp, emerging into the light from their various battery-powered lamps, they all look up.

"Good news," Liz announces, shoving me forward a few steps. "Came to an understanding with this one—she's with us."

Protests rise around the circle, and Javier stares at me intently, but I'm trying so hard not to look at Jules that their voices fade into a blur. After I blurted out his name, he'll have no problem believing I've switched sides. *Good*, I think vehemently, clinging to that sense of betrayal, the knowledge that he brought me here with a lie. *Let him twist.* But the thought brings little comfort.

"We'll keep an eye on her," Liz continues, "but she's one of Mink's scavvers, like us, and smart. Smart enough to have got this far. Another set of eyes and ears in this place can only help."

In the end they still tie me up. Liz is too cautious to just welcome me into the fold with a word and a handshake. But they only bind my hands, and they bind them loosely in front of me, almost comfortably. Just enough of an inconvenience that I'll make noise if I try to slip away in the night. But it's enough that I can hold the breather Liz drops into my lap, enough that I can fit its mask to my face and take a deep breath. Looking over at the camp, I spot Jules's breather—they haven't given it back to him yet.

And that's what brings me up short, my anger and hurt draining away. Because once we get to the center of the temple, once Jules has served his purpose and brought Liz and the others to whatever loot or revelation lies at its heart, they won't need him anymore. He'll be one more loose end, a witness to testify against Liz, against her gang, against Mink herself. They won't just let him go.

They'll kill him.

I force myself to look at Jules, willing him with everything I have to understand, to trust me, to let me do what I do best. To understand I've already won us one small advantage, and it's the best kind of advantage: one the other side doesn't know you have. But he gazes at me for a long moment, ice-cold, then closes his eyes. Though I wait and wait, he doesn't open them again—I can't imagine he's asleep, but he refuses to look at me.

I stare hard at the ground as talk eventually drifts away from this change of events. I sit there in silence as the mercs start to relax, to talk about past adventures, to laugh over in-jokes. To enjoy themselves a little, now that they're on top.

Liz's voice rises, catching my attention—they're all laughing over something, loud and coarse. "Sure, Hansen." She's snickering, pausing to take a swig from her water bottle. "Your *girlfriend* back home," and the way she leans on the word makes it clear said girlfriend is fake, Hansen's wishful thinking at best, "can hang out with our new friend's little sister. Imaginary friends always get on like a house on fire."

There's more laughter, as the bottom drops out of my stomach.

I turn my head, knowing what I'm going to see. Jules's eyes are open, and he's staring straight at me. She just took my lie—my denial of Evie's existence—and she spoke it out loud. She laughed at it.

And Jules heard her turn Evie into an imaginary girl.

One by one the lanterns start going out, as the tired mercs turn in for the night. It's not until there's only one left that I gather up the courage to glance across at Jules, to see where they've settled him.

Despite everything, despite the fury still lingering in my core for his lies, I don't want to pile on the betrayal—he's just seen how ruthless people can be, and it makes me shrivel inside to be a part of it. My mind is so desperate for him to see, to understand what I'm doing—or at least to trust I'm not turning on him like it seems—that I can imagine his wink, his flicker of a smile, his quick nod of acceptance. They're so vivid I almost think I'm seeing them for real.

But then my eyes focus, and I see him bound to a boulder twice his size, with scarcely enough give in the rope to let him lie on his side on the bare rock. Someone's draped a blanket over him, but it's already falling off.

His journal and pencil lie on the ground next to him now, and though they've finally strapped his breather over his nose and mouth, I can still see his eyes, red-rimmed and hard and boring back into mine. And it turns out the anger I saw earlier, the fury and hurt at being followed by Mink's crew and led into this trap, was nothing.

Because the way he's looking at me now . . .

I tear my gaze away and curl up under my blanket, all too aware that Jules has barely anything to warm him in the underground chill of this ancient place. Cold, shivering, I close my eyes and try to sleep. But all I see is Jules's face, half-hidden behind his breather, and the disgust in his eyes.

10

JULES

BY THE THIRD ROOM THE NEXT MORNING, I'M STUMBLING. I BARELY SLEPT last night, partly because I was so cold I was shaking, and partly because of the pain. My muscles were screaming for a change of position by the end of the first hour. This morning, when I tried to stand, two of them had to hold me up until the feeling rushed back into my legs, agony spearing down to my feet. We're still behind on time with our breathers, and my limbs are heavy and sluggish as a result.

But most of the reason I couldn't sleep was because I spent the night rehearsing furious, accusatory conversations with Amelia, in which I threw at her every withering insult my mind could conjure, and she utterly failed to defend herself. I keep hearing her voice, asking me about the Undying, about violence and deception. The irony of that memory is so thick it nearly chokes me. I can't believe I trusted this girl, this—this criminal.

Perhaps that's rich, coming from me, but there's a world of difference between our two deceptions. I needed her help for the sake of our whole world—I had to put the work I'm here to do above anyone's needs, including my own. And even if that excuse wasn't enough—and perhaps it wasn't—I promised myself that despite the lie that brought her to this temple with me, I'd find a way to get her the money she needed.

She, on the other hand, threw me to the wolves the first chance she got, and then did it again.

I can't believe I made a fool of myself over her. Liking her, admiring her, even—*god, I'm such an idiot.* She threw my name at them like a shield, like a bribe—if Liz hadn't already known who I was, that would've sealed my fate.

I've let everyone down. Charlotte, who believed I could do this, who argued on my behalf to convince Global Energy to back me and spend unthinkable amounts of money to smuggle me here, who bet her career that I could bring back enough information to help her keep her job and prove my father right.

My father.

My eyes burn. I went against his wishes in coming here—or what his wishes would have been, if he'd known what I was planning—I've helped a looter find her way into the heart of this temple, and I let her distract me enough that I lost sight of what I came here to do.

All I can think of right now is my father, imprisoned as surely as I am. And he's not some cardboard cutout of an academic, an imaginary man standing up for a highbrow ethical argument.

He's my *dad.* He's my dad, who forgets his coat on the way out the door when he has an idea. Who daydreams until he falls asleep on the couch, his cup of tea cold by his side. Who still turns to talk to my mother, even though she hasn't been there in over a year.

He's alone, stubbornly, desperately holding out against pressure from the IA and the world, worrying about me, about what will happen while he's locked away and powerless. I'm all he has, and I've let him down.

But I have to stay alive if I want any chance of rectifying that, so I force my mind back to the hallway in front of me.

So far we haven't hit another puzzle like the musical bridge, just simple instructions to be decoded in order to avoid traps—keep to the right-hand side of the room, step only on the dark stones, that sort of thing. I've spotted the Nautilus symbol tucked away in corners, or up high, scratched as if nobody was meant to see it. Each time it has a line radiating from it on a slightly different angle. Each time I've taken a picture. Last night I sat with my journal, drawing the spiral over and over again, and inventing and dismissing ciphers to explain the seemingly random lines radiating outward. I didn't get anywhere.

On the upside, the thugs behind me are taking my instructions a little more seriously since one of them—Alex, I think—took off his pack to hunt for a snack while I thought, and let its weight ease onto an unmarked stone.

Sixteen razor-sharp spikes in a four-by-four grid shot up from the stone his pack was resting on, sliding into it like a knife through warm butter. So now Alex's belongings are nicely aerated, and everyone's listening more carefully.

I've been translating for what feels like hours, while trying to force my tired brain to think its way out of this. But I can barely concentrate on the glyphs, something that's usually second nature to me, let alone think strategically. When the toe of my boot catches on a loose flagstone, and I nearly fall into the next room before I've had the chance to read the instructions, Liz calls for a halt.

We're in a wide hallway between chambers, and it's as safe a place as any. I sink down to a crouch, leaning my back against the wall, lifting my bound wrists so I can scratch my jaw. The bindings aren't helping with my balance, but apparently they're non-negotiable.

Javier crouches down in front of me to check my circulation and loosen my bonds a little, and hand me a few crackers and a hunk of cheese from my own supplies. I make myself chew and swallow, resting my aching head against the cool stone behind me, and try to make myself *think*.

It's going to be the devil's own work getting out of here, climbing back up cliffs and jumping over crumbled rock. It can be done, but with pursuit on my tail, and without Mia's climbing expertise? It's going to take almost as much brainwork to get out of here as it did to get in. I'm counting on Liz thinking the same way, and keeping me alive long enough to navigate them out of this place once they're looted whatever's at the center, but I know that as soon as we're out, my usefulness drops to nothing.

Come to that, I don't even know what we'll find at the middle of this temple. The answer to my Nautilus puzzle, certainly. But tech? Valuable loot? I honestly don't know. She might lose her temper before it's time to exit, if I'm unlucky.

If I'm going to survive this, I need to think about ways to even the odds. It's not just my father depending on me, but—if his theories are right—potentially the rest of humanity as well. I can't afford to stop fighting. I can't afford to shout my hurt at Amelia for her betrayal, or throw my life away in some stupid lunge for freedom, because if I get shot there's no one else. I have to *think*.

And I have to be prepared to act.

A moment later the fourth guy, who they've been calling M.C.—in my head it's because of the bushy black muttonchops visible below the edge of his hat—is hauling me to my feet. Soon we're underway once more, the stone passage ahead lit by our head torches. I'm out in front, trained lab rat that I am, and Amelia's walking back with the rest of them, her hands now unbound, though she's flanked by Javier and Alex. It pleases me that they don't quite trust her.

And it kills me that they're right in believing that however badly she's betrayed me, I don't think I can bring myself to abandon her to the mercies of this place, knowing what it will mean. Clearly they think she'll work as collateral to ensure my good behavior. And they're right.

As we arrive in the next chamber, it's immediately obvious it's another grand puzzle rather than a simple set of instructions. Warning glyphs parade across the ceiling, and cover the walls, and the floor is a complex but very deliberate pattern of stone pavers, many of them carved as well. I angle my wrist up to snap a Nautilus carving half-hidden in the shadows, etched over the doorway on the far end of the field of pavers.

Crystalline stone glints back at me as I shine my head torch over the floor, and when I look up, I can see hints of cables up in the dark recesses of the ceiling high above us. Metallic veins dance through the stone of the walls, and everywhere I look, there's more to take in.

I stop in place, staring, my heart sinking. This looks impossible. "Well?" Liz says behind me, impatient.

"This will take a while," I reply, and though she growls under her breath, when she walks up to take a look over my shoulder, evidently the sight before her satisfies her that I'm not stalling for time.

They set up lights so I can see the whole cavern, and sit down for another round of snacks while I work. A tiny part of me—the very small part that's not preoccupied with either trying not to die, or dreaming up exotic, impossible plans for revenge—wishes I could film every section of this cavern, preserve every glyph and every stone for study. Beyond his warning about the Nautilus, about what the glyph beside it meant—*Catastrophe. Apocalypse. The end of all things*—my father spent endless hours trying to argue with the International Alliance about the sheer value of exploration, the infinite possibilities afforded by the opportunity to study such an ancient and vast civilization.

It's a conversation he and I have had many times. The first time I remember it was when I was twelve. It was my school holidays, and he and I had joined an expedition in Spain from the University of Valencia. My father's friend Miguel headed it up, and to me, he was the king of all he surveyed. We were excavating a series of centuries-old homes near the university itself, recently—and briefly—uncovered due to some building works there. In the gap between demolition and construction, the archaeologists had swarmed in.

Miguel and my father let me assist a couple of the grad students, and when I got back to our hotel that first night, I was brimming with things to tell him. I swiped through picture after picture on my phone, filling him in on every artifact we'd uncovered, parroting what I'd learned about which museums might want them, and what they were worth.

He listened, and he nodded, and when he spoke, he said the last thing I expected to hear. "That's a long list, Jules. But what did you *learn* today?"

I remember the feeling as if it happened just moments ago—the way the ground slipped beneath my feet, and suddenly I was uncertain. I'd done something wrong. But I didn't know what. I glanced down at my phone, with its catalogue of pictures, silent.

"Each one of these pieces will play an important part in a museum," he said, his voice gentle. "But together, they tell a story that's even more important. Look here, at these things you all found in the bedroom. I see five different hair combs. What does that tell us about the person who lived in this room?"

"They were probably rich," I ventured. "Or they cared a lot about doing their hair."

"Or both," he agreed, with a smile. "Let's look at what else is here, and see what kind of story we can build. You never know what we'll find out."

And I couldn't have imagined how much we would find. We were up until well after midnight constructing stories about the people who might have lived in that house. Learning about them, viewing them through first one lens and then another.

Without that late night, we'd never have discovered that the home we were excavating belonged to a fifteenth-century poet still studied today. Other scholars would never have found new interpretations for his works, knowing where he'd lived. We'd never have seen the beauty of his work refracted back at us, or learned more than we knew before about the world he inhabited. Which taught us in turn about the world we inhabited.

"Humans exceed themselves when they open their minds to discovery," my father said, that first night. "When we immerse ourselves in the wonders of curiosity, rather than moving straight toward the goal we've chosen. Toward the goal we imagine is most important, because it's the one we can see. When we allow ourselves to explore, we discover destinations that were never on our map."

My father changed the way I saw the world that night. That night was the reason I understood when he called for the exploration of Gaia to slow down, even before we found the hidden warning, the Nautilus spiral. I still wonder how everything might have unfolded—how our lives might be different—if even a handful of the officials at the IA had ever had an experience like that night in Valencia.

My father and I dreamed for years of exploring a room like the one laid out before me. But now I don't get the luxury of exploration, because I have to pour all my efforts into survival. Which is exactly what the International Alliance has been doing on Earth, focusing on the immediacy of saving lives, theirs and the rest of humanity. After years of arguing against my father's critics, now I sound just like them.

So I take what photographs I can manage, and start to read. The problem with reading conceptual glyphs—signs and signals that don't mean any one particular word, but change in relationship to one another—is that you have to read the whole inscription and hold it in your head in order to translate it. And I have no idea where to start. So I let my eyes run over the glyphs, consider their various meanings, and wait for the pattern to emerge. I really wish I had my father's gift for mathematics around now—or Amelia's, come to that.

The puzzle is something to do with time, I realize after a while. The glyphs are talking about the nature of time—I think they're saying that it's linear, that one can go forward or back along it, like a road, but that makes no sense. Then again, they're aliens, and I'm lucky they conceive of time in a manner that makes any sense to me at all. They might be talking about literally moving forward or back in time, but more likely they're talking about something abstract, like imagining the future, or remembering the past.

I can't travel back in time, but I want to. I want to go back to the moments I trusted Mia. I want to go back to smiling at her across our campfire. I want to go back to not knowing just how far she'll go, who she'll betray, to get her money.

I step out onto the first stone, feeling the attention behind me focus as I start to move. "Don't follow yet," I say, holding up my bound hands to signal they should stop. "I might need to back up quickly if I get this wrong."

The first few puzzles are simple—repeats of those I've already seen. *Step to the left here. Stand on the dark stone. Tap this one with your foot before transferring your weight to it.*

And then I'm staring down at a familiar curve, my eyes widening. I've seen this before, too, but it's not a glyph. This is the graph Mia deciphered, the key to tuning the pipes and the bridge that opened that immovable door. Why is it here again?

There's no wind here this time, no music, but it *is* a puzzle that lies in my immediate past. Just as the instructions I've seen so far have been repeats.

In a flash, I understand what this room is. A journey through time, from behind us, to in front of us, though how I'm meant to understand puzzles I haven't come across yet, in the future, I don't know. But I can start with what I do know. Maybe the rest will become clear. Or I'll figure out a way to run.

"I need Amelia, and a bottle of water," I call over my shoulder. I can hear the frost in my voice, and I'd like to drop it a couple of degrees further, use her surname, rather than the intimacy of her first name. But I'm realizing I can't call for "Ms." anything, because I don't have any idea what her last name is. *There's a lot I don't know about her. Hell, how can I be sure I know anything about her at all?*

"What do you want her for?" Liz calls, from the entrance behind me.

"It's referencing the first puzzle," I say. "She helped me unlock it. I can't do it on my own."

There's quiet consultation behind me, a murmur of voices I can't make out, and then footsteps. Amelia carefully makes her way across the stones I've locked into place, fetching up beside me. Her hands are still free, and she holds a water bottle in one.

"We have weapons trained on you," Liz calls out. "Careful, Amelia. Wouldn't want your *sister* to come to any grief without you, would we?"

I can only assume Liz is one of those people who think that I'm a genius in one area of my life, and an idiot in every other. That now, I'm not going to hear the way she leans on the word *sister*, like she's putting it in quotation marks. My anger is like a visceral thing, heavy in my chest, closing my throat. The sister I silently promised myself I'd find a way to help. The sister Amelia offered me, as a look at the deepest part of herself. The sister that sealed her lie. The sister that doesn't exist.

"Got it," Amelia calls back, her voice tight, without looking up. Instead, she looks straight ahead, so that I can hear her, but Liz can't see her mouth move. "Jules," she murmurs. "I'm doing this to keep us safe."

I snort, though I keep my voice down, indignation surging up. "Us? I'm already safe, they need me. And I was still ready to try and keep you safe, but you've thrown me to the wolves twice now, and you're standing free with them while I'm at gunpoint. I hope you'll forgive me if I'm not too sympathetic to your needs right now."

Her jaw squares, but her voice stays low. "You have every right to think that. But I promise, I won't abandon you. I know what it's like to be the only person who can help someone you love."

"Do you?" My tone is pointed, and makes her already-large eyes widen even more. *Don't,* I think, anger tensing my muscles. *Don't pretend to be shocked or hurt. Don't look at me like we're friends.*

Before Amelia can muster a response, Liz's voice cuts across the space between us once more. "Enough chitchat, kids. Let's get moving, if you already know how to complete this section."

The frustration that's been simmering inside me breaks like a wave, tumbling me over and submerging me. "Listen," I snap. "If you want this done, either do it yourself, or bloody well wait until I'm ready. If you want to bring the ceiling down on us all, which is what one wrong step will do, then just get on with it."

There's no response from behind us, but I have no doubt I've just earned myself some manner of punishment—a meal lost, a kick to the ribs. It's worth it. No doubt they're looking up at the shadowy cables and glints of metal above us, impossible to make out in the darkness, and drawing the conclusion that that's a lot of ceiling to land on top of anyone. Perhaps they'll give me a little room to concentrate now.

I point out the curve to Amelia, who understands straightaway— the next five stones have holes in them, and she's careful to fill each one with the same fraction of water she used in that first puzzle. The next few pavers click into place, and together we step forward onto them. Behind us, a couple of the thugs raise a cheer for the progress, then fall abruptly silent as Liz snaps something.

Mia tilts her gaze up and sideways at me, her mouth curving to a smile, and for a moment I wonder if one really can go forward and back in time, just as this room seems to suggest. Because just for an instant, I'm traveling back to that moment I wished for, when we trusted one another, when we worked together without doubt.

And then that moment's gone, and I'm translating the next paver, stepping forward onto it. Amelia stays beside me, and nobody calls her back yet, though I know the guns are still trained on us. I take a long swig from the water bottle, because I'm thirsty, and not feeling particularly motivated to conserve the supplies of my allies, earning a growled warning from Liz.

We make it another six pavers—a good two-thirds of the way across the hall—before we arrive at the next major puzzle. And immediately, I know we're in trouble. "Mehercule," I mutter, lifting my bound hands to run them through my hair.

"Jules?" Mia whispers, before Liz cottons onto the fact that I've stopped for too long.

"I think this is from the puzzle that had already collapsed, the cliff we climbed down," I murmur.

It only takes a second for the implication of that to register on her face, as her mouth falls open. We never solved this puzzle, which means we have no idea how to solve it now. And if we try, there's a decent chance we're going to bring this whole thing down on our heads.

"So if we mess this up . . ." she whispers.

I nod fractionally, rolling my eyes up to the ceiling above us. Most of it's hidden in the darkness, but there can be no doubt that the designers of this room paid some very serious attention to that ceiling. Cables glint, seeming to move and sway for a moment in the shaking light of my head torch. Mia swallows hard.

"Problem, sweetheart?" Liz shouts across the space between us.

By silent agreement, we ignore her. "Keep thinking," Mia whispers. "Look at the whole picture, maybe there's something."

"Alex, get out there," Liz snaps, when neither of us reply. "Bring the girl back."

The next few seconds slow to a snail's pace, as my mind flips through a thousand thoughts, one after another.

The short blond thug, Alex, is stepping out onto the path I've locked into place behind us.

We've only got a few moments before he'll drag Mia back to the others, and leave me out here alone. For those few moments, until he reaches us, he's walking across a literal deathtrap. He's vulnerable.

Vulnerable.

It's a simple word, and it avoids the unthinkable reality of what that could mean: this is my chance to improve the odds against me.

This is my chance to take one of them out.

Another second ticks past.

This isn't just about my survival. This is about my father. About the danger of the Undying tech, and the chance to prove it. The future of my planet, our planet.

"Mia," I whisper, head down, looking sideways at her.

She turns her head properly now, hesitating, looking back up at me. She's tired and dirty and her eyes are scared, and she looks lonely, and it makes my throat tighten. I wish I knew if she were playing me, sticking with whichever side she thinks will get her further.

I know I want to believe.

I know she stopped and helped me before she knew I could offer her anything.

I know I'm furious she sold me out to these criminals.

But whatever she's done, she doesn't deserve to die. I won't be a part of that.

I draw a shaky breath. "Do you trust me?"

Another second slips away as I scan her features, drinking them in. Silently, she rests one of her hands on my bound ones, giving me her answer in the squeeze of her fingers through mine.

I squeeze back, the only warning before I'm gathering myself to move. "Run!" Together we sprint for the archway ahead of us, for safety. In the same instant there's a thunderous roar above us as the ceiling starts to give way, a rock ricocheting off my shoulder and knocking me off-balance. I stumble forward, nearly losing my footing, and Mia shoves her shoulder into mine without breaking stride to knock me back upright.

In the next instant, the floor's giving way beneath us. *Perfututi, we're screwed, I didn't see any glyphs about the floor.*

I missed one detail, and that's what's going to kill us: it wasn't just the ceiling that was rigged, but the floors as well. We're leaping from stone to stone as they drop away beneath us, momentum sending us flying toward safety, but not fast enough, *not fast enough.* Somehow Mia has her multi-tool in her hand, and we're just a few steps from safety, and we're not going to make it.

The final stone drops out from beneath me, and I throw myself toward the archway that's suddenly a ledge above me as I fall—*I've miscalculated, this is my fault, this is it*—when Mia suddenly punches her hand between my bound wrists, driving the multi-tool into the rock face.

The ropes around my wrists snag on it, and my arms are on fire, my shoulders screaming as I'm jerked up short, the floor gone from beneath me, the ceiling still raining down, hanging from the knife wedged into the rock. Her momentum carries her down, down, and my heart's stopping, and I can't do anything—and then she manages to grab at one of my legs, sending a bolt of agony through my shoulders at the extra weight. I can't stop myself from crying out, but there's as much relief in it as pain.

She doesn't even pause to acknowledge the fact that she nearly plunged to her death and scrambles up my body, climbing me like a ladder. As soon as she's on the ledge she spins around to reach for my arms. She's too small to pull me up, too light, and my weight drags her toward the edge of the cliff. I kick wildly, my boot finding a tiny ledge, and I jam my foot onto it, scrabbling upward as a chunk of rock from above plummets past my head.

Then somehow I'm over the edge of the cliff, and we're safe together in the archway, lying in a tangle of limbs as she reaches past me to yank the multi-tool out of the rock. The ceiling is still falling, and soon the room we've just come through will be packed solid with fallen rocks.

And somewhere in there, Alex is dead. We're safe on the other side, separated from Liz, her remaining men, and most of our gear, but we're alive, and—

And then it really hits. *Alex is dead. And I killed him.*

In all likelihood I'm the first murderer on Gaia. *Take one of them out,* I thought to myself—*murder* one of them, that's what I meant. I dodged the word. I can't dodge the deed.

I crawl free of Mia, propping up on my elbows and knees, and my coughing turns to retching, my skin ice-cold, damp with sweat. Wordlessly, Mia eases my arms to one side, so she can get at the ropes binding me. It takes her three tries to cut me free, her hands shaking so badly her fingers won't work.

"We should keep moving." Her voice is shaking too, and I don't think I can look at her or I'll lose what little remnant of calm I have left. "Liz won't give up. We need a head start."

A man is dead. Liz is on our heels, angrier than ever.

And I'm trapped on the wrong side of a rockfall with an uncertain ally.

Did she save me because she still needs me, or . . . I'm not even sure of the end of that sentence.

As we climb to our feet, the questions racing around my head are pounding as hard as my pulse.

11

AMELIA

I LEAD THE WAY FOR A WHILE. NOT EVERY ROOM IN THIS PLACE IS A PUZZLE requiring Jules's expertise, and while I can't read the glyphs, I am starting to know what their patterns indicate. Like Jules said, the glyphs are based on math, and once I started to recognize the equation for their language, their simpler instructions—*step here, don't walk there*—aren't hard to translate. And the spread of ordinary traps like hidden spikes and pitfalls are becoming easy to spot and avoid—it's almost like the Undying put them there so we can see them, and know we're still on the right path.

Maybe it says something about me that the easier it gets, the more uneasy I feel. Like even an ancient race that died out before humans used tools could somehow be out to get me. "This doesn't bother you?" I say to Jules, shattering the silence.

"What?" His voice comes from behind me, distracted.

"It's like they're playing with us," I say. "This part is so easy."

"Maybe," he replies, sounding tired, an edge to his voice. I don't know if it's frustration with my continued suspicion, or if it's this new barrier that's formed between us, or both. "But we can't assume they were anything like us, Amelia. Or that they were putting in these tests simply to torture us. They weren't human, there's no reason to think they'd understand the kind of cruelty we're capable of."

He only calls me Amelia when he's being formal, or when he's annoyed. Otherwise it's Mia, his accent leaning into the vowels. *Cruelty*, I think, feeling sick, and I fall silent once again.

I tell myself that I'm leading to test myself, to make sure that I've got some chance of getting through this place alive without Jules, if he decides I can't be trusted after all. But the truth is that I'm walking in front so that I don't have to look at him. He's so tired, so ragged, and so *changed*. That trusting nature of his, the one I scoffed at and predicted would get him killed—it's gone. When I look at him I can see it in his posture, his body language. That slight scholarly stoop to his shoulders now looks like he's carrying the weight of the entire cave-in that killed that man.

Of course, with him behind me, it means I can feel his eyes boring into me. Or I imagine I can, anyway. Despite the warmth of his hand as we ran for the edge of the last puzzle, despite his nod when I suggested *we* keep moving, all I can see in my mind's eye is that burning look of his last night as I lay down with Liz's gang and he stayed tied to a rock, barely able to move. When everything we'd built started to crumble, beneath the laughter over my "imaginary" sister.

You don't owe him, my mind insists, flashing frame after frame from the moment he admitted he'd lied to me so I would help him, so I'd get him to this temple for his altruistic dreams. *There's nothing to explain.*

And even if I wanted to explain, we don't have the time to stop. We're moving. That's enough.

My feet feel unsteady, and it's not just exhaustion making my legs shake. For all my swagger, for all the time I've spent scavenging in the ruins with murderers and thieves, I've never actually seen someone die. And true, I didn't see that guy—Alex, Liz called him—die either, or even hear him scream. A part of me insists that maybe he survived, maybe he leapt out of the way back toward the safety of the other side of the puzzle even as Jules and I ran for it. But we were closer to the edge than he was, and thanks to Jules, we were ready—and we only barely made it.

That guy is dead.

I want desperately to stop, turn, grab for Jules's hand and pull him in against me just to feel his warmth, despite the fact that I hate him for his lie, for dooming me and Evie, for the crimes of his father, for all of it.

But it already feels like centuries ago that he slipped that arm around my waist in our sleep and it was all I could feel for an instant before Liz's flashlight brought reality crashing in. I know there was a chemistry between us, and I think he knew it too, but we're too different. And there have been too many lies now.

Though it was for all of a second, I miss the feel of his arm around me. I'd been keeping myself apart from him, this boy who's so goddamn brilliant and so goddamn naïve all at once, this boy who's both the best possible candidate to make it to the center of this temple and also the most likely to stride into danger with no idea what he's doing. I've kept that distance there on purpose, because my sister comes first, and when it comes down to it, I've known there might come a moment when I'd have to choose between her and Jules.

And it has to be Evie. It *always* has to be Evie. It's me and Evie heading for our Amsterdam, and then everyone else, the people who don't matter.

But that night, his arm around me, my head tucked under his chin . . . For the first time, and not just since landing on Gaia, I wasn't alone. Just like Evie wished.

I mean, when all's said and done, we've only known each other a few days, and what we don't know about each other far outweighs the stories we've told so far. But there's something about him—I can sense the potential of what we could be together, as a team, or more, and I know that for a while, he did too.

I wish I could tell him that. Our trust's so badly damaged now that he wouldn't believe me—I don't know if he believes anything I've told him was the truth.

But that night we were a *we*. And now that I'm a *me* again, I feel lonelier than ever.

I'm forced to set all these thoughts aside when we come to an archway signaling one of the rooms with the larger, more complex puzzles, and as Jules comes up beside me, we shine our lights in to size up the challenge ahead.

The huge chamber seems empty, but each of the paving stones has something carved on it, and I can guess the nature of the puzzle easily enough: Step on the right stones, you make it through. Step on the wrong ones, you don't.

Jules must be thinking of Liz behind us, and perhaps of Alex, but he takes his time, studying each of them in turn, frowning. "These aren't glyphs," he says eventually, and when I look down, I realize he's right. I had just assumed, but now I study them, they lack the mathematical precision of the glyphs, the patterns that I'm starting to recognize. This writing is something entirely different.

My heart sinks. We don't have time for Jules to teach himself a whole new language to get us across the room. I crane my neck up, checking the roof, trying to pull together a backup plan. Perhaps there's a way we can climb, get around the puzzle somehow. I don't like our chances. We're both exhausted, and we've hardly got any equipment left.

"There are patterns," Jules says eventually, very slowly, like he's trying the idea out. He lifts a hand to point to the rows of characters as they stretch away. "See how they change a little, the letters? And the words, for want of something better to call them?"

"I see," I agree. "If we can't read them, does the pattern help? They could say anything."

"They might not mean anything at all," he admits. "Human brains look for patterns everywhere, it's how we're wired. That doesn't mean it's how the Undying see things."

I make myself stay quiet, trying not to hurry him along as he works through it, mentally giving him about ten seconds more in lecture mode before I cave. "They heard music the same way we do," I point out. "They made us harmonize, to cross the bridge. So perhaps we should assume it's a deliberate pattern. I mean, if it's not, we don't have any other options, and we're in a lot of trouble. So we might as well hope it is."

"Agreed," he says, still staring down at the floor. "Look here. Do you see how there's one dot, and beside it, there's these three . . . I'm going to call them words, though they're not any language I've ever seen. They might not be a language at all, they might just be for the puzzle."

"Yes," I say, forcing myself to be patient. "A dot."

"And then there's two dots," he says, pointing at the next stone along. "And then these three words again."

"Are we counting dots?" I try, squinting at the stones past the first two. Most of them seem to have one dot, or two, sometimes three, and then the list of words beside them.

"I think . . ." He falls silent again. As I try not to scream, and dig my nails into my palms, and wait.

Eventually I'm rewarded, when he speaks again. "I'm trying to think what I'd notice about these words, if they were in English, or French, or Chinese, or something I speak," he murmurs. "How do they change from when they're beside one dot, to when they're beside two. Because they're quite similar otherwise. I think it's . . ." Abruptly he trails off, nodding slowly.

"Jules?" I prompt.

"Conjugation," he says, breathing the word like it's a prayer.

"It's—it's like verbs. You know the way a verb changes? *I run, she runs?* Or in some languages, it changes even more dramatically. Think of French—*j'ai, tu as, elle a, nous avons,* and so on."

"If you say so," I agree, and he snaps out of lecture mode, returning to something more useful.

"The Undying handle verbs the same way we do, in some cases. It changes, depending on whether it's *I, you, we,* and so on. I think this is a nonsense language that uses that sort of pattern, and we have to learn it."

"We're having a *grammar lesson* right now?" The urge to laugh bubbles up inside me, and I clamp down on it. I think if I start, I might not stop.

"Yes," he says, more enthusiastic than I am. "The ones with one dot, they're *I. I run.* And the ones with two dots, they're someone else, second person. *You run.* Three, third person. *She runs.* So all we have to do is learn the endings for each, and then step on the stones with the correct ones. When we see three dots, step on a stone with the third person ending."

"Easy as that," I murmur. I follow his gaze as he traces out the pattern he's found, the series of words with endings that change. We find it once, then twice, and once we're sure enough, we step out onto the paving stones, making our choices for each stone with one dot, or two. Every nerve in my body is jangling, but there's no grinding, no sudden crack—the floor beneath us holds steady. And one by one we find each new word, work out how it should conjugate, and step across those stones. It's almost like a mathematical puzzle, once I get the hang of it.

When we reach the other side, I let out a breath, leaning against the arch of the doorway and glancing back. Our footsteps mark a clear path to follow in the dust, if Liz and her crew get past the rockfall, but there's nothing we can do to hide our trail without potentially setting off whatever fatal traps lie in this room to punish mistakes.

We're quiet as we keep moving down the endless mazes and

corridors. The next few rooms are far simpler—we come to a puzzle with square blocks of stone to be transferred back and forth between different pavers until their combined weights are equal. It's a little difficult without any way to weigh them, but we heft them in our hands, and it doesn't take us long. Clearly, math and logic are universal between our two species. Maybe universal among any intelligent species, I don't know.

We continue on, coming eventually to a branch in the path with two forks with swaths of glyphs carved above them. This time I'm the one who recognizes the puzzle type—it's a variation on the one where there are two guards standing in front of two tunnels. One always lies, one always tells the truth, but you don't know which is which. So when they both tell you there's death down their tunnel, you have to figure out which to believe. Jules mutters softly to himself as he translates the rows of glyphs beneath them. Their meanings change, depending on context, he says—like kanji in Japanese, or a bunch of other Earth languages. He's trying to translate for puns in an alien language, as best I can tell. I hold my breath, and try not to show my impatience, until finally he nods hesitantly at one tunnel.

We move gingerly, ready to run or dodge if something shifts in the path, but it seems we've chosen correctly. The next few corridors are filled only with the typical pitfalls here and there, and my mind starts to wander—until I see Jules, just ahead of me, walking straight onto a pressure plate.

I dart forward, grabbing at his pack and yanking backward with all my strength. I'm so much lighter than him that I only shift him a little, but it's enough—when the plate triggers, and a shower of head-sized boulders rains down, Jules and I are in a heap just beyond its edge.

Half-dazed, Jules stares dumbly at the pile of rubble for a moment before groaning and rubbing at his head. I risk a glance at him and see again the exhaustion there. We haven't stopped moving since we ditched Liz and her cronies, and it's been at *least* a day.

What little sleep we did get before our capture got cut short when they snatched us, and neither of us slept much the night they had us as their prisoners. Especially not Jules, bound as tightly to that boulder as he was.

"We've got to stop," I gasp.

Jules coughs, the dust from the rockfall settling in around us. "Liz." He's still prone, shaking his head.

I know what he's saying. Liz's company managed to cross the chasm beneath the music puzzle, despite the bridge being destroyed. They rappelled down into the broken puzzle where we were camping so silently they didn't wake us. They'll find a way through that rockfall sooner or later, and we can't be within grabbing distance when they do.

"We'll hear them," I say, sounding more certain than I feel. "They're going to have to tunnel through all that rock, and that'll take time, and they'll make a lot of noise when they break through. That kind of sound echoes, and we'll hear it."

"But we've already solved the other puzzles, cleared the way and left a trail for them. If they do get through the rockfall, all they'll have to do is catch up to us."

I swallow hard. It's like he's speaking my own fears aloud. "I know. But Jules, look at you. You were two seconds away from being a pancake. Look at *me*—I was half-asleep, I could've just as easily not even seen that plate. We got lucky. And I don't know if you've noticed, but our luck hasn't been all that great so far. I don't want to count on it. We need sleep. We need time with the breathers. Even if you could force yourself to keep moving, if you don't get some oxygen, you won't be able to think straight."

Jules lets his breath out, then slowly drags himself into a more upright position. "Mehercule," he mutters, one of his incomprehensible curses. "You're right," he concedes finally. "Looks like another chamber up ahead—if it's safe, we can stop there."

I can see the darker hole he's indicating through the gloom. The chambers themselves, the ones containing puzzles, all share similar doorway-like entrances with carved rims like a warning, whereas the connecting corridors of tunnels seem more like simple passageways from one room to the next. I drag myself to my feet and offer Jules a hand, but he waves me away and stumbles up on his own. The shape I'm in right now, I wouldn't have been much help to him anyway, but the gesture just serves to remind me of what's changed between us. We inch our way toward the next chamber, on alert. Pausing at its entrance, Jules gazes around, searching for the glyphs of warning and explanation that have marked each puzzle room before.

There are none.

The walls and ceiling are completely and utterly *bare*. The floor's empty, no paving stones or pressure plates or pits. There are no carvings, no paintings, no glimmers of metal or crystalline rock, no shadowy cables in the ceiling, nothing. Nothing but an empty room. Its only feature is another archway at its far edge, but instead of darkness on the other side of it, it contains a sheet of rock, carved with the most complex glyphs we've seen yet. If it's a door, it's not one with an obvious keyhole.

This chamber is totally different from any other we've seen so far, and though I don't know what it means, Jules doesn't need to tell me to be careful—we both move forward slowly, gingerly, waiting for the catch. But we reach the center of the room without incident. And after tapping at the stone around us, then stomping on it, then—finally—jumping up and down on it, Jules drops his pack wearily to the ground. "I guess it's safe. We can look at those carvings after we've slept."

"You think it means something, that this room is so different from the others?"

"I can't be sure," he says. "But we must be very close to the center now. Whatever's significant about this temple, whatever the Nautilus is warning us against . . . I think it might be on the other side."

His gaze snags on the door, and I feel that same pull toward it—all this way, and our prize is finally within our grasp. "All the more reason to sleep," I make myself say. "If there's some kind of test coming, let's give ourselves a fighting chance."

Jules nods slowly. "Mehercule, I'm exhausted."

I let my pack slide from my shoulders too, and sink to the stone floor. "What does that mean? You keep saying it. One of your languages?"

He looks mildly embarrassed. "It's, uh, Latin. 'By Hercules.' We'd catch it bad from our teachers if we were caught cursing, so I guess we just . . . got creative."

I eye him sidelong, not sure whether to laugh or cry or collapse in exhausted hysterics. "Every time I think you can't get more . . ." But I'm not sure what the word is that I'm searching for. More *Jules* is what I mean. He's the most *Jules*-ish person I've ever met.

We both fall silent as we settle on the floor. It's frigid to the touch, but I'm so tired I'm ready to sleep right there, cheek pressed to its chilly rock surface. But though my body's screaming for sleep, my mind knows at least part of the exhaustion comes from lack of food and lack of oxygen. So I force myself to open my pack and start sorting through it.

"It's a good thing they were lazy and made us carry our own stuff." I break the quiet, the meager light from my wrist LED throwing shadows around the gear in my bag and confusing my tired eyes.

"They took the wave-stove," comes Jules's reply from the gloom a distance away. "No hot meals for us anymore."

I physically flinch at that reminder—something hot in my stomach would have been like a ray of light in the endless night of this underground labyrinth. Trying not to sigh too loudly, I dig out my breather. I slip its strap into place and suck in a few lung-fuls of richer air.

I know all it's doing is injecting a little extra oxygen into Gaia's thin air, but it makes such a difference I imagine myself dizzy with the sudden influx. I can hear Jules sorting through his own pack, see his head lamp moving this way and that in the dark. I pull out my blanket roll and a few protein bars, then crawl toward him. He's setting up his lantern, pulling his flashlight apart so it casts a yellow glow around the empty room; then he switches off his helmet and tucks it beside his pack.

He's deliberately set up the lamp between him and me, and he's pulled out his little journal and pencil, fumbling with it in his tiredness as he tries to grip it to write. Drawn back to his translations as if he can't help himself, doggedly continuing to work as if somehow it might save us, prepare us for whatever's on the other side of the door.

I try not to shiver at the thought of sleeping alone on this cold stone. I toss him one of the protein bars, and it hits the floor and skitters to a halt against its leg. He doesn't react.

"Eat," I say, my voice distorted by the breather mask in place around my nose and mask.

"Not hungry," he replies shortly, dropping his head into his hands.

My mind's working so sluggishly that it takes me a few moments before I understand why his voice sounds so different from mine. "At least put your breather on," I suggest. "You'll be hungrier after your blood's got more O_2 in it."

He looks up wordlessly, eyes meeting mine for a second before sliding away toward his pack. Then I figure it out.

When I negotiated with Liz, my only demand—apart from not being shot in the face—was that we get our breathers back. I got to see mine put back in my pack. But Jules . . . I was so busy trying to avoid the accusation in his stare that I never saw what they did with his when they got us up and moving again.

His breather's gone.

My thoughts spin as the bottom falls out of my stomach. Mink outfitted me with a breather tank delicately balancing carrying weight against time so that it would have just enough oxygen to see me through to the scheduled rendezvous. Which still has to be more than two weeks away, though I'd need to get back to the surface to know exactly what day it is. As long as I'm careful with it, limiting myself to the eight hours a day my body needs, rather than the many more hours my body *wants*, it's enough.

Enough for one person.

Sharing my breather cuts that time in half, and I don't make it to the rendezvous. I don't make it off Gaia, and I don't make it back to Evie.

My next breath is shaky and loud, its sound amplified by the mask over my face. Then I'm crawling forward, my shadow in the lantern light swinging around the surface of the rock wall as I cross to Jules's side. I pull off the mask and hold it out to him, hand shaking.

His eyes flick up, surprised confusion there.

"You breathe," I whisper, "while I eat. Then we'll switch."

His gaze holds mine for a long moment, searching. Our lies are there, like layers of dust and debris left by time and neglect, concealing the truths engraved beneath. I can't help but wonder if we've buried ourselves too deeply, if the honesty of that moment waking with his arm around me is as lost to history as the race who built this place.

Then he sets down his journal and pencil and reaches out with both hands—one comes to rest against my shaking fingers, steadying them, while the other takes the mask. I exhale, and some of the dust choking my heart drifts away on the air sighing past my lips.

Our dinner is necessarily silent—and at this rate, it seems like conserving our air is a good idea. We switch after I finish my dinner, then switch again. Jules's head is bowed, hands dangling from his drawn-up knees, breath shallow in the confines of the mask.

For the first time since Liz's gang jumped us, I pull out my phone. It's an old, battered junk-heap of a thing. Years ago everyone had one of these—they were so universal they were like ID back before everything went digital. Now there's a dozen different companies making newer, better versions, with cutting-edge technologies this one lacks. Jules's wrist device, for one, with its holographic interface and its kinetic energy charger so that its battery never runs down.

But the nice thing about these phones, even though they're ancient in technological terms, is that they're so universal you can always find parts for them. They're sturdy, and they're cheap, and when you're a scavenger you don't sport fancy tech unless you want some rival gang to rip you off in your sleep.

It runs on solar power—solar power that it hasn't seen in days. When I swipe my thumb over the screen, the little battery icon flashes a red warning before the circle for my thumbprint unlock appears. I probably only have a few more minutes before it dies on me.

Even if the station were directly above us now, we're so far underground that there's no chance of a signal. I can't call anyone or get any data. If I tried to watch Evie's last video message, the battery would die instantly. I hunch over the screen, though, turning the brightness down to conserve power, and swipe until I get to my photo gallery.

There's the selfie I sent to Evie right before I boarded the ship, and before it, a few promo shots of bits of salvage for auctioning online. I keep scrolling until I find the picture I'm looking for.

It's the last time Evie and I were together. She's still got her makeup on from work, the dark, smoky eyes and red lips making her look way older than fourteen. You can see her tracker bracelet at the picture's edge—the bracelet the club put around her wrist, attached to the bone in her arm by dozens of micro-anchors. The only way to remove it is by paying her impossible debt, or lopping off her arm.

Though it's hard to look past the makeup and the bracelet, she's wearing pajamas with pink elephants on them, and I'm in my PJs too, and we're snuggled close on the crappy couch in her room under the club that holds her contract. Our heads are together and you can see my arm where I'm holding the phone up, and we're grinning. We'd been laughing about something right before I took the picture, and the smiles are real.

I can't remember what we were laughing about. My eyes blur as my mind sticks on that, turning over and over and over. *Why* can't I remember the joke? Why can't I remember the last thing my sister and I laughed about together?

My breath catches and I choke, drawing my knees up and cradling the phone so that its dim picture is right in front of my eyes.

"So she's real."

I jump at the voice, reaching up to dash my tears away. But Jules's eyes are already on my face—he's already seen me crying.

"She's real." I look back at the phone, eyes hungry for the sight of her face. Trapped behind a rockfall, with bloodthirsty mercs on the other side, under countless tons of rock and sand on a planet so far from home I can't imagine the distance, without enough air to catch my ride back even if we could get back that way—I'm just trying to look at Evie, and not at the battery symbol flashing urgently in the corner of the screen.

"You were right," Jules says, lowering the breather mask from his face. He's moved over to my side so he can look at the picture of my sister. "She's beautiful. She looks just like you."

That makes me laugh, but I'm still crying, and I end up half snorting and lifting my arm so I can wipe my nose on my sleeve before I start dripping snot. "Liar."

"I'm not lying." His voice is quiet as he says it, and abruptly I remember why there was distance between us, and the warmth of him seems to pull away even though our bodies are still. "Not this time."

I keep my eyes on my phone, knowing it could go dark at any moment, but I wish I could look up at Jules, too. "I was never going to join them, Jules. I wasn't lying to you either, about Evie or about me. That was the lie, back there with them. Not this."

It feels more important than ever that he knows this, that he hear the truth from me even if he's already seen it in my face or felt it as I passed him the breather. It feels strangely vital that he understand without having to dig for it, or guess, or decipher my expression. I don't know what waits for us on the other side of that door, but I need him to see me truly before we go through it.

Jules lifts the mask for another breath, but I can tell it's as much to buy himself time to answer. But even after he's done, he's quiet for a while before letting that air out in a sigh. "I don't know what's real anymore. I just know I have to be here. I have to find answers for my dad. For myself."

"I'm real." My voice sounds thin and quiet against the stone. "And I'm here." I lift my head, searching for his face in the dim lantern light. *I'm here*, I said. What I meant was: *I'm with you*. The words I'd meant as reassurance sound instead like a promise.

He opens his mouth to reply, but before he can, the light flickers. I know before I look down that it's not the lantern—it's my phone.

The screen's dark. Evie's face is gone. In a moment of blind panic, I can't even remember what the picture looked like. And I wasn't watching when it went away—I wasn't looking at her, those last precious seconds. And I can never get it back.

I'm crying again, holding the phone in my palm like it had been a living thing, cradling it like it's the loss of this pile of plastic and circuitry and computer chips that's broken my heart. Then Jules's arm is around me, and he's easing the phone away from my hand with the other, and pulling me in against his chest.

We lie down that way, pressed together, legs entwined in the warmth of his sleeping bag, the breather mask between us. We pass the mask back and forth in the dark, finding each other's hands and fingers and faces by touch. And when I sleep, he wakes me after a time to press the mask against my face, and after an hour or two I do the same for him. Binding ourselves together, as we prepare to face whatever waits on the other side of that final door.

All night we learn each other's hands and lips as we share this single tie to life, the warmth of his skin still on the plastic mask each time he fits it to the curve of my own face. Each touch is more intimate than any kiss, our minds half-waking, half-dreaming, our two bodies sharing one breath.

• • •

I'm torn from sleep by the ground quaking beneath me. I gasp, eyes flying open to meet Jules's, his fingers still splayed gently on the mask over my face. Sleepy, confused, I would think I was dreaming but for the alarm written so clearly on Jules's face it's like I'm looking in a mirror.

Then the air's split by sound—a massive boom followed by the roar of falling rock, and the ricocheting, multifaceted echo of the initial crack of stone.

We both bolt upright, tangled together but moving as one. My voice is hoarse from the dry air in the breather, and hoarse with exhaustion, and hoarse with sleep. "That was an explosion," I gasp. "That wasn't a natural rockfall."

"I know," Jules replies, disentangling himself from me so he can grab his pack and shove his gear back into it. "That was a demolition charge."

I'm struggling up as well, the breather in one hand, my dead phone in the other, staggering in the sudden cold outside his sleeping bag.

If they've blasted through the rockfall, it means one thing: we're out of time.

12

JULES

"Okay," I mutter, trying to force myself to calm down. "Okay, the door." *Why didn't I look at it last night?* But I know the answer to that—because I was so tired and so short of oxygen I couldn't think straight. But now, we've only got the time it'll take Liz, Javier, and the others to navigate the traps we passed on our way here, and given the trail we left them, that won't be long at all.

Mia lifts her flashlight to shine it on the door for me, stepping back so the beam takes in the whole of it, silent as she waits for me to translate the glyphs—the ones carved on the door are the only features in this otherwise empty chamber. I can feel her presence at my back, but now her silence is supportive. Something's changed between us, in the night. We both still have questions—we both still see the chasm between us. But somehow, we're a *we* again.

The glyphs seem to swim together, new combinations I've never seen tangled in with the old. Translating them isn't like reading any language I know—it's about absorbing all their possible meanings and then allowing them to sit together in your mind, until suddenly, like one of those optical illusion puzzles, you can see what they say.

"It's talking about energy," I mutter, frowning. "About . . . not the sun. Mia, I don't know."

She stays silent, and for that I'm grateful—this isn't the moment to point out to me that *I don't know* could be a death sentence.

"Here," I say softly, lifting my free hand to trace a line that curves down to the lower right-hand side of the huge double doors. "There's something I'm supposed to focus on here, as if I—"

There's a small square carved into the wall where the curve of the glyphs ends, and I press my fingers against it. With a soft click, the section I'm touching slides out, a rectangle not even as big as my hand, and it's hollow. Something glints inside—crystalline, something resembling the Undying artifacts we've studied—and my heart sinks. *No, no, no.*

"What is it?" Mia asks, stepping forward to look down at it, then glancing back over her shoulder, as if Liz is only steps away, rather than several rooms.

"A piece of tech goes here, I think," I say, barely able to speak the words. "A piece of Undying tech. Which we don't have. We must have missed something, perhaps there was some key we were supposed to pick up, and we didn't see it, or it was in one of the collapsed rooms." I'm stumbling over the words. "I don't know."

"What?" Her voice is sharp. "No, it can't! Jules, we haven't come across bridges made of songs and past spikes shooting up from the floor and through rocks falling from the ceiling to hit this door and not have a stupid key. We don't need a key, we'll break in, we'll pick the lock. There *has* to be something!"

Pick the lock . . . I'm staring at the circuitry in the slot.

I yank off my wrist unit, which is Earth tech, but at least conductive, holding it over the little chamber, but it's no good—it won't stretch one end to the other, I can't even pretend to make it fit. I need something the right size—and an instant later I know what, the realization a second punch in the gut. "Your phone," I say. "I think your phone will fit."

"But it's dead," she protests, and I know that's not her only reluctance. Of course it's not.

"It's still conductive," I reply. "I'm sorry—but you're no use to Evie if you die trying to hold on to a picture of her."

She nods, and though I can see what it costs her in the tightness of her mouth, she doesn't hesitate. She digs the phone out from her pocket, shoving it into the hollow, and it's a perfect fit.

We exchange a glance—surprised, relieved, confused—as it retracts back into the stone once more, and inside the huge doors we hear the familiar grinding of gears and machinery that tells us the temple's about to unleash something new. We tense, ready to duck or leap, to make a quick and desperate play for survival, but then the doors simply slide open, retracting into the rock on either side.

We both flick up our lights to look through, but they illuminate little of the dark chamber waiting beyond it, and we don't have time for the caution we've both learned over the last few days. I reach down to curl my hand around hers, and she weaves her fingers through mine and squeezes. Whatever this is, we'll do it together.

We take one step through the archway, onto the first paving stone inside. I feel it click, and a jolt of fear goes through me— are we standing on a pressure plate? Is something swinging at us through the darkness even now? But all that happens is a rumble of stone as the doors grind back into their original position, sealing behind us once more.

Mia turns—I let go of her hand reluctantly—and uses her whole body weight to shove against one of the doors, failing to budge it. "Well," she mutters. "At least we'll hear them trying to get through." She doesn't say what we're both thinking—her phone is lost now, sealed into the wall on the other side. "Let's see if this place has, oh, I don't know, maybe an exit sign somewhere."

Together we swing our flashlights up once more, illuminating a chamber with huge, vaulted ceilings, and something in the center, a large mass that I can't make out. The room itself is immense, but I don't see a single glyph to explain why this place should be important. My twin goals beat like drums in my head—I *have* to find out why the Nautilus led me here. What could possibly justify a warning hidden in a transmission, in a temple, in the very architecture of this place.

And we have to find a way out of here that isn't back the way we came, because if Liz catches up with us, I don't think she's going to be in the mood to negotiate.

"Come on," Mia mutters, edging out carefully, testing every step before she commits her weight, as she's learned to do, a little slower now we've got more solid rock between us and Liz. I keep my flashlight down, examining the floor in front of her, making sure I'm following in her steps exactly. When she stops abruptly, I fetch up behind her with a bump, sliding one hand quickly around her waist to make sure I don't knock her forward onto untested ground. She tenses a moment, then leans back into me.

"What did you see?" I ask, lifting my gaze.

"There's something . . . Hold on." She shuts off her light, and at her gesture, I do the same. "Up there, Jules."

And so there is. Very faint, high above us, there's a steady, pale spot of illumination that does nothing to dispel the darkness of the room, but has an entirely different quality to the light from our flashlights. My heart thumps. "It could be some sort of residual power signature from the door," I make myself say. "Or a trap." Because what I want it to be so very badly, and what I know she's thinking too, is that it could be sunlight. And if it's sunlight, it might be a way out.

"They *would* give us light, after all this time, and make it a trap," she mutters, cynicism almost as thick as the darkness surrounding us. "Come on, what do you want us to do with it?"

"Maybe a stone just came loose up there," I suggest, but we

both flick our lights back on, swinging them around the chamber in search of a clue. It's Mia who finds it, letting out a little victory cry, as she squeezes back past me to hurriedly retrace our steps to the door once more. And now I see what she sees.

Running down from the blackness of the ceiling, there's a set of cables made of a strange, silvery-gray material that looks almost wet in the light. She swings her light across to the other side of the door, and there's a second set—they both rise to meet one another at the top of the huge doorway, and disappear into the dark above. Beneath each set of cables, sitting parallel with the wall, is a huge lever.

The old Mia would have simply started hauling on it without a second thought, but she's learned, and she looks back at me. "Can you see any reason I can't pull on this?"

"I can think of a dozen nasty things that might happen," I admit. "But we can't stand here for eternity either. The cables are visible, and so are the levers, so they're not intended to be a hidden trap. I think we might as well pull as not." I've made my way over to join her now, and by the light of my torch I can see her faint, wry smile. Perhaps I was supposed to say something slightly more comforting. I'm not good with cues. "Just in case," I add, "it's been a pleasure knowing you."

She snorts. "It's been a hellish nightmare, Oxford."

"Well, I'm English," I point out. "I'm quite good at enjoying myself under even the most miserable of circumstances. And I did like riding the skimmer bike." I'm joking, playing for another chance to see one side of her mouth tug up in that reluctant smile, but it's true. Parts of this trek *have* been a pleasure. Though I've learned things I wish I didn't know about my fellow human beings, I've learned some things I'm glad to know, as well. I've met Mia.

Together, we're something more than we are apart, something more than I've ever been before.

Something I don't want to give up.

I'd like more time to parse that thought, but she's grabbed the lever, and after a gentle pull on it does no good, she's applying all of her weight to trying to move the thing down to a horizontal position. Ancient machinery groans above us, and the light up at the apex of the ceiling intensifies ever so slightly, like a beam being focused.

There's not enough room for two sets of hands on the lever, but I reach up to grab the cables, leaning backward and letting them take my weight. It's not like any material I've ever felt—strong and unyielding as metal, but somehow seeming to squirm under my touch in a way that makes my stomach turn. But slowly I take up more slack, and the light brightens, the beam growing stronger and broader. There's no mistaking it—it's daylight, but so far above us we have no hope of reaching it. This set of cables is attached to something like a retractable roof, or a sunshade over a skylight. "What's it for?" I mutter. "Why did they want us to do this?"

But when I glance across at her, Amelia's not looking around. She's visible in the dim light, looking at the second set of cables on the other side of the door. "I've got a feeling . . ." she murmurs, and I know to wait as she pauses, let her complete the thought. I've picked up on these little cues, over the last few days; she's thinking, and the further outside the box her thoughts go, the more intensely she goes silent.

I'm repaid for biting my tongue when she continues. "In Chicago," she says, voice taut with excitement, "cell reception sucks. Something to do with protons or ions or something in the desert winds, I don't know. Anyway, sometimes I'd earn some cash playing lookout for one of the gangs, and since you can't just text, and you definitely can't shout to raise the alarm, you need a visual signal. At night, it's this." She flickers her flashlight on and off, the change still visible in the faint daylight. "But during the day . . . during the day, you use mirrors." She swings her flashlight up to where the cables divide, branching out and angling every which way around the room.

I have absolutely no idea what she's talking about. "But there aren't any—"

She walks across to the other side of the door, grabbing the lever there, and throwing her weight back against it. "If there is one, it would be a way to redirect—" she says, then falls silent to swing her weight against the second lever again. It doesn't budge for a moment, and then with another round of grinding machinery, slowly it begins to lower from vertical to horizontal, Amelia's small frame hanging off it. The beam of sunlight begins to strengthen and brighten, and I can make out the outline of a reflective disc, and another set to catch its light once it rotates into place, before the reflected sunlight grows too bright for me to look at it. Then, between one heartbeat and the next, as the mirrors align, the chamber transforms into a sea of rainbows.

Sunlight shatters across every surface in the room in a dazzling, shocking flash, and from somewhere to my left there's an undignified shriek as Mia comes barreling straight into me. My arms go around her automatically, and they stay there as our surroundings blaze to life with a brilliance that's momentarily blinding. My vision's dancing with stars and sparks, and as I try to blink away the tears and focus, she turns in my arms to gaze out at the chamber of light.

"Holy . . ." She trails off, staring at the beams of light, lips parted in awe. As the cables above us groan and settle, the rainbows glimmer, and Mia's wonder is writ clear on her face. "It's so beautiful," she whispers, face tilted up toward the domed ceiling and walls covered in the fractured rainbows. "Do you think they knew?" She finally tears her gaze away, just enough to look up at me. "Knew what beauty was?"

My heart's slamming against my chest, and it's not just that I'm holding her in my arms again, that I'm gazing down at her, her mouth only a breath from mine. It's that in this instant, she's me, back in Valencia. Opening herself to exploration. To curiosity. It's not just that for a moment she's sharing in my thrill of discovery. She's *experiencing* it. She understands.

As she reaches out across the millennia to the Undying, to wonder if they knew what beauty was, to wonder why they created something so delicate and perfect, she's opening her mind to all the possibilities they represent.

She's communicating with them, by picking up the stories they left behind and adding her own words, asking her own questions. This is what I do—what exploration and archaeology is—and in this moment, Mia's in it with me. In this moment, all our questions and suspicions about the Undying are set aside, as we share this thing with them, left for us all this time. "I think they must have," I murmur. "Known what beauty was. Look what they made."

"Whoa, Jules. Look what *else* they made," she murmurs, eyes no longer on the ceiling but staring toward the center of the room.

Illuminated by the refracted sunlight, a huge monolith stands there, a towering, jagged piece of black stone. Invisible in the darkness before, the massive stone structure is impossible to miss now that we're not distracted by the beauty of the lighting. It's nothing like the red and blue-gray and creamy colors of the Gaian bedrock in this area, or the metallic stone the Undying use to build—it's nothing like I've seen anywhere on this planet.

It's at least twice my height, and its edges are jagged, save for one side, which has been cut and polished to marble smoothness. It stands atop a low stone plinth, and a huge circle made of the same stone frames it like a picture. It's the centerpiece of the room, no doubt, but I have no idea what it's for.

Mia steps away from me, and we both move cautiously across the floor, though we're more and more certain there are no traps here. This is the end of the hunt, it's whatever we came to find. We've passed the tests, and the traps are behind us.

The secret Nautilus equation buried in the broadcast, each hidden spiral scratched into the stone rooms of this temple and woven into its very architecture, they all led me here. And now I'll find out why.

We shine our lights up, and now that we can trace the cables across the vaulted ceiling, we see that instead of the one or two mirrors Mia supposed might be used to light the chamber, there are dozens upon dozens, all angled now toward a multifaceted crystal set up near the ceiling. It scatters the sunbeam into rainbow fragments that paint the walls in swaths of color, daylight-bright.

The purpose of the huge chunk of rock and the stone frame that arches around it is considerably less clear. I stand in front of the polished side, staring up at it, but it's completely free of glyphs or instructions. "This must be what we're meant to see," I say. "There's only one thing in the room."

"This is the final room," Mia says. "But . . ." She trails off, turning in a slow circle, taking in the rainbow-clad walls that enchanted her a minute before. "Nothing," she says, her voice dropping suddenly. "No way out. There's just this hunk of rock."

"There must be something," I say, but I'm echoing her movement, spinning in a circle, and my heart's dropping with every second. *How did I fail to look for another door?* Because it was dark at first, and then the rainbows, and Mia's wonder at them, and my own anticipation, and I . . . *There's no exit.*

We're trapped here, and Liz is on her way. And there's no sign of the Nautilus—or what it means.

"The vent," I try, squinting up at where the sunlight is, pushing aside the question of the Nautilus for a few moments. It's of no use to us if we're dead.

"It's too high," Mia replies, voice still quiet, staring at the huge rock in the middle of the room as though it's to blame for our predicament. "We don't have a rope long enough. Our climbing gear wouldn't reach, even if we had a way to toss it up and secure it." She doesn't even have to look up to be sure. "We're going to *die* here, Jules." The scattered light does nothing to hide the distress on her face, her reddened eyes and nose, the exhausted desperation in her gaze. *So much for the wonder of discovery. Impending doom will do that to you.*

Her voice breaks as she speaks again. "We're trapped in a place nobody but you could ever reach, except for the trained scavver crew that's coming through that door to kill us as soon as they get here and plant explosives. And even if they pick the wrong passageway, or they can't break in, we've got food for maybe a week, a breather that'll last less than that, and there's not even a pebble-sized scrap of tech here we could use to bargain our way off the planet, let alone for Evie!"

Her whole body's tensing, hands curling to fists at her sides, and when I take a step toward her she turns sharply, stalking around to the other side of the monolith, putting it between us.

"Deus," I mutter, running one hand through my hair, grabbing a handful of it in frustration. There *has* to be a way out of this. And we have to find it now. Liz won't hesitate to shoot Mia the moment she sees her. And I won't be far behind, either because I won't stand by and let Mia be hurt, or because Liz will realize I'm done cooperating.

Which means we need to find an exit, and find it fast. I close my eyes.

If this whole journey is the Undying's version of a test, determining our worthiness as a species, then there must be an answer. *Unless we're not worthy,* my panicked mind supplies. *Unless the solution is beyond what we can reason.*

Then Mia's voice cuts through my tangled thoughts, coming from the other side of the rock. "Jules, what does *'pergite si audetis'* mean?" She speaks the words haltingly, cautiously.

I blink. "When did you learn to speak Latin?"

"I didn't," she says, her voice thin, and as I make my way around the plinth to find her, she looks across at me with huge eyes, then points down at the base of the plinth. "It's carved right there."

I look down, and sure enough, there the letters are, carved into the base of the stone.

PERGITE SI AUDETIS.

My throat is dry, my heart a frantic drum in my ears. Mia's looking at me, her alarm spiking when she sees whatever's written on my face. She's waiting for me to explain, and it takes all my effort to force myself to speak. "It means—it means 'onward, if you dare.'"

13

AMELIA

LATIN. IN A TEMPLE ON THE OTHER SIDE OF THE GALAXY BUILT BY CREATURES who went extinct long before Rome ever existed.

My mind's spinning, and I know Jules is as thrown as I am.

"This message is for us," I say, my voice hoarse. "For humans."

"Yes," he whispers.

"I mean, it's freaking *Latin!*" I actually squeak the last word. "What the *hell*, Jules?"

"They used the same words in the broadcast," he says, dazed, his gaze barely focused. "'Onward, if you dare.' And now here it is, it's . . . The test was always for us. It was *us* they were testing for worthiness."

"I don't like this," I murmur, staring up at the black monolith like it might move. "I don't trust it. We've been doing our best to explain everything away—fifty thousand years, convergent evolution, but—"

"*I've* been explaining it away," he corrects me, still soft. "You've been asking what other ways they might be similar to us. Whether they could lie. Deceive. We have your answer, now."

"But the answer's impossible," I reply. "The answer is that they've been seeking humanity, targeting Earth, all along. That's *impossible.*"

"And yet there it is." I think something's broken in his head—intellectual overload, or whatever. He just keeps shaking it slowly, staring at the Latin.

A sound, tiny and far away, yanks me back to myself. Maybe I'm imagining it—Jules certainly doesn't hear it, too lost in his own mind—but it reminds me nonetheless that whatever we've just discovered, we're still in a race for survival.

I want to give him a shake, to shout that Liz is on our heels, and she won't bother to solve the door puzzle—she'll just blast her way through it. But I need him thinking.

"Okay," I say, trying to make myself calm. "It says 'onward, if you dare.' That means there's got to be a way to actually *go* onward, right? I mean, I don't like this, and I have more questions than I can count right now, but we know Liz will *definitely* shoot us if she catches up with us, so onward's still looking better than our other options."

Jules's mouth opens a few times before he actually manages a response. "Right. Yes. There should be a way."

"So maybe there's a puzzle here, too. Something to do with this thing." I move forward toward the hulking stone structure in the center of the room, forcing myself to look at it and nod toward the letters carved there. "It'll turn into a ladder, or a trapdoor, or it'll open some invisible second door in here, or something. Maybe we could try and climb this frame." But even as I say it, I'm eyeing its smooth slope, without so much as a crack or chip for a toehold.

"Maybe." Jules is still so shaken he's barely registering my words. "But I don't . . . The Latin just says 'onward,' there's nothing about a puzzle, no glyphs like in the other rooms. If this is the end of the maze, where are our answers? The Nautilus . . ."

"Okay." I take a breath, coming up alongside him. Part of me wants to take his hand, drown out my fear with the feel of his fingers twining through mine, but I need him thinking about that statue-thing, not me. "Okay, Jules—forget the Latin. Forget the glyphs, forget the Nautilus, forget the Undying, forget Gaia. Forget everything else in this temple. You're an archaeologist. Where do we start?"

Jules gives himself a little shake, as if shedding the confusion and fear and wonder. "We . . . we observe. We look for wear patterns that might tell us if this was used for anything, we look for any fragments around it of other artifacts. Anything that might suggest why this would've been important to the civilization that built it."

He starts poring over every centimeter of the thing, and while I do the same, I have no idea what I'm looking for. It's obvious as I get closer that the structure does *something*—sections of the stone are cut through by narrow, almost invisible lines that would allow the different parts to move if operated by some invisible mechanism.

Another distant sound, muffled by the thick stone door, slithers into the quiet and jacks up my heart rate. Jules hears it this time, and his eyes meet mine, widening.

"Ignore it." I'm talking fast, but trying to sound calm. "We've got time. Focus."

But inside I'm screaming. *Figure this thing out or we're gonna get blown up or shot or tied up and left here to die.*

It feels like hours before Jules gives a little exclamation, though I know it's only moments. I'm quick to join him where he's crouched at the base of the statue, inspecting something half-concealed in the shadows. It's another of the scratched carvings he's been tracking—the curve of the Nautilus shape, a line radiating out from it. Taking a breath to steady his hand, he angles his wrist unit so he can photograph it.

Then his finger trails across to hover above a shape next to it that's similar, but definitely not the same. This shape isn't scratched into the surface—it stands out in relief, like it's been embossed on the stone.

"See this?" His voice is quiet, tense with concentration. He's gesturing, without touching, at the curl of carving and the shadow it casts. "I think it's an *alpha*."

"A what?" This time, I'm not able to keep the impatience from my voice.

"It's the first letter of the ancient Greek alphabet."

The curl he's indicating looks kind of like a stick-drawing of a fish, but it could also be a badly drawn lowercase *A*. "Didn't the ancient Greeks speak Latin?"

"Well, no, they spoke Greek, actually. A number of different forms of Latin were the dominant languages during the Roman Empire that followed, although it depends on which area of the empire you're talking about, because at times it occupied territories that stretched into what's now—"

"Jules!"

"Right. Right. I think this statue *is* another puzzle. I think it might just be a simple alphabet puzzle."

"Starting with this alpha thing?"

He nods, tracing the shape of the letter in the air by the carving.

"Good enough for me." I reach for it, and I know we're both holding our breath. It stands out from the stone, so it's easy enough to grip. Under my fingers, the letter gives a little, the layer of stone it's carved into seeming to separate from the rest, and I wrench harder. The small tile with the alpha on it twists a quarter turn to the right, then clicks inward.

The frame encircling the polished surface of the monolith shudders, and suddenly the stone sheds a cloud of ancient dust and sand and comes to life. More stone carvings push their way to the surface until Greek letters ring the entire frame.

Before we have time to inspect them, a rumbling and shower of dust from the cavern wall behind us makes us both jump to our feet, ready to run if the ceiling's coming down—though I know we're both thinking, *Run where?*

The source of the sound is another set of characters, emerging from the stone wall, a foot high at least, suddenly there at head height where there was nothing before, just like the letters on the statue. The words aren't Greek—they're written in another alphabet I can't read—but I recognize it.

"What—is that *Chinese?*" I gasp.

Jules is staring at it in silent, baffled awe.

But before either of us can speculate, we hear a sound that leaves absolutely no doubt that Liz and her people are close: voices.

They're on the other side of the door.

Jules's gaze swings to meet mine, and in that moment we have no need of speech.

I'm immediately turning to scan the frame. "What's the next letter in the Greek alphabet?"

"Beta. It looks like an uppercase *B* with a longer tail. . . ."

We search the ring-like frame, moving fast, Jules calling out descriptions and both our eyes searching for the letters that came to the surface when I twisted the alpha stone. He finds most of them, eyes trained to see them, but every so often I'm the one who leaps forward and twists the next piece of the puzzle.

Each time we turn a new letter, more words emerge from the walls around us, sometimes four or five sentences at a time. They appear on every wall of the chamber, until the whole place is covered with words in more languages than I knew existed. At one point a series of lines pop out that look barely more than chicken scratch, but as I stare at them, I remember vaguely a lesson from before I dropped out of school. Cuneiform, it's called. From some ancient civilization before even the Greeks and Romans.

What the hell is going on?

The fact that Liz and her people aren't already inside means they haven't found the little slot that contains my phone, the key to unlocking the door. But I doubt they only brought enough explosives for one cave-in, and if they blast their way in here, we're dead—if the explosion doesn't kill us, Liz will. She might keep Jules alive for a little while, but only until he's outlived his usefulness.

"I'm telling you," shouts Jules, urgency lifting his voice, "it looks just like a lowercase *W*."

"And I'm telling *you*," I retort, "that the only *W*-looking thing was the *psi* we just pushed. Like a *w* and a *y* got busy with each other."

"Look harder, it's got to be here. Omega. It's the last letter."

I'm searching, eyes watering with the effort and the brightness of the refracted sunlight flooding the room, when my gaze suddenly snaps into focus—not on the frame around the monolith, but on the wall behind it. There's a phrase there . . . in English.

The worthy will rise into the stars. . . .

I don't stop now to marvel at the fact that I'm reading something from an ancient temple. I can't worry that it's cryptic, that I can only think of it literally, that a naïve college student and an uneducated scavver girl are clearly not "worthy" in any possible way.

I just look up.

"Jules—what does an uppercase *omega* look like?"

"All the rest have been lowercase—"

"I know, but it's the last one, and those words . . . it says *rise* . . . What's that at the top?" I'm pointing—*rise into the stars*—to a semicircular carving at the very center of the top of the frame.

"Mehercule," Jules mumbles.

"Give me a boost," I demand, hurrying to his side. He kneels and cups his hands obligingly, and then he's heaving me upward, grunting with the effort. I can just barely touch the top of the frame, but it's enough—my fingers graze the *omega*'s edge, and the letter twists and sinks into the frame.

The ground beneath us quakes, and as Jules cries out and I

go tumbling down, I'm thinking, *Oh god, they've blown a hole in the wall. . . . This is it . . .*

But when I land on top of Jules, who half grunts, half gasps at the impact, I'm scrambling up to discover that the door is still intact. The rumbling is coming from the *structure*. I've been so focused on Jules, so desperate to keep him working, translating, thinking—that I haven't had time to process my own fear. So the sudden wave of hope that washes over me is so visceral I'd fall to my knees if I weren't already in a heap on the ground with Jules.

The structure *is* a puzzle, and it *is* doing something. Opening a door, creating a staircase . . . I don't care what it is, as long as it gets us out of this dead-end deathtrap.

We stumble to our feet in time to see a mind-bending ripple flow through the solid rock of the monolith. I jerk back, Jules staggering with me—his fingers are tangled through mine, I realize, but I have no idea who grabbed for whose hand.

Another ripple flows through the polished center of the statue, and abruptly it doesn't look like stone anymore. Its surface looks like an oil slick, semi-reflective and fluid.

I take it back. I want a goddamn staircase.

"What the hell is that?" I draw in close to Jules's side, his warmth a comfort in the chill air that's humming now with a strange sort of energy, like we're standing beneath a set of power lines or on an open field in a thunderstorm.

"I don't—" But Jules stops abruptly, his eyes widening. "Wait . . . I *have* seen this before. Don't you recognize this? It looks like the surface of the portal, the one that brought our shuttles here to Gaia."

"I spent that trip sealed up in a packing crate, remember?" I reply. For all my dreams of exploring space, all I got was the inside of a box—and the utter, gut-wrenching, mind-searing pain of going through the portal.

The memory of it makes me want to shrink back from the

oily-looking thing in front of me. *I can't do it again. I can't. Not unless it's to go home—to go back to Evie.*

"We can't just leap in blindly," Jules is saying, gazing at the portal in wonder. "We don't know why they built this place, we don't know why they were testing us, not anymore. We still don't know what danger the Nautilus was warning against. This is the room, Mia, this is *it*. Why I came here. They led us here, and we have to find the answer. This portal could be the very threat we're meant to avoid—the spiral's carved right there in this thing's base. We need more time."

"We don't *have* time," I remind him, hating that I have to be the one to say it. "We're out of options."

"Mia, we *can't* go through this thing not knowing where it goes. It could take us to some other planet, one where we'd need more than breathers to survive. It could send us straight into a black hole. It could send us into the middle of outer space to die, for all we know."

At least I'd get to see what space looked like before my eyeballs exploded in the vacuum.

"Look at these walls." I give his hand a tug to turn him, so the light on his helmet scans across the multiple languages and characters that emerged while we were unlocking the portal. "These are *human* languages. I have no idea what that means, but I also don't know why the Undying would have a path leading straight to this portal, and a message telling us to keep going, in a language we understand—in literally *dozens* of languages humans might understand—if this portal were going to kill us."

"You're assuming their motives—"

"We have no *choice!*" I interrupt him. "I don't know what's going on, but I do know that we *are* gonna die when Liz and her people come through that door. I'd rather take my chances with the portal."

But he's shaking his head, setting his jaw and gazing around at the walls. "The answers are here, Mia." He's taking pictures again—*pictures, for the love of . . .*—of the walls and their multi-language messages, his eyes burning with that fervor that lights them every time he gets buried in the secrets of the Undying. "These walls . . . this is why I came to Gaia, what I risked my life to find. Translating these messages could be the key to proving my father was right not to trust blindly the technology the Undying left us. These temples were built long before these languages ever existed. You can't tell me to leave this behind."

I close my eyes, trying to take a deep breath. If this room were filled with valuable artifacts, I'd be grabbing every single one I could fit into my pack, for Evie. These messages are his version of that—I can't deny him the chance to do what he came here to do just because I've failed. And beyond that, he's right—there are questions here we *have* to find answers to.

I glance at the door, which still stands between us and Liz, and let my breath out slowly. "Maybe there's a place to hide that we missed," I say softly. "I'll look around now that we've unlocked the—"

But I don't get to finish. I'm interrupted by an ear-splitting crack and a roar, and the ground shakes again—this time enough to knock me down, though Jules keeps his feet. When I lift my head, part of the door is gone, enough that I can see flashlights in the darkness beyond. The rest of it is covered with a web of cracks, and before I can even catch my breath, the clang of pickaxes penetrates the ringing in my ears. Half the mirrors have been mis-aligned by the blast, and the remaining shafts of light aren't aimed at the refractory crystal—the rainbows are gone.

Jules's head lamp swings toward the door, the air now so dusty from the explosion that his helmet's beam looks almost solid as it quakes and wavers.

I can hear Liz shouting orders on the other side of the door, though my ears are still ringing so badly from the explosion that I can't make out what she's saying. I lurch unsteadily to my feet, still dazed from the shockwave.

"We have to go!" I shout at Jules, stumbling toward him until I can steady myself by grasping at his arms. "Now!"

He's staring at me, forgetting for the moment that his light is blinding in my eyes—but I don't need to see him to know he's torn, body rigid with the warring needs to flee and stay to study this room of secrets.

"I can't," he says back, barely audible to my explosion-dazzled ears. "Mia—we can't just dive through a thing like this without knowing where it leads. Especially not after seeing all this." He gestures around at the walls. "You'll talk to Liz again—we can convince them to wait, to keep us alive long enough to—"

"To what? Find another miraculous way to escape four trained, armed mercenaries with no qualms about shooting us? Jules, don't make me go through the portal alone."

But still he hesitates. A shot rings out, fired through the widening hole in the door and pinging off the stone some distance behind us. I gasp and reach up, switching off the lamp on his helmet so at least they won't be able to see where we are so easily.

I tighten my grip on Jules's arms, trying to pull him toward the portal—but even if he wasn't a foot taller than me, he's strong, and I can barely budge him. "There's a time for study and planning and waiting and going over every detail, like you do, and there's a time for answers, but sometimes you have to go by your gut, your—"

I'm interrupted by a shower of rocks and a shout, as one of Liz's men knocks another section of the door down. The hole's going to be wide enough to squeeze through in another few seconds.

Now that his bright helmet's off and out of my eyes, I can see some of Jules's face in the half light left by the mirrors high overhead. His dilemma is so clearly written there that my heart aches for him. And in that moment I know what to do.

"Sometimes you have to go on instinct," I whisper. Then I lean into him and stretch up onto my toes, sliding one hand up his arm to curl around the back of his neck and pull him down into a kiss.

For an instant, there is no portal. There's no Liz, no armed crew ready to kill us, no loved ones waiting for us on Earth. He's motionless for a heartbeat. Then he slides his arm around the small of my back and pulls me in against him, our bodies colliding and robbing me of breath.

His other hand cups my cheek, as gentle as his embrace is fierce, and my skin burns where his fingers rest. I meant to shock him, distract him, interrupt his frozen indecision—and instead I'm the one who's melting, my body fitted against him, my lips parting with his, a heat washing over me so intense I have to break away or else catch fire. . . .

I stumble back, dizzy. I'm staring up at him, and his eyes are burning, and my voice is somewhere far away, making me hunt for it amid the wreckage of my thoughts. "Instinct," I whisper.

Then, before I can talk myself out of it, before I can think again about the agony of my trip through the portal from Earth to Gaia, before Jules can grab for me and stop me, I turn and break into a run.

Please, Jules. It's all I can think as I make for the dark, roiling surface of the portal. *Don't make me go through alone.*

14

JULES

PANIC SWEEPS THROUGH ME AS MIA LEAPS INTO THE OILY BLACK SURFACE of the portal, disappearing with a ripple, leaving me staring after her with my mouth open.

My body's still electrified, my heart hammering, and I can still feel her lips against mine. We were only together a few seconds, and already there's an aching absence where she was.

This room holds everything I've been searching for.

Everything my father feared.

Everything our world needs to see.

The Nautilus. A warning. Languages that weren't born for tens of thousands of years after this place was abandoned. If I run, I'm throwing away everything it took to get here.

But Mia went through the portal.

There's only one choice to make, and so I make it. I stumble half a dozen steps, then break into a run. I make for the black shimmer where Mia vanished, and pray I'll find oxygen on the other side. A voice shouts from the wreckage of the chamber door, but Liz is too late—the blackness swallows me up, and I'm alone, and silence is all that's left.

Pain shoots down my arms and legs, pounds at my temples, rips at my insides. My stomach lurches with nausea as I lose all sense of which way is up. Waves of green and gold ripple across my vision even as I squeeze my eyes closed, even as I reach for something, anything to grab on to—but nothing's there.

Just as I'm about to scream, I hit something hard. The impact drives the breath from my lungs and sends me rolling, an intense cold slicing at my skin wherever it's exposed. I come to rest face-down, and as I pry my eyes open, I'm still not sure I can feel my arms and legs. All I can see is a blur of white. The sand beneath me is white.

No, my brain supplies, the sharp pins and needles of cold stabbing into my forehead. *The snow is white. You're facedown in snow.*

I can't summon anything more coherent than that—I can't remember where I am, or where I'm supposed to be, but everything hurts, and I'm positive that for some reason, I'm supposed to move.

There's a huge black monolith standing in the icy landscape just behind me, jagged stone polished smooth, and I squint at it, waiting. Then the information arrives with a sudden surge of adrenaline: it's the portal.

Mia.

I twist my head around to look for her in the dim light, shove over onto my other side, and there she lies a few arm's lengths away, huddled in a small pile on the ground, completely unmoving. I scramble up onto all fours to crawl across to her, the snow stinging my hands and soaking through the knees of my trousers, my pack trying to tip me over sideways like a too-heavy shell on an oversized tortoise. "Mia," I gasp, grabbing for her shoulder with one hand. "Are you okay?"

She moans; it's a long, low sound, her throat raw, as if she's been screaming. On the ship here, half the crew were incapacitated on the way through the portal, and evidently Amelia's on the side of the sufferers. I found the sensation thoroughly unpleasant, but then, as now, I recovered quickly. And right now, I have to think for both of us.

I twist around to look back at the portal once more, coming up onto my knees as I realize my hands are starting to turn numb, pressed against the snow. The monolith behind us looks solid, a black mass in the near darkness. *No going back.* But there's no guarantee that just because it looks like stone on this side, it isn't still a portal on the other side. It's hard to imagine any mercenary who'd choose "unknown alien portal" over "retrace steps and go home," but theirs is a world I clearly don't understand.

Theirs is a world that just sent us through a portal because the fear of the humans behind us was greater than the fear of the unknown ahead of us. Or perhaps that's not their world. It's our world.

At any rate, I've left behind the thing I came to see, but I have to believe that where there's life, there's hope. So my priorities are to find a place to hide, in case Liz and her cronies do show up, and then to figure out where the hell we are, and what to do next.

I turn my glance on the landscape around us. We're in a kind of frozen gully, lying in thick snow, walls of ice rising on either side of us. Even in the faint light, I can see the places I've kicked up the snow. Anywhere we move, we're going to leave footprints behind us, a trail straight to our hiding place.

I stagger to my feet, not bothering to brush off the frost clinging to my clothes, and twist to look in each direction along the gully. Behind the black stone of the portal, the ground rises a little, turning to frozen brown earth, or stone, the snow dissipating. *That way, then.* We'll have to hope there's a hiding place somewhere up in that direction.

"Mia," I say, crouching down to speak in her ear, resting one hand on her back. "We have to get out of sight. Liz could follow us through."

"C-c-c-can't," she manages, curling into a smaller ball, graduating from shivering in the cold to outright shaking. She doesn't protest as I carefully pull her pack free of her shoulders.

"I'll help you stand," I murmur, drawing out her hands—they're ice-cold, even to my half-numb touch—and wrapping them in mine. "Not far, then we'll hide and wrap up warm. Come on, you can do it."

It's a tribute to her determination—it's a tribute to everything I've come to admire about her—that she tries to get to her feet. I can see how much every movement costs her. I hook my hands in under her arms and mostly lift her, holding her steady until she can uncurl her legs underneath herself, and stand in the snow, leaning in against me. I wrap my arms around her, tucking her in under my chin, simply holding her for a moment, letting her gather herself.

"Th-thanks," she manages after half a minute, her voice husky and whisper-thin. "For following me."

She would've gone through this on the way from Earth to Gaia, and she *still* leapt through the portal, knowing what it would do to her. And not knowing, not for certain, that I would be behind her and here to help her on the other side. Although she did a pretty good job of making sure I'd follow.

"Well," I say, holding her steady with one hand while I dig in the pocket on her thigh with the other, pulling out the last of her granola bars. A smile wants to creep into my voice despite the adrenaline still flooding my system, simply because she's near. And I let it, just a little. "I had to follow you. I wasn't sure the kissing was over, and I didn't want to risk missing any of it."

Her breath is a white cloud on the air as she exhales slowly, but she doesn't reply. Neither of us speaks. And as the white mist of her breath dissipates, so too does the warmth inside me.

I can't believe that kiss was just a ploy—I know that dizzying rush was as strong for her as it was for me, I *know* it. But that doesn't mean she wants to do it again. She's so single-minded in her pursuit not just of survival, but a way to save her sister, that for all I know, the very intimacy of the moment might be what's frightened her away from it. She can't afford to let me be a distraction. Maybe I can't let *her* be a distraction.

I use my teeth to tear open the wrapper on the granola bar I'm still holding and peel back the packaging with one hand, holding it to her lips. She takes a bite, though chewing's clearly an effort. I take a couple bites too, then shove the rest of it into my pocket. I want to wolf it down, but some part of my brain knows to stop myself. We've got to ration our supplies all the more strictly now that we have no idea where we are, or how to get back to Mia's rendezvous point with Mink. All I know is that we can't stay here forever. We've got to keep moving—I can't think past that, the impossibility of our situation too overwhelming to contemplate.

"Ready to try moving?" I ask.

She nods, but as I lean down to retrieve her pack, so I can sling mine over my left shoulder and hers over my right, she sways in place. We need a hiding place nearby—our first few, faltering steps confirm that.

"Jules," she whispers, hoarse, but audible. "Why is it dark?"

For a moment the question doesn't make sense, and then I realize she's right. We lost track of all time inside the temple, but right before we leapt through the portal, the place was lit with a thousand rainbows. With sunlight, refracted through the crystal up at the ceiling. But now we're either right before dusk, or just after dawn, judging by the light. "I don't know," I admit. "We must still be on Gaia—the air feels the same and we're not asphyxiating, but this snow . . . I don't know."

We keep to a slow but steady pace, and when we reach the frozen ground on the far side of the portal stone, I glance back, reaching up to turn on my head torch. Now that we're on ice instead of snow, as best I can tell we're not leaving footprints, or at least, not footprints that will be visible until daylight.

We make our way about ten minutes along the crevasse we're in, icy cliffs rising on either side above us several times our own height. If we weren't in such rough shape we could climb up and out of the crevasse entirely, though what we'd find above us I don't know. But I don't think I could climb that high right now, and I'm certain Mia can't.

I'm straining my ears for the sounds of pursuit, and using my torch to methodically sweep the cliffs for any sign of a crack, a cave, or anywhere we can hide. Mia's steps are starting to drag, and I'm taking more of her weight, when I finally spot it. There's an opening in the icy cliff just above my head height, which means it must be about two meters above the ground. It's barely more than shoulder width in size, but if we can slither in feet-first—and if it's stable, and deep enough—it'll be a workable hiding place until we can regain some strength.

I gently lower Mia down to sit on the frozen ground with the packs, leaning against the ice, and look up at the cliff face. It's not a long way, but the fall could still do considerable damage. Assuming it doesn't just collapse when I try to climb it.

Mia lifts her head to look up at me, her face white in the darkness. She's pressing her fingertips to the ice, and I realize that if she's grown up scavenging in deserts like the one that decimated Chicago, she's probably never seen ice before in person, or snow, and certainly not in quantities like this. I've only been in a landscape like this once, on a geological expedition with my father in the Antarctic. For Mia, who nearly had a stroke when she tried to imagine me in a swimming pool, this much fresh water, frozen though it is, must be almost incomprehensible.

I reach up to test the ice, and it's not as slippery as I feared, though the cold is biting. I yank my sleeves down to cover part of my palms, set my foot on an outcropping only a couple of fingers wide, and reach up, every muscle in my body protesting as I tentatively hoist myself off the ground. The cliff holds.

I don't have to work my way up far off the ground to get a look inside the crack—I can't even really call it a cave—but by then I'm sure the cliff face is solid, and relief washes over me like warmth when I get a look inside our prospective shelter. It goes back far enough for us to fit inside, and given I'm not moving Mia any farther in a hurry, it'll do.

I climb back down and pick up the packs, slinging them over my head and into the shelter, and then help her to her feet. "More climbing," I tease, drawing a faint smile from her. "You love climbing."

"You hate it," she murmurs.

"I do," I agree. "Here lies Jules Addison. He died in the name of archaeology, when he tried to climb an ice cliff and landed on his head."

"I'll make sure that's what the plaque says," she replies, her voice a little stronger, and when I lean down to lace my hands together to boost her, she's strong enough to lift her foot and set her boot on them, reaching up to take hold of the two highest outcroppings on the cliff she can reach.

"In Latin, please," I say, bracing, then lifting her up, so she can grab at the edge of our little nook, slithering in headfirst with a kick of her feet, then twisting inside there to stick her head out a moment later.

"You'll have to write it down, if you want it in Latin," she says, as I glance down at the ground, use my boot to scuff out a hint of a footprint, and start to climb after her. "And based on our day so far, seems like more Undying would've understood it than humans."

It's a tight fit, climbing in beside her—I can squeeze in headfirst well enough, but there's a lot of shuffling to turn myself around. I can only just rise up onto my hands and knees without smacking into the ceiling of our hiding place.

Eventually we're wedged in next to each other, with me on one side of her and the packs on the other, my blanket wrapped around the pair of us. We finish off the granola bar in silence, and she doesn't protest when I hand her the breather.

Its presence reminds me—and her, I have no doubt—of our limited resources, and as my limbs start to defrost a little, I turn my mind to the next question in my triage list.

Mia alive, check.

Place to hide, check.

Figuring out where the hell we are, and what the bloody hell is going on . . . no idea.

As if she's reading my mind, Amelia switches off the breather after a couple of minutes, pulling it down from her mouth so she can speak. "So," she says quietly, breath steaming in the frigid air. "We have limited oxygen, limited food, and no loot to buy our way off the planet. We're still on Gaia, but this snow means we're a long, long way from where we started, which means we have no way to contact Mink on the station anyway." Her voice is low, almost monotone, her gaze fixed on the cliff face opposite the mouth of our little cave.

"That's about it," I agree, settling on my side to face her. "But we're not dead yet."

She wriggles around, settling down to face me, nose to nose. "If you say something like 'where there's life, there's hope,' I'm gonna punch you," she warns me.

"Fair enough," I concede, my mouth wanting to quirk a little when I cast my mind back to my earlier thoughts as I tried to get her moving. Good thing I kept them to myself then, or she might've stayed facedown in the snow out of spite.

What I want to do is bridge the gap between us, to brush my lips against hers, feel her warmth and share mine with her. But I don't know if I can, if I should. She said nothing when I brought it up before, leaving room to joke in case she really was only trying to get me through the portal. So instead, I curl an arm around her, and bring her in closer, share my warmth that way. We're speaking again, she's teasing me again, and that much I'll take. Physically, we're close as I could wish—*well, almost*—but it's cold comfort without knowing whether she truly wanted that kiss or not.

"Are we gonna talk about what happened back there?" Mia murmurs.

For a wild moment I wonder if she can read my thoughts, if her mind keeps circling back to that kiss too. Then I look down and see her staring ahead, eyes distant and fearful, and I realize she's talking about the portal room. Like any sane person would be.

Get it together, Jules.

When I don't answer, Mia straightens, pulling away from me just a little. "Those were Earth languages written on the walls, Jules. I mean, I don't speak Russian or Chinese, but I know what they look like. Not to mention the French and whatever else that uses normal letters."

"I know." The words slip out, soft and helpless, before I can stop them. I'm lost.

"There was English, too," she goes on. "I saw only a flash of it, but something about rising into the heavens? Wasn't that in the original broadcast?"

"Yes, at the end of their message to us. We thought it meant to build and use the portal."

"But . . . we've done that. We're here, aren't we? Why are they still giving us those same instructions? Rise up?"

"I . . . I can't explain it, Mia." My voice sounds small and grim, and as much as I'd like to find something reassuring to tell her, I don't know what's going on. I don't even have a hypothesis, however far-fetched. For the first time in my life, I'm adrift in a sea of *not knowing,* and it's a terrifying, sinking feeling.

"You're the expert," she protests, her exhaustion making her sound accusatory. "Could they have heard radio broadcasts from Earth and learned about our languages that way?"

"We're not even in the Milky Way galaxy anymore—it'd take millions of years for radio waves to travel here from Earth."

"Well . . . it's only been fifty thousand years since the temples were built, and we still heard the Undying broadcast that led us to Gaia. Maybe they can use the portals to send and receive transmissions, too."

I lift my free arm so I can rub at my aching head. "Even if they had some reason to come find us, use their portals and listen to our radio signals . . . Mia, their civilization crumbled before mankind even *had* radios. Before we could do more than make stone tools. The temple that brought us here, whose walls tell the story of their race's destruction . . . it's over fifty thousand years old."

"Then *how* are there human languages on those walls back there?" Her voice is high with confusion and weariness, and I can feel her looking at me, waiting for me to supply the answer she feels certain is coming. "All your Nautilus symbols, they led us to a room full of carvings in our languages, which could only be for humans, but how is it possible if they did it before these languages even existed?"

"I don't *know!*" The words burst out, sounding angry and small.

I expect her to lash back, to pull away from me entirely, to accuse me of not fully understanding the level of screwed we are because of my upbringing. Instead she's silent for a few breaths until I hear her inhale. "Well," she says finally, "we should keep moving."

"What?" I look across at her, and she's got that game-face on again, the *bring-it, I-can-take-whatever-you-throw* face. "Moving where?"

Mia shrugs, spreads her hands. "Anywhere. Look, you said that temple was important. That it held the key to the hidden warning inside the broadcast, to proving your dad right or wrong. That the important thing in it was all the way at the center, at the bottom. That was the portal. They wanted us to end up here—there has to be a reason. We won't find it sitting in here."

The logic is like a life raft appearing in my sea of uncertainty just as I'm getting too tired to tread water. "Maybe there's another temple here," I say slowly. "Maybe that room wasn't the final piece of the Nautilus puzzle. Maybe it was just a stepping-stone. The satellite imaging at the poles is sketchy at best, because of Gaia's magnetic fields, so they could've missed something. Perhaps we can make for higher ground, get a better vantage point."

Mia nods, eager to seize on any possibility. "Well, then, let's do it."

I take a long, slow breath and find myself nodding. But before I can open my mouth to respond, a sound breaks the quiet. It's quiet, distant, muffled—but unmistakable.

Voices.

Liz and her men have come through the portal.

15

AMELIA

WE BOTH FREEZE. WE'RE CLOSE ENOUGH THAT I CAN FEEL THE MUSCLES IN Jules's body stiffen, can feel the catch of his breath like it's my own. I can hear one of Liz's men hurling his guts out somewhere down below, a side effect of going through the portal, and the sound of his retching makes my own stomach roil in sympathy.

Yeah, I feel you, buddy.

Liz, however, seems as immune to the portal's side effects as Jules, or else she's just so used to shoving aside physical discomfort that she powers through it. I can hear her giving commands, ordering her men to fan out and search for tracks.

Tracks . . .

The moments after I wound up in a snowdrift on the other side of the portal are a bit of a blur—Jules talking about climbing is the first thing I can remember with any clarity. But we're some distance from the portal, and we had to get here somehow.

Tracks.

"Tracks," I blurt, my mind finally catching up. "We've got to move. They'll see our footprints in the snow and find us in no time."

Jules is moving quickly, twisting in our tiny ice hole so that he can return my pack to me. "I concealed them as best I could. The last few minutes we were moving over ice, so the tracks will be harder to find, but not impossible. If we climb back down, we'll certainly hit snow again, and leave more prints. And if we go up, we'll be out in the open, where anyone can see us if they climb to the top of the crevasse."

I tighten the straps of my pack around my shoulders once more, poking my head out cautiously from our hiding place to make sure they haven't found our trail yet. Though the occasional beam from a flashlight ricochets through the ice, the voices don't seem any closer. I crane my neck, inspecting the crevasse. I don't have anything like the kind of gear we'd need to climb the ice safely. "Your pick," I whisper, pulling my head back in so I can make out Jules's silhouette in the dark. "The one you brought for artifacts and stuff."

"What?" He's staring at me like I've lost my mind—and maybe I have.

"If we can't go down and we can't go up, we'll go sideways." I'm grabbing my multi-tool from its pocket, twisting it until I can unfold its mini hatchet blade. "Across the ice."

Jules is muttering something under his breath, something I recognize now as probably Latin. *Latin.* We have so, so many questions that need answering right now, and as soon as we're not running for our lives, I'm going to make him turn that enormous brain of his to figuring them out. Right now, though, survival's top of the list.

I wriggle my top half out of our hole and jab the blade of the tool into the ice some distance away. I ease a leg out, trying to find purchase with my boots and scrabbling until I get the leverage to kick at the ice and make myself a tiny dent of a toehold. Jules follows, breathing harsh just behind me. We're not high off the ground at all, but a fall will leave a telltale sign for Liz to follow, and make enough noise for them to hear. And that's a death sentence as certain as any life-threatening drop would be.

I've seen plenty of movies with ice climbing, and it always looked so much easier than scaling skyscrapers—you just make your own holds, wherever you need them, with your ice picks. But as we make our way horizontally across the face of the crevasse walls, I realize those movies were bullshit. For one thing, each of us has only one pick. We have to stick close together so I can use Jules's holds while freeing my ax, and vice versa. For another, half the time the ice gives way as soon as I put any weight on the handle of my multi-tool, causing a shower of ice to skid to the bottom of the crevasse. Fortunately, bits of ice litter the sides of this canyon from years, or even centuries, of shifting winds. I don't think the trail we're leaving is one Liz will easily follow. At any rate, it's a better bet than trying to hide our footprints.

Our progress across the cliff face is slow, and at times I swear I can hear my breathing echoing back at me off the opposite wall—we're in a narrow gorge in the ice, snow on the ground below us, sky visible above.

When the crevasse branches, and branches again, we're forced to stick to the same wall, always heading right through this ice maze. But as Liz's voice, and the voices of her men, fade into the distance, I'm feeling better and better about our chances of getting out of this.

Well, away from Liz, at any rate. The rest—I can't think about the rest, about anything beyond surviving the next few hours.

Eventually, my shaking limbs and burning lungs force me to give up. "I think that's far enough," I gasp, trying to sound like I'm not as winded as I am. My only consolation is that Jules drops to the snow almost immediately after I speak, slumping over with exhaustion.

I drop down beside him. By my estimation there's at least half a kilometer between our last tracks and these, and the crevasse branched twice. Liz only has four men now, after losing Alex to Jules's rockfall. It's gonna take her some time to find us. We take a few minutes to pause, share the breather between us, and stretch. The horizon is definitely getting lighter, though the blanket of stars overhead is still brilliant against the deep violet sky. I gaze upward, trying not to think about how alien it all looks, how there's not a single constellation from the Chicago skyline up there.

I feel like I should say something to Jules—not about the impossible languages we've just seen or how we're going to get off this planet, but about what happened before we jumped through the portal. I kissed him. He kissed the hell out of me right back. But I don't know what I *could* say.

In the end, I give myself a shake and tuck my multi-tool into its pocket. "Let's move."

• • •

Jules and I keep close to the wall, picking our way among the ice shards fallen from the lip of the crevasse. Our tracks are still visible, but at least they're not as obvious. Once found, our trail will be easy for Liz to follow. But we've put enough distance between us and them that our tracks should take hours to find.

We abandon stealth in favor of speed, trying to widen our lead over Liz's gang. While I'm geared for cold weather, I'm geared for desert cold—sub-zero, yes, but not *this* far sub-zero. My feet are numb before too long, and my face quickly chapped by the freezing wind.

The crevasse narrows, then narrows again, forcing us to sidle through single file, until I hear Jules hiss a warning behind me. I stop, but the ice is so narrow I can't turn my head. That's when I realize it's gotten so narrow that he can't follow. My hips barely fit, and his broader shoulders just won't squeeze through anymore.

I wriggle backward until I can tip my head back and turn it over my shoulder. "Dammit," I groan, conceding that we've reached a dead end. "How far back was the last branch?"

"Couple of Ks" is Jules's brief reply, his own head tipped back so it can rest against the ice, sending his breath steaming above us as he pants.

"Shit." I let my head fall back, too. We stay that way for a while, watching our exhalations rise and vanish into the sky, which is distinctly lighter now. "Well. I guess we go up now."

"We do need to get to higher ground," Jules points out. "See if we can spot another temple. For all we know we're wandering in circles."

The fact that we're nearly wedged in makes the upward climb far easier than the sideways scramble of a few hours before. I don't even bother with my multi-tool, just wedging my boots sideways against the opposing walls of the crevasse and wriggling upward. The top is the hardest part, and I'm so eager to pull myself over that I slip and manage to kick Jules in the face before his bulk stops my slide.

His grunt of pain and effort makes me flinch and grab for the edge of the crevasse. I haul myself up, praying I didn't break his nose. That's the last thing I need to add to my list of sins. Once I'm up, I flatten myself on my belly and dig the toes of my boots into a crack in the ice, and offer Jules an extra hand as he scrambles up after me. Then we're both rolling over onto our backs, ignoring for the moment the cold of the ice beneath us, breathing hard and staring up at the silvery blue of the early morning sky.

When I finally find the strength to sit up—and look around—my breath sticks in my throat as a strangled gasp.

The suns hang just over the horizon, which is marked by distant mountains that look as though I could reach out and touch them, the air is so crystal clear. Gaia's two suns are overlapped in the sky, red and orange where they sit low above the mountain peaks, and their light paints the edges of the ice a fiery crimson-gold.

Before us spreads an expanse of flat ice, marked with crevasses like the one we just climbed out of, each one gilded in fire that drops quickly into a deep aqua in their depths.

I reach for Jules's hand without thinking, to pull him upright.

And though he takes my hand, he rises to his feet on his own power, keeping my fingers wrapped in his.

We say nothing. My mind is dazzled by the sudden beauty of this place, and there are no words to fill the silence. It's a silence that doesn't need filling anyway, a silence so full of awe that to speak would only lessen our wonder.

The crevasse field spreads behind us into what seems like infinity, but ahead of us there's a line in the white expanse that suggests a change in terrain. We set out for it without needing to discuss it.

While there's no snow to slow our steps, we quickly discover the reason for that—unshielded by the crevasse walls, the wind is fierce up here, too fierce for any snow to collect on the icy plain. We have to hunker our shoulders and lean into it to make any progress, though the winds rise and fall and give us occasional reprieves in which we can move considerably faster.

The change in terrain proves to be a drop-off, but we're still too far to see into the valley beyond. We're moving for an hour at least when Jules pauses, his icy fingers tightening in mine to give me some warning before I'm forced to jerk to a stop too.

"The suns aren't rising any higher," he notes, brow furrowed as he inspects the horizon. "They've moved, but only along the mountain ridge."

Tired, my mind refuses to interpret what he's saying. "So?"

"So, that's strong evidence we're near one of the poles. The southern one, I'm betting, based on where the suns are. That's why it went from light to dark when we went through the portal. It wasn't time travel or anything like that—we just teleported to a part of the planet where the suns hadn't risen yet."

"The south pole?" I echo. Numbly, I'm trying to remember my studies of the planet. I knew the terrain by the drop-off point like the back of my hand, but damned if I remember where that actually *was* on the planet's surface. "That's . . ."

"At least fifteen thousand kilometers from where we were."

It ought to be a blow. It ought to drive me to my knees, confirming how far we are from the rendezvous point. It ought to make me want to lie down on the ice and wait to freeze to death.

But I think some part of me already knew. Even back in the prism chamber, as we activated the portal, I knew. The old plan—get in, grab the loot, get back to Earth—was long gone by then, lying in ruins at the bottom of one of those pitfalls in that temple.

It started falling apart way before this—before Liz found us, before we even stepped inside. It started falling apart the moment I teamed up with Jules and headed for the hidden temple. It disintegrated when we found all the languages of Earth at the center of the temple, an impossible sight. "Is this part of the planet even covered by the satellites?" I ask, dully sure of the answer.

Jules shakes his head slowly. "Gaia's magnetic field is so strong at the poles that they don't have any surveillance here at all."

I absorb that new blow with barely a waver. There's no way to call Mink even if she would still pick us up. And even if we could call her, she wouldn't have any maps or images of this terrain. We might as well actually *be* on a different planet.

Jules gives my hand a squeeze, then lifts it to his lips. He wraps my fingers in both of his, pressing them to his mouth where his skin is warmer, and his breath warmer still, exhaling life back into my numb body.

Then the air's rent by a crack, and we both start, half dropping toward the ice. It sounded like a gunshot, but after a moment its echoes are overtaken by the crackling roar of ice. Somewhere behind us something just broke a big chunk of ice from the crevasse. And while it's impossible to tell how far away it was, the sound's echoing all around us now, and buried inside the noise of falling ice is the warmer patter of surprised voices.

Jules and I meet each other's eyes for half a heartbeat, then break into a run. It's only a few moments later that a shout rings through the air. Liz's men have not only picked up our trail, but have done as we did and climbed the crevasse for a better vantage point. We turn as one, looking behind us—they're about a kilometer back, just specks against the ice. But if we can see them, they can see us.

My footing gives way without warning—I was looking behind us, and not where I was running. Jules is falling even before I am, the ice shattering beneath our feet and dropping us with a bone-bruising thud onto a sheet of ice below.

Our momentum carries us into a slide and we go shooting into darkness, kept together only by our linked hands, even as the force of the fall threatens to separate us. We've fallen into some sort of meltwater cave system within the ice sheet, and with every passing moment we're gathering speed as we slide downhill.

We crash into a series of delicate ice stalactites that serve only to daze us, not slow us down. Flashes of light streak by as we pass shafts leading upward into the dusky daylight, but we're moving too fast to see anything else. Jules tightens his grip on my hand and pulls and our bodies come together.

We smash through another sheet of ice and slam into a wall before careening sideways and down another chute. I blink ice and tears from my eyes and see the darkness starting to give way, not in a bright flash like we're approaching a vertical shaft to the light above, but gradually, like we're rapidly approaching the end of . . .

"Hold on!" I scream, reaching for my multi-tool. Jules wraps an arm around me, yanking me in against him, and as the hatchet blade comes shooting out of the tool, his other hand wraps around both mine and the haft of the ax. Together we swing downward and the blade strikes ice, not catching but screeching through it like nails across drywall, and with about as much effect.

Then daylight dashes over us—after the utter blackness in the caves, even the dusk of the polar spring is dazzling. The ax's haft vibrates once against my palm, my only warning before it catches in the ice and jerks to a halt. My arm would've been yanked from its socket but for Jules's added grip—even so, the pain of it wrenches tears from my eyes and a moan from my throat. Jules's own grunt of pain tells me he's barely holding on.

And that's when I realize why: we're dangling over thin air.

The caves open up into the valley wall beyond the ice sheet, and we're hanging from the handle of my multi-tool over a drop so high my eyes can't even track the chunks of ice dislodged by our slide as they fall to the valley floor far below.

I moan again, though this time it's half a scream, and it's enough to make Jules glance down and echo it. Together we scramble, adrenaline giving us the strength to haul ourselves back over the lip of the tunnel and retreat, boots scrabbling against the ice and debris, until we can lie still, shaking and coughing.

The multi-tool is wedged into the ice so far I can't get it out, and Jules has to help me pry my own fingers from its handle. I gently wriggle it to and fro, and he uses the edge of his pick to chip away at the ice around it.

I huddle in against him as much for comfort as for safety, and he's not pulling away, his own body shaking as hard as mine is—we're both fumbling every movement, taking longer over this than we have to, but this is a small, concrete action we can cling to, and so we do. The multi-tool is valuable, and whatever happens, we're going to need it. Eventually it comes free of the ice, and bit by bit we unwind enough to creep back toward the lip of the cave, to look at the valley spread out before us.

The ground far below would have looked like a huge, unbroken expanse, like a frozen inland sea, but for a slab of rock jutting out of it at an angle. My dazzled eyes see it as a pillar from Stonehenge, something finite and understandable.

But as I make out the fine spiderweb of cracks in the ice radiating out from the thing, as my mind reasserts just how far up off the valley floor we are, how far away we must be, the true scale of the stone starts sliding dizzily into place. It's massive—far larger than any of the temples, even the decoy complex I'd originally intended to loot. It's not the right shape for one of the temples, either. Now that I'm looking at it, the sleek lines of the thing curve where it's buried in the ice, spiraling around on itself like the stone is a half-concealed serpent, coiling to strike.

"That's not a rock." Jules's voice is hushed. The shape of that curved base is familiar, and I can feel both our minds trying to figure out why. "It's . . ."

He reaches for the multi-tool, easing it out of my unresisting fingers. His breath is catching, as though he wants to speak, but he can't. He fumbles with the tool's grip, and out springs the blade. He can't find the words, but slowly he drags the blade across the ice between us, etching out what he wants to show me.

The Nautilus symbol. Curved, spiraling, twisting in on itself.

I stare at it, then my gaze trails down to the thing in the ice once more. That curve at its base . . . He's right. It's an exact reflection of the Fibonacci spiral he found scrawled all over the temple. On a scale like we've never seen it before.

Then my mind tips the object on its side, and everything else about its shape becomes clear. The elongated section snaps into perspective. It's the body of a bird, a fish, a fighter jet. Designed to move through the air, the water, the substance of reality, with scarcely a ripple.

Designed.

"Rise into the stars," Jules whispers at my side, for once our two minds following the exact same trajectory.

This is what the Undying broadcast and the temples meant us to find—and it's also what they tried to warn us about, whoever slipped the equation for the Nautilus—for the shape of this thing—into their broadcast, and etched spirals into the temple walls.

Catastrophe. Apocalypse. The end of all things.

This is the treasure they guarded, the prize at the end of the maze, the discovery that will change the future of Earth forever. Because it's not a temple, or a monument, or a rock formation at all.

It's a spaceship.

16

JULES

I'M REELING, MY HEART TRYING TO HAMMER ITS WAY OUT THROUGH MY chest as I lie beside Amelia, staring down at the plains below us, and it's not because we nearly just plummeted to our deaths.

Everything has been leading us here.

Every test we passed, every note we tuned, every step we took, every puzzle we solved. They were all leading us to the portal in the rainbow chamber, to the path that would bring us to this spot.

We gaze down at the valley floor, our breath puffing out in front of us, the mist of mine mingling with hers. Amelia has her goggles on, and no doubt she's magnifying the view, but even without that, I know what I'm seeing. It's a craft, unmistakable, and after the dozens of languages all telling us to *rise*, there's no question the Undying meant for us to find it.

Us—humans.

And that's where my mind stalls, where my thoughts keep beating futilely against the walls of logic. The Undying were long gone before we'd invented those languages, and more than that, I can't think of any way a species on the other end of the galaxy could have even known about primitive humans evolving on Earth while they built these temples. Beyond logic, what truly makes my stomach shrivel in fear is that they *lied*.

Their broadcast seemed designed for any intelligent species to decode, and yet the planet it led us to proves they could have just sent their broadcast in English, or any of the dozens of other languages we saw in that temple. Why lie, why deceive, unless the truth would keep us from coming here?

I'm exhausted, and part of me wants to suggest we just stop here, on the ledge that saved us from a fatal drop onto the valley floor. But Liz and her men are still out there, and if they get to that ship first, we'll never get inside to unlock its secrets.

This ancient, frozen lake and the ship half entombed inside it is what the Nautilus symbols were warning me about. I thought I'd lost my chance to answer all its questions, and now hope's surging up inside me once more, melting away the pain, the disappointment. I *have* to be the first one inside that ship. I have to know the truth. No matter what it costs me.

Finding this ship exists is only half of the answers I need to prove my father right. Showing the International Alliance that the Nautilus shape and its warning are attached to something real won't be enough. I'll need to show them *why* the ship is dangerous, and for that, I have to live to reach it.

I'm gathering my breath to speak, to suggest we keep moving, when Mia's head lifts abruptly. She pulls her goggles off, and I see her eyes go distant—she's listening. I catch my breath and listen too, and that's when I hear it.

A humming, faint but unmistakably artificial, like the whisper of a fan or the whirring of tires or—the sound is growing louder—the distant roar of an engine.

"They couldn't have snowmobiles or something," Mia whispers, her eyes wide. "We saw all the equipment they had with them, and they couldn't have known we'd end up at the pole. . . ."

I'm turning my head this way and that, trying to pinpoint the source of the sound, but in all these ice caverns and tunnels it's impossible to tell echo from origin point. "I don't think it's a snowmobile," I say slowly, mind shying away from the truth. "I think it's . . ."

The sound has grown to a low roar that rumbles in my stomach, and with a jolt of understanding I poke my head out of the hole we're huddled in, out over the drop-off, and look up. There I freeze, and Mia takes one look at my face and joins me.

In the sky, descending with dizzying speed, is a shuttle.

No, not *a* shuttle—*multiple shuttles.* Two, three . . . four . . . the sky is suddenly full of them.

None are the gray, chunky supply shuttle that dropped me off on Gaia's surface from the space station overhead—neither are they the triangular white shuttles the IA uses for its exploratory missions. These are sleek and black, more like fighter jets than space-faring vehicles.

They sweep across the valley floor, then circle in formation and land not far from the half-buried ship.

Mia's the first to find her voice. "Are they from your company? Energy World or whatever?"

Global Energy. I'm staring, shaking my head. "They didn't have private ships like this, they had to bribe half a dozen station officials to get me smuggled down in an IA shuttle dropping scientific equipment." The gears in my mind are scraping together, feeling horribly misaligned, the machinery of my thoughts jarring. "Could—Mink? Liz's crew could have signaled her somehow, after following us through . . ."

But Mia's already shaking her head, in echo of mine. "No way does Mink have this kind of tech at her disposal. That's no salvage op. That's military, that's . . . that's government."

"The IA." At least a dozen shuttles have landed, looking tiny and unimportant now next to the massive ship in the ice. A handful of ant-sized people are emerging from the fleet, throwing the scale of the Undying craft into even sharper focus. "How could they have kept something like this a secret?"

"They didn't show up until we did," Mia replies. "Maybe they didn't know. Maybe Liz was working for them all along—maybe she . . . maybe . . ." But we're out of answers, out of possibilities.

My only comfort, adrift in this dark, sucking ocean of uncertainty, is that Mia's adrift with me.

One thing does swim up to the surface, flashing in my mind like a beacon. Whoever those people are, they'll have food. Water. Breathers. *A way home.* "Those ships," I begin slowly.

"Right," Amelia agrees. "No way can we go down."

"Wait, what?" I blink across at her. "Are you kidding?"

She pushes her goggles up into her hair, so she can get a better look at me. "Jules, are *you* kidding? That's the freaking IA down there. We're scavvers. They'll shoot us in the face."

"Well, how else do you propose we get out of here? They've got the only transport I can see. Can you fly a shuttle, Amelia? Even if it were possible to steal one, can you navigate it past the security on the portal, handle reentry on Earth, and set us down somewhere nice and discreet? Because I can't." I can hear my voice—I know I sound as English and officious as it's possible to sound—but I can't help myself. "Whatever the odds are, we're out of options."

"Not yet, we're not," she counters. "We're not desperate enough to risk that."

"*I* am!" I pause to drag in a breath, and she digs for the breather as I speak. "We have barely any food, a couple more days with the breather, we're exhausted, and Liz is back there somewhere looking for us. If you really want to find somebody who's going to shoot us in the face, just head on out and she'll take care of that for you. At least there's *some* chance the people down at that camp have some sort of moral code."

"Moral code," she echoes, as if I'm simple, pressing the breather into my hand. "Moral code, now I've heard it all. What planet are you from?"

"Not this one," I snap, yanking the breather strap around the back of my head and pulling it down over my face. It's enough to stifle conversation, and we both stay propped up on our elbows, staring down at the camp.

As the light grows, so too does the activity below. Teams set up tents and equipment while others search the hull of the ship, moving across it in squads, patrolling the edge of it. They're looking for a way in, I suppose.

Despite everything, a part of me is desperate to be down there. To be a part of the thrill of this discovery, to be there when they find a door they can open, to see it unsealing, opening for the first time in millennia. There must be a way in.

And the chosen will know the final test, and rise into the stars . . .

Mixed with my wonder, though, is my father's voice in the back of my head. If carrying pieces of Undying tech back to our planet, like ants carrying precious grains of sugar down into our nest, is dangerous, how much more dangerous is something on this scale? For all we've explored, we have more unanswered questions about the Undying than ever. We know nothing about this ship, except that someone among the Undying hid a warning in the broadcast that led us to it.

As I stare down at this ship, my amazement starts to give way to something darker. I feel like the huge, beautiful creature I've just met has bared its teeth, and it turns out it's a carnivore.

"Look, can we at least give it a little longer?" Amelia's voice breaks the quiet, and I realize that while I've been speculating on the future of humankind, she's had her mind on more practical questions. "Let's gather a little more information on this operation before we make any decisions. We have a few more hours to scope them out." But I can already hear the concession in her tone—she knows what we'll have to do in a few hours.

"Sure," I say from beneath the breather, because what's the point in arguing? "You need a little time with this?"

"You keep it a while longer," she says. Again, unspoken: *We'll be able to refill it down there.*

And so we lie side by side, occasionally propped up on our elbows, our chins sometimes resting on our folded arms. We hand the breather back and forth, and let our bodies rest, and find some crackers in my pack to share. And again, I try not to notice her closeness. Try not to think about the moment I smiled, and mentioned our kiss, and she said nothing at all. My tangle of feelings for her is more complicated by the moment, and every time I find a string and tug on it, the knots grow tighter.

She, on the other hand, is busy studying the camp below us. It will be a risk going down there, and it'll be physically challenging, especially as tired as we are. We'll have to wriggle all the way up the tunnel we slid down, and then find a way down onto the plains and out toward the camp, all while avoiding Liz and her team. Neither of us relishes the prospect.

I'd guess it's two or three hours later that Amelia nudges me with her elbow, and I realize I've been dozing. "Look," she murmurs, pulling down her goggles and pointing out at the ship below. It takes me a long moment to see what she's looking at, but when she points, I lean in to press my temple to hers, feeling the warmth of her skin a moment, and follow her line of sight.

There are two figures making their way from the base of the cliffs below us, out toward the campsite. They're not dressed in black like every single other person we can see—they're in the same dirty browns and khakis as us, both carrying packs on their backs, their arms stretched out wide to either side in the classic *look-I'm-unarmed* pose.

"Who is it?" I whisper, as though they'll hear us.

"Liz," Amelia replies, just as soft. "And one of the other guys, not Javier, not Hansen. I never caught his name."

"M.C.," I supply absently. He was the one with the mutton-chops. "I guess Javier and Hansen didn't make it." I'm wondering if I killed them. Whether my rockfall caught them, along with Alex. It doesn't matter how they died, if they're dead . . . except that it does, to me. Of course it matters.

"I wonder what Liz is gonna tell them," Amelia says, as a detachment of figures in black peel away from the camp to trot in formation toward Liz and her companion. They've been spotted. "What she'll tell them about *us*."

I go cold at the thought of that. She may not have any more credibility than we do, but whatever she says to warn them about us, it'll be a first impression we have to try and break. "Perhaps we can convince them . . ."

I trail away, because far below the two groups of figures have come together, and though we can't hear them, the pause must be because they're talking. The figures in black stand arrayed around them in a half circle, and one of them—the leader, I suppose, because this figure's still in black, but wears a different coat, lon-ger, more generously cut, reaching to the knees—is speaking to Liz and the man she's brought with her.

Then, without warning, Liz and her companion fold to the ground.

The sound reaches us a second later, the deafening slam of gun-fire echoing off the ice and rolling around inside our tiny hollow, setting the cliff face trembling all around us. There's nothing we can do but press ourselves down low, cover our heads with our hands, pray the whole thing doesn't cave in on us.

When I eventually crack open my eyes, Amelia's staring down at the icy plain below us. The figures in black are already on their way back to their camp, led by the one in the longer coat, who's striding away without a backward glance. Even without the magnification of Mia's goggles, I can see the blood washing the snow around the two bodies a bright crimson.

"Holy shit," Mia's whispering. "Oh son of a . . . they *can't* . . ."

She'd begun to believe it would be all right if we went down there. So had I.

If we had—if I'd won the argument—we'd be dead right now.

"They . . ." I echo in a whisper, as if the shooters below will somehow hear us.

And then, though I can't believe I'm saying it out loud: "They left their gear on them. Their breathers. Maybe when it gets dark, we could—"

Mia twists around, and she's staring at me as I fall silent. "Holy shit, Oxford," she mutters.

"I didn't—"

"No, you're right," she agrees quietly. "I just didn't think you had that in you."

"I think I'm in shock," I murmur.

"Fair enough," she replies quietly, pressing her forehead down onto her folded arms.

We're both silent, processing what we've just seen, trying to understand it, and it's several minutes before Amelia speaks. "Look, maybe—"

She gets no further, interrupted by a soft sound, as icy debris comes sliding down the way we originally came. We both hold still to see if there'll be more, though the low-ceilinged cave we're in seems solid enough.

There is more, and then a scraping sound, and then abruptly, a pair of boots coming into view. Amelia grabs her multi-tool, and I grab my pick, both of us twisting around at once to face whoever's coming, the image of Liz's blood on the snow fresh in our minds.

The boots wedge in against the wall, slowing their owner's descent, and before I have time to register his clothing isn't black, I find myself staring down the barrel of Javier's gun.

17

AMELIA

FOR A FEW SECONDS NO ONE SPEAKS—JAVIER'S BREATHING HARD, FOCUS
switching between us. He's wearing goggles, making it near impossible to read his expression, but his body is tense and ready. It's
clear he's a pro. A mercenary, rather than a simple scavver. Or, at
the very least, someone who's been doing this sort of work for a
long time.

"You fire that thing in here and you'll bring the whole cave
system down on our heads." I'm speaking before I know what I'm
hoping to get out of him.

"Maybe," he replies. "But *you'll* definitely be dead if I pull the
trigger."

"Why come after us?" Jules is staying still, not risking a movement that could make Javier's twitchy finger slip. "That's what
you're after, down there. You don't need us anymore."

"You're our bargaining chips." Javier's head turns a little—
I'm guessing he's glancing toward the relatively bright hole in the
cave that overlooks the valley. "Liz is going to trade you two as

prisoners and hopefully make a deal with the Alliance forces down there. This operation's out of our league."

"Liz?" I exchange glances with Jules, whose brows are raised. He lifts his eyes to the hole through which Javier descended, and I'm right behind him. Tunneling his way through the ice, Javier would've heard the gunshots, but in all likelihood, he won't have seen what happened.

For a few wild moments, my mind flips through half a dozen ways to use what we know against him. On this, at least, Jules and I agree: knowledge is power. But I'm so tired, and so shaken, and the last few hours are catching up to me faster than I can think.

Javier's got his attention back on us, and after a few more seconds of silence, he reaches up with his spare hand and lifts his goggles up onto his head. He squints at us, though the gun doesn't move. "What?"

Now I can see his eyes, I'm remembering the gentler voice he had, the way he loosened my bindings. My resolve to fight him is failing. I have so much else to fight already. "Liz is dead. The guys down there shot her and M.C."

Javier's eyes narrow. "Shot?"

"See for yourself." Jules gestures to the ledge.

Javier inches toward it, keeping his eyes on us. It'd be easy to lunge forward the moment he shifts his attention to the valley, and shove him out over the drop. But when I glance at Jules, and meet his gaze, I know we're thinking the same thing. Under Liz's leadership, her team was ruthless, efficient, and smart. And those soldiers down there shot her after a couple of minutes of conversation, and evidently with no warning.

Liz was a nearly insurmountable threat to us, and they just took her out like it was nothing. On our own, Jules and I don't stand a chance.

It takes Javier only a few seconds to find the distant pool of crimson surrounding the two bodies in the snow on the surface of the frozen plain. He scans the area, then pulls himself back from the ledge and slumps back against the cave wall. "Well, damn." His gun clicks as he thumbs the safety back on, and he shoves it back into its holster inside his jacket.

I swallow, my throat dry and lips chapped from the cold air. I sneak another look at Jules, who looks relieved—though thanks to recent events, he seems no more eager to trust Javier's apparent change of heart than I am.

"Sorry," I say eventually, though even I can hear the lack of feeling in my voice.

Javier's eyes flick up, and the corners of his mouth twitch in a smile. "No, you're not. Tell the truth, I can't say I am either. Knew it was a mistake as soon as she started giving orders. I'm a merc, I go where the money is. But killing a couple of kids?" He grimaces and shakes his head. "I've got kids of my own. Not what I signed on for."

I'm sensing now's not the time to protest the word *kids*. Instead, I let my breath out in a long, shaky sigh. "So you're gonna let us go?"

Javier shrugs, eyes creeping back toward the valley, though this far back in the cave we can't see the spot where Liz's body's still lying in a pool of her blood. "Go where? That's black-ops down there. There's a lot the world doesn't know about the Alliance, and those teams down there make the old organizations, like the CIA and your MI6, look like kids at playtime. Show ourselves, and we get the same treatment as Liz. Pros like that won't care how old you are. Keeping the secret's the mission, and taking prisoners requires resources. They've got to feed you and find a place to stash you and waste manpower guarding you. They'd need a helluva reason to keep you around. They're more likely to shoot you, like they did her."

"Well, we're running out of choices." My voice sounds every bit as exasperated as I feel, though, thankfully, nowhere near as terrified. "Stay here, we miss Mink's evac and either starve or die of eventual asphyxiation, whichever comes first."

"Go there, and get shot in the face." Jules's voice, despite the grimness of it, still manages to warm a little of the ice in my stomach. At least I'm not alone.

"Only if they see us." I inch forward toward the ledge, and feel Jules's hand wrap around the ankle of my boot to keep me from sliding out into empty air. Scanning the ship and the tents being erected around it, my gut tightens. There's dozens of them, not to mention however many have yet to land—probably hundreds, altogether. But when you run out of options, you have to get creative. And desperate. "It'll be dark again soon, right? The days here are short, at the pole? We can at least sneak in and steal some supplies, and maybe find out more about what's going on. There's no reason they'd have a perimeter set up in a place like this yet, because who were they expecting to come calling, but we don't know what Liz told them about others being here. We should act fast, before they change their routine, and make it harder for us. If they've got shuttles running up to a station and back maybe we can stow away."

"That's a lot of maybes," Javier points out.

"Hey," I snap back, wriggling away from the ledge until I'm at Jules's side again. "We've made it this far on maybes, a lot farther than you guys would've gotten without us."

"True." Javier exhales loudly, letting his head thunk back against the ice. After a few seconds, he announces, "We'll back you up."

That brings me up short.

"We?" Jules echoes him.

"Me and Hansen. He's back at base camp. We've lost over half the team now. Hansen's a pilot, if we can get to a shuttle . . . I'd just like to get off this planet with my skin in one piece and see my family again, and your plan sounds as good as any."

Jules looks at me, but I'm so stunned that I just shrug, too tired to think through the ramifications of joining forces with the remnants of the gang that was, less than a day ago, trying to kill us.

"Fine," Jules says eventually. "But Mia and I, we're giving the orders."

Javier shrugs. "Won't be the first time someone half my age is in charge."

"And we get weapons."

"Done."

Jules's eyes narrow. "And no more tying us up."

Javier's half quirk of a smile comes back. "That's fair."

I drag myself up onto my knees, readying myself to move out and follow Javier back to his camp. "One more thing," I add, feeling around for my multi-tool, and the blade that pops out of its haft. "Your guy Hansen tries to cop another feel and he's gonna lose that hand."

• • •

By the time we reach the camp, the suns are back down below the mountains again, and night's falling fast. It's an uneasy truce at best. Hansen's initial confusion at seeing us unbound only deepens as Javier explains the situation. But after a few outbursts—*how do I know you didn't just switch sides, and Liz'll come through any minute and shoot all of us?*—it seems to sink in, and Hansen subsides with his back against the wall of the crevasse we're nestled inside.

Jules and I retreat to the opposite side, though the spot's narrow enough that we're only a few meters from where Hansen sits. We pass my breather back and forth in silence for a time, until a squeak of boot on snow summons my attention. It's Javier, crossing toward us in the dark and stooping to hand us something. Aside from a dim LED lantern, we're not risking any light, so it's not until I reach up to take it that I realize what it is: another breather.

I nudge Jules, whose head jerks up with a start before he reaches up to take the breather. "This isn't mine."

"Yours is in Liz's pack, out there on the ice." Javier's voice is quiet. "This one was Alex's."

If Alex's absence from the little group wasn't proof enough, the truth is in Javier's voice. Alex, the guy who was halfway across the puzzle floor after us back in the temple when the roof caved in. The guy we killed.

Jules is staring at the breather in his hand like its tank is filled with poison gas. I don't blame him. Every breath out of that mask is one Alex's never taking again.

"Switch with me," I hear myself saying. "I'll take that one."

But Jules is shaking his head. "The mask's for a man. It'll fit my face better than yours." He only hesitates a moment longer before fitting it to his face and leaning back against the wall behind us.

I look across at the two new members of our little group. Javier's busying himself checking our remaining gear, inventorying what stayed here when Liz went out to talk to the forces excavating the ruined ship. Hansen's got his shoulders pressed back against the crevasse wall, like he's bracing himself. He's got an automatic rifle clutched to his chest like it's the only thing standing between him and certain death. Back in the temple, when it was a gang nearly half a dozen strong tying me up, he was an asshole with wandering hands and an attitude. Now he's just a guy a few years older than me, stranded like we are on a planet so far from home our galaxy isn't even a smear in the countless spread of stars overhead.

My breathing sounds shaky to my own ears, echoing against the plastic of my mask until eventually I pull it away. Though my brain knows the air from the tanks is better for me, the masks get hot and moist and just now I *want* the frigid chill of the frozen air against my face.

"We need a plan." My voice sounds a lot stronger than I feel.

Hansen's gaze flicks up, eyes wide enough that I can see the whites of them rolling in my direction. "A plan? A plan? We're gonna *die*, how's that for a plan? Shit. I almost went with them. I almost went *with* them."

I'm assuming he means Liz and M.C., whose bodies are probably frozen solid by now, out on that windswept plain. I take a breath, resisting the urge to join Hansen in what is, admittedly, a justified descent into panic. Take his badass, hardcore boss away and he's more scared than we are.

I realize I'm shivering, and not from the cold. *Okay, maybe not more scared than we are.*

"We're not dead yet." Jules lowers Alex's mask from his face. "We need to know more about the layout down there if we're going to get our hands on more supplies, and ultimately, a shuttle."

"Gonna *die*," groans Hansen.

"Shut up, kid." The gruffness of Javier's voice is undercut by the fact that he drops down next to Hansen and hands him a flask too small for carrying water. Then, to Jules: "You've got an idea?"

"Well," says Jules, thoughtful. "I assume their first step will be to try and get inside the ship. I don't know how they'll do it—I haven't seen it close up—but I have a better chance than most of figuring it out." He pauses, and we exchange a glance in the dim light. We're both thinking of the clues we've already seen—of the human languages carved into a fifty-thousand-year-old temple. I'm wondering if Javier and Hansen even saw it all, or if the mirrors were knocked so askew by their explosion that they weren't lighting up the walls anymore. Neither of us mentions it. Nor do we mention the trail of Nautilus symbols that warned us about the ship. About a danger we still don't truly understand.

"Right," Javier prompts, gentle, and Jules continues.

"I'm assuming *you* have the best chance of guessing how an armed camp of this sort would be set up. Of reading the landscape of it, so to speak."

Javier nods slowly. "So you think we team up and scout."

"I don't love it," Jules admits. "But I don't have a lot of better ideas."

I don't love the plan either—a lot has to go our way for it to work—but I'm one of the best *get-out-of-this-with-my-skin-intact* scavvers I know and I can't think of a better one.

Javier doesn't seem much more enthused than I feel, but

eventually he grunts and nods. "We'll want to observe them for a few hours before we get close enough to scout properly. Time to see what their security measures are now, avoid being spotted by the guys with guns, that sort of thing."

"Tomorrow," I say firmly. "Thanks to you lot, we haven't slept—not *really* slept—in days. I don't particularly feel like walking into a fully armed patrol because I'm half-asleep on my feet."

At that, Javier actually laughs—and though it's brief, it's a quiet, gentle laugh rather than the harsh bark you might expect from the big, burly-looking guy. "You've got a point. Hansen, go easy on that stuff." He tugs his flask back from Hansen, who still looks too shaken to process much of anything.

"Better put out the light, though," I note, nodding toward the little LED lantern. "Don't really want anyone over there spotting an odd glow on the horizon or anything."

We settle down on our opposite sides of the crevasse, Jules and I sharing the inflatable warmth of his high-tech sleeping bag, and using my blanket roll for a pillow. He wraps his arms around me, for warmth as much as anything—that is, until I feel him sigh, and pull aside Alex's breather, and duck his head until his lips are against my hair.

"We're still alive," he whispers.

I swallow, feeling my fingers curl around the fabric of his shirt as though I might be able to somehow draw him closer that way. "Even if we do make it off this planet, there's no way I'm doing it with enough loot to help my sister. And whatever's going on here, it's something far, far worse than anything your father could've predicted. You don't set up elaborate, multi-stage lies for altruistic reasons—somehow I doubt the Undying hid their foreknowledge of humanity and its languages because they wanted to throw us a surprise party. Whatever's happening here is a con. And I can't think of any way it ends well."

Jules's jaw tightens. "I can't either."

"There's nothing more in the transmission? Nothing in the translations from the temple?"

He frowns. "No, but . . ." He stops as his eyes widen. He wriggles his arms free so we can both look at the wrist unit, bringing up the display and the hundreds of photos he took inside the temple. He flicks through them with quick movements of his fingers, pulling out the ones he wants, and I watch in silence.

He has about ten of them when he's done, and he's gazing so intently at them that I don't dare interrupt. They're just the pictures he took of the Nautilus symbols from the temple, scratched into the stone in so many of the chambers we passed through.

He turns the images semi-transparent. And then, with a series of slow swipes, he begins to layer them, one on top of the other. All the Nautilus swirls fit neatly on top of each other, as if they were just one shell. But all the lines are in different places. And when all the pictures are layered together, those lines join up.

They form the body of the spaceship, rising up from the Nautilus at the base.

"It was always there," I whisper, staring. "If we knew how to look at it."

"The spiral was hidden in the broadcast," he whispers in reply. "And the spiral carvings in the temple were all hastily made and unobtrusive. We've been thinking of the Undying as a single cultural entity with a single goal, but look at human history—look at you and me, even. We barely agree on anything half the time. We might not know what the ship is for, but clearly it's important—and at least one member of the Undying race tried to warn us that it's dangerous."

I want to cry, to rail at the impossibility of the puzzle the Undying have left for us. The tangle of timing and probability is worse than any temple maze or pitfall. And even Jules—brilliant, clever, Undying specialist Jules—can't offer any explanation that makes sense.

Instead, I draw a shaky breath. "The question is, which faction—the engineers of the broadcast or the ones who warned us away in secret—was telling the truth?"

He swallows and shakes his head in reply, then with a quick flick of his fingers, dismisses the images. He looks so determined, his jaw squared, his gaze fixed on the horizon. And with that quick bob of his throat, he looks nervous—more than nervous, afraid.

I turn my head so that just my eyes are peeking out the top of the sleeping bag. Looking up, I can see a sliver of sky beyond the walls of the crevasse stretching up above us. "You know what I miss?" I whisper.

He clears his throat with an effort. "Pizza?"

I laugh, more than his attempt at humor really deserves, relieved he's trying at all. My breath against his neck makes him shiver. And knowing I did that to him makes my skin prickle in response. I turn a little in his arms so I can look up more easily at this alien sky. "I miss the moon."

Jules's head shifts where it rests against mine, and I know he's looking up now, too. Both of us, scanning the heavens for anything familiar, knowing that there'll be nothing there to bring us any comfort.

Our whole lives, the International Alliance has been a group of bickering, petty politicians more concerned with buying votes than helping mankind—but there was a time, long ago, when they were Earth's best hope. When all the nations of the world turned their eyes toward the stars and worked together to reach out toward Alpha Centauri. Toward the future.

It's when we stop looking up that we fall apart.

I turn in Jules's arms and he gathers me in, so that we can wrap the sleeping bag up around our faces while keeping our eyes on the alien constellations. Strange, how familiar and how comforting he feels, this boy I still barely know. As familiar as my own stars.

For all I know, tomorrow we'll get caught sneaking in by one of those patrols, and our bodies will be left to freeze in the snow like Liz. For tonight, I'll close my eyes and pretend I'm lying here, looking up at the moon, with Jules.

• • •

A tiny noise wakes me. My mind cycles through a dozen possibilities, getting closer to the truth with each lap of my thoughts. Then the noise comes again and I recognize it as the blip of a walkie-talkie, the quickly stifled burst of quiet static. I don't remember anyone in Liz's group using walkies.

Then I hear the sound of feet on snow. And the squeak of this boot is different from the squeak of Javier's earlier, and I can see Hansen in the starlight, passed out where he was sitting when I fell asleep.

The gun I insisted Javier give me is in the sleeping bag with us. I'm not good with guns—I wasn't exactly a seeker of confrontation, back on Earth. I reach for it anyway, grabbing for Jules's arm as I do so, gripping it in such a way that I hope he'll wake quickly, and silently.

I'm listening for more footsteps, trying to figure out where their source is, but all I hear now is quiet. Then the starlight glints off something metallic, and I'm moving before I can talk myself out of it. I draw the gun, yanking it free of the folds of our sleeping bag, and swing it toward the glint.

Instantly a light beams directly into my face. "Drop your weapon!" demands a voice, harsh and slightly muffled by a breather mask buckled in place.

"You drop yours!" I shout back, hoping my hands aren't shaking visibly.

The light shifts to fix on Jules, and for a moment, blinking with afterimages, I can make out three, four . . . maybe as many as six figures, black clad like the patrol that killed Liz, spread throughout our camp. No badges that I can see, but that only supports Javier's theory that these are special forces, some kind of secret elite military. Each soldier holds a laser-sighted rifle—I can see the little red dots swing here and there until we're all in their sights. I'm the only one with a weapon drawn.

The guy with his gun on me gives a little laugh, breathy behind the mask. "Next time, take the safety off, kid."

I glance at the gun, but I know before I even see it that he's right. My thoughts are spinning. Static crackles again, and this time the guy nearest us replies. "Four hostiles. Armed, not dangerous. Orders?"

I can't hear what order he's given, only the crackle of a voice in his ear. But the guy shifts his weight, then sighs. "Sorry, kid."

For a heartbeat all I can think of is the flash of a gun going off, the sound it'll make, whether I'll even hear it before I'm dead. Then I'm throwing my gun into the snow and lifting my hands. "He's Jules Addison!" I gasp, voice hoarse with fear.

The guy pauses. He probably expected at least a little begging for our lives, but probably not that. "What?"

"Jules Addison." I can feel Jules at my side, tense—but silent. I used his name to keep us alive once before, and I nearly lost Jules because of it. This time, he waits. This time, he's trusting me. "This is Elliott Addison's son. There's nothing he doesn't know about the Undying. Tell me he won't be useful to you guys down there. Alive."

The guy's light swings over toward Jules's face once more, letting me see for a few precious seconds. "Huh," is all the guy says, inspecting Jules as he blinks in the brilliant light attached to the guy's helmet. Then the light's swinging back toward me, and the last thing I see is the big black shadow of the butt of his gun slamming down toward my face.

18

JULES

THE TENT WHERE WE'RE BEING HELD IS A THIN PREFAB THING THAT DOES little to block out the cold. With my hands bound behind me, I can't move enough to keep warm. I can't tell whether my fingertips are numb from cold or because the plastic zip ties they've used have cut off my circulation. Hansen and Javier are nowhere to be seen—the last glimpse I got of either of them was of Hansen being dragged off into the dark.

Mia, still unconscious, is slumped on the ground next to me. The best I can do to check on her is to scoot across the tarpaulin floor to be closer to her, to see the steady, minute rise and fall of her chest that tells me she's alive.

They've set up floodlights outside, and without any light in here, it throws every movement of the camp beyond our tent into a nightmarish shadow play against the canvas walls. The only steady shape is the outline of the guard at the tent's entrance. They haven't gagged us, but I don't call out. Mia's quick thinking clearly spared our lives—the guards took extra care not to harm me—but I don't want to attract more attention to myself than necessary.

Maybe they'll forget we're here.

Unlikely.

Mia . . . wake up.

She's the one with the silver tongue. I may be able to puzzle our way out of an eons-old alien temple, but she's the one who can bluff her way out of captivity. *Mia. Mia. Wake up, please wake up.*

A second shape joins the guard outside. I catch a brief murmur of conversation, and then the flap's lifting to admit the new arrival.

The floodlights outside blind me, and I jerk my face away, blinking tears. When I look back, the newcomer's bent over a crate, back to me, turning on a lantern. With a stomach-lurching jolt I recognize the long black coat I saw earlier—this is the person who shot Liz.

Then the figure turns around, and everything goes still. I know this face.

Her face.

A long, thin face with an aquiline nose, thick brows to accentuate her sharp eyes, lips that speak of competence and certainty without uttering a word. Her hair is brown, not the blond I remember, though the sharp bangs framing her face are still the same. In her military uniform I wouldn't know her but for the way she looks at me, appraising, gauging, needy . . . except now I see it isn't need. It's a chilling mix of greed and triumph and drive.

"Ch-Charlotte?" I croak, too stunned to do anything other than stare at the Global Energy employee who recruited me. The last time I saw her was over coffee at a tiny café in London. To see her here is like seeing a thoroughbred racehorse in a police station waiting room—so jarring I can't begin to draw the line of connection between them.

"Mr. Addison." Her voice would almost be warm, but for the remoteness of her gaze. I remember our conversation so clearly— she was as passionate as me, dedicated to using her corporate reach to back my trip. Prepared to sell the idea to her bosses however she needed to. She was committed, one of us. All that's gone now. She's brisk, efficient, and calm. "You are every bit the treasure we thought you'd be."

I'm staring at her, unable to stop looking between her face and her uniform, trying to connect them in my mind. These soldiers wear no symbol or badges, but then, a black-ops force wouldn't. And the only group left on Earth with the resources to be here in such numbers and with such precision and skill is the IA.

But Charlotte isn't in the International Alliance, my mind protests again. She's as disgusted by their politics as I am. She believes in my father. She's like me . . . she wants to save the world. . . .

The dark brows lift. "Did they give you a concussion? I specifi-cally told them not to harm you."

I swallow hard. "They didn't." A pause, my mouth open, and she waits expectantly. "How . . . What are you . . ."

". . . doing here?" she finishes, looking almost amused. *Almost amused.* She doesn't answer the question, though, waiting for me to figure it out instead.

"You're not with Global Energy Solutions," I say slowly, my exhausted, numb mind trying to catch up.

"Global Energy Solutions doesn't exist." She moves away from the lantern, letting more of its light illuminate the interior of the tent. "I'll be honest, Jules, I didn't think you existed anymore either. We lost our lock on your tracker once you went too deep inside the temple, and there was no report you'd come out again."

"Tracker?" I repeat, echoing her like an idiot.

"You were supposed to *think* you were unobserved," she says with exaggerated patience. "Not *be* unobserved. There was a tracker on the breather we supplied you with. When we found your breather on the mercs we sent to tail you, and their leader refused to say where you were, I assumed she was covering for having killed you."

"Liz?" I'm trying desperately to put it all together, blinking up at her. *Yes, Liz had my breather. With this tracker on it, apparently. And she wouldn't have told them where I was. She'd sent Javier to find me, so she could trade me.*

"Yes, Liz—keep up, Mr. Addison." Charlotte rolls her eyes. "I thought you were the brains of the operation." She nods down at Mia's unconscious form. "Perhaps we shouldn't have hit your girl-friend so hard on the head."

"My—" All my confusion condenses, and when it solidifies in my gut the knot is full of fury and fire. "What the hell is going on? Who are you, and why—" Why *everything*, my mind wants to demand.

Charlotte's lips quirk, and she slips a hand into a narrow slit at the hip of her long black coat. Then there's a click, and a blade pops out from her hand as she advances toward me. My body jerks automatically, straining against bonds I already know I can't break even as my eyes hunt for Mia, hoping against hope that her own eyes will open and meet mine, that she'll have a way out—or that I'll at least see her look at me one more time.

But Charlotte snorts. "Calm down, you big baby. I didn't bring you all this way to kill you."

I'm still tense, my muscles screaming at me to run, when she leans down over my shoulder and grasps the bonds behind my back. She smells of shuttle fuel and resin, acrid and chemical and nothing human at all. After days curled up with Mia, growing used to the scent of her, even sweaty and dirty and "gross," as she'd say, Charlotte smells sterile.

I must smell like a sewer to her.

Then there's a pressure on the plastic zip ties that makes them dig all the more sharply into my wrists, making me bite my lip. And then my arms are falling to the sides, the pressure gone, my hands dangling like lead weights.

Charlotte steps back, folding her knife back up and stowing it once more. "We don't really have time to waste on explanations, Mr. Addison. Nothing has changed, except for the resources at your disposal. We still want what you want: to uncover the technological abilities of the Undying."

"To *use* them, you mean." She's IA. She's part of the group that threw my father in jail because he wouldn't guide them through the temples. She has *no* idea what we're dealing with. *She doesn't know about the warnings left in the spirals leading to this place.*

I bite my tongue on that particular piece of information. Liz might've died because of it, but she had the right idea not telling Charlotte everything she knew. The IA never believed my father and his decades of expertise—there's not a chance in a thousand Charlotte will pay any attention if I tell her to hold back from exploring the ship. She'll think it's a delaying tactic, or else an all-out lie, and she'll end up watching me all the more closely to make sure I'm not sabotaging their mission. The only weapon I have is knowledge—if there's a chance I can use what I know to stop them, or to get Mia and me out of this mess, I've got to hold on to it.

"You want to exploit the technology, whatever it is," I say. "Whatever the danger."

"You want to know, don't you?" Charlotte raises one eyebrow. "Whether your father was right. Whether your lives can go back to what they were. This is your chance to find out. The answers are in that ship, Mr. Addison, if you can find a way inside."

"Hang on." My mind's catching up, slowly, too slowly, like thinking through treacle. Looking for a way out. I push myself to speak again, stalling for time with indignation. "You lie to me, you track me here, you tie up my friends, and now you want me to *help* you?"

Charlotte's lips purse, and she shrugs. "We could always just blast our way in, if you prefer."

Some part of the scholar is still in my brain, because even though I know the most important thing we can do here is find out what the Undying knew about us—*how* they knew about us and what we would become, why they deceived us—her words make my heart shrivel. The idea of blowing up part of this astonishing artifact still carries with it a visceral, tangible pain. But fear reasserts itself and I swallow. "You want me to open the ship for you. What then?"

"Not really your concern, is it?"

"I mean—what about me? What about M—my friends? Somehow I doubt you'll just let us sign a nondisclosure and walk off into the sunset."

I'm thinking of Mia, mostly, but a part of my brain—not one I'm enormously proud of—is still aware that Hansen's a pilot. That Javier can fight. That the two of them could be a way out of here, if I keep them alive.

Charlotte smiles. My heart shrinks just a little more. "Believe whatever you like, Mr. Addison. But a choice between certain death now and possible death later isn't a difficult choice at all. I'm sure we'll come to an arrangement."

My lips press together. I feel the rage building in me, some distant relation to the anger I felt when I thought Mia had betrayed me to join Liz's group; related the way a forest fire is related to a scented candle.

And suddenly my whirling thoughts coalesce, and my father's voice, his face, is all my mind knows. Every warning of his is ringing in my ears. I can see the refracted rainbows back in the temple, the words in a hundred languages engraved, impossibly, into fifty-thousand-year-old walls.

My every exhausted sense is screaming that this place, this planet, is *dangerous*. And after everything the IA has done to me, to us, they want me to open up the ship for them. Open the Nautilus, unleash the danger every hidden symbol warned about.

My mouth is opening to tell this woman to go jump off a cliff, that she can kill me if she wants, that the day I open up that ship for her is the day they discover mind control—

—then Mia stirs at my side, with a whispering groan of pain and confusion that pops my fury like a pin held to an overfilled balloon. I lean over, reaching out to lay my hand on her arm and give it a squeeze. And I find that hand isn't numb after all, that I can feel the warmth of her against my palm, the brush of her rib cage as she takes a deeper breath.

"Jules," she mumbles, before her eyes even open, recognizing my touch. "The hell . . . think I'm gonna hurl."

She's got a concussion, of that I'm certain. I'm no doctor, but she was out for the better part of an hour, and the way she's trying to sit up and can't make her limbs work is all too familiar. People scoff at water polo, but they've never seen a guy take a blow to the temple and finish the point streaming blood, then desperately make for the edge of the pool so he can puke on the concrete.

"Here, let me," I whisper, forgetting Charlotte but remembering my hands are free. I slide my arm under Mia's shoulders and help her sit up. They zip-tied her too, and her fingers look unnaturally pink and puffy. She leans against me for support.

"Jules, what's going . . ." But her dazed, unfocused eyes have wandered away from my face. "Wait," she says, struggling to form the words. "Am I halluci—halloge—hillocillat . . . Shit, am I see-ing things?"

I follow her gaze, which is fixed on Charlotte. The woman's standing right there, arms folded loosely, watching us with what looks like amusement. Like someone's aunt, watching the antics of her little niece and nephew with bemused patience. If that aunt had a knife, was dressed in black-ops military garb, and had a fleet of dozens of shuttles at her command.

"It's okay," I murmur, keeping my voice low but not really car-ing if Charlotte hears. "I'm going to handle this."

"But . . ." Mia's still staring, and after a few seconds of struggle, she blurts, "*Mink?*"

Now I *know* she's concussed. And hillocillating. "Mia," I say gen-tly, trying to encourage her to look back at me. "This is Charlotte. She's the one who recruited me, the one whose company backed my trip here."

Except, of course, they didn't. Because Global Energy Solutions doesn't exist. But I can't explain that to myself yet, much less the concussed, half-conscious girl leaning against my shoulder.

"No," Mia says, blinking hard. "No, that's Mink. My backer. She hired me. Hired Liz and them. How is she . . . Are we still at the south pole?"

But I'm staring at Charlotte again. She doesn't look confused. She doesn't look surprised. She doesn't look like anything—except, perhaps, that patient aunt, waiting while her charges work torturously through a primary lesson, like one of those cardboard books that teach small children how to read. *See Jane,* my mind supplies, absurd and out of control.

"Mink . . . Mink is Charlotte?" My mind's spinning so much I wonder if somehow Mia's concussion could be contagious.

See Jane play.

"We were hired by the same person?" Mia's leaning harder against me, and somehow I know she wants to take my hand but can't. I wrap an arm around her instead.

Charlotte—or whoever she is—sighs. "When we were recruiting Mr. Addison here, he kept on asking whether it was really possible to make it to Gaia in secret with the IA monitoring travel through the portal."

Mia leans in against me. "So you gave him proof," she says quietly.

See Jane jump.

"We recruited a few scavengers to head for the planet," Charlotte says. "Pointed out that it was his own father's breakdown on live television that leaked all the info a scavenger would need, and that the record was already being contaminated. We took care to pick out those who had nobody of consequence to report them missing, back home."

Mia goes stiff beside me, and all the breath leaves my body, as if I've been punched in the gut. Nobody was ever coming to pick

Mia up. And Mia didn't win her chance to come here because of her skill, as she thought.

Charlotte—Mink—chose Mia because she was disposable. Expendable.

The woman's eyebrows lift. "Think about it this way, Amelia. Everybody else we recruited is out there right now, waiting for a pick-up that will never come. In your case, perhaps Mr. Addison will negotiate your way off the planet before all this is done. And you'll be able to go back to . . . Evelyn, right? The precious sister."

In this moment I don't have to look at Mia's face to know what she's thinking—it's what I'm thinking. We haven't crossed a universe, traversed an alien planet, crawled through an ancient temple, and thrown ourselves into an unknown portal that could have obliterated us just to let someone like *this* pull us apart.

Charlotte unfolds her arms and steps toward the tent flap, making no move to untie Mia and instead gesturing at me. "Come with me, Mr. Addison." Her voice is polite and remote and, right now, more terrifying than a dozen armed and faceless soldiers. "It's time to go to work."

See Jane run.

"I need her," I blurt, not moving from Mia's side. "She knows the glyphs as well as I do now. She knows their maths. I—I need her." A deep breath. "And I need proof of life for the others, if you want me to do anything for you." *My pilot and my soldier. My escape.*

Charlotte—Mink—Aunt Jane Doe—narrows her eyes a fraction and looks from my face to Mia's, lingering, considering. She heard which one of the three I named first. She heard the desperation in my voice.

Her lips move, just the tiniest bit. It looks like she's smiling. "Very well."

Run, Jane. Run.

19

AMELIA

My head is spinning, aching. The ground feels uneven, not just because of the crunch of old snow beneath my boots, but because it keeps tilting crazily, my vision and inner ears fighting a doomed battle whose first casualty is my stomach. I don't know if it'd be more humiliating or satisfying to turn and hurl all over Mink's sleek uniform.

I stay close to Jules, and every now and then he puts a hand out to steady me. They still haven't untied me, but even if I could use my hands for balance, I think I'd choose holding on to Jules instead. I'm not sure it was smart of him to demand I go with him—I'm not sure it was wise to let them know there's any connection between us at all besides coincidence.

I'm not sure it was the best idea. But god, I'm so glad he did it I could weep.

The ship looms above us, even from a distance. It's more massive than I'd realized, with only the IA shuttles to use as reference. It could house hundreds—thousands of people. Or Undying. Or . . .

I don't even know anymore. It's sized for us the same way the temple was. The fifty-thousand-year-old temple that had English engraved on it.

I've never been what anyone could call honest—I dropped out of school illegally, I worked jobs that paid under the table, I outright stole once I made it to Chicago. But the depth, the complexity, of the tangle of deceit binding us to Gaia makes my body start to shake. The Undying, posing as a race who couldn't have known about humanity, creating an elaborate set-up to get us to this spot—they knew us well, to know that a race for treasure would make us ignore our instincts, ignore our better natures, ignore any warnings just to get to it first and claim it for our own.

Mink—or Charlotte, or whoever she is—letting me believe I was chosen to go to Gaia because of my skills, my quick thinking, my drive. The gut-wrenching blow of learning I was sent simply because the only person who'd notice I'd disappeared was a child in illegal bondage with no means of getting me back. *God, Evie, I'm sorry.*

Even Jules. Jules, who lied to get me to help him. Jules, who told me the spiral-shaped temple being ignored by the other scavvers would contain wealth beyond my wildest dreams. Jules, who let me follow him, knowing that it meant I was abandoning my sister.

My eyes burn, and for a moment I want to tear myself away from Jules's supportive arm—I want to run, anywhere, into the snow and ice, not caring if the soldiers shoot me in the back.

Jules, who told me the truth as soon as he realized his lie was putting my life in danger. Jules, who gave up the chance to find his answers so that I wouldn't jump through that portal alone. Jules, who's lying even now to keep me alive, keep me safe, knowing that if he's found out he'll likely be killed.

I draw a quaking breath and blink back my tears, pressing my body close against Jules at my side. I feel his eyes on me, just for a second.

This, at least, is true.

The suns are just breaching the horizon, somewhere beyond the mountains. Their light paints a distant streak of clouds peach, and for a moment it's so much like being home—despite the alien ship, despite the zip ties cutting into my wrists, despite the frigid air burning the insides of my nose and steaming my breath—I want to stop and stare at it, gaze at this sight one last time. In case it *is* the last time.

And then we're in the shadow of the ship, and it's twilight once more.

"There's a door." After so long with only the background noises of the base being set up all around the ship, Mink's voice sounds like the crack of a whip. "We've done a sonar sweep, but without knowing how stable the ship is, we're hesitant to use a larger charge. We do know there's a chamber beyond the door—most likely some form of airlock."

"Great," replies Jules, voice flat. A few days ago he'd have given his left arm to get even the tiniest scrap of information on a find like this. It's how much his priorities have changed, more than the tone in his voice, that leaves me shaken. "I don't need to know any of this to translate your glyphs."

Mink lets out a snort that puffs into the cold, then streams away behind us as we keep trudging toward the ship. "You think it's just about translation? You and your dad don't have that skill cornered anymore, Mr. Addison. Hell, I can translate them myself reasonably accurately, given enough time. But whatever this locking mechanism is, there's more to it than the glyphs. Which is where you come in." I catch, out of the corner of my eye, her head turning a little to look at me. "Both of you."

"Fine." Jules reaches out to take my arm, almost absently tugging me upright—I hadn't noticed I'd begun to tilt. "But I want to see a vid on someone's phone of Javier and Hansen saying they're alive and not being mistreated. I want proof of life, if you want us to keep working."

Mink's laugh is soft, and if I didn't know better, I'd think she was genuinely touched by his concern for them. "Whatever you wish," she says, spreading her hands in an expansive gesture.

"In that case, I need my pack. Our packs." Jules's fingers tighten around my arm a little. I'm trying to think, remember what's still in there after Liz's gang got through ransacking them.

"Tell me what you need from your pack and I'll have it brought to you," Mink counters, cutting my ties so I can climb. With a squeak of her boots on the icy slush, she comes to a halt at the base of some scaffolding. When I look up, I see only the ship, rising like a wall before us. Despite the dark I find myself squinting, trying to focus. The hastily erected prefab scaffolding blocks end at a sleek round panel—the door, I'm guessing.

It isn't that high off the ground, though my dizziness makes it seem like a climb twice as treacherous as the pit we scaled in the temple. Jules reaches the top first and then reaches down to grab my hand and pull me up after him. He hesitates there, my hand in his, as though he'd like to pull me in against him. I wish we could stop, breathe, figure out what it means that the woman who hired him and the one who hired me are the same person, figure out what the languages we saw in the temple meant, what it means that this ship is here at all, how it connects to the Nautilus warnings.

I wish we could be alone again. But Mink—Charlotte—whoever she is—is standing at the base of the scaffold, watching us.

So when Jules tightens his hand around mine, I shake my head, ignoring the way my concussion makes my vision dance in response. *Not here. Not when it's ammunition for them. Don't show them your cards.*

Jules understands. He lets go of my hand with a shaky breath out and turns his attention to Mink, listing what we need from our packs—he tries for as many of our possessions as he can. I lean my head against the pole beside me while they fetch our gear, along with a video of a wary Javier and Hansen telling the camera they're still alive.

And then, Jules and I both look up at the doorway.

It's a large round thing with glyphs circling it and minute cracks radiating outward from its center. For half a second I wonder if the IA actually did try to blast their way in, when I realize they're not cracks—they're seams. The door's meant to iris outward, like the door we short-circuited in the temple with my phone.

As one, Jules and I both glance down and to the right—and there it is. A small, barely noticeable indentation at chest level, gleaming with crystalline circuitry.

I have to fight the insane urge to laugh, hysteria trying to bubble up inside me. All this buildup—all the drama of Mink's strong-arming, all the posturing and the threats, spoken and unspoken—and it's not even a puzzle. It's a simple lock, one we've known how to pick since before we even discovered the ship.

It makes perfect sense—if the Undying wanted to be sure that whoever found this ship was "worthy" of their prize, then they'd use a puzzle said worthy ones had already solved when we were approaching the portal through their temple, passing their tests.

I draw breath, but Jules lifts a hand abruptly, gesturing above us. I pause.

"There are glyphs here," he says, conversational, gesturing to the glyphs circling the doorway. Mink's close enough that she'll hear every word, and we can't risk whispering to each other. "I'll need to translate them, and compare them against the notes I have from the carvings in the temple."

"Right." My poor brain is struggling to keep up, but whatever he's doing, I'm in. "I'll get your journal." It's among the things he asked for, to help with deciphering the way through the door. I crouch down to retrieve it from the bag, and find my multi-tool in there as well. He must have put it on the list he gave them while I was zoned out. No need for Mink to find out about the modifications I made to it—she'd never have handed it over if she'd known how truly useful it is. I settle it in my hand for a moment, the grip blessedly familiar, but when I look down, Mink's staring straight at me. I can't slide it into my pocket while she's watching, so I reluctantly leave it where it is.

"Okay." Jules takes a long breath, a dramatically weary sigh. *Easy there, Macbeth, we're not onstage.* "So this one here . . ."

He's dictating slowly, translating them one by one, taking his sweet time and double-checking what I'm writing. Jules, who I've seen read the Undying script like it's English, like he grew up reading it—which, come to think of it, he did. Then my struggling brain catches up.

He's stalling for time.

Mink—or Charlotte, or whoever the hell she is—doesn't know how easily he can read the glyphs, and she doesn't know we already have the answer to opening this door. But the moment we do open it, Jules and I become just that much less important, less useful.

Less worth carrying.

Fighting the urge to look down and see if Mink's watching, I flip back to some of his earlier translations, where hopefully they won't look if they decide to double-check his work here.

We can't stall forever, I write, trying to stop my hand shaking through sheer willpower.

Jules is still "translating," droning on in a voice that makes me want to tear my hair out—good lord, he must have had some boring-ass teachers in his life, to learn that. He glances down. "Yes, good, that looks right. This next one . . ."

Way too many of them to fight. I'm cramming the words in the margins of a sketch of the Nautilus, some unreadable glyphs copied down next to it. *And we can't run—even if we get away we'll die with no food/water/O_2.*

Jules nods, looking down at the page, his eyes grim. But there's hope there too. We're still together, and right now, in this moment, they *need* Jules. Which gives us power. However tiny. I feel that hope kindle a spark somewhere inside me, too.

"This grouping of glyphs here has something to do with an

exchange, I think. A trade, a deal? Of course, that's if you trust the glyphs . . . There were plenty fake messages in that temple that were just there to trick us."

None of the glyphed instructions in the temple were false—we survived their traps. And though we don't know which faction to trust, the Undying who made the broadcast to get us here, or the Undying who left the Fibonacci spirals to warn us away, Jules isn't talking about the Undying right now, not really.

Definitely not, I write, flipping a page and turning the journal sideways so I can write along the border of a sketch of one of the puzzles. *I wouldn't trust these ppl as far as I could throw this ship.*

Jules snorts, and turns it into a cough, and when I look down, Mink's frowning up at us.

"Can we get some water?" I call down. It's a long shot, and I'm not surprised when instead of leaving her post at the foot of the scaffold, she just talks into a communications unit tucked into her collar.

"Hmm." Jules scrubs his hand over his face, resolutely keeping his eyes on the glyphs. I'm pretty sure they say something like *Please use caution when opening the doors,* but he's not budging. "This one's new, I'm stuck."

I make a show of looking up, staring in the direction he's staring, though my mind's racing, as I'm sure his is too. There has to be a way out of this. There's always a way out. But sitting on a rickety scaffold at the south pole of a planet on the opposite side of the universe from home, surrounded by some of the best-trained soldiers in the world, for once I'm drawing a complete blank.

I've accidentally kept the pen pressed to the journal page, and there's a blot of ink there when I finally twitch my hand away. I turn the page.

Jules, I write, letting the pen dwell on the curves and lines of the letters. Letting my hand memorize the pattern of his name, letting my eyes drink it in. *I'm scared.*

When I look up, his eyes are on mine and not the journal, and he swallows hard, the hand resting against the side of the ship curling until it's a fist. He nods, wordless, and his eyes say, *Me too.*

I turn another page and find a sketch there, but it's not of a series of glyphs, or an architectural anomaly, or a diagram mapping the floor tiles. It's me.

The face is stylized, not quite realistic, but precise and instantly recognizable. I'm looking down, in profile, my hair falling forward, and I look sad—so sad I almost feel it for real. The pen strokes emphasize and darken certain parts of my face: the angularity of my jaw, like I'm clenching it, determined; my eyes, large, reflecting the light he must have drawn this by; the freckles on my cheek, in a pattern I didn't know I recognized from the mirror until now, seeing it here, captured in perfect detail. And my lips—his pen lingered there. He turned the slight blot of ink into a shadow, smoothed it out, went over them again and again.

The drawing is beautiful. I've never been beautiful before—but I am, here, on this page. In this picture that looks exactly like me.

I look up to find Jules's eyes on the journal, fixed there, not meeting mine. His lips are tight, and I know under any other circumstances this moment would be a violation. I've never tried to sneak a peek at his journal—not least because I'm pretty sure I wouldn't understand half the stuff in there—and that must be why he felt it was safe to draw this . . . this declaration.

I swallow hard, and fight against the tears burning my eyes.

I grip the pen again, and as a drop patters against the page, blurring part of my hair, I write:

me too

There's just enough time to look up again, for him to look at the journal and then at me, a universe in those eyes, a language that doesn't need translating. There's just enough time to remember the moment before I leapt through the portal, when his arms tightened around me, when I forgot where I was and what I was doing and who I was and what I was. There's just enough time for the corner of his mouth, his perfect mouth, to lift.

There's not enough time at all.

The scaffold gives a sudden jerk and I gasp as I reach out for one of the supports. Mink's on her way up, the added weight making the whole thing groan and sway. Without thinking I scrub my sleeve across my eyes and flip pages with my other hand, back to the end of the journal, writing down the few glyphs I have learned over the past few days, the few I can recognize from up there, so it looks like we've done something.

I stop just as she reaches the top. "Water?" I ask, my voice sounding remarkably bright and normal, for feeling like there's a howling gale inside my chest.

Mink's frowning. She unslings a canteen from over her shoulder and tosses it at Jules, then reaches down to pull the journal from my hands. I cast a brief, panicked look at Jules, whose own visible panic is enough to bring me back to myself. I gesture at him to drink—who knows when we'll get water again—and rise up on my knees.

"This is all super weird, Mink," I say, trying to emulate Jules's tone when he's lost in thought, danger forgotten in favor of academic zeal. "We can't make sense of these phrases, they're all—"

"Bullshit." Mink's voice is hard.

"Uh, well—"

"You haven't done anything." She looks up from the journal page, eyes going from my face to Jules's, and back again. "You honestly think, after all of this, that I'm stupid? Ordinarily I'd point out that we've got all the time in the universe, that you can stall as long as you like but there's no cavalry coming and you're going to get pretty cold eventually. But I'm getting impatient. Open the door, Mr. Addison."

Jules swallows his mouthful of water and steels himself. "I'm trying, Charlotte, I just haven't seen—"

"Try *harder.*"

"Look, I'm doing my best!" Jules's voice cracks, despite the water, and my heart gives a little aching ping in response.

Mink watches him for a moment, lips together, eyes thoughtful. Then, before either of us can react, she reaches down and grabs my upper arm and drags me to my feet. She's absurdly strong for someone her size—like her whole body is muscle. I reach out for one of the scaffold supports out of instinct, though even if she shoved me off, it's not high enough that the fall would kill me. Maybe break something, if I landed funny, but probably not. I've got practice falling, I know how to land.

My mind's calculating all of this in a fraction of a second, because in the next second, it all drains away.

Her gun's out, and she's pressing it to my temple.

"Open the door, Mr. Addison."

Jules's face goes ashen. He's staring at me, and his heart's in his eyes, and even if it hadn't been on that page I'd see it now as clearly as the sunrise I didn't want to leave behind, as clearly as the unfamiliar stars overhead the last time he had his arms around me.

Mink smiles, and cocks the gun.

"Open the door."

20

JULES

I'm STUMBLING ALONG IN A FOG. I SHOULD BE FASCINATED, RIVETED, I
should be stopping at every intersection, every doorway, every crack
in the wall—I should be reading every scrap of text I can find. I
should be back in Valencia, discovering wonder all over again.

I'm walking through the corridor of an alien ship, tens of thousands of years old. I'm seeing something no human has ever seen
before, walking where no human has ever stepped. At the wildest
heights of fancy as a child I never dreamed of this.

Open the door, Mr. Addison.

I should be lost in the stories this place is waiting to tell me.
Instead I'm just lost.

I—I need a phone.

In theory, Charlotte's got me out in front so that if there are
traps waiting for us here like there were in the temples, I'll either
see them—or get hit by them first. I'm holding the bag containing my journal in front of me like a shield, but somehow I know
there aren't any traps. This is what the broadcast wanted us to

find—or else, this ship is what its hidden message told us to fear. Me, Charlotte, and a half dozen of her operatives, helmeted and faceless, their torch beams crisscrossing the air.

Air that's been still since the last Undying stepped off this ship and closed its doors. Until I opened them.

Just trust me—it's a lock, that's all—don't shoot her. Yes, okay? I was stalling. We're bloody well scared, what else would we be? But I'll open it. A phone—the conductivity—it's a—a—a key. Please, I . . . I'm telling the truth.

The door opened on an octagonal room that could have been an airlock—beyond it, corridors branched out in a fan. I chose one at random. And now we're walking. Exploring. Doing what I've longed to do since I was a child, and my father first told me tales of ancient beings who left us stories to solve and lessons to learn.

And I'm at gunpoint, and I'm alone.

Wait—wait! I did what you said! What are you doing with her? I need her with me, she's my maths . . . I did as you asked. I did . . .

The corridors all look alike, crystalline streaks running through the metallic stone like frozen rivers, like the whole ship is made of ice, like it might melt once the suns rise a little higher in the sky. Outside I can hear charges detonating, as the IA soldiers clear the ice away from the hull.

A part of my brain is firing off questions, a hundred a minute. For what purpose did the Undying bring us here, to this ship? Why is this ship so important? What did they intend us to do with it? And the heaviest question of all of them: who left the Nautilus warnings, and what danger were we meant to escape?

What were their intentions, these aliens who knew how to deceive us so perfectly?

And what were the intentions of the ones who left us the warning about this gift? Were they members of the Undying too? What did they know that I can't guess?

But I can't focus on my endless questions, because there's just one that's living at the forefront of my mind, taking up all available real estate: How do I keep Mia safe? I can still hear Javier's voice ringing in my ears, talking about how disposable we were, after they killed Liz. *They'd need a helluva reason to keep you around*, he said. So I need to show them a helluva reason.

I know I should be trying to memorize the ship's layout. I know I should be doing *something*. Stalling them. Ingratiating myself. Finding weak points among Charlotte's soldiers. Doing what Mia would do. What Mia . . . My ears are ringing, echoing.

My memory won't let it go. The soft click of the hammer releasing as Charlotte slowly lowered the gun and tucked it into her holster again. As my heart started beating again.

I need her.

The last I saw of Mia was a flash of her white face as they shoved me into the ship. I saw her eyes, large and dark in the low light, saw the faded pink in her hair glinting as the sunrise on the other side of the ship bloomed. Saw her open her mouth to call out for me—and then she was gone.

Charlotte's voice echoing in my head. *Don't worry, she'll be alive. Kill her, and we lose our power over you. Hurt her, though . . .* Her face, serene, almost whimsical, as she lifted a shoulder.

I have to focus. I do my job, Mia lives. Right now, that's all I know. Right now, that's all that matters.

21

AMELIA

THE HOURS CREEP BY, AND I'M LEFT CUFFED TO THE SCAFFOLDING BY THE
entrance to the ship. I yank at my bindings a few times, and eventually a soldier just points his gun at my face until I stop. Message received.

I'm so used to the commotion passing me by that I don't notice when one of the uniformed soldiers stops in front of me until he grasps my wrists to untie me from the scaffolding. The motion sends twin jolts of pain up my arms into my shoulders, and I let out a hoarse sound of protest or surprise or exhaustion, I'm not even sure. He ignores it, double-checking that my hands are still tied securely to each other.

The IA soldier says nothing, choosing to give his orders in the form of brute force. He hauls me to my feet by my bound hands, then shoves me through the ship's entrance and down one of the multiple corridors that branch off just inside.

My mind is blank. All those years, dodging the cops and talking my way out of scrapes, and I've got nothing. Any second now

I'm going to see Javier and Hansen, dead, stashed wherever they stash the people they don't need anymore. Any second now I'm going to join them. And I've got nothing.

They lead me in a circuitous route that takes me through the long corridors. I lose all track of where we are, though the hallways are far from featureless, marked by the same strange metallic stone and crystalline circuitry we saw in the temple.

I suppose I ought to be glad that they're leading me into the ship rather than taking me back outside—if they were planning on killing me, surely they'd do it out in the snow, and not where my brains would get splattered all over their precious artifacts.

They bring me to a door not unlike those in the temple, and pry it open with a crowbar and a screech of scraping rock. They cut the ties binding my hands and toss me inside. The door slams closed behind me, the air battering against my ears and making my abused head spin all the more.

"You okay?"

I whirl around at the voice and immediately regret the sudden movement, groaning and trying to feel at the scabbed-over spot where they hit me. My arms are like wet noodles, my hands numb and tingling. I blink and find Javier there, a few steps away. He's got one hand outstretched, like he's ready to catch me. Like I look ready to drop where I stand.

I suck in a deep breath and steel myself, blinking again and scanning the room. Both Javier and Hansen are there, unbound but stripped of their gear, like me. *Not dead*, I think, with a surprising depth of relief, given that a day ago we were running for our lives from these guys. The way our luck's been going, I was pretty sure they'd been shot the minute they were done telling the camera they were alive.

"I'm okay." I pause. "Well, I mean, as okay as I can be."

Our cell is a small, pod-like room as featureless as the snowy plain outside, lit by a simple LED lamp—the one from Javier's gear. The door has a small indentation next to it—not like the one

Jules figured out how to crack, though, even if we did have something conductive. This one's a bit bigger than a hand, but pushing against it does nothing. If it were some summer sci-fi blockbuster the door would go whooshing open at our touch, but apparently the Undying never watched those movies. Or else the batteries are dead.

"Home sweet home," Javier says, as I look around. "Your boy Jules came through here early on, apparently said there was nothing worth seeing in here." His mouth quirks. "Guess they're counting on the fact that it'd be a lot harder to escape from stone walls than canvas ones."

I try to pry at the door's edge, but even after both Javier and Hansen add their strength to mine, the stone doesn't budge. It's impossible to get much purchase on it without something to pry with. What I wouldn't give for my multi-tool right now.

"Well, at least they seem to think your boy is as important as everyone else does." Javier drops down onto the floor, putting his back against the wall. "Pretty sure we'd be dead if they didn't."

"I hope you're right." My suspicious mind can come up with half a dozen reasons they might keep us alive that have nothing to do with Jules—bait for more traps, lab rats to send down unexplored corridors. But my money, if I had any, is on Jules.

Hansen's looking between the two of us, face blank, before he suddenly blurts, "How the hell are you two so freaking calm? I mean, what the hell, guys? We're screwed. We are so goddamn screwed I can't even—"

"Well, what do you want?" I snap. My temper is frayed beyond tatters as it is, and he's not helping by echoing the thoughts I'm not willing to speak aloud. "Us to burst into tears and wail and rend our clothes and beat ourselves to death against the door?"

Hansen scowls at me. At least pissed off is better than panicking. "This is all your fault anyway."

"My fault?" I sputter. "You're the ones who ran us ragged—no one *made* you follow us through that portal!"

"*She* did. Liz made me."

"Well, she's dead!" The words seem to echo despite the confines of the room, spilling into a sudden silence as thick and impenetrable as the stone door entombing us. I'm regretting them already for more than one reason—shouting makes my head throb. I try to take a calming breath. "Look. I'm sorry, I just—"

"She's right." Javier stays on the floor, though he lifts his head to glance between me and Hansen. "Liz is dead. She's gone. We have to assume that Jules is too, as far as we're concerned. Whatever they're using him for, it doesn't involve us. His identity may have kept us alive this far, but it's on us to get out of here on our own."

"I'm not going anywhere without Jules." The words come out automatically, before I even register the thought. I ought to be surprised at the steel in my voice—and Liz's remaining men clearly are—but I remember that drawing, and I remember that little smile when I wrote *me too*, and I'm not surprised at all. I clear my throat. "I'm not leaving him here."

Javier's brows lift, but he doesn't protest. "One step at a time," he says instead. "We're not going anywhere inside this room. But they'll have to open it eventually. There's no food slot or anything—this wasn't built as a prison. They'll have to open it to feed us, take us to the bathroom, that sort of thing. Now, when they brought me and Hansen to this cell, they had six guys on us. But I noticed only one with you."

His eyes are on me, and I glance away at Hansen, who's suddenly watching me with renewed interest.

"Yeah, but one guy with an automatic rifle and body armor and a crapload of training." I take a step back. "I climb, I sneak, I scramble . . . I don't fight. Besides, I'm like half their size. I wouldn't stand a chance. You'd do better against six dudes."

Javier grins, shaking his head. "You're quick, and that counts for a lot more than size or strength. I noticed you had a gun on them before they had one on you, when they took us at camp."

"Yeah, with the stupid safety on," I mutter.

"Well, I doubt these guys leave their safeties on."

"Is that supposed to be a comfort to me?"

Javier gets slowly to his feet. "You're right that these guys are well trained. But I don't think their training really involved what to do with prisoners. One of the ones guarding me actually had his gun pressed against my back while we were walking—a dumb mistake. I can show you what to do, how to get the jump on them."

"Yeah, and send me home sporting some lovely new piercings in the shape of bullet holes."

"Me and Hansen, we're pros, clearly trained. They watch us too carefully, put too many guys on us. But you . . . you're small, you're quick, and most importantly, they're underestimating you just as much as Liz did."

I can feel my stomach shriveling. "Wait, you're *serious*? You want me to overpower a fully armed, fully trained guard twice my size without so much as a freaking spoon for a weapon?"

Javier beckons to Hansen, who groans as though he knows what's coming. "Watch me," Javier says. "And pretend Hansen here's your guard."

• • •

"I'm *out*." Hansen's on the floor, and rolls over until he's facedown on the stone. "Somebody else be the guard for a while."

Javier ignores him, grinning at me. "Not bad. You're getting faster."

I'm gazing down at Hansen, but more because I don't want to look at Javier, and the hope and desperation there in his face. He's so certain I'm our best chance of getting out of here. I wish I could feel so sure. "Yeah, but we're pretending his arm's a gun. Arms don't shoot very fast. Pretty sure a real gun's gonna go off before I'm out of the way."

Javier shrugs. "Maybe."

I stare at him. "Okay, dude, you've got to get better at lying."

"There's no point in lying." He's somber now, grin fading away.

"But I also wouldn't be suggesting this if I didn't think it stood a good chance of working. If one of us tries something and fails, it'll be the only excuse they need to shoot the rest of us to avoid any more trouble. We're in this together now." His eyes soften a bit, and I remember what he let slip before we were captured—he's got kids of his own, somewhere back on Earth. "You can do this."

We've been through the movements so many times it's like instant replay in my mind. With the guard close enough for the barrel of his gun to press into my back, I can twist, sending the gun to the right as I dodge left, which throws the guard off-balance and lets me charge my shoulder into his rib cage and knock him down. Then I can get my foot on the gun barrel, pressing it down against the guard with all my weight so he can't possibly lift it up to aim it at me again.

But all of that—that's just step one.

We let Hansen have a rest so he can sit at the far edge of the room and nurse his bruises and glare at me. My heart's pounding from the exercise, and from the adrenaline. I lean back against the wall, letting it take my weight.

"You can do it," Javier repeats quietly. "The only question is . . . will you?"

I swallow, lifting my head from the stone wall behind me so I can look at him. "What?"

"It's one thing to hold a gun, even aim it at someone. It's something else to pull the trigger. Especially when you're standing so close."

Each one of our practice sessions with Hansen has ended with my foot on his arm, pressing his outstretched finger against his throat, and Javier saying, "Bang! Okay, good job. Now, next time . . ."

But it won't be Javier saying *Bang*. It won't be someone's arm, and it won't be Hansen getting back up afterward, groaning about his bruises and rubbing his chest. It won't be me grinning and breathing hard and high-fiving my coach.

It'll be an ear-shattering explosion, and a jolt that makes my leg go numb, and the top of a guy's skull splattered against the floor. It'll be me killing someone.

I haven't stopped feeling nauseous since I woke up, since I saw Mink standing in front of us in an IA black-ops uniform, but I'm not so sure it's the concussion anymore. I shut my eyes, hoping that it'll cut the dizziness, but instead it leaves me feeling like I'm in a dense fog that only grows thicker with every passing moment.

Before I can answer, before I even know what the answer is, a sound outside makes all three of our heads snap toward the exit. Footsteps, the clang of metal on metal, then the faint creak of a crowbar settling into the seam of the door. I tear my eyes away to find Javier looking at me.

I exhale, long and slow. "I guess we'll find out," I whisper, and turn toward the door.

22

JULES

I'VE BEEN CLIMBING STAIRS FOR HOURS. THE INSIDE OF THIS PLACE IS A maze the size of our biggest skyscrapers back home, and without any power for transport between levels, I'm reduced to climbing up and down what I assume are emergency stairways. I have two guards trailing after me, and we're not the only team exploring. We cross paths with half a dozen other groups, the corridors echoing with booted footsteps and the occasional burst of static from comms radios.

Twice I catch a glimpse of Charlotte, heading up one of the exploratory teams, and her gaze swings over toward me, eyes narrowed, speculative. This must be the first time she's personally entered an Undying structure. Does she find it as unnerving as we did, our first day in the temple, when Mia asked me why it seemed so like our own ruins? And what would she think if she knew what we'd seen before we jumped through the portal? The languages of Earth's past and present. The Nautilus warnings.

Pergite si audetis.

Onward, if you dare. But onward to what?

I force my thoughts back to the hallway ahead of me. I don't know how much time I have to come up with something she deems useful before she starts making good on her threats against Mia.

I'm following my instincts, absorbing what I can from the glyphs—though there are dozens I've never seen before. It's like one giant puzzle to solve, and it turns out I was training for it by surviving the temple.

My legs are groaning and protesting as I force myself up yet another staircase, trying not to think about the descent that's yet to come. I pause on the landing to brace my hands on my knees, casting a resentful look at the closed doors of what I'm pretty sure is a powerless elevator, then straighten to force myself onward.

"Where are we going?" The soldier behind me is as sick of climbing as I am.

"That way," I say, trying to make my tone confident, to make up for the lack of specificity. I don't want him reporting back that I seem unsure.

"And what's that way?" the other asks, taking a swallow from her canteen, then handing it across to the first guy, who follows suit, and then hands it to me.

"Maybe the ship's bridge, or something like a control room," I say. "Maybe something else to do with the ship's hierarchy. It's important, that's all I can tell you."

I trace a line of silvery glyphs. They indicate power and control, and the concept of change, which I speculate might mean something to do with making adjustments, perhaps to the engines or the power source of the ship. That power source has to be what the IA's after—they want the tech that could power a ship this big, and damn the lessons that could be learned by exploring it properly.

They couldn't create a future for humanity with their mission to Alpha Centauri. Now they're hoping this ship, and the tech it holds, will be Earth's salvation. That it will do for the world what the first power cell did for Los Angeles.

The IA wants this to be the treasure the Undying promised us in their broadcast. They need it to be the answer. But the words in that broadcast echo over and over in my mind, sounding so changed now that I know what I know: *Unlocking the door may lead to salvation or doom . . .*

Whatever the Undying's ultimate plan, at least one of them took great risk in trying to warn the target of their deceptions. To warn us. And I'm not about to ignore that warning—not anymore.

The corridor leads to a small room, and the beam of my head torch swings across its interior. On the far side is what I think must be a control panel, backed by a reflective wall. My escort checks there's no other way out of the room, and then settles down in the hallway outside to wait. The controls sit at about waist height, a long bench covered in carved grooves and depressions. Perhaps if it were powered, you could drag your fingertips along it like a sensor pad. I already know from the temple that this strange, stone-like material can sense changes in pressure.

I glance at my reflection in the reflective wall—my curls are wilder than usual, I look wrecked—then realize a moment later I can see *through* the wall. It's a window, but the dark and my head torch transformed it into a mirror. I risk a quick glance over my shoulder to check I'm unobserved—one of the guards has vanished, but the other is in the doorway, murmuring into his radio. I lean in to press the torch against the glass, blinking to focus on what's on the other side.

It's a dull gray wall a couple of meters away from the glass, gleaming with circuitry that crawls over every square centimeter of it. It's Undying tech. I tilt my head up, then down, studying it by torchlight. It goes as far as I can see in either direction. *Mehercule.*

The solar cell that revolutionized the Los Angeles water purification plant was about the size of my head. As best I can tell, this goes hundreds of meters up and down, and in both directions. This could power a *continent*.

"Anything in there?" A voice rings out from the hall, and I snap back from the glass, startled, fumbling for words.

"I, uh, I don't think so. Nothing of interest."

"You sure about that?"

That voice cuts through the thrill of discovery and I turn, going cold. Charlotte's standing there, the guard that had been on his radio a few paces behind her.

Perfututi. I'm an idiot—it doesn't take a genius to see that this room is important. I should've been listening to my guard, keeping track of what he was saying. He was calling Charlotte. Telling her I'd found something.

"I—" My mind's blank. I keep seeing Charlotte on the scaffolding with her gun to Mia's temple. I can't lie. I *have* to lie. Give them what they want and eventually I stop being useful—eventually their reason for keeping Mia alive vanishes. But give them nothing, and I'm already of no use.

Charlotte's expression is unreadable, not flinching even when I look over at her. Her pupils dilate in the beam of my torch, but she doesn't move. "Yes?"

"See for yourself," I say finally, feeling like the centuries-old chill of the ship around me has settled into my bones. "I think this is what you've been looking for."

She moves into the room, keeping her distance from me, one hand at her side—resting on her weapon, I've no doubt. I back up, making it clear I have no intention of trying to get a jump on her. She peers at the panel full of glyphs and then the glass—and then she stops. Her eyes sweep across the massive structure beyond the room, hungry.

"How do you turn it on?" Her voice comes whip-like through the quiet.

"Turn it—" I'm left staring at her, aghast. "Turn it *on*? This has been here for centuries, for millennia. The probability that it'd be operational is—"

"The Los Angeles cell was." Charlotte tears her eyes from the ship's power core to fix on me. "How do we turn it on?"

"I swear to you that I'm not stalling—trying to start this up after so long, such a complicated piece of technology . . . the amount of power involved, it's as likely the whole thing'll just explode, and take us all with it."

"Your warnings have been taken under advisement." Charlotte shifts her weight, jaw hardening as she lifts an eyebrow. "Think about where you are, Mr. Addison. Think about everything we've done, all the pieces I had to set up and execute in order to retrieve this single artifact. I've fought for this chance, I've pleaded and begged and killed for it—this is our salvation, and when the rest of the world sees it, they'll know I was right to do everything I did to find it. When I bring this ship back, I'll be saving the human race. Would you like to tell me again to give up and go home?"

Her face all but gleams, the singularity of her purpose sending a shiver down my already chilled spine. When I decided to come to Gaia, I believed I was giving everything, sacrificing all I had and all I'd ever be, for the good of my planet. No one could possibly be sacrificing more. But this woman, this Charlotte—Mink— whoever she is—there's a light behind her eyes that I recognize, that makes my heart sink. Because I've seen that look in the mirror.

Would I have let anyone stop me?

I swallow, taking a breath, trying not to think of Mia, some- where back in those tents, or on the ship herself by now, being used to test for traps, or even dead, for all I know, though my gut refuses to accept that as a possibility.

I lean down to brace myself against the control panel. There's no guarantee that I can power the ship from here, but the impor- tance indicated by the glyphs leading to this room, and the view from its window, make me think I can.

Pergite si audetis.

Charlotte's waiting.

"Listen," I say, desperate, my words tumbling over one another. "There's more to the Undying than you know, Charlotte. Only a few people in the IA know that my father found a second message, a warning, hidden in the broadcast—this ship could be dangerous, catastrophically so. We can't just . . ." But there is no *we*. Charlotte was never interested in those questions like I was. She was never the person I thought she was. She's not going to listen.

"You're stalling." Her voice is grim.

"No, I promise—there were warnings all through the temple, warnings I should've . . . Even if you can't accept that we were being warned, at the heart of the temple we found messages in Latin, Charlotte. In Greek, in English and Chinese and Italian and Malaysian, and—"

"In a temple that predates humanity." Not grim, anymore—disbelieving.

"Yes!" I hold up my wrist unit. "I have pictures, I can show you. We have to understand why, before we turn it on. The hidden message, it was a coded spiral, and there was a glyph with it, it was warning us about the end of the world, and—"

"It was some sort of technology that created your Latin, your Malaysian," she says, dismissive. "Pulling from the languages the temple heard us speak, translating."

"But nobody in there spoke—"

"Enough!"

I meet her gaze, and though her expression is as grim as ever, there's a fire in her gaze that frightens me. I always saw the International Alliance as a bunch of politicians, arguing with one another. I never understood that behind the scenes were people like Charlotte. Driven. Committed to their cause, whatever the cost.

"I don't know if I can start it," I try.

"Lives depend on your success," she says quietly. And I know she's not talking about the people back on Earth this tech might save. She means Javier, and Hansen, and most of all, she means Mia.

I can't do as they ask, and I can't refuse.

As long as I stand here, unmoving—as long as I say nothing, I don't have to choose between my planet and Mia.

Then Charlotte's radio gives a little pop as she presses the transmit button. I look up to see her head tilting down toward the receiver clipped to her collar—as she speaks, though, she's watching me. "Alpha-oh-four to prisoner lockdown. Status report?"

The response is immediate, and Charlotte's adjusting the volume up so I can hear it. "Secure and stable. About to take the prisoners to be fed."

Prisoners, plural? *Javier and Hansen*, my mind supplies, with a surprising gust of relief. They're alive, too.

"Leave the men," says Charlotte, her eyes on me. "Take the girl—bring her to Benson."

My heart stops. Fear slashes at my chest, as sharp as a blade, cutting my lungs to ribbons as I try to breathe. Dimly, I can hear the soldier's response on the walkie, but my thoughts are too consumed with imagining ways they could hurt Mia to force me into compliance. *I should've hidden it better, how much I . . .* I swallow hard and taste bile at the back of my throat.

Charlotte lifts her head again and leans back against the wall, one hand on her gun, the other falling from the radio control. Her gaze is ice. "Well?" she says.

I clear my throat, trying to keep my words even, trying not to let the fury making my vision spark show in my voice. "You'll have to give me some time."

23

AMELIA

THE JOLT OF FEAR WHEN THE GUARDS HAUL THE DOOR OF OUR CELL OPEN IS nothing compared to the icy fingers that wrap around my throat when they single me out to go with them, alone. I want to glance at Javier, to get a nod or a wink or some last bit of reassurance, but I can't do anything that might arouse suspicions, so I trudge out the door like my spirit's broken.

My two guards are both bigger than me—one's a woman, about a head taller, and the other's a lanky guy with quick, darting eyes. My heart's sinking, because there's no way I can take out *two* on my own—but part of me tingles with relief, too. Because there's no way I could be expected to deal with them both. I won't have to risk getting shot. I won't have to risk shooting someone.

I've seen no sign of Jules. I have to assume he's okay, though, and that he's still insisting I be kept alive in exchange for his cooperation. Otherwise the manpower they're wasting keeping an eye on a bunch of useless prisoners makes no sense.

They bring me back outside, down a long, enclosed ramp they've erected to make accessing the airlock door easier. The IA camp is still being erected around us, but I guess the soldiers are at least human enough that they're worried about lunch, because the kitchens are up and working. We walk to the tent serving as a mess hall, where a skinny military chef called Benson gives me a bowl of tasteless protein mush.

I'm about halfway through the meal when an electronic crackle sounds from the guards' earpieces. The guy rolls his eyes over toward his partner. "No way—I'm calling in that favor. I heard it's twenty-five flights of stairs, maybe thirty."

She lifts her eyebrows. "Yeah? You want to take this one to the ladies' room, then?"

The male guard's eyes flick back toward me, and he groans. "Cheater," he accuses.

The woman shrugs. "Up to you. If you've got a handle on her feminine needs, then I'm happy to go up there instead."

The guy mutters something uncomplimentary under his breath and gets up, presumably to answer the summons from his earpiece. The female guard grins at his retreating shoulders, then leans back, watching me finish my breakfast.

"Feminine stuff," she comments. "Gets 'em every time. Guys are such idiots."

I'm inclined to agree with her, but the tasteless mush of a meal is suddenly sticking in my throat. I'm down to one guard.

"Done?" she asks, after a few long moments of me staring into my bowl.

I probably should finish the meal, but I'm not hungry anymore. I nod wordlessly.

"Then it's to the latrines, then back to the cell. C'mon, on your feet." She approaches, grasping at my arm to help me up from the bench. Her other hand's gripping her gun—she might sound casual, but she's on the alert. These soldiers aren't stupid, that's for sure.

I tell myself I'm going to wait until after the bathroom visit because she might have relaxed by then; that there might be fewer guards patrolling that section of the base; that it's nearer the ship, so easier to get back to the cell undetected. But in my heart of hearts I'm stalling for time.

The bathrooms, also still being set up, are little more than tents with holes dug down into the ice, and are small and stark and smell overpoweringly of disinfectant. But we find one that's ready to use, and there's even lukewarm running water hooked up to a washbasin, so I spend some time splashing my face.

You can do this, I tell myself as firmly as I can.

Yeah, comes the answering thought before I can stop it. *Sure you can, in bizarre upside-down world where you're a freaking superhero and not some high school dropout who specializes in running the frak away when things get dangerous.*

My hands are shaking as I dry them on the damp rag hanging as a towel next to the basin. My legs feel rubbery as I step toward the door. My guard's waiting for me, and she falls into step behind me. She's not close enough, though. She needs to be right on my heels for me to execute Javier's plan.

I slow my steps. "I don't want to go back," I hear myself saying as we reach the umbilical-like tunnel leading up into the Undying ship.

"Orders," replies my guard. "Sorry."

"What is all this, anyway?" I'm talking just as much to distract myself from what I have to do as anything else. My steps echo on the ramp as we ascend into the dark, icy ship once more.

"Confidential."

"Come on," I reply over my shoulder. "No games. We're all dead anyway, me and the guys—once you've got what you need from Jules, you're gonna kill us, right? What harm is there in telling a dead girl?"

My guard hesitates—or, at the very least, doesn't answer right away. "I don't even really know," she says finally. "I'm not high on the list of need-to-know personnel. But this mission—we're saving the human race. This tech, this is how the International Alliance fulfills its promise to the world. It was created for projects bigger than all of us, like Alpha Centauri. And this is even bigger than that. Not just a new colony. A cure for our whole world. We're doing the right thing."

"And yet you're planning to kill us eventually."

Her silence is answer enough, though she doesn't exactly look happy about it. I keep my steps slow, hoping she'll prod me along with the barrel of her gun, giving me my opening. But she doesn't, hanging back and letting me dawdle. Despite my best efforts to stall, we're turning the corner into the hall that houses our make-shift cell before I can come up with another plan.

There's a crowbar leaning against the wall outside our door, the tool they use to pry our cell open. My guard gestures with her gun for me to pick it up and open the door myself. I heft the tool in my hands, toying for an insane moment with the idea of turning and swinging it at her head—but she's far enough back, too canny to get within range. She'd shoot me before I got anywhere close.

So I fit the edge of the crowbar into the groove along the door and haul with all my weight. I wiggle it into the widening crack bit by bit, until the curved end is well inside the cell—then I let go with a gasp, grabbing at my wrist. The door goes slamming back on the crowbar, wedged in firmly now.

"I think I pulled something," I groan.

My guard mutters something, shifting her weight. "No dramatics, please." She sounds tired. I guess I would be too, having to be on the alert all day like her. "If you think you're getting me close enough to take me out with a crowbar, take another look at this and think again." She hefts her weapon, a rifle as long as my arm.

"The crowbar's stuck," I point out, lifting my arms and taking a step back. "See for yourself."

The guard scowls at me, but after a few breaths steps closer, then closer still. After a brief inspection, she puts her attention back on me. "Well, try again."

"Give me just a sec," I mutter, panting. "Catch my breath."

"No, *now*." The woman's on edge, suspicious. But the flare in temper is all I needed; she gestures with the barrel of her gun, just centimeters from my chest.

The move Javier taught me used contact between my back and the gun—had me spinning so the barrel went one way while I went the other.

But this is as close as I'm gonna get.

For the briefest instant, I look up to meet the guard's eyes. And in a heartbeat I know it's a mistake. She reads my intention there, in my face, and suddenly I'm committed. I'm moving, slamming my arm up against the barrel so that when she pulls the trigger it fires up into the ceiling with a deafening crack. My head's spinning from the noise, but my body knows what to do next. I lower my shoulder and slam into her, my momentum combined with the recoil from the rifle knocking her flat onto her back. And just like in our practices, I'm wresting the butt of the gun from her lax hand and pulling it so the strap around her shoulder is taut, and my boot is pressing the barrel into the underside of her chin.

But then my finger touches the trigger and I freeze.

Sorry, she'd said. And *guys are idiots*. And she'd grinned when she got her way and sent the guard off to answer the summons, like she'd drawn the longer straw, like escorting me was the better assignment. She waited for me to finish my breakfast. She let me take my time walking back to the cell. *We're saving the world.*

And now she's looking up at me, still half-dazed. The impact with the floor knocked the wind out of her and her eyes are watering as her lungs try to reboot.

I can hear the guys on the other side of the door, the scrabbling of the crowbar against stone, someone shouting something through the crack. But it all fades to a dull buzzing as I stare down at the woman.

It's not like we practiced.

Then a body barrels into mine, coming out of nowhere and

knocking me aside. I slam into the wall opposite the cell door, and an instant later there's a second gunshot. Shaking, I blink and blink again until I can see properly. Hansen's propping the door open with the crowbar and Javier's standing where I was a second before, the rifle in his hand. The guard isn't staring at me anymore—she's staring at the ceiling, still looking surprised. There's blood on the floor beneath her, and as it spreads it finds a crack in the stone floor and slithers toward me like it's a live thing.

I stumble away until a hand grasps at my shoulder.

"You okay?" Javier's face is close to mine. I can smell the tiniest hint of something acrid in the air. Smoke. Gunfire. "Sorry I knocked you aside so hard."

"I was gonna do it." I swallow, unable to take my eyes from the dead guard. "I was."

Javier's hand squeezes. "I know. But you don't need to become a murderer, kid. Not today."

Then I'm retching, whirling around and ducking back inside the cell so I can puke in the corner, my mushy breakfast just as vile coming back up as it was going down. I end up with my head in between my knees, forehead resting on my balled fists.

By the time I can stand back up, Hansen and Javier have dragged the body into our cell and wiped up most of the blood in the hallway with the guard's jacket. Hansen's looking a bit white in the face, as I can only imagine I am too, but at least he's not hurling his guts up.

"We should go," he's saying, reaching out to touch my elbow, hesitant.

I nod. "Yeah. Yeah. Okay."

"Follow me," Javier orders. "If anyone heard those shots, they're already on their way to investigate. If we get separated, try to get outside to the shuttles."

"Shuttles?" That word cuts through my fog like a welding torch through copper.

"Hansen's a pilot, remember?" Javier waits until I'm out of the cell before yanking the crowbar free, then tossing it to Hansen as the door slams shut. "If we can get one of those shuttles working, we've got transportation."

"Jules," I manage. Single-word sentences. I swallow, tasting bile and fear, and try to pull myself together. "We can't just bail yet, we need Jules."

"Look, I know you want to help your friend." Javier's keeping his voice low, eyes scanning each end of the corridor. "And we will. But we don't even know where he's being held. We've got to get out of here ourselves first. He's the valuable one—they're not going to kill him because we escaped. We get out, we find more gear, we survey the place, we get intel . . . then we've got half a chance of rescuing him."

My throat's like sandpaper. "If we get to a shuttle, you're telling me you're going to come back for Jules?" I don't believe it for a moment—I can barely even blame them—but it still feels like a punch when Javier looks away, won't meet my eyes.

"He kept you alive," I say, trying to force strength into my voice. "He made them keep you alive. So you could just leave him?"

Javier and Hansen exchange a glance, and Javier's the one who speaks again. "Kid, if he were here, Jules would tell you to run," he says quietly. "Save yourself, if you can."

And perhaps he would. I'm sure he would. But that's exactly why I can't.

I stare at Javier and Hansen, thoughts spinning. They just want to get out of here alive, and I can't blame them. Javier just spared me having to kill someone at point-blank range. He's got no practical reason to bring me along on this escape attempt of theirs, a girl with no training, an extra mouth to feed with whatever supplies we can steal on our way out.

He's not a bad man, but I can't go with him. I can't leave Jules. Slowly, I shake my head. "He's in here somewhere," I say quietly. "I have to find him."

Javier's shoulders drop, but he doesn't look surprised. "We'll

289

head along this hallway," he says. "It's the best way out, and it'll get you closer to their command post. If you can listen in on their plans, maybe you'll get a handle on where they've got him. We'll stay together as long as we can. And if we can wait for you at the shuttles, we will."

I nod. Then, trying to forget the image of the guard's body slumped in the dark next to her blood-soaked jacket, I fall into step behind Javier, with Hansen bringing up the rear. We don't have a lot of time.

The IA's only been in the ship a day, so most of the corridors are untouched by footprints or trekked-in snow or other signs of humanity. We try to stick to less marked-up hallways, but we have to follow the footsteps—the more there are, the more likely it is the hallway will lead to weapons, or an exit, or for me, some kind of command post I can eavesdrop on for hints on where to find Jules.

We dodge soldiers in the maze of corridors, navigating as best we can by the frequency of footprints in the dust, until my head starts to spin. Maybe it's the concussion still, or dizziness from trying to mentally map this place, or just plain exhaustion. *If we can wait for you at the shuttles, we will,* Javier said.

A day ago these men were my enemies, and now the thought of leaving them to fight on my own again makes me want to crumble. But I can't. We're coming up on the exit to the ship, and the moment when we'll part ways. And I'll be left alone, without any kind of a plan, hiding on an alien ship, dodging soldiers and trying to save a boy I didn't know a few weeks ago. I told Jules that the ability to make snap decisions is what keeps a scavver alive, but I've never been less sure what to do.

Suddenly a door a ways up the corridor creaks open and a handful of people pour out into the corridor. We're too far from the last junction to hide. And there are only three of them. Javier's already got the rifle to his shoulder, moving to stand between me and them.

"Wait!" My heart's leaping and I'm darting forward to grab at Javier's arm. Because not all the figures are wearing the black of these soldiers. One of them is wearing head-to-toe khaki, and though it's as dirty now as if it's been through an entire excavation season, I'd know it anywhere. "Don't shoot—it's Jules."

24

JULES

I FREEZE IN MY TRACKS, MY ESCORTS PAUSING HALF A SECOND LATER AS they register the others down the corridor. I'm staring at the gun, and it takes me a long moment to realize it's Javier behind it—and that Mia and Hansen are behind him. *Mia's alive, Mia's still alive.*

In the same instant I'm gaping, the soldiers are lifting their weapons, the guns level with my face, and I realize I'm standing between them and Javier—whoever shoots, I'm in the line of it. I hold perfectly still, heart hammering, searching his face for a signal, wondering if I'm dispensable to him.

Then there's a deafening crack and I throw myself to the ground, and a soldier's hitting the ground beside me, eyes wide and staring, a red, bleeding spot directly between them. *Oh god, he's dead. He's dead, that's a bullet hole.*

His vacant eyes are fixed on my face, and I'm biting down hard on the inside of my cheek, suppressing the urge to retch, and Javier points his gun at a place over our heads that must be where my other guard's standing. I can only assume she's aiming hers right back at him.

Wait, Mia's not behind him. I drop my gaze, and she's at my level, crouching on one knee, trying desperately to pull Hansen's arm around her shoulders and drag him backward. There's blood all over his throat, running down his chest, his eyes huge.

Javier and the soldier still standing must both have fired at once.

But Hansen took the bullet meant for Javier.

Mia's cursing under her breath, her voice frantic and terrified, and I don't dare move, lest I get a bullet in the back of my head, and everyone's frozen in place, Javier and the soldier standing with weapons trained on each other.

Then noise explodes all around me, the soldier's gun firing somewhere above my head. Javier spins back to slam into the wall, and with a crash, the soldier hits the ground behind me, her gun clattering from her hand. I lunge for it, fumbling, trying and failing to wrap my fingers around it, and in desperation I give up and just swing at it, sending it skittering along the floor, back and away toward Mia and Javier and Hansen.

But the soldier doesn't even try to stop me. She's dead.

Everything's silent.

Mia's the one who breaks it, her voice hoarse. "Shit, shit, Hansen, *no!*"

I spin around, scrambling to my feet to stumble toward her. Javier's pushing away from the wall, his right hand clamped against his left arm to stanch the flow of blood from a new wound, the rifle hanging from his shoulder by its strap. Mia and Hansen are on the floor now, her hands, covered with blood, trying to stop the bleeding at his chest. The flow of blood is slowing—but it's because Hansen's eyes are blank and still, staring into the nothingness beyond her.

"We have to go," Javier says, swaying on his feet.

"But Hansen—" Mia chokes.

"We have to go," Javier repeats. "*Now.*"

"Dammit," Mia shouts, slamming her palm down onto the floor beside Hansen, leaving a bloody handprint and staring down at the man who died in her arms. This is the guy whose hand she threatened to remove if he groped her again—and now she's got tears in her eyes, shock coursing through her and making her shake.

"I'm sorry," Javier says softly, and I have no idea if he's apologizing to Mia or Hansen. I'm not sure he knows either.

I want to break down, just seeing Mia here. Charlotte made me think they were torturing her, that they were willing to do anything to her to gain my cooperation. And here she is, alive. Unhurt, as best I can tell, but for her anguish.

I crouch down beside her, pulling my handkerchief from my pocket and offering it to her. Wordlessly she takes it, doing her best to clean her hands, dragging it along each finger in turn until it's soaked red, then setting it on the ground beside Hansen. I reach for her hand, ignoring the fact that it's sticky with blood, and turn it over so it's palm up. Then I dig in my pocket and pull out her multi-tool. I've been carrying it since we parted ways, like a promise to myself that I'd see her, and give it to her.

And now I do, curling her fingers around it and squeezing her hand. Restoring this small seed of who she is to her, though I don't know how much it can mean, surrounded as we are by such horror.

But she looks across at me, face white, jaw clenched, her eyes a little more focused than they were before. Fixing on me, seeing *me*.

Then she nods, and together we rise to our feet.

"Javier's right," I say. "We have to go. There are more of them coming. These two were just my escort. And—Mia, everything's gone wrong, we need to—"

"Hansen was our pilot," Javier says quietly, ripping off the sleeve covering his injured arm so he can inspect the wound. "We need somewhere to hole up. We can't take a shuttle now."

"We can't just hole up," I snap, my voice cracking. "That's what I'm trying to tell you. They—they made me show them. How to turn on the power core. They're going to start up the ship." *I did it to save you.* I can't say it out loud. *Charlotte called my bluff.*

"They what?" Mia breathes, my own horror mirrored in her

face. "You said there's no way to know what will happen—what if the whole thing just explodes?"

I meet her eyes, and I know she sees my own fear. "Then we lose all hope of understanding what the Undying wanted with us, or what this ship was for."

"This explosion," Javier says, eyes flicking between us. "About how big do you think it could be?"

Jules shakes his head, hollow-eyed. "I have no idea. But given the raw power the Undying were capable of creating . . . for all I know it'll take out half the planet."

Javier sniffs, scrubbing a hand across a couple days' worth of stubble on his jaw. "I'm thinking let's go steal that shuttle."

"But Hansen—" Mia's voice shakes on the dead man's name.

"Look, I can get it into the air. I can't fly it through the portal, but I can get it off the ground. I'd rather be on a shuttle we barely know how to fly when this thing blows up than sitting in a makeshift cell a few yards away from ground zero."

I take a deep breath, shaking my head. "We can't just leave. If they manage to get this ship running and it still flies, they'll take it back to Earth. An explosion in orbit would be the biggest disaster since the extinction of the dinosaurs."

Mia suddenly leans forward, grabbing my arm. "Not if we warn someone. Mink's not listening, but if Javier can get a shuttle moving, we don't have to be able to fly it back to Earth—we just have to get far enough away from the poles for us to send a transmission without it getting scrambled. We broadcast through the portal."

I glance from her face to Javier's. He nods, approving the plan—and I swallow my fear. "Let's get moving."

.   .   .

A quarter hour later we're half a dozen floors down and two sectors over. Javier holds up his good hand to signal a pause, and we all stand in silence, straining to listen. No sounds of pursuit, at least not yet.

"This way," I say, pointing to the left, into uncharted territory, where no footprints lie. No snow has been tracked this far in, no dirt mixed with dust to show where the soldiers have been. We're looking for a way out that won't be covered by the IA guards, a place we can slip through unnoticed on our way to the rows of IA shuttles.

"Are you sure?" Javier asks.

"No," I admit. "But I think these symbols here are talking about movement. I think they mean an exit."

"We have nothing better," Mia points out. "Go, I'll handle the footprints."

She peels her jacket off, and as the three of us make our way along the hallway, she uses the back of it—the front's bloody—to carefully wipe out our tracks, until we're beyond the vision of any-one who might stand at the crossroads looking for signs of where we've gone.

Just as I did when I was finding the way to the control room, I'm following the vibe of this place. The glyphs I'm watching become more prominent, promising my goal is closer. *Out*, or *door*, is the best translation I have for the characters along the wall.

I force my mind to remain on the goal. I can't think of Hansen behind us, of the dead soldiers, of Charlotte and everything she's done, and forced us to do, to find this ship. I can't think about the fact that our best hope is a million-to-one long shot that then hinges on someone back on Earth listening to reason. We have no other options, except surrender.

We make our way down a flight of stairs and along another corri-dor, and when I stumble out of tiredness, Mia grabs my hand again.

"We're close," I say. "I think we're close. I . . ."

My words die in my throat as we round the corner. The hallway ahead of us stretches into the distance, ending at a blank wall. The beams of our torches reflect off black patches in the walls at perfectly even intervals. Otherwise, the corridor's bare, devoid of glyphs, devoid of anything. A dead end.

"This isn't a way out," I say stupidly, staring. *How did I get it wrong?*

Mia and I walk forward together to the nearest black slab, about twice the width of a door. It looks like black, polished rock. It looks familiar, but I'm so tired my brain can't place it.

"What is it?" asks Javier from behind us, keeping an eye on the corridor leading here.

"It's the other side of a portal," Mia says, lifting her free hand to brush her fingertips across it, keeping her other hand wrapped firmly in mine. "This is what it looked like out there, after we came through from the temple."

"These are all portals leading here?" Javier sounds nervous.

I look again, remembering the other black shadows along the hallway, and this time I know what I'm seeing by the beam of my torch. Black portals, evenly spaced, running down both sides of the corridor all the way to its end.

"It didn't mean 'exit,'" I say slowly. "It meant 'a way through.' That's what the movement was. That must be the glyph for *portal.*"

Beside me, Mia makes a noise in the back of her throat. I know that sound, and my heart's sinking before I'm even turning my head. She's seen something, something important. Her eyes are on the corridor ahead of us, though, and aside from the lack of exit at the other end, I can't see what's caught her eye.

"No footprints leading this way," she whispers, eyes still on the corridor ahead. "We saw all the footprints stop, back the way we came. No one's been up here since the Undying a bazillion years ago, right?"

"Right." But I know her voice, I know the answer isn't going to be that simple.

"Then what left those?" Mia's lifting her arm, so that her LED flashlight sweeps across the corridor before us. It's subtle, and some of the dust has obscured it, but when I glance back to look at our own path, it's impossible to deny what she's pointing at.

There are tracks in the dust.

25

AMELIA

"**Tell me those are bazillion-year-old tracks.**" **Javier breaks** the silence first, and though I can't take my eyes from the smudges on the floor in front of us, I can hear the metallic click and squeak of a strap that tells me he's tightening his grip on his stolen rifle.

"I . . ." Jules is looking at the tracks, which aren't exactly clear, so it's impossible to make out what shape of foot made them or even if it was a foot at all. But then, our tracks behind us aren't exactly clear either. What we do know about the smears in the hallway ahead—what *matters* about them—is that they're in a corridor that had no tracks leading to it. Which begs the question: how did whoever or whatever made them get here?

Jules swallows hard and tries again. "I'd have to do a study on the weather patterns, on—on how much snow makes it inside the ship on a weekly, monthly, yearly basis . . ." His voice is betraying him. And though it's been only days—*god, can that really be true?*—it still feels like I've known him my whole life. He's freaking out, and

I don't blame him. Either something else, yet another intelligent species, followed the same trail we did and found this ship, or . . .

"Never mind." I keep my voice firm, commanding. At least there's one thing I can take away from Liz's reign over her thugs—I'm channeling her voice now as I speak. "It doesn't matter. This clearly isn't what we're looking for, and we can worry about what all this means when we're *not* wanted fugitives lost in an ancient alien spaceship that might explode as soon as someone flips a switch."

"Right." Jules swallows hard, and I can almost see him forcing away the thousand questions he has. It's just another piece of one huge, confusing puzzle—one that began with the Undying broadcast, continued in the temple, and hit a whole new level when we found all the languages of Earth surrounding the portal. "We've got to get out of here first. Figure out what all of it means later."

But then, as if on cue, a shudder runs through the stone beneath our feet. It's small, barely enough to make the soles of my feet tingle inside my boots, but then it comes again. Unmistakable. Vibrations.

Jules's head snaps up, looking first at Javier, then at me. For a moment all three of us are still, waiting for the vibrations to die out—waiting to realize they were from the excavations outside, or some part of the ship collapsing, or anything other than what we know it is: the ship powering up. The switch being flipped. The eons-old power source beneath our feet coming to life.

A row of lights, spaced evenly and built into the rounded edges of the corridor ceiling, flicker on. I flinch away, half expecting them to burst like lightbulbs in a power surge, but they just glow a calm blue, illuminating the corridor and us.

"Okay," I manage, my feet still tingling—but now with the urge to run. "I vote we get the hell out of here."

• • •

We're sprinting back, following our own tracks the way we came to renew our search for a way off the ship.

I'm about to round a corner when a hand grabs the back of my collar and yanks me backward—the fabric cuts off my air, turning my shriek of surprise into a quiet gurgle. I stumble back to find Javier holding Jules back as well, and once I meet his eyes he lets go of my shirt in order to press a finger to his lips.

It's then that I hear what he heard: booted feet, marching—no, running—toward the intersection we were about to cross. One of them has a comms channel open, and I hear Mink's voice snapping orders. "All personnel to evacuate *immediately*—repeat, immediate evacuation for all . . ."

And then they're gone, the radio-distorted sound of Mink's orders vanishing with them.

I glance first at Javier, then Jules. We've been trying to find a different exit from the airlock we first unlocked on Mink's orders—but I've never seen a group of guys in full black-ops body armor running so fast.

"That can't be good." Javier shifts his grip on his gun. "Addison, why're they all bolting?"

Jules shakes his head. "I don't know. Maybe Charlotte's taken my warnings that it's dangerous to heart. Getting her men out, testing the ship remotely somehow."

"I'd rather not be a lab rat, if it's all the same to you two." My voice is taut and sharp with fear. "I'd rather join the rats fleeing the ship, thank you very much."

Jules is nodding before I'm done speaking. "I can't argue with that sentiment."

"We know where the main airlock is. It'll be a lot faster than searching for somewhere with fewer guards—it'll be crawling with IA, but if we can make it there without being seen, maybe we can get lost in the crowd."

"We can worry about stealth after we're not sitting on top of a ticking time bomb." Javier ducks his head out into the hallway to make sure there's no sign of the retreating IA squad. "Let's go."

26

JULES

WE RACE ALONG THE HALLWAY, PAUSING AT THE TOP OF THE STAIRS AS MIA creeps down, the smallest of us, the best scout. She's turned off the light at her wrist, and she's silent and invisible in the near darkness, startling me when she suddenly rematerializes by my side. "Clear," she says, and Javier slips forward to take point once more, his torch turned down as dim as it'll go.

We're following the tracks left by the retreating IA personnel, aiming for the main exit. There's a chance, in the confusion and haste to evacuate, that they might not notice three people in the crowds slipping away.

I'm following on Javier's heels, my hand wrapped around Amelia's once more, on automatic pilot. When she stops suddenly, Mia yanks my hand to make sure I do too. I look up to see Javier gesturing urgently backward with his hand, and Mia and I reverse several steps. She pulls me into a room on one side of the hallway, Javier hurries in after us, ducking into the shadows beside the door, gun at the ready.

"Another squad coming," he whispers, easing out to take a careful look. He's gritting his teeth when he withdraws. "Wait here, I'll track them and make sure they're gone."

He's visible in the faint light of the hallway, but the room itself is dark. Mia's hand tightens around mine, and I follow as she leads me over toward the far wall, into the shadow. I can only see the barest outline of her—the gleam of her eyes, the line of her nose and mouth. I half see, half sense the movement when she lifts her free hand to trail it down the wall beside us, fingertips moving slowly.

"What is it?" I whisper. I know she's thinking, but we don't have time to waste.

She shakes her head, the movement slow. "Jules," she murmurs, so soft she's nearly inaudible. "Whatever's about to happen once the ship warms up, it'll be what all the spirals were warning us about, won't it?"

"I don't know," I admit. Three words I've spoken more in the past week than in the rest of my life put together. "But I'm afraid of that."

"And we still don't know," she whispers. "Who tried to warn us. Why."

"No," I agree, soft. "But you were right when you said that there's no way they hid everything they knew about our languages just to give us a nice surprise."

"What if . . ." Her voice trails off, and she shakes her head as if denying her own words before speaking them.

"Go on," I murmur. Mia might not have the education on the Undying I do, but she's seen more of them in the last few days than any scholar alive except for me.

"What if we're doing exactly what they wanted us to do, when they built this place? We're already sure we were passing tests back in the temple, tests to lead us here. *Us in particular*—humans— because they left us instructions in our *own languages*. They led us to a ship made to feel familiar to us, with rooms and halls and doors. And now we're starting up the ship so we can take it home to dismantle or study or put to work. Jules, any race that's even remotely like us would recognize Earth as a freaking *jackpot* of a planet, despite all humanity's done to it. It's still got oxygen, oceans, resources, life . . . what if all the temples, all the puzzles, they were putting us through our paces to check we were *us*? That we were humans? To make us lead them to Earth?"

I try to swallow, I can't. My hand's clammy where she's holding it, my mind racing ahead, now I can see where she's leading me. But she speaks the words anyway.

"We proved we hear music like humans, we do math like humans, we speak languages belonging to humans. We've been like rats in a maze, only instead of a reward at the end there's just a trap. Now we're going to take this ship straight to Earth for them, and just like you said, all it has to do is blow up to wipe us out, and leave our planet totally defenseless. You were talking about what would happen if it blew up by accident, because it's old . . . but it could do that damage on purpose too."

"But they're dead," I protest, voice hoarse. "Extinct, long ago."

"Are they?" she counters. "Somebody had to leave us messages in Latin, and English, and French, and Chinese, and who knows what else. You've been telling me that the radiation dating doesn't lie—and that those languages didn't exist fifty thousand years ago—so we're already dealing with an unsolvable paradox. What's one more impossible thing?"

"I can't just throw all logic and reason out the airlock because I don't understand yet. It doesn't make sense, it's not *possible*."

"What about the footprints?" she whispers. "No footprints leading to that hallway, but footprints right there in it, beside the portals."

"We don't know they were footprints," I try, but it's not much of a protest.

"Markings, then," she replies. "None of this adds up. Unless you're heading to one conclusion."

"Which is?"

She shakes her head again, but speaks on anyway. "What if they named themselves the Undying for a reason? What if they didn't mean their legacy would live forever, that their broadcast meant their story would never die? What if they meant *they* would never die? What if they're not extinct?"

"If they're . . ." My mouth goes dry. It took an outsider to see it. I've always been told they were gone. I've always known it. Because *everyone* knew it.

"If they're alive," she finishes for me, wide-eyed, "what if we're leading them straight to Earth?"

27

AMELIA

JULES IS STARING AT ME LIKE A GUY BETWEEN THE MOMENT WHEN HE'S
punched and the moment when he falls down, lips slightly parted,
breath shallow. Then Javier hisses to get our attention.

"Let's go," he whispers. "We don't have much time—they're leg-
ging it like their tails are on fire—evacuation must be nearly done."

My blood feels like ice in my veins—I don't need anyone telling
me to run like hell, but my feet won't move. I know what I've just
said is insane. The Undying are extinct. We're alone in the universe, picking at the remains of their civilization like me and the
scavvers in the ruins of Chicago. Except . . . what if, like the people of Chicago, the Undying didn't die out? What if they just . . .
moved on?

Then the corridor lights flicker, on and off, in a rapid succes-
sion of flashes. "That can't be good," mutters Javier, easing out to
double-check that all the guards are gone. And Jules is following,
until our joined hands and my unmoving feet bring him to a halt.
I feel, rather than see, his eyes on me—I'm staring up, at the lights.

They're flashing almost too quickly to track, but there's a pattern there.

I'm counting under my breath, and when the flashing stops for a beat, I whisper the number aloud. "Twenty-nine."

He must be used to my seemingly random outbursts by now, because Jules doesn't give me the whole *crazy-scavver-girl* sidelong eyeball he used to. He crouches down at my side instead, ignoring Javier's increasingly urgent summons to follow him. "Twenty-nine what?"

"Flashes. Hang on." The sequence is starting again, and I'm so tired I don't think I can count and hear Jules's voice at the same time. This time there are twenty-eight flashes—and this time Jules is counting them too.

Our eyes meet, and then as one we're scrambling back to our feet and taking off down the hallway, bursting past Javier. "It's a countdown," Jules is shouting. "The flashes—they're counting down each time."

Javier scrambles after us. "A countdown—what, like for a shuttle takeoff or something?"

"Exactly like." Jules's voice is short, as he saves his breath for running. "I guess not everyone's evacuated—someone's initiated a launch sequence."

Javier slings his gun over his shoulder so he can run faster. "Or they've rigged up a remote piloting system."

Jules stumbles, spitting out an oath so strangled I can't even identify what language he's speaking. "I guess she did listen to my warning after all. Just . . . not enough."

Oh shit, oh shit, oh shit. It's the best of all possible worlds for Charlotte—she sends home her prize through the portal without risking herself or a single one of her men. Assuming the ship flies—assuming it doesn't blow up on liftoff—and assuming it doesn't wipe out half of life on Earth.

I don't want to get blown up leaving Gaia's atmosphere on an ancient alien spaceship. I also *really* don't want to get blown up on an ancient alien spaceship in orbit around the planet my sister and I call home. I guess I just don't really want to get blown up at all. Mostly I want *off* this goddamn creepy-ass alien deathtrap. If I'm going up into space again it'll be as god intended it: in a nice, carbon-fiber and steel shuttle with noise-canceling headphones and, preferably, enough sedatives coursing through my veins to knock out an elephant.

The halls of the ship are empty, with only the well-traveled boot prints of the Alliance forces to tell us anyone was ever here. Though I know we can't run any faster, my mind's tracking the countdown anyway, like some perverse reminder that there's *not enough time*. For the first time in my life I wish I wasn't good with numbers. I wish it didn't come naturally. I wish I didn't have this realization echoing around inside my skull, reverberating to the rhythm of my pounding feet.

Nineteen.

I try to comfort myself by remembering that it's not a one-to-one countdown—it takes nineteen seconds to count out nineteen flashes, then another eighteen to count down eighteen, and it'll keep going, flashing out each number in full right down to zero. We've got a few minutes, not just a handful of seconds. But each step seems to take forever.

Jules's boots squeal against a puddle of melted snow and he goes careening into the wall instead of rounding a corner, his hand tearing from mine—Javier's there before anyone else, grabbing at his elbow to haul him upright again.

But neither of them starts moving again, and an instant later, I see why.

The airlock's ahead of us, and it's still open. A way out.

The ramp has been pulled away already, but if the doors are going to automatically close, they haven't yet. I'm trying to remember how high up the scaffolding was—I know I thought I could make it, if Mink pushed me off. But the white, featureless snow below us is almost impossible to gauge now.

"We have to get to a shuttle," Javier shouts, lifting his voice over the roar of the engines. "I've got a family on Earth. I've got kids. My sister, my nephews. I don't care if they arrest me, shoot me. Someone's got to try to send a warning to Earth, that they shouldn't bring this thing through the portal until they're sure it's not dangerous."

Not a word we've said to Mink has made any difference so far—well, except to make her cautious enough to evacuate herself and her troops—but she's not the only member of the IA with pull. If Javier can get us to a shuttle so we can send a message to whoever her commander is, there's a chance they could abort the launch, or at least make sure the ship stays far from Earth.

Slowly, Jules nods. His eyes are distant, and I know he's thinking. I wish I knew what to say—how to tell him in this instant that staying alive, bringing this message back to humanity, is more important than the answers this ship could give us. But I'm not even sure that's true anymore.

Javier drops to his knees, grasping at the edge of the drop and then falling. My heart stops for half a second—then starts pumping again, frantically, as I see him land harmlessly in the snow only a few meters down. He's shouting something, but out here the hum of the ship has risen to a roar. He gestures for us to follow, then takes off along the outer hull, aiming for the shuttles lined up a few kilometers away. But when I start to make for the drop, I realize Jules is just standing there, unmoving, eyes fixed upward on the lights overhead.

Seventeen.

"There's not enough time," he says softly, so softly I mostly just read the words on his lips, half deafened by the sound of the ship preparing to take off. For half a moment I think he's reading my mind.

Then I snap out of it. "Not if you stand there gaping like a dumbass!" I gasp, lungs burning from our headlong flight.

"No—not enough time for Javier to get a message through, even if he gets past the guards, even if he can figure out instantly how to launch one of their shuttles. He won't be able to get someone in charge to stop this, not before it's already happening. He won't even *reach* the shuttles before this thing takes off." He takes a quick, bracing breath. "But there's still a chance I could shut it down from inside."

"From inside—" I stop short, all my glib replies and oh-so-witty rejoinders fleeing. I'm rooted to the spot, one hand on the wall of the corridor as I stare at him. Suddenly I understand what he's planning—with the time we have left, it'll almost certainly be a one-way trip to the control room. Sabotage, not shutdown. If this ship is meant to destroy a planet, better it destroy lifeless Gaia than the only home our species has ever known.

His eyes snap down to meet mine, and after a heartbeat, he manages a little smile. "Sometimes you trust your instincts," he whispers, then steps in close so he can wrap a hand around my waist and pull me in against him, hard. His mouth finds mine, and this time the kiss is real—the first time, neither of us knew what was happening, not even me, and I was the one who started it. This time . . . this time there's a heat there, a longing, desperation in the way his lips explore mine, the press of his hand against my back.

I step back, not because I want to pull away but because my knees feel like they're about to give out, and I hit the wall of the airlock with a little gasp. The stolen rifle drops from my nerveless hands and clatters to the floor.

Jules presses in close for another breath, but the lights are flashing again—*fifteen*—and I know we don't have time to stay in this moment. No matter how utterly, completely, heartbreakingly much I want to. I give a little moan and he pulls away, though his arm is still around me. He lifts his other hand to brush a lock of gross, sweaty blue hair out of my eyes, his fingertips gentle, tracing my cheek. "I'll see you around, Mia."

Then he's turning me toward the edge of the drop-off, ushering me toward freedom. I can see Javier already dwindling into a tiny figure as he heads for the shuttles.

My knees are still being uncooperative, and for a moment I get a flash of horror that Jules actually thinks he's gonna dump me off this ship and go back to the control room by himself.

I give a wordless noise of protest and kick out, hitting him in the shin and causing him to stagger back with a grunt of pain and surprise.

"Screw that, Oxford," I gasp, then reach for the panel beside the airlock. The same panels that I observed next to all the doors, the ones I thought might be door controls if this were a science fiction movie. The ones that did nothing . . . before the ship powered up, that is.

Now, my palm connects with a tingle, like the pad senses the conductivity of my skin—and the airlock doors slam shut with all the force of an avalanche. The bright glare of the snow is gone, leaving us bathed only in the blue glow of the lights of the corridor, pausing between countdown numbers.

"Dammit, Mia!" The words fly from his mouth as he stares at me, horrified. It's the first time I've heard him swear in a language I actually understand, and for a wild moment that fact delights me, makes me want to grin, to laugh, to throw myself at him with insane and, I'll admit, inappropriate enthusiasm.

"You think you're gonna leave me behind *now?*" I'm still panting for breath; panting from the run, from the kiss, from the decision to die with him, if that's what we're about to do. "Stupid academics, always thinking everything's some dumbass fairy-tale legendary epic with the chosen sacrificial hero. You really want to stand here and fight me? You know I'll win."

Fourteen.

Jules's horror is fading to surprise, and as my eyes adjust to the blue-tinted gloom, I realize that he's always looked at me that way. Always *surprised.* Always like I've caught him off-guard. At first I thought it was because he was an asshole, some elitist jerk who thought no uneducated criminal chick could possibly have anything to contribute to his precious expedition.

Then I thought it was because he was automatically dismissing me as just another scavver, someone trying to play him for his expensive gear, his knowledge of the temples. Then I thought maybe it was because he was surprised at himself, at what he was really capable of when things got real, when the choices we were facing were about murder and death and sacrifice and loyalty to our families, and maybe he saw me as a symbol of how he'd changed.

But now he's just gazing at me, and as his mouth closes and curves into a smile, brown eyes warming, he murmurs, "I am never going to figure you out, am I?"

Maybe I was just always a puzzle. Exactly the kind of puzzle that calls to a guy like Jules.

"I hope not," I reply.

He reaches out, and I slip my hand into his, and together we sprint for the control room, and for our last-ditch effort to stop this portable apocalypse from lifting off.

28

JULES

SEVEN.

We barrel through the door to the control room, ricocheting off each other and sending Mia's smaller frame into the wall. She waves a hand to urge me on as she gasps for breath, and I stumble forward to stare at the huge control panel. The metallic stone is lit up from within now, circuitry gleaming. The pause before the lights flash for the next sequence in the countdown is interminable, stretching for eternity, but it's still not long enough.

Charlotte had me at gunpoint last time I was here, but that wasn't the real threat—the real threat was hanging over Mia's head, though she didn't know it. I worked out how to power up the ship, and the launch sequence was only a few steps from that. I said nothing, hoping they wouldn't make those next few connections themselves. But Charlotte told me they had people who could read the glyphs, and clearly that was true. They managed to initiate the launch, compete with autopilot. My problem is that I didn't have enough time to learn how to turn this thing off.

315

And if Mia's guess about the Undying is right, perhaps there *isn't* a way to shut down the launch.

As I stare, more panels light up, signaling their readiness.

Okay, maybe I can work backward—it's showing me which areas are involved in the launch, maybe I can shut them down.

I run my fingers over the panels and along the grooves carved there as the lights dim for another flash, feeling the current tingle through my fingertips. Mia's standing beside me, her hand resting on my back, waiting to be told what to do, not wasting an instant on asking questions.

Six.

"Down there," I snap out, stumbling over the words, pointing to the other end of the small room. The lights dim again. "The section lighting up blue, second from the top—yes, that one. Hit that on my word." We both ready our hands above what I hope are the instruments for measuring altitude and trajectory. Maybe. They're something to do with moving quickly, and I *think* they specify movement in a particular direction. Maybe if they don't work, the ship will pause until it can fix them.

Five.

"Now!"

Our hands slam down in unison.

Four.

The start-up continues without a pause.

I don't know what I'm missing, and it could be anything. I could be a fraction off in my guess, or a world away—or I could be absolutely right, and whatever Charlotte and her team did to control the ship remotely has rendered it impossible to shut down the sequence. And I have about ten seconds to work out what to do.

We try another combination, and another, moving together in perfect synchronization, Mia hitting the panels almost as I speak their names, but we might as well be fleas on a dog for all the difference we make—less than fleas, we don't even cause an itch.

Three.

"Come *on*," Mia shouts, smacking both hands down on the control panel in unison, frustration taking her over.

Two.

If this were a story, the ship would magically shut down in this moment, her hands having incredibly found the perfect combination. Instead, as she turns huge eyes to meet mine, the lights give us our final flash.

One.

We both stagger back against the walls as the huge ship pulls itself free of the ice, our ears ringing with the roar of its ascent. I push off my side of the room to stumble over to her, planting my hands on either side of her head to stop myself from crushing her against the wall when the floor tilts. She reaches up to grab my collar, hauling my head down so she can shout in my ear.

"What now? Fry its circuits or something, short out its engine?"

I lift my head to look down at her. It's not a bad idea—if we can cause an error, maybe . . . but if we destroy the ship's ability to pilot itself, there's no chance she'll land safely.

"Maybe," I shout back. "We could crash it, or get it to self-destruct on this side of the portal, instead of above Earth."

"How long do we have?" she shouts in my ear, up on her toes.

I have no idea how fast we're climbing, though my body's protesting the G-forces like we're in an old-school rocketship. I shake my head. I don't know how long we've got. Seconds? Minutes?

Not long enough to say the things to her that I want to say.

The wall's shaking against my hand, the ground bucking beneath my feet, and it's as if every thought in my brain has been shaken loose, landing together in one enormous pile, too tangled to ever be picked apart again.

I want to tell her what it means to me that she's here.

I want to tell her how much I wish she weren't.

I want to tell her how glad I am I met her.

I want to apologize that I ever did.

"Mia," I try. "It's been—I mean, I'm—"

I stare down at her, helpless, and she slings her arms up around my neck, pulling me into a fierce hug. "I know," she says in my ear. "I know, Jules. Me too."

And so I draw back, and I nod, because we don't have time. "Whatever system they rigged up to get it to fly unpiloted, I don't think we can undo it. But I think I can at least feed it some additional commands. Perhaps enough to confuse it. If we can fool it into trying to accelerate and reverse at once, maybe we can cause a fatal power surge."

We push apart, grabbing at anything we can to keep our balance as we turn back to the console. "The ship's so unstable, a power surge would . . ." Even shouting, I can hear the knowledge—and the determination—in Mia's voice.

"Destroy it," I agree. "Before it makes it through the portal. Before it reaches Earth."

And with us on board.

The earthquake beneath our feet abruptly stops, the roaring dying back to a loud but even hum, the floor suddenly still, and we're left standing there—Mia gripping the doorframe, me braced against the console, blinking.

We're past the point of no return, our commitment already made, and neither of us hesitates. There's no time to think anymore, no time to imagine what will happen if we succeed—whether it will be quick.

We stagger upright, turning toward the console—and the world goes black.

Green and gold bursts across my darkened vision, and pain explodes down my arms and legs, pounding at my temples, trying to turn me inside out. I'm dimly aware of my body hitting the floor, and then I'm spinning, my gut churning like I'm cresting the top of a roller coaster, and falling down, down, down. I want to run, but I can't remember how to move.

I'm not sure if I'm dead or not, but it strikes me a moment later that the fact that I'm thinking about it means I'm probably not.

Cogito, ergo sum.
I think, therefore I am.
I am . . . alive, hopefully.

There's a groan somewhere nearby, and then some cursing that includes a couple of words I've never heard before, though I'm too dizzy to take notes. Then reality snaps into focus, as the voice snags in my brain: that's Mia's voice.

And I've felt this way before. This is how I felt after passing through the last portal.

Oh, deus, the portal.

"Mia," I groan, rolling over onto my front. "Mia, we have to—it went through."

She's lying on her back, eyes closed, and when I speak she manages to roll onto her side to face me, curling into a fetal position. The noise she makes isn't a word, but I know she's trying. I force myself up to my elbows, and try to sit, the world swimming.

"We have to what?" she mumbles, and that's when it hits me. We have to *nothing*. If we destroy the ship now, so close to Earth, we're doing the Undying's work for them. Maybe I can find a way to prevent it, to turn it around, to take it back. Even as I climb unsteadily to my feet, moving on automatic, I know I haven't a hope.

I couldn't even abort the launch sequence. Turning off the autopilot and managing to steer this thing back through the portal would take years of study.

There's nothing else to do, though, so I grab the control panel for balance and stare down at the lights racing across it, blinking to clear my vision.

"Everything hurts," Mia mutters on the floor, still in a ball. "I was supposed to be dead by now. This hurts a lot more than dead. At least it didn't blow up. . . . If it was a bomb, if they meant us to take it back to destroy Earth, it'd be blowing up now, right?"

The crystalline circuits on the panels before me are blinking on and off, the sections used for launch dimming, and new areas slowly coming to life as power's diverted to other systems. I trace the glyphs with my fingers, trying to make myself understand what they might mean. And then I see one I know. The same swooping line I followed, thinking I was leading us to the engines. The swooping line that led to the long hallway full of portals. *Why is power diverting there?*

Hope surges through me, followed a moment later by horror.

"Mia," I say slowly, and I know she hears it in my voice, because she rolls to all fours, and with a gasp, pushes herself to her feet to join me, wrapping an arm around my waist for balance—the portal's taken her as badly as it did last time. "I don't think it's going to self-destruct—I don't think it was ever meant to be a bomb at all. I think it's a Trojan Horse."

"A what?" she whispers, staring down blearily at the panels before us.

"It's . . ." I grasp for the quickest explanation. "All right, it's this ancient story from Greece, it was called *The Odyssey*, and these—"

She cuts me off, shoving an elbow into my ribs and gasping, "I know what the damn Trojan Horse was! What the hell are *you* talking about?"

"The—the Trojan Horse," I repeat, like an idiot. "The Trojans brought it inside their walls, and all the Greeks hiding inside poured out to slaughter them. The power's diverting to where the portals are. I think it's bringing them all online."

"But they're one-way portals," she replies, staring at me in confusion. "They look just like the one we came through from the temple. They don't lead anywhere, they lead . . ." The words die in her throat.

I say it anyway. "They lead here. From wherever the Undying are now, if they *are* still alive like you said, to this ship. Currently in orbit around—"

"Around Earth," whispers Mia.

"If they're trying to take Earth, they're not using the ship as a bomb. They're using it as a gateway to come here themselves."

"No," she murmurs, pushing away from me, and I follow her as she stumbles through the doorway, picking up speed as we run toward the portals.

I've never wanted so badly to be wrong.

I've never been so sure I'm not.

29

AMELIA

I CONCENTRATE ON TRYING NOT TO PUKE, BECAUSE IT'S HARD TO RUN WHILE you're heaving your guts out. But focusing on the side effects of the portal that brought this ship back to Earth also means I don't have to think about what's happening.

Yeah, right. If there's anything I can do while trying not to die, it's think about how utterly goddamn screwed we are.

All this time. Every puzzle, every step through their carefully laid-out temples. The temples themselves, designed to be tantalizing clues—tantalizing *traps*. The ship, with its doors, and its hallways, and its controls simple enough that a teenager—albeit an academic genius—figured out how to fly it in a matter of hours. At least—enough to fly it straight back to Earth.

Exactly where the Undying intended it to go.

This is what the secret warning was trying to point us to. The Nautilus spiral in the code, the glyph that warned us about the apocalypse, the unspoken catastrophe that Jules's dad feared. We've helped deliver the end of the world.

The prize was never a lump of Undying tech that would save my sister or exonerate Jules's dad. The prize was always Earth. We were just wrong about who the raiders were.

The blood pumping through my veins, with its healthy dose of adrenaline and utter panic, is proving to be a potent antidote to the portal hangover. If only Jules had known that all he had to do to get me moving after we came through the portal back at the temple was scare the shit out of me.

I want to laugh, a hysterical reaction, but I just gasp for air. All I can hear is the harshness of our breathing over the hum of the engines, purring gently now that we're in orbit.

We pass the intersection where Javier knocked out that Alliance soldier, but he's gone. Either he came to, or one of his comrades got him out.

Jules and I are alone.

I wish I hadn't left the other rifle at the airlock. Of course, at the time, the ship was empty, evacuated for launch. We had no reason to think we'd need weapons. And, given how I froze during the escape plan with Javier and Hansen, no reason to think I'd be able to use one in a pinch.

I may not be able to shoot a person, but damned if I wouldn't shoot whatever freakish alien bastard comes squirming through those portals.

We round the corner that opens onto the portal corridor, and Jules has to reach out and haul back on my arm to counteract the momentum that tries to send me plunging onward. I blink sweat and tears from my eyes, dropping into a crouch so I can peer around the corner. The rows of portals are still solid, dark.

"Nothing's happening." I'm panting from the run, from fear, from relief. "You were wrong."

"They only go liquid when something's coming through," Jules replies, breathing as hard as I am, but struggling to get it under control. "Remember the temple portal? Looked like stone on the exit side after we came through, but Liz and her gang still came through after us later. Just because it looks solid now doesn't mean it won't change in a few seconds."

I actually don't remember what the other side of the temple portal looked like at all, being too busy having a seizure on the ice, but in this moment I'm willing to take his word for it. "Then what do we do? We can't just sit here and wait, what if——"

"The lights." Jules points, hand outstretched over my shoulder. He's crouching just behind me, voice in my ear. Any other moment and the sound of it would give me shivers, make me want to lean back a fraction and feel the warmth of his chest on my back. Just now, though, his tone only makes me feel colder. "The lights over the portals. They're on, and they weren't before. They're active."

He's right. But before I can reply, the portal at the far end of the corridor ripples with a sound like a distant earthquake, like a shockwave in reverse. It's so low I feel it in my gut, through the soles of my boots, in the marrow of my bones.

And something steps through.

Jules's hand on my shoulder tightens, but I don't need the warning. We both pull back out of sight, taking turns to peek around the corner for a heartbeat here, a breath there.

It's wearing a suit of some kind, though nothing like what our astronauts wear. Bipedal, like we thought. Tall, taller than Jules. I can't see if it has arms or a face or anything else. Then, between one glance and the next, a second figure appears, the sound of the portal rebounding against my eardrums and settling into the pit of my stomach.

They're making noises, harsh, distorted sounds that mean nothing, but do suggest they can hear each other—and us.

I take a careful breath, exhaling the words as softly as I can: "There are only two of them."

"And only two of us," Jules replies. His hand on my shoulder is shaking, his whole body is shaking—or mine is, and the tremor I'm feeling is my own terror.

Two unarmed kids, neither of us exactly trained in combat, against two alien members of a species capable of creating the largest-scale hoax in the known galaxy, capable of insane cunning and patience just to find the right kind of life-form, the right kind of planet to take over. We don't stand a chance. But without us, neither does Earth.

Because Earth doesn't know what's up here. If Javier does manage to steal an IA shuttle, it'll take him time to get it away from the magnetic signal-scrambling effect at Gaia's pole; it'll take him time to transmit the message, time for the IA honchos to get it, discuss it, make a decision. And even *if* he manages all of that, he's still only warning them that the ship could explode. Now that we're in orbit, and the ship hasn't turned into a bomb, his warning will be meaningless except to make the IA all the more cautious about sending an exploratory team up here. They'll take their time, making sure to get it right. They could spend months developing exactly the right bomb squad team to explore what they think is an empty ship.

By which time the Undying could have a hundred, a thousand, ten thousand troops ready to swarm through, carrying god knows what kind of tech-powered weapons to obliterate us all.

I can feel tears running down my cheeks, as though my body's already decided that it's hopeless, that we'll die, that everyone we love on Earth will die. That I'll never see Evie again. That I'll never have the rush of standing atop Chicago's tallest skyscrapers again. That I'll never eat lime chicken and porcini wild rice again.

To hell with what my body thinks.

"We're *not* letting them take Earth," I hiss.

"Wait." Jules's grip on my arm is still tight, as though he expects me to go barreling into the corridor without a plan. And just now I'm not sure he's wrong. "Look."

The two figures seem to be conferring, then one turns and slots something into a groove beside the portal they arrived through. The surface shimmers and turns oily, and then one of the figures casually tosses something through.

"They're the advance team," Jules whispers. "Sending back a message that it's safe."

The two figures move up the corridor toward us, checking each of the portals, acknowledging the operational lights over the archways, and continuing to speak to each other in those distorted, muffled voices. Without further warning, more Undying start to appear, and not just from the single portal in the back—the whole corridor is filling fast, and the two original scouts are about to reach the end of the portals. And the corner where we're hiding.

Their heads are bulbous, their featureless faces jet black and almost metallic-looking, like the portals. There's nothing to distinguish one from the other—they look like clones, like robots, like . . . aliens.

Then the pair stop, just a few steps from where Jules and I are crouched, holding our breath.

One of them has its head bowed, examining a device on its suit. It gives a little beep, then flashes green. The Undying scout makes one of its garbled sounds, then reaches up—oh god, it has arms . . . hands?—and unbuckles something with a hiss of released, pressurized gas.

Then it pulls off its helmet.

"At least the air's safe." Its voice is heavily accented, but unmistakably speaking English.

Not its voice—*her* voice. Jules's grip on my shoulder falls lax. We're both staring, forgetting for the moment that we're supposed to be hiding, that we're only a couple of meters from invaders trying to take our only home from us.

Because the Undying scout standing right there, where I could almost reach out and touch her, is a woman. A tall, golden-skinned woman who could walk down any street on Earth without attracting a second glance.

Because she's human.

She glances at her partner, who's in the process of removing his helmet too. "Well?" she says, taking a deep breath and then turning her back to survey the stream of Undying soldiers pouring through the portals behind them. "Ready to take Earth back?"

ACKNOWLEDGMENTS

Sorry about that. (Well, not really. We're pretty unapologetic.) Rest assured, though, for Jules and Mia will be back in the sequel.

There's nothing in this world (or any other) that we'd rather do than write stories together, and we're so grateful we get to do it for a living. This truly is a dream come true, so first of all, dear reader, we'd like to thank *you*. Without readers, booksellers, librarians, and reviewers, none of this would be possible. Thank you from the bottom of our hearts for all your support.

There are so many people who help us take these stories from our first ideas to the book you're holding in your hands now, and we owe a huge thanks to all of them.

First, our incredible agents Josh and Tracey Adams, as well as the wonderful Stephen Moore, and the network of foreign scouts and agents who've helped *Unearthed* find overseas homes. We'd be lost without you.

In the United States, our wonderful editorial team are Laura Schreiber, Emily Meehan, Mary Mudd, and Deeba Zargarpur. Thank you for your wisdom, your patience, your insight, and occasionally for catching ridiculous mistakes before they make it out into the world! A huge thank-you as well to the whole Hyperion team—from sales and marketing, to the copy editors who save our bacon over and over, to publicity and everyone in between. We love working with you. A special shout-out to the amazing Cassie McGinty.

In Australia, our other home, we are eternally grateful for the fantastic Anna McFarlane, as well as Jess Seaborn, Radhiah

Chowdhury, and every single member of the Allen & Unwin team. We don't know what we did to deserve you.

We also had help from all kinds of experts—everything we get right is down to them, and of course everything we get wrong is down to us. Thanks in particular to Yulin Zhuang for checking our Chinese, Megan Shepherd and Esther Cajahuaringa for checking our Spanish, and Soraya Een Hajji for teaching us to curse in Latin. Dr. Kate Irving helped with all things medical, Anindo Mukherjee made sure we weren't sending Mia and Jules to their deaths rappelling down cliff faces, and Christopher Russell helped design our musical mathematical puzzles. Alex Bracken and Megan Shepherd provided fantastic feedback on the manuscript at the exact moments we needed it—thank you, ladies!

We're so lucky as well to have a pile of friends who are always there to cheer, celebrate, and kick our butts when needs be. They include Marie Lu, Stephanie Perkins, Jay Kristoff, Leigh Bardugo, Kiersten White, Michelle Dennis, Alison Cherry, Lindsay Ribar, Sarah Rees Brennan, CS Pacat, Eliza Tiernan, Shannon Messenger, Alex Bracken, Sooz Dennard, Erin Bowman, Nic Crowhurst, Kacey Smith, Soraya Een Hajji, Peta Freestone, Liz Barr, Nic Hayes, Megan Shepherd, Beth Revis, Ellie Marney, Ryan Graudin, the Roti Boti gang, the Melbourne retreat crowd, and the Asheville crew.

And finally, of course, we have to thank our families, who cheer louder than anyone—our parents, our siblings, Brendan (an extra *I love you* here from Amie for the world's best, most patient, supportive husband), the Cousinses, Kaufmans, McElroys, Miskes, and Mr. Wolf—we love you, and we're so grateful for you.

And now, if you'll excuse us, we hear other worlds calling our names—we'll see you all in the next book!